THE
NEXT
KILLING

Books by Rebecca Drake

DON'T BE AFRAID

THE NEXT KILLING

THE
NEXT
KILLING

REBECCA DRAKE

PINNACLE BOOKS
Kensington Publishing Corp.

PINNACLE BOOKS are published by

Kensington Publishing Corp.
850 Third Avenue
New York, NY 10022

PINNACLE BOOKS and the Pinnacle logo are Reg. U.S. Pat. & TM Off.

ISBN-13: 978-0-7394-8893-5

Printed in the United States of America

For J^2 and M^1

All my love

ACKNOWLEDGMENTS

Thank you to my agent, Evan Marshall, and my editor, John Scognamiglio. I'm constantly aware of how lucky I am to be working with such considerate yet shrewd members of the publishing world. Thanks to Diane Burke for her great copy-edits and for the beautiful cover art of Lou Malcangi.

Many thanks for the help of my local Sisters in Crime siblings, especially fellow authors Sandra Stephens, Meryl Neiman, and Kristine Coblitz, for their perceptive edits and advice. Also, thanks to fellow members of Mysterywrights, including Mike Crawmer, Joyce Tremel, Jan Yanko, and Brian Mullen, for listening to the ideas and not being afraid to tell me when they didn't work.

Thanks to Nancy Martin, whose boot camp for aspiring authors drop-kicked me toward publication and to J. A. Konrath, whose hands-on guerilla marketing workshops prepared me for any challenge.

Nat Drake, Margaret Hallisey, Avram Machtiger, and Lathrop Haynes were instrumental in the early plotting of this novel and the first one. Mary Alice Mertz answered many questions about teaching. David Axelson, M.D., and Joel Rosenbloom, D.O., offered valuable medical advice.

Thanks to the towns and people of Summit, Chatham, Madison, and Morristown, New Jersey. Their enduring charm and my own fond memories contributed to the fictional town of Gashford.

Thanks to my local offices away from home, Enrico's Tazza d'Oro in Highland Park and Make Your Mark in Point

Breeze. Great coffee, food, and conversation. And thanks to my office at the beach, Coffee Talk in Stone Harbor, New Jersey. I value that quiet corner booth.

Finally, thanks to my husband, Joe Mertz, for all his support, emotional, technical, and financial, and for our children, Joey and Maggie. None of it is possible without you.

Prologue

The shed was dark. She couldn't see a foot beyond the door where she peered in, the murky shadows at the front giving way to deep black, hinting of strange things hidden in corners. It had an awful musty smell that reminded her of a dead mouse her father had trapped once under the sink.

"No," she said, turning back to look at the others. "I don't want to go in there."

They were watching her with predatory smiles. "But you do want to join the club, right?"

She swallowed hard, shifting her backpack. She'd been so excited when she got the note, pausing near her locker between classes to pull the little square from its hiding place under her math book.

"Meet us this afternoon near the track." She'd read the single sentence over and over again, amazed that they'd asked her, thrilled to be chosen.

She lingered when school ended, waiting for others to leave before slamming her locker and hurrying out the side door. The track was empty, but one of them was sitting in the bleachers, waiting. The other stood just beyond the fence.

The walk across the playing field beyond the track was so

quiet that she could hear the crunch of grass underfoot. They hardly talked, smiling occasionally if she asked a question. In the silence she heard the slight, wheezy sound of her own breathing.

Beyond the playing field the grass came up higher, tickling the skin at their ankles. The shed came into view, standing alone in the shallow basin of land below a slight rise.

"Wouldn't that make a great clubhouse?" one of them said, stopping in front of it. Gray clapboard with faded green asphalt shingles peeling off the roof, it had a double door held together by a wide chain and a heavy padlock. The lock hung open.

"Maybe," she said, her voice betraying the doubt she didn't feel free to express. The sun beat down on them. She could feel the heat underneath her uniform blouse, sweat trickling into the new space created by the small buds appearing on her chest that was swaddled in what her mother stupidly called a training bra.

"Why don't you go inside and look it over?" they said, making it sound like a suggestion, though one hurried to unhitch the padlock and the other pulled the chain through the metal loops. The door squealed as it opened and she'd leaned cautiously inside.

"No," she repeated. "It's too dark."

"That's just because your eyes haven't adjusted. Step all the way in or you won't be able to really tell."

She looked from one to the other, searching for some indication that they were joking. They stared back at her with those strange, fixed smiles. Like alligators, she thought, and wished she hadn't come.

"Don't you want to be part of the club?"

How many times had she wished to be popular like they were? Yes, she wanted to be part of the club. She wanted to sit at the good seats in the cafeteria. She wanted teachers to smile at her the way they smiled at them. She wanted girls to feel envy when she walked down the halls and for boys' heads to turn on the streets.

She let her backpack slip from her shoulder and drop to the grass. The door creaked, swinging slightly on its rusting hinges. She looked at the gloom and thought of wolf spiders and bats. She swallowed hard.

"Go on," one of them said. "Hurry up."

She took a deep breath and stepped inside.

The sudden shove in her back knocked her forward and she fell hard, slamming her knees onto rough wood floor. The door banged shut, the entire shed shuddering with the impact.

Blackness engulfed her. She screamed, struggling to her feet, and stumbled around, hands outstretched, trying to find the door. By the time she reached it they'd restrung the chain and fastened the lock.

"Let me out! Please!" She pounded the door and it shook in its frame, but didn't budge. Her begging and pleading went unanswered, though she could hear their muffled voices outside.

"You stupid wannabe," one of them called. "This will teach you to stop following us around."

Their laughter rang through her sobs as she lurched around in the blackness, slamming her shin against something hard, stabbing her hand on something sharp. Things clattered to the floor, smashing her foot, rolling around her. Something splashed her legs.

The smoke surprised her, a gentle waft against her face. She coughed and shied away from it, nostrils quivering at the scent.

There was a cracking sound, like a tree branch breaking, and suddenly there were flames racing along the floorboards, tongues of orange licking at the juncture of old walls, climbing the leg of a rickety workbench, lapping at her feet.

Choking on the billowing smoke, tears streaming from

her eyes, she tried to stamp out the flames and beat them back with her hands. A sweet smell, like meat on a grill. Her own flesh burning. A line of fire reached the roof, turning a rotting beam to ash, which fell like hot, black raindrops on her head and shoulders.

Above the angry hiss of the fire and her own cries she could still hear their laughter. She would hear that sound forever.

Chapter One

The school had stood on the hillside for more than a hundred years. It had been there for so long that it looked as if it had sprouted from the woods surrounding it, the tops of stone buildings appearing suddenly above the trees like lichen in a sea of green.

Lauren Kavanaugh pressed her face against the taxi window to catch a glimpse of it through the rain while running her hands down the horizontal pleats creasing the pale linen skirt of her borrowed suit. She tried not to believe that wrinkled clothing was going to cost her the job.

"You visiting someone up the Hill?" the cabbie asked. His had been the only cab idling outside the local train station, where most of the commuters had been heading the opposite way, north into Manhattan. He must have seen her confusion because he laughed. "I mean St. Ursula's. We call it the Hill because it's up there." He gestured out the window, but the road had turned again and the buildings had disappeared. All she could see was a mountainside covered in trees.

"It looks like a forest," she said.

He chuckled. "Oh, the school's in there. It's a big campus—close to two hundred acres. You got a sister there?"

"No, I've got an interview."

"Oh. Well good luck."

She could see his eyes appraising her in the rearview mirror. "You look a little young to be a teacher."

She didn't reply to that, just stared out the window as they passed through the outlying streets. It was quite different from the packed streets of Hoboken, where she paid a fortune to rent a tiny apartment on the third floor of an old row house.

The center of Gashford was the intersection point of two long, wide streets lined with small businesses, a bank, and a post office, and no building was higher than ten stories. They'd sped past it and past the tree-lined, residential streets surrounding it and then on past the larger homes spaced farther apart with sweeping lawns. Now they were outside town, where civilization was encroaching on less desirable land; in either direction were cockeyed realty signs stuck in patches of sparsely covered mud.

The edges of the road were sprinkled with late summer wildflowers drooping under the continuous downpour. She could smell the unfamiliar scent of wet grass through the cracked windows.

The cabbie chattered on about the mild weather they were having for August and Lauren made murmuring noises of agreement, but all the while she was thinking about how greener this was than Hoboken and how she needed this job.

The taxi slowed and turned between two large stone pillars. A tall sign with black Gothic letters announced St. Ursula's Preparatory Academy and then they were climbing up a winding strip of blacktop between towering oaks and pines.

"There she is," the cabbie said, pointing ahead out the windshield, and Lauren caught another glimpse of a stone building before it, too, vanished as the road curved around the hillside.

The same building appeared again between the trees and then another building near it and then they crested the hill and the campus was before them, a large complex of stone buildings, the most massive of which sat at the peak of a semicircle driveway. The other buildings surrounding it stretched out at different points on a mandala of concrete pathways.

The taxi pulled to a stop in front of the main building. "Good luck."

"Thanks." She paid him with money carefully counted and then he was gone and she was alone, making one last attempt to smooth the wrinkles out of her skirt.

Only she wasn't alone. A girl dressed from head to toe in black was hunched in a corner of the wide stone steps under an overhang, tucked so close to the wall that Lauren almost missed her. The hair was what she noticed, an astonishing coppery red color. The girl was smoking, the acrid scent of tobacco unmistakable, but she had the cigarette cupped under the hand resting on the lower step, hiding it without putting it out.

"Hi," she said without smiling and Lauren repeated the greeting, wondering if she should say something. The girl was obviously underage. Was this some kind of test for prospective teachers? Should she tell the girl to put out her cigarette?

The front door of the building suddenly opened and a tall, horse-faced woman with a gray suit that matched her iron-gray hair stepped out.

"Morgan, you know smoking isn't allowed. You don't want me to report that to Sister Rose, do you?"

The girl stubbed out the cigarette with a hostile look and the woman suddenly seemed to notice Lauren.

"May I help you?" she said and her eyes flicked up and down like a laser, zeroing in on the wrinkled suit.

"I'm here for an interview."

"The main office is inside and down the hall to the left." The woman held the door for her and gave a faint sniff as Lauren passed.

The hall was dark and empty. Wood was her first impression, dark wood and lots of it. Front and center was a large wooden crucifix with a marble Christ figure hanging above an intricately carved wooden console table. On the center of the table was a foot-tall marble statue of the Virgin Mary; she stood on a wooden base with her arms extended, head bowed submissively, and lips curved in a slight, Mona Lisa smile.

Lauren's heels clicked loudly on the ivory marble tile floor and she wished she'd thought to check her hair in the bathroom at the station. It had finally gotten long enough to pull back and she'd fastened the unruly mass of gold curls at the base of her neck with a silver clip, hoping it made her look more mature.

The headmistress's office was marked with a discreet black-lettered sign. A young woman with sleek black hair, wearing a blue twinset and matinee-length pearls sat in the outer office at an old wooden desk, looking for all the world like someone out of the 1940s, except she was typing away on a state-of-the-art desktop that seemed to be giving her trouble. She looked up with a pleasant smile and adjusted the stylish tortoiseshell glasses slipping down her small nose.

"May I help you?"

Lauren introduced herself. "I've got an interview with Sister Rose Merton?"

The young woman consulted a spiral-bound black appointment book. "Yes, of course, you're her nine o'clock." She gave Lauren a broad smile and adjusted the glasses again. "The headmistress will be with you in just a moment. If you'd like to take a seat?"

She gestured behind Lauren, who suddenly noticed the brown velvet sofa near an arrangement of large potted ferns.

The door to the inner sanctum was at the far end of the sofa. It was open a crack.

Lauren took a seat on the couch and placed her slim briefcase carefully beside her. She sat up straight and took several deep breaths, looking at the painting in a gilt frame hanging on the wall. It was a vaguely familiar scene, a cluster of whey-faced, robe-wearing young women with oil lamps. Something from the Bible, Lauren thought, and hoped that there wouldn't be questions that tested her religious knowledge. Thank God she was being interviewed for a history position, not religion.

She realized she could hear voices through the door. Or one raised voice and the murmuring of another, clearly placating.

"—excuses being made for the way my daughter has been treated!"

Lauren glanced at the secretary but she was engrossed in her typing again, seemingly oblivious. She looked back at the door and jumped as the voice continued. "What I'm asking is that everything not be blamed on Morgan."

So it was the mother of the smoker. Lauren tried not to listen, but the lower the voices got the greater her urge to hear what they were saying. She caught fragments about rule breaking, about suspension, about other girls.

All at once the door opened and a tall, elegantly dressed woman with the same striking coppery hair and a frown marring her patrician features strode out. She was followed by a shorter, rounder woman wearing a look of resigned patience.

Lauren stood up and the shorter woman smiled at her.

"I'll be right with you," she said. She followed Morgan's mother out of the room. The secretary caught Lauren's eyes and rolled her own with a slight smile. Who or what that referred to Lauren wasn't sure, but she smiled back.

A few minutes passed while Lauren waited, flipping through the magazines on the coffee table, a strange combination of religious and secular. She was barely able to focus. The headmistress came back into the room and spoke quietly to the secretary for a moment before turning to Lauren.

"You must be Miss Kavanaugh," she said, extending one deceptively soft-looking hand for a firm shake. "I'm Sister Rose Merton, the headmistress at St. Ursula's."

She ushered Lauren into her office and closed the door. This time, Lauren noticed, it really was closed.

"Please, have a seat," Sister Rose gestured toward two upholstered chairs that sat in front of a large mahogany desk that dominated the room.

Lauren took a seat in one as Sister Rose moved silently behind the desk, noticing that unlike the headmistress's own leather office chair, the chairs in front of the desk were rigidly upright as if not to lull any visitors to the office into a false sense of security.

The wall to the left of Sister Rose's desk was lined, floor to ceiling, with bookshelves. The wall opposite was hung with tasteful, if somewhat bland, landscapes in gilt frames. Directly behind her desk, hung so it appeared to be looking over her shoulder, was a sepia-tinted photo of a grim-faced nun in full habit. Directly above her was a large gold crucifix.

"Sister Augustine Clement," Sister Rose said, following Lauren's gaze. "St. Ursula's founding headmistress. A smart and tenacious woman."

The two nuns were a study in contrasts. Unlike her predecessor, Sister Rose wore no habit. She was dressed simply in a plain navy blue suit with an unadorned white blouse. She wore earrings, small pearl studs, and a gold circle pin was affixed to her lapel; a crucifix was at its center. The pin and the plain gold band on the ring finger of her left hand were the only official markers of her membership in a celibate community devoted to God. To the casual observer, she could have been just another grandmother.

She had short, dove-gray hair and piercing steel-gray eyes that were at odds with the soft and crepelike quality of her pale skin and her benign smile. She rested her plump arms on the desk and folding her hands, turned her intense focus on Lauren.

"As I mentioned when we spoke, one of our teachers unexpectedly retired and we have an unanticipated, and unwelcome, vacancy for this academic year."

Lauren nodded. She'd been thrilled to get the call, anticipating another year of substitute teaching. She was in the bind that all new teachers were in, anxious to get a full-time job in a system that only wanted to hire the experienced. She'd never imagined that she'd get the opportunity to teach at a prep school. Submitting her résumé to St. Ursula's had been pro forma, nothing more. She'd simply canvassed every school in Northern New Jersey and sent them her résumé.

"Usually, we'd only consider a more experienced teacher," Sister Rose said, as if reading Lauren's thoughts, "but circumstances dictated that we broaden our search."

The "circumstances" were just how close it was to the start of the academic year. School was slated to begin in just two weeks. More experienced teachers had their teaching jobs lined up and ready.

Sister Rose opened a file on her desk and pulled out Lauren's résumé.

"I see that you've done a full year of substitute teaching in Hoboken."

"Yes, it's been a great experience." It wasn't a lie, not exactly. It had given her enough experience to know that caring about your students wasn't enough to transform their lives. Poverty, burned-out administrators, and limited funding had a lot to do with academic failure. Not that these things would have deterred her from accepting a full-time job there, but teachers in these districts seemed to die in their posts.

"As I mentioned, Sister Agnes was the history teacher for our upper school for over twenty years," Sister Rose continued. "It will be difficult to fill her shoes, but we must."

She outlined the teaching responsibilities and Lauren listened, nodding when it was expected, asking intelligent questions when a pause indicated she should, while trying to appear interested but not overeager.

It was going well. They needed her—that was clear. She'd thought she was one of many candidates, but it didn't sound like it.

"We are a traditional Catholic school, Miss Kavanaugh. Parents send their daughters here to receive the finest education in a setting that prepares them spiritually as well as intellectually for the challenges of adult life. Our girls attend Mass twice a week, on Wednesdays and Sundays, as well as on the holy days, of course."

"Of course."

Lauren couldn't remember all the holy days. How many were there? The last time she'd been to Mass was while touring a church in Spain with Michael. He'd whispered "hocus-pocus," during the priest's blessing of the congregation and she'd erupted into giggles, so they'd fled the building for the hot sunshine and cobble streets outside.

"As I think I explained, this job includes an apartment in one of our dormitories." She looked inquiringly at Lauren, who nodded. Rent-free accommodations were definitely part of the appeal.

"The resident faculty member for each dormitory is responsible for the girls in that house—we call our dormitories houses—and will generally oversee their welfare while in the dormitory."

Lauren wondered what welfare meant. She had a sudden vision of herself armed with a thermometer and a bottle of aspirin.

"Of course we have an infirmary," Sister Rose said as if

reading her thoughts. "You would not be responsible for the care of sick children, but you would see to it that the girls in that particular house would abide by the rules of St. Ursula's, particularly as they pertain to curfews."

"Are the girls allowed off school grounds?" Lauren asked.

"Yes, but there are rules regarding this as well. As you can see, we are not an easy walk into town. There is, however, a bus that runs at the base of the hill and girls do use this bus to go into town on the weekends."

And she would have to use it, too, Lauren thought. She didn't own a car and until this moment it hadn't occurred to her that the job might require one. She was used to walking to the grocery store around the corner from her apartment in Hoboken, to going to the neighborhood bar for a drink in the evening. If she got this job she would be isolated during the week.

"I'm not familiar with St. Mary's Academy," Sister Rose said, glancing back down at the file open on her desk. "It's outside Pittsburgh?"

Lauren nodded. The memories came in a rush. Rows of uniformed girls kneeling in the shadows of a dark church. *St. Mary's girls do not follow, they lead.* A golden orb of incense swaying gently at the end of a long chain clutched in a priest's veiny hand. The overwhelming smell of lilies.

"I see that you attended school there when you were younger, but you finished your education at a public institution?"

"Yes." Lauren said. She'd anticipated the question, the need to know why she'd given up a religious institution for a secular one, and she'd prepared an answer. "I moved far away."

She was sure that Sister Rose would ask more, but the headmistress just nodded briskly and looked back down at the open file.

"And you attended university in England?"

"Yes. The University of London."

The headmistress nodded, fiddling with the thin silver chain that held a pair of black reading glasses against her chest. "Why did you choose to go overseas?"

"I'd always been interested in seeing Europe. It seemed like a great opportunity."

Sister Rose seemed to consider this for a moment, nodding and looking down at the file in front of her. Lauren surreptitiously wiped her sweating palms against her skirt.

"And you studied history and education, but completed your teaching certificate last year once you'd come back to the United States?"

"Yes," Lauren said, her hands relaxing against her lap. "I knew by then that I wanted to teach."

A few perfunctory questions about her education classes and then Sister Rose abruptly closed the folder.

"Congratulations, Miss Kavanaugh. I trust you'll be able to move in by next Tuesday at the latest?"

Lauren's mouth fell open and then she thought how idiotic she must look and snapped it shut. "What? You mean I've got the job?"

Sister Rose gave her a small smile. "Yes, that's exactly what I mean. I'm afraid that this interview was pro forma. I had reviewed your credentials already and quite frankly you're the only qualified candidate available at the moment. We simply had to meet you in person to be one hundred percent sure."

She had the job. She had a full-time teaching job! The tension in Lauren's shoulders eased and she felt them drop a bit.

"I'm sure you'll understand that with your relative lack of experience, we can offer this position only on a probationary basis," Sister Rose added. The smile vanished in place of a serious look. "We will see how the first semester goes and decide at the end of it whether or not you'll continue at St. Ursula's."

That stung a bit, but still—it was her first full-time teaching job! If she had to prove herself in it, well, that was probably to be expected. Any school would want to evaluate her competence.

Sister Rose abruptly stood up. Lauren scrambled to her feet, still stunned. The headmistress stuck out her hand and gave Lauren's a surprisingly firm shake. "It was a pleasure meeting you, Miss Kavanaugh. I look forward to your arrival next week."

On the train journey back to her cramped apartment, Lauren replayed the interview in her head and wondered at having gotten the job. She needed it so badly and she'd gotten it.

All the way out here on the train, she'd kept up an internal pep talk, telling herself that if she didn't get this job, there would be another. Only not this year.

It was too late for any other job to come through. The most she could have expected was for some regular teacher to go on maternity leave and free up a long-term substitute position.

So what that she had to live so far from a town. There were buses—she'd manage. And she could save money and pay off the credit card companies breathing down her neck. Every day she'd checked her messages and the mail, hoping to hear from a school, but now she wouldn't have to bother.

Thinking of the mail reminded her of what had arrived in yesterday's post. There'd been such a gap between this letter and the last that she'd gotten a shock when she saw the slim white envelope stuck in the middle of a pile of bills. She thought—she'd hoped—he'd forgotten all about her, but he never would.

It had taken him so long to find her and now she would be leaving again. Maybe this time he wouldn't be able to find her. She stared out at the dirty window at the wet landscape streaking past, hands clenched in fists in her lap. Maybe at the school she would finally be safe.

Chapter Two

At night the lights go out and the school rests. From the sky, spotted by low-flying planes, it looks like some great coiled beast, the peaks of the rooftops like scales on a dragon's back.

Lights must be out in the dormitories at ten; that is the rule and that is the official end to the day.

The first day was over. The hustle of moving in, the rush of old girls finding one another and the stress of new girls finding their way around—all of this noise was absorbed by the stone buildings and dissipated into the woods surrounding them. The day was over and everything that has happened now slipped into the past.

At night the school rests, but not everyone. There was movement in the dark hallways. Hours have passed. Those who were watching waited and then wait some more. Fifteen minutes after midnight they slip out of the doorways from different houses. They are used to carrying their shoes and stepping silently. They are used to pulling hoods over their faces.

Out of the houses they came, silent figures moving through

the darkness. They don't speak until they're past the buildings, until they're in the shelter of the trees.

"Hurry," one of them said. "We're late." She held a small
flashlight pointed at the ground. A round beam of light, eight
inches across, is all that guides them. Still, they are used to
this. They found the path they needed and moved along it.

"How do you know she's even going to be here?"

"I heard her telling someone."

Their feet crunched quietly against the crushed limestone, but they didn't worry. No one will hear them out here,
well, maybe not *no one*.

They found her near the pond. She was taking off her
clothes slowly, piece by piece, and they watched her in the
darkness. One of them giggled as the girl stripped off her bra
and panties, adding them to the pile of clothes she left on the
bank. She didn't hear, though, because she was moving toward the water.

"You couldn't pay me to swim in there," one of them
whispered only to be hushed by the others. The girl looks as
if she might agree, lifting her foot out as soon as she put it
in, obviously cold, her pale arms wrapped around an even
paler torso. But this was only for a second. In the next, she
stepped into the water, moving forward until she was swallowed by the dark liquid.

"What's she doing? Where did she go?" A hiss in the silence.

"Ssh, there she is."

Up again, emerging from the water like a sylph, like
Venus, her hair hanging about her pale shoulders as she
stood for a moment. And then she began to swim, careful
strokes with her head above the water. She floated on her
back and they could see that she was staring up at the sky.
She was saying something. She was talking to the moon.

"God, she's so weird."

"Where's the rope?"

She doesn't see them until she's swimming back to the shore, until she's stepped forward in the soft mud of the bank, until it's too late to run, too late to do anything but scream.

Chapter Three

There are flames licking her hands, curling around the pale pink of her skin like orange petals on some deadly flower. The heat is curling the tiny almost invisible hairs on her bare calves. Something sizzles and there is a smell she doesn't know, a charred scent, steak on a grill but with something sweet overlying it.

Lauren woke with a start, breathing hard. For a moment she didn't know where she was, expecting to see the brightly colored Matisse poster she'd hung over a long scar in the chipped plaster of her apartment in Hoboken. Instead there are bare, cream-colored walls.

She didn't see the battered chest of drawers she'd rescued from someone's garbage. There is only a single bed with a nightstand tucked beside it and a closet. Above the bed, hanging above her head, is a crucifix in dark wood with the Christ figure in silver. She reached up a hand and ran it over the cool metal. The clock on the nightstand glowed five o'clock. Her first class as a full-time teacher would begin in just under four hours.

Moving day had been yesterday. She'd arrived along with most of the students. The sound of car doors slamming and

teenage voices squealing echoed through the halls. Boxes
and trunks were hauled into rooms by drivers. Music began
playing almost as soon as the first girl arrived.

There were ten dormitories, called "houses," all of them
in the same Victorian Gothic style as the main building, all of
them named for Doctors of the Church. Six began with "A":
Ambrose, Anselm, Augustine, Aquinas, Anthony, and Avila.
The remaining four began with "B": Basil, Bonaventure,
Bernard, Bede. Lauren's apartment was in Augustine House.

The inside of the building was relatively modern. The
long hallways were carpeted and each room was outfitted
with twin beds, desks, dressers, and a shared bookcase. The
windows were casement style, but they were double-glazed
and the house smelled of fresh paint.

At one end of the hallway was a large common room,
where girls could watch TV or play the board games that
were stacked on a shelf. At the other end was her apartment.

"I know it's small," Sister Rose said, producing a key
from some hidden pocket as she led the way down the hall
toward a single wooden door painted a dark red, "but I think
you'll find it comfortable." She jiggled the key in the lock,
saying, "it sticks sometimes," before the door suddenly
swung open.

"I think these apartments are pretty charming." The older
woman stood back so Lauren could pass in front of her. The
postage-stamp entry gave way to a larger living room.

"You've got a fireplace," Sister Rose said, but Lauren had
already seen it. "It's gas—they were converted years ago—
but it works and all you have to do is flip a switch. It's
around here somewhere." She strode across to the white
wooden mantel.

"That's okay," Lauren said quickly. "I don't like fire."
Flames shot up, crackling around realistic-looking logs.

Sister Rose shut off the switch. "You might change your
mind when it gets colder," she said.

As soon as she'd gone, Lauren rearranged the beige love seat and two dark brown armchairs in the small living room so they blocked the hearth. They were comfortable, if a little worn, as was the cheery oriental rug on the floor. All of it was better than anything she'd had. Bookshelves flanked the fireplace and the other blank wall. There were plenty of books on the shelves and a wooden desk in one corner.

Lauren got out of bed and padded into the tiny kitchen that was adjacent to the living room. Small fridge, small stove, and sink. Soap underneath and a fresh sponge. The refrigerator was empty save for a box of baking soda and the carton of milk she'd picked up at a convenience store. The cupboards were lined with white shelf paper and her single box of Cheerios. There wasn't a crumb in sight. Sister Agnes had left the place immaculate.

The photograph album was on the table where she'd left it after unpacking. It had taken her only an hour to settle in. Lauren wondered what that said about her that her entire life could be unpacked in an hour. At the bottom of a box of books she'd found the small photograph album she'd put together one rainy day in London.

Sitting down at the table, she'd turned the pages, looking at the photos of her and Michael on a hillside in Dover and at a café in Paris.

It was an indulgence, looking at Michael, at his smile, at his eyes. She knew there would be a time when she looked at these pictures and simply thought of him as her first lover, not her only. There would be a time, but that time was not now.

She put the album aside and sat down with a bowl of cereal, listening to the silence. Back in the apartment even at this early hour there were the noises of neighbors' televisions and children. All she could hear now was the soft sound of rain slapping against the windows.

Between the kitchen and the bedroom, off a narrow hall,

was a small bathroom with a shower. Lauren splashed water on her face and brushed her teeth, grateful that she didn't have to share the students' communal baths.

Stripping off her pajamas, she dressed quickly in a T-shirt and exercise pants, pulling a sweatshirt over her head and lacing up a pair of running shoes.

She was used to running early in the morning—she'd done it for years, kept it up when she was overseas, and didn't stop when she returned to the States, running the streets of Hoboken every morning. She'd done it for so many years that sometimes she forgot why she'd started, the need to escape that had driven her when she was younger. It was still good for that, still a way to shut off the stress. She had to face a classroom in a few hours, but first she would run.

Locking her apartment door behind her, Lauren slid the key into her shoe and tiptoed down the hall to the front door. She slipped outside, closing it quietly behind her, and paused on the steps to do a few stretches.

It was so incredibly still. She could hear the far-off cooing of doves, but otherwise the only noise was from the faint patter of a soft rainfall. It was nothing more than a drizzle and she didn't let it stop her from starting off at a good pace.

Up the path, away from the dormitory toward the main building, then cut across the asphalt road in front of the school and into the woods across the street. She'd discovered yesterday that the acres and acres of woods had crushed limestone paths running through them, a nature lover's sanctuary and a perfect place to walk or run.

Morning fog had settled around the trees and there was a chill in the air. She was glad she'd worn the sweatshirt. Such strange weather for August, but she wasn't complaining. Anything beat the summer heat.

Her feet crunched along the limestone and she breathed in the heavy loamy smell of wet earth and the underlying odor of wet wood and decaying leaves. Soon the paths would be blanketed by the leaves that were only starting to turn.

She wondered what it would be like to run up here in the winter.

When she came to a "Y" she hesitated for a moment before bearing right, only to be startled into a full stop when something large and ghostly rose from the fog ahead of her.

It was only a statue, she realized, laughing at her fear and moving forward to run a hand lightly over the cold marble. She recognized the tableau. Jesus is Condemned to Death. She peered through the fog and saw another statue a few feet ahead. The Stations of the Cross cut in intricate detail on expensive stone. They'd probably been here since the beginning days of the school, if the dark green moss edging the marble's surface was anything to judge by.

She ran slowly past the remaining eleven statues, looking at the story of Christ's passion worked in stone. And then it was only trees again and the wind whipping lightly across her face. She ran hard, blanking her mind to everything but the movement of her feet. When a large pond came into view on her right she slowed and pulled off the path, feeling the grass cold against her ankles as she headed for the water's edge. There was a small stone bench and she took a seat, breathing hard.

The water of the pond, murky and algae laden where it merged into grass, was a still oval of silver. Leaning against the bench, feeling the cold stone press into her back, she looked out over the water and went through the mental checklist of everything she needed to finish prepping for class that morning.

Something caught her eye. A glimmer of color between the trees. She stood up and squinted, trying to see it more clearly. A coppery red color. Something bright, but it couldn't be a bird, could it?

She stood up and circled slowly around the approximately quarter-mile loop, running at a slower pace in an attempt to keep sight of it, but the trees blocked her view. Once she was on the far side she slowed to a walk, looking around in vain for that color and then back across the pond to find the bench where she'd been sitting so she'd have a reference point.

This was where it should be, but she saw nothing but green as she walked toward the trees until suddenly there it was again. Just a splash of color. She moved past the trunk of a maple and saw it clearly this time, that bright coppery red that should have seemed familiar.

It was hair, hanging damp and heavy. But Lauren didn't notice that as much as she did the naked body it was attached to.

Stephanie was making love with Alex when the phone rang. They were in bed, half-asleep, a slow, sweet, good morning suddenly and rudely interrupted. The noise echoed through the small town house, a chorus of phones jangling in tandem. He ignored it, trying to hold her attention, but she couldn't. Cursing, he slipped out of her as she plucked the phone off the nightstand.

"Detective Land."

"It's not even six," Alex complained, grunting as he climbed out of bed and stalked to the bathroom still semi-erect.

"Got a call from the Hill," the nasally voiced dispatcher said. "Detective Plane said ten minutes."

"Okay."

Stephanie hung up and swung her legs over the side of the bed, slipping into her panties and reaching for the pair of khaki pants she'd left on a chair the night before. She walked toward the bathroom, avoiding Alex's work boots and fastening a bra as she went.

"What's it this time? Someone shoot their neighbor's dog?" Alex flushed the toilet and moved roughly past her.

"I don't control the calls," she said, but she was speaking to the air.

He was in bed, lying with his back to her side, when she

came back out, fully dressed with her long brown hair twisted into a knot at the base of her neck. His short dark hair was disheveled and she could see the rigid set to his shoulders through the T-shirt he'd put back on. She took her weapon from the nightstand and checked it before slipping the holster around her shoulders with the ease of long practice. A light blazer on top, badge in the breast pocket and comfortable shoes on her feet. Nine minutes and thirteen seconds.

She leaned down to kiss Alex, but he didn't open his eyes.

"Sorry," she said in a whisper, breathing in his scent for a moment.

"S'okay," he murmured, turning to press a brief kiss to her lips, but he sounded sulky.

Detective Oswald Plane, known as "Oz," drove up in an unmarked sedan as she was pulling the door to the town house closed behind her.

"You gotta move closer to town, Land," he said, shaking his grizzled head as she got in the passenger door.

"Yeah, move my paycheck closer to a living wage and I'll see what I can do."

Plane grinned, his walrus mustache parting to show large teeth yellowed from too much coffee. "Why don't you just sleep with the chief?"

"And spoil the fun I'm having with your brother?"

This time he guffawed. Stephanie smiled and reached for the cup of take-out coffee closest to her. "You remember my sugar this time?"

"Oh, I know you like it sweet."

"Sweet and hot, Oz, don't forget it."

Sometimes she wondered what Alex would make of this banter, whether he'd be appalled or embarrassed by the sexual innuendo that his girlfriend participated in with such relish. Fiancée, not girlfriend. She kept forgetting that. They'd been engaged for barely a month. The diamond solitaire sparkling on her hand was still new to her.

"Stop mooning at your ring, Land, and tell me where we turn off for the Hill."

Stephanie flushed and looked up at the road ahead. "Another two miles at least. You need GPS. What's up?"

"Some kid's dead. Probably offed herself."

"Shit. I hate those."

"Yeah. If they're going to kill themselves why can't they go off a cliff in Morristown and spare us the cleanup?"

He reached toward a white bakery box sitting on the dash. "You want one?" he said, rustling around in it as the car swerved slightly on the road.

Stephanie steadied the corner of the wheel closest to her. "Way to be a walking stereotype."

"They're Danish, not doughnuts." He took a big bite out of a pastry that managed to look pint-sized in his beefy hand.

"Same difference."

"Now that's just plain ignorant. They're not the same thing at all."

"It's still just sugar and fat."

"My two favorite food groups." Oz grinned and waved the half-eaten Danish at her. "These are from Rosenbaum's—best bakery in town. C'mon, have one already."

"You shouldn't be eating them."

"Yeah, yeah—who are you, my mother?"

A patrol car was waiting by the stone-pillared entrance to flag them down—evidence that Oz's notoriously bad sense of direction was known beyond the detective squad.

In the two minutes it took to climb the hill, Stephanie loaded up with latex gloves and checked to make sure that she had Vicks in her pocket. Oz shoved the rest of the Danish in his mouth and brushed crumbs off onto the floor.

They passed the main building, where a small crowd stood on the steps, and drove by a patrolman signaling them to go farther up the road. It ended in a large parking lot where Oz pulled up behind two black-and-whites, lights flashing. An EMS van was nearby and one of the paramedics was sitting on the back bumper smoking a cigarette. A sheriff's department vehicle signaled that the crime scene unit had beaten them to the scene.

A uniformed officer, young and eager, practically hopped up and down next to an entrance in the woods.

"This way!" he called. "Crime scene's this way!"

"Okay, junior, stand down," Oz muttered, checking his weapon and adjusting his tie. Stephanie moved ahead of him, straightening her blazer as she walked.

"What is this, a nature hike?" Oz complained when they'd walked twenty feet along a footpath and still weren't at the crime scene.

"Nice pond," Stephanie commented.

"Yeah, fucking beautiful." Oz was huffing and despite the coolness of the morning sweat was trailing down his broad face. He was a big man, both tall and broad, and he carried a gut. "Gotta lose this."

"I'll pick you up for the gym tomorrow morning."

"I was thinking something easier. Like one of them gastric bypasses."

"The only surgery you need is to staple your mouth closed."

"Bitch."

"That's skinny bitch to you."

"Laugh now. It's all going to catch up with you when you hit my age and I'm going to be the one laughing when your tits droop and your ass spreads."

Stephanie laughed. "You still going to be around?"

Oz was saved from replying because they suddenly came upon the crime scene. Another paramedic was standing there with a couple of cops and a young woman in running clothes. A crime scene investigator was expanding the perimeter of the scene, but that wasn't where Oz was looking when he said, "Shit."

Stephanie followed his gaze and swallowed hard. The

naked body of a teenage girl was tied to a large oak tree, her red hair garish against the paleness of her skin. Very white, but with a purplish-blue sheen, it reminded Stephanie of skim milk.

"I thought you said it was suicide?" Stephanie said, ducking under the tape and drawing gloves on her hands. She stepped carefully toward the body, looking out for footprints or other evidence, and stepping around investigators taking pictures. She stopped short at seeing something else on the ground. "Look at that."

A large circle had been scratched in the dirt and thin grass surrounding the tree. Within the circle was a five-pointed star. There were words scratched in each point of the star. "Water," Stephanie read out loud the word in the point closest to her. She followed the circle.

"What is that?" Oz squatted down over a point with "Air" written in it, rocking back on his heels to take a closer look.

"It's a pentagram. The other points say Earth, Fire and Spirit."

"What is this, some satanic thing?"

"I don't know." Stephanie looked up and called to the investigator with the camera. "You get pictures of that?"

The guy nodded and she stepped carefully into the circle and closer to the body. The girl's pupils were fixed and her skin and hair were wet. There was a small tattoo of a butterfly on her left shoulder, the brightly colored wings another startling contrast to the skin. The rope binding her to the tree looked like nylon. Approximately an inch thick and made of multicolored orange strands, it looked like something used by rock climbers.

It had been wound tightly around the body, compressing the collarbone and shoulders, cutting sharply into the skin just below the small breasts, digging into the softer skin of the lower abdomen, and wrapping twice around the thighs. It was knotted tightly behind the tree and Stephanie noticed that some of the bark was worn against the knot as if the girl had struggled.

"What's the cause?" Oz asked.

Stephanie moved close to the body, trying to get a closer look at the girl's neck. "Looks like there might be some blood back of the head. Maybe trauma and exposure?"

Oz stepped next to her and looked where she pointed and then peered at the other side of the girl's head.

The medical examiner's arrival was signaled by an impatient cough behind them. Dr. Harriet Wembley was wearing a bright blue tracksuit that did nothing to mask the fact that she looked tired, cold, and impatient.

"Whenever you're done, detectives."

Oz grinned at her. "Early enough for you?"

"I was having a nice dream, made nicer by the fact that you didn't factor in it."

Oz staggered dramatically, one beefy hand to his chest. "You wound me."

Harriet rolled her eyes. "If only it was so easy to insult you." She stepped past him with her case and then, seeing the victim, suddenly swore.

It was completely out of character for her and Stephanie's eyes jerked from the victim to the older woman.

"Who called this in?" the medical examiner demanded. "This poor girl may not be dead at all!"

"What? But her pupils are dilated and she's already in rigor." Stephanie pointed at the girl's eyes and the clear rigidity of her body.

"Severe hypothermia can mimic death. This might not be real rigor. Jesus H. Christ, we've got to get her down from here and warm her up. Get those paramedics over here," she said to the air, "and see if they've got a Bair blanket!"

"We need to get photographs," Oz said, even as he shuffled backward.

Dr. Wembley turned on him, blue eyes flashing. "I don't

give a rat's ass about photographs! I'm trying to save this kid's life!"

Oz held up his hands in defeat and hustled off, calling to the paramedic standing on the outskirts of the crime scene tape.

"Are you done with pix of the body?" Stephanie asked the investigator with the camera. She didn't recognize him; he had to be new, which explained why he had a sheen of perspiration on his upper lip and looked like he might lose whatever breakfast he'd had time to grab.

He nodded in response and looked away from the body as if he'd seen enough. Poor kid was going to have to toughen up if he wanted to stay on the job.

"Okay, we can take her down," she said to Dr. Wembley, who was practically shaking with anxiety. The paramedics hustled in with a stretcher and Oz pulled out a knife he was carrying and sawed away at the rope.

Stephanie signaled the young investigator to get some more shots of the girl once she'd been pulled away from the tree and then of the tree itself.

Then they hustled the girl away with some sort of heating blanket wrapped around her and Dr. Wembley rushed after them, promising over her shoulder to call Oz and Stephanie from the hospital.

"No way is that girl alive," Oz said. "I'm sorry, but that is just wishful thinking."

"Yeah, maybe." Stephanie looked again at the crime scene, now devoid of a body, and walked over to one of the uniforms. "Who found the body?"

The female officer jerked her thumb over her shoulder toward the path where the woman in running clothes was standing with another officer. "A teacher. She's pretty shook up."

"It would be news if she wasn't," Stephanie said. "Did she touch anything?"

The officer flushed, an ugly color climbing her neck, all

the way to the roots of her hair, which Stephanie could see because she was taller. The woman had obviously forgotten to check and Stephanie was glad that she'd asked and not Oz or one of the other detectives. There weren't that many women on the force and she knew how quick some of the guys were to assume that your genitals determined your judgment.

Schaeffer, the officer's badge said. Somebody Schaeffer. Stephanie searched her memory, but couldn't come up with the first name. Pam? Jan? Something short like that, but she didn't risk trying one out.

"No problem. I'll talk to her."

The teacher was young enough that in her sweatshirt and exercise pants she could easily be mistaken for a student. She was average height and skinny to the point that she needed to put on a few pounds, with curly blond hair pulled back in a short ponytail.

Stephanie introduced herself and the other woman shook her hand, turning wide blue eyes on her with a look that Stephanie recognized as shock.

"Did you know the victim?" she said gently, but the woman still winced at the word.

She shook her head. "No. I'm new." Her voice trembled, but she paused and it toughened. "I don't really know any of the students, not yet."

Stephanie talked her through the discovery of the body, taking notes while watching the woman's body language and tone of voice, weighing almost unconsciously the truth of what she was saying. There was no deception that Stephanie could detect, at least not about this victim and this crime scene. There was a hint of fear, but it probably had as much to do with being the focus of police attention as anything else.

"Did you touch anything?"

"The rope. I tried to undo it." The woman's eyes filled with tears and she blinked them back. "I thought, I mean, I didn't know if she was—" Her voice trembled again and she stopped talking.

Dead, Stephanie finished for her mentally. "Did you see anyone else this morning?"

"No."

"Do you always run at this hour of the morning?"

The woman shook her head, blond curls escaping. She tucked them back behind her ears. "This was the first day of classes," she said. "I have to teach this morning."

Again, it sounded like the truth. She didn't look like she'd spent the last couple of hours tying someone to a tree and her clothes weren't wet.

"I need to get going. Can I leave?" she said, arms wrapped around her body again. She was shivering, but Stephanie doubted it was from the cold.

"I think you're a little shocky," she said. "You should probably see someone. Why don't you let one of the officers take you over to the hospital to get checked out?"

But the teacher was shaking her head before Stephanie was finished. "No, thanks, I'm fine." She forced a smile. "I've got to teach this morning."

Stephanie thanked her and signaled for Officer Schaeffer to walk Ms. Kavanaugh back to the school. Then she retraced her steps to Oz, paying close attention to the ground around her. The grass was short and sparse in places, the ground softer the closer she got to the water. There was at least one visible footprint and she pointed it out to the CI taking shots. It made her wonder how the vic had gotten here. Walked? And if she were going for a swim, wouldn't she have brought a towel?

Suddenly Stephanie thought of something and looked up. Circle. Tree. Naked body. Rope. "Where are her clothes?"

"What?" Oz turned from the body.

"The vic. Did she walk up here naked?"

He looked around. "And without shoes? Her feet weren't cut up."

Stephanie felt a little glimmer of excitement that faded when she found out that the clothes had already been bagged by an overzealous investigator.

"Stupid shit," Oz grumbled once they'd taken a look. "Watched too many episodes of *CSI* and think they run this show."

"So she comes up here and leaves her clothes in a neat little pile, takes a swim, and then someone comes along and ties her to the tree—"

"And what? Waits for her to die?"

"Unless she didn't wasn't supposed to die," Stephanie said.

"What do you mean?"

"What if was a game or some sort of ritual?"

"Like hazing?"

"Yeah, something like that. Maybe it's a club initiation."

Only the headmistress denied that such a thing was possible at St. Ursula's. "There is no hazing at St. Ursula's," she said, shaking her head at them as if they were foolish even to suggest such a thing. "Our girls simply would not tolerate anything like that."

They were sitting in the headmistress's office, admitted to the inner sanctum because she wanted them off the front lawn and away from the all-too-curious eyes of other students and teachers. A carafe of good coffee had been brought in by the secretary, along with porcelain cups with saucers and a silver cream-and-sugar set. It was all very dignified and seemed completely incongruous after the scene in the woods.

The crime scene investigators had been packing up when the captain called in on Oz's phone to let them know that the victim couldn't be revived. It was once they'd finished explaining this to the headmistress that she'd invited them into her office.

Oz looked like he didn't know where to put his feet and

the chair he was sitting on had creaked ominously when he sat down.

"I understand that the police have to ask these questions," Sister Rose Merton said, "but it's completely out of character for our school."

Stephanie recoiled inwardly at that statement. The way Sister Rose said "the police" sounded suspiciously like someone saying "the help." Like any good detective, she schooled her features so they wouldn't reveal the hostility she felt toward this woman. It wasn't personal as much as a knee-jerk, blue-collar bias from the daughter of a cleaning lady.

"We'll need you to identify the body, Sister," she said.

"Oh? But is that really necessary? I have trouble believing that this poor person could be connected in any way to our school."

Stephanie blinked and even Oz looked stunned. "Well, we think she's probably a student," he said slowly. "She's pretty young."

"What? One of our girls?" Sister Rose sounded truly shocked. "I mean, I know she was found on our campus, but I just assumed . . ." her voice trailed off.

That tragedy only happened to other people? Poor people? Stephanie purposely slurped her cup of coffee before letting the cup clatter into the saucer. Coffee splashed onto the small table and Sister Rose's eyes flickered to it, but she didn't say anything.

"She had very distinct red hair," Stephanie said. "About shoulder length. And a small tattoo of a butterfly on her left shoulder."

Sister Rose frowned. "A tattoo? That doesn't sound like a St. Ursula's girl, we don't allow—" She stopped short and her face changed.

"What?" Oz said. "Do you know who it is?"

A hand crept to Sister Rose's mouth and she nodded, eyes

large. "But it can't be," she whispered. "Not one of our girls."

"It might not be," Stephanie said. "But if you think you know who it is we really need to contact that girl's family."

"Morgan Wycoff."

"She's a boarder?"

Sister Rose nodded. "Just started last year. I think her mother thought it might help her fit in." She fiddled with the pin on her lapel and looked up at them with concern. "That poor girl. Her poor mother."

"Her family lives in town?"

"Yes. Her mother. It was just the two of them."

"Do you have Mrs. Wycoff's address? We're going to need it."

"Of course, of course." Sister Rose went into the other room.

"That's a little weird," Stephanie commented in a whisper.

"What?"

"That she didn't just assume it would be one of the students."

Oz shrugged. "Nobody thinks it's going to be someone they know."

Stephanie thought about her own happy or at the least indifferent memories of attending the local public school, and wondered what it would be like to attend a private school like this one, with its uniform and tradition and the weird commingling of religion and education. She wasn't a Catholic, though. Maybe it was normal for Catholics.

They drove straight from the school to the Wycoff residence, which turned out to be in the wealthiest neighborhood in Gashford, Briar Ridge. This was the land of large empty homes with security systems and housekeepers that commuted all the way from poor neighborhoods in Jersey or the boroughs.

The Wycoff home was a large frame Colonial in yellow with black shutters and front door. They parked behind a green BMW and the front door opened before they were halfway up the walk.

A red-haired woman in a business suit, who looked like an older version of the girl tied to the tree, greeted them without preamble. "Have you found her?"

Oz glanced quickly at Stephanie with a look that conveyed how shitty this was going to be. Then he said, "Are you Mrs. Wycoff?" Not because either of them were in any doubt, but you had to ask, you had to follow procedure.

"Yes, yes. I called last night and this morning. Where is my daughter? Have you found her?"

"Could we speak inside, Mrs. Wycoff?"

"Oh, God." She was a tall woman with good posture, but she seemed to fold in on herself a little. "Yes, okay, yes." She stepped back for them to pass and Stephanie stepped inside the cool hallway while trying to compose her own nerves.

"Is there a Mr. Wycoff?" Oz asked.

The woman frowned. Her trembling lips drew together in a thin line. "We're divorced."

They were standing in a tiled entranceway, the beige of the floor complementing the walls, which were painted in a corresponding shade of cream. On one wall was a painting of a placid landscape in a gilt frame, on another a gilt-framed mirror. All very ordered, very serene.

Oz glanced at Stephanie. She took the lead. "Mrs. Wycoff, when was the last time you saw Morgan?"

"Yesterday afternoon. I helped her move in. She was supposed to call me last night, but she didn't. When she didn't call this morning I phoned the police."

"Instead of the school?"

Mrs. Wycoff nodded. "Morgan wasn't happy there. She threatened to leave more than once." One hand moved to her mouth in a fretful gesture. The other thin arm was pressed against her stomach. "Please. Has something happened?"

"I'm sorry to have to tell you that the body of a girl matching Morgan's description was found this morning at St. Ursula's."

The woman uttered a groan so deep that it sounded primeval. She shook her head slowly at first, then faster, whipping it back and forth.

"We'll need you to identify your daughter," Oz said gently.

"No, no. God, no."

Stephanie reached out a hand to steady her, but Mrs. Wycoff jerked out of her reach. "No!" she said again, screaming it this time.

"We're so sorry," Oz said.

"It isn't Morgan," the other woman said. "It isn't!"

"Do you have any family member that we could call?" Stephanie asked.

Mrs. Wycoff shook her head and for the first time tears sprang to her eyes. "It's just us. I'm an only child and so is Morgan. My mother's in a nursing home."

"How about a friend?"

In the end a neighbor came with them, a seventy-some-year-old woman in a baby-pink twinset with a matching headband in her iron-gray hair. She smelled faintly of menthol and gin, but she clutched Mrs. Wycoff's hand firmly.

They took them both in the back of the car to the medical examiner's offices. By the time they got there the body had been delivered, cleaned up for identification, and a sheet drawn over the pale limbs, the livid marks left by the rope hidden from view.

Mrs. Wycoff took several deep breaths, holding her friend's hand before nodding for the sheet to be pulled back. After the briefest look she fell over backward in a full faint, pulling her friend down with her and hitting the floor before Oz or the lab assistant could catch her.

"Oh shit," Oz said and the elderly friend gave him an affronted look. She accepted his arm to get to her feet. "Poor Janice," she said. "Poor, poor Janice."

It took waving a bottle of smelling salts under her nose to get Janice Wycoff to come to. She moaned as she sat up and tears ran down her face. Stephanie felt nauseated and had to fight the urge to run from the building.

Instead, she and Oz drove Mrs. Wycoff and her friend back to their pristine neighborhood and the friend took over, leading all of them into the living room, instructing them to place Janice on an upholstered sofa and disappearing into the kitchen only to return in a few minutes with a slug of whiskey.

Stephanie saw Oz looking longingly at the glass, but the woman had brought only one and she held it to Janice Wycoff's lips as if she were a baby who needed to be suckled.

"Was your daughter depressed?" Stephanie asked after the woman had dutifully swallowed and grimaced on the harsh burn of liquor.

"She's—she was—a teenager," Janice Wycoff said in a dull voice. "They're all depressed. Hormones."

"Did it seem worse lately?"

"No. I don't know. She didn't tell me everything." Tears welled up in her eyes and she didn't blink them back. They slipped onto her cheeks and trailed down the powdered face, disappearing around her jaw and down her neck.

"Did she have any enemies?" Oz said.

More tears. Janice covered her eyes for a moment, her shoulders shaking. "She was different," she said after a moment. "She was a smart girl, creative—not a joiner. She didn't like school."

"Was she religious?" Stephanie handed Mrs. Wycoff some tissues from the box on the coffee table.

Janice mopped at her face and shook her head. "Not as a Catholic, if that's what you mean. She stopped going to church—outside of school, I mean—more than a year ago.

She said it was hypocritical and frankly I couldn't argue with that."

She shot them a red-eyed but defiant look, as if expecting them to find this objectionable.

"Perhaps I should have forced her," she said. "I'm sure her father would have argued for that, but I'm a single parent. I did the best I could."

"Of course you did," her friend said stoutly.

"Besides, she'd found another religion," Janice Wycoff added.

"What was that?"

"Wicca. She was a self-proclaimed Wiccan."

Chapter Four

The news of Morgan's death spread to every member of the St. Ursula's community before Lauren made it back to her house. She could feel the eyes of dozens of students, not to mention the other teachers and staff who had gathered around the main building.

"We'll need to talk to you later," the female cop had said, handing her a card just as if she were some insurance broker and not a homicide detective.

Back in the privacy of her room, Lauren locked her door, tossed the card on the table, and gave in to the temptation to cry.

She sank into the armchair and curled up, dropping her head into her hands and allowing the tears that had been pricking at the back of her eyes since she'd first found the body to spill over.

She didn't know how long she sat there, but the tears weren't cleansing. She felt just as sick when she forced herself up and into the bathroom to shower, but as soon as she'd stripped off her sweaty clothes she had to run to the toilet to retch.

Her hands shook on the tap as she started the water and she stood under the hot spray until it ran cold, trying to stop the tears that kept falling down her face, trying to forget the sight of that pale body tied so cruelly to the tree.

She had lied to the police when she said she didn't know the girl. She knew her, there was no mistaking that red hair. It was the girl who'd been smoking on the steps when she came for the interview, the girl whose mother had been meeting with the headmistress.

Who could have done something like that? It was so strange, so cruel, the rope cutting so tightly into that pale skin. She pressed her hands against her closed eyes, trying to stem the tears, trying to push the vision away, but the girl's pale body appeared over and over again in shocking detail, a slide show of images that began to merge with others until the sound of rushing water became instead a roar of flames and she saw the flickering of reddish orange before her eyes and she opened them with a gasp.

Panting, Lauren stared at the flow of water down her arms, turning her hands so it collected in her palms, where she could just barely see the etched spiderweb of white lines, like trace embroidery or the nearly invisible veins of a leaf.

She felt just as sick when she got out of the shower. She had less than an hour to get ready for class, less than an hour to forget what had happened and focus on teaching.

When she was dressed, with her hair curling in wet strands against her back, she padded into the small kitchen and made a cup of tea, unable to bear the thought of anything stronger.

She carried the cup into the living room and sank into the chair behind the small desk. Spread out on its surface were her lesson plans for the week, meticulous notes in neat, even printing.

Staring down at the page, she remembered the scrawl that

had been Amanda's handwriting, the large, loopy letters racing across hastily written pages. Laughing over silly notes. A lifetime ago.

She shook her head, trying to forget. Amanda was gone, the flat in London was gone, and Michael was gone. They were the past but the past didn't want to let her go. And alone in the woods coming upon that body in the fog had brought it all rushing back. Amanda, she'd thought when she saw the girl. Amanda.

The sound of paper tearing brought her back. Lauren stared down at the meticulous notes now crumpled in her clenched hands. She dropped them, springing back from the desk.

What was she thinking? She couldn't teach, she'd been stupid to apply for this job, stupid to leave the safety and anonymity of the city schools. How long before the police showed up asking more questions? They already seemed suspicious that she was running around campus so early in the morning. How long before one of them accused her of the murder of that poor girl?

The small stack of bills neatly arranged on the opposite corner of the desk caught her eye. All she could afford was the minimum payment and on some of them she hadn't even been paying that.

Lauren sank back down at the desk and smoothed the crumpled pages with hands that trembled. She willed them to be steady. The important thing was not to panic. The police didn't know her. No one knew her here. She needed this job and she needed to succeed at it. There was no going back.

Early American History was in the main building of the school, in one of the older classrooms. Taking a deep breath, Lauren pushed open the door and walked in. The hum of conversation ceased, just like that, and the sudden scrape of a chair's legs against the linoleum floor was loud.

Walking briskly to the front desk, her heels clicking like little castanets on the floor, Lauren put her briefcase down and turned to face the class. Twenty girls stared back at her with frank curiosity, none of them looking especially friendly.

"Good morning," Lauren's voice sounded loud and falsely cheery in her own ears. She was unprepared for all the students to repeat her greeting in unison. She jumped and someone tittered.

Feeling her face flush, Lauren turned to the blackboard and picked up a piece of chalk. It broke with a squeak as she drew a capital "L" and a muffled wave of laughter rolled behind her. She could feel the color in her face climbing her neck and ears and wished that she'd left her hair down instead of pinning it up so she looked more mature.

Scrawling her name quickly across the board she turned. "I'm Lauren Kavanaugh," she announced, "your new history teacher. Let's begin with the roll."

She picked up the list that had been left in the center of the desk and read off the names, trying to still the shaking of her hands.

Each girl responded with "here," some of them sounding bored, some of them cheerful, some like automata, as if they were just doing time. When she called out Nicole Morel there was silence and her eyes swept the classroom, looking and failing to find anyone responding to that name.

She'd reached Bonnie Wharton when the classroom door suddenly opened and a small girl with short dark hair slunk into the room, books clutched to her chest. "Sorry, Madame," she said, with an accent. "I got lost."

A few titters over this. Lauren frowned at the class then smiled at the girl. "No problem, it's a big campus. I'm Ms. Kavanaugh and you are?"

"Nicole Morel."

"Aah," Lauren checked her name off. "Please take a seat, Ms. Morel."

She looked back down at the roll and without thinking about it called out, "Morgan Wycoff."

There was sharp intake of breath from a girl in the front row and someone else gasped. Lauren realized her mistake. So this was the girl. She hadn't heard the last name before. She moved hastily to the next name.

"Rachel Yarrow."

A plump, sleepy-looking girl raised a languid hand. "Here."

When the list was done, Lauren turned immediately to her textbook. "We'll begin with chapter one."

By noon, with two classes under her belt, Lauren felt as if she'd been running a marathon. She paused at a drinking fountain on the way to the dining hall, stepping out of the waves of students flowing past and waiting behind a tiny freshman before hastily swallowing some water.

"You should bring a bottle to class with you." The voice above her was cool.

She straightened and looked at a dark-haired man in a pinstripe suit grinning at her.

"Ryland Pierce," he said, sticking out a hand. His nails were manicured. "And you must be Lauren Kavanaugh."

"Must I?"

He laughed. "Well, you match the description I got from our dear headmistress. I'm St. Ursula's guidance counselor and I've been sent in that capacity to guide you through the hazards of your first official school lunch in our dining hall."

He laughed again and suddenly gripped her just above her left elbow, steering her in the direction of the cafeteria, chattering about the school and traditions and lots of other nonsense that Lauren didn't hear because she was so annoyed by his handling her that she could concentrate on nothing but extricating herself politely from his grip.

She got her chance when he paused to reprimand a student for running and she briskly stepped ahead of him so that he had to hurry to catch up as she crossed the campus toward the dining hall.

"We're so sorry that you found Morgan Wycoff," he said in a stage whisper once he'd caught up. "Not that it would be pleasant for any of us, mind you, but for a new teacher here—" He grimaced and then held the door open for her.

In some ways, the dining hall was much like other school cafeterias, complete with trays, food being kept warm under heat lamps, served by grumpy-looking, stolid ladies wearing hairnets. The similarities ended just past the cashier.

Instead of metal-and-Formica molded cafeteria tables, there was row upon neat row of wooden refectory tables with wooden chairs. The tables were laid with white linen, real flatware, and cloth napkins, and every table had a centerpiece of a small flowering plant.

"There are two prefects chosen from both the sophomore and junior classes and four from our senior class," Pierce explained. "These girls take turns monitoring the dining hall."

Pierce led her toward the faculty section, identical to the rest of the seating except that the long tables were separated from the students by a raised platform. It gave the teachers a clear view of what was happening across the dining hall, but it also afforded them little privacy.

"One of the downsides of being a teacher," a middle-aged woman wearing a tweed suit said with a grin as Lauren sat down. "They say being on this platform is putting us in a place of honor, but the truth is that we're really just on display for the herd. Feels strange, doesn't it?"

"Alice, you'll scare her," an older man admonished. He stood up and extended his hand across the table. "Leonard Whitecliff, and this is my esteemed colleague in the English department, Alice LaRue."

"Oh Leonard, you're the one who'll scare her with your *Masterpiece Theatre* manners." Alice laughed and offered her right hand to Lauren while taking a small roll from a basket with her left. "Personally, I still eat here for these." She broke open the bread and steam rose from it. "Aah. Warm bread is the true mark of civilization."

A tall, quiet man seated to Lauren's right chuckled at that. "My vote goes to indoor plumbing," he said. "James Bolton, science."

There was a flurry of other introductions and she promptly forgot most of the names. She'd gotten a salad to eat and there were sweating glass pitchers of iced tea and water with slices of lemon floating in both.

"We understand that you're the one who found Morgan," Alice LaRue said. The others paused in their eating and looked expectantly at Lauren.

"Yes," she said.

"We've heard that she was naked? Is that true?" Ryland Pierce asked.

Lauren's hand faltered and the iced tea she was pouring splashed onto the linen cloth. A pool of amber spread around her glass as she dabbed at it with her napkin.

James placed a hand gently on hers, stilling Lauren. "It's okay," he said in a low voice. "They've seen worse stains."

Lauren looked up to see a row of expectant faces. "Yes," she said. "She was naked."

Her appetite shriveled as she said it. She had managed to push the image of that girl's drawn face and purplish skin far from her mind while she was teaching, but now it rushed back with a vengeance. She could feel bile rising and thought she might be ill.

"She was a very strange girl," Leonard said. "She really didn't fit in here."

Alice grimaced. "Oh, Leonard, just because she was a free spirit."

"Flouting all the rules, repeatedly—that goes beyond being a free spirit." Natalie Myers, a startlingly thin math teacher said with a moue of distaste.

"I'd say that's the very definition." Alice countered, slathering another roll with butter. She munched on it placidly.

"I'm afraid I'll have to agree with Leonard and Natalie," Ryland Pierce said, but he didn't sound at all regretful. "She was quite a handful. It's just like her to cause controversy even in death."

Natalie suddenly said, "She's dead. Let's not speak ill of her."

"I'm surprised the media hasn't shown up yet," Ryland said as if she hadn't spoken.

"St. Ursula's doesn't need the publicity," Alice said with dismay. "Not just when we're recovering from what happened two years ago."

Lauren asked, "What happened two years ago?"

"Two stupid kids killed driving drunk," Leonard said.

Alice added, "They crashed into a tree on campus. For some reason it made the national news—you probably saw it."

Lauren shook her head. "I was out of the country."

"Oh? Where were you?" Leonard gave her an inquiring smile.

"Studying in London."

"Lucky you," Alice said. "Did you get to Paris? I adore Paris—I got these there some twenty years ago." She fingered the string of long, swirled-glass beads around her neck.

"Heavens, Alice, she was a baby twenty years ago!" Natalie said with a laugh. "I'm surprised Sister Rose hired someone so young to replace Sister Agnes. No offense." The last directed at Lauren with a little laugh.

She was spared from replying by Alice. "Poor Agnes. That was really awful. It's amazing how fast the mind can disintegrate."

"What happened?" Lauren asked.

"Alzheimer's," Leonard said. "And the worst part was people didn't understand, well, at least not until the paranoia."

Ryland Pierce interrupted him. "Goodness, this is de-

pressing lunch conversation. Let's turn to something more
pleasant, shall we?" He shone his capped-tooth smile on them
all and Alice gave a little harrumph under her breath.

"Tell us about your background, Ms. Kavanaugh," he
said. "I understand you attended a prep school outside of
Pittsburgh?"

Lauren nodded and took a bite of salad. She hoped he'd
move on, but it appeared that he'd just started.

"Where was that?"

"St. Mary's Academy."

"Oh, I'm not familiar with that one. It must seem like old
times coming to St. Ursula's. Is it similar?"

"A bit," she said while thinking, too much. It was too similar to her past, too much a reminder of the girl she'd been
and of everything she'd hoped to forget when she went to
Europe. *"Aah, Catholic schoolgirls wrapped so tight in their
little plaid skirts." Michael laughing as he looked at a class
picture.*

"Was it a boarding school?" Alice said.

"No." She'd longed to go to boarding school, wanted desperately to get away from that picture-perfect house and the
expectation that it would hold a picture-perfect family. When
she thought of those years it was often of the hours spent in
a spacious, cold dining room, sitting ramrod straight at that
vast polished table while being forced to endure formal
meals with older parents for whom she'd been an unwelcome surprise.

They'd had their three children, the five of them a perfect
tableau for family portraits and the annual Christmas card.
Her mother was forty-two when she found out she was pregnant again. Lauren's arrival disrupted the plan and she'd
grown up with the burden of knowing that it was only because of allegiance to their Catholic faith that she'd been
born at all.

"I'm sure many of our traditions will be familiar to you,"
the guidance counselor said.

"Yes, we're very big on tradition at St. Ursula's," Alice said. "Everything must be done in the same way as it's been done for the last one hundred years."

Leonard rolled his eyes. "Not if left to you, Alice. I'm sure we'd be doing liturgical dance in chapel if left to you." He shuddered. "As a history teacher, Ms. Kavanaugh, I'm sure you'll find the history of St. Ursula's very interesting."

"St. Mary's didn't have any ghosts?" James said. "Tell her about our ghost, Leonard."

"What ghost?" Lauren said.

"Oh, for heaven's sake," Ryland said with an uneasy laugh. "That's just an old story."

"I've seen her," Alice said with conviction. "It's not just a story." She leaned toward Lauren. "When the school was founded there were eight nuns living on the top floor of the main building. One of them, the youngest, hanged herself from the railing over the main stairs."

Lauren's mouth was dry. "Why?"

"She was pregnant," James said.

"Rubbish!" Leonard wiped his hands briskly with his napkin and threw it down on the table. "There's no evidence of that, no evidence at all."

"What are you talking about, Leonard?" Natalie argued. "Her grave's clearly marked—"

"Okay, one of the sisters died and died young. That doesn't mean she committed suicide, and as for the pregnancy story, it's just that."

"I know what I saw," Alice said.

Ryland gave a condescending chuckle. "Shadows, Alice. We've all seen them in that building late in the day."

"They weren't shadows," Alice insisted. "If Candace was here she'd tell you."

Lauren saw Natalie shift in her seat. "I don't know what you saw, Alice, but I do know that there are some things that fall outside our understanding of science."

"Throwing out the scientific method?" Leonard said, but

there was a twinkle in his eye. Natalie smiled, but Alice just shook her head dismissively and leaned across the table toward Lauren.

"She walks the halls at night," she said. "If you listen you can hear her footsteps on the marble floor."

She watched the new teacher with the intensity of a scientist studying a specimen under the microscope. It was entertaining to observe somebody new, to note the obvious physical differences and uncover the nuances.

The teacher was eating a salad, though she was already thin. A poor appetite or some sort of medical problem? Perhaps she was prone to anxiety. That would be useful to know.

She took her little notebook out and jotted down "health?" as a reminder to check for this when she went through the files. Nervousness could be exploited.

Miss Kavanaugh spilled some iced tea. That was interesting. What had caused that little accident? She peered over the cover of her book at the teacher, watching for and spotting the faint tremor in the woman's forearms. The new teacher hid it by tucking them in her lap while sad little Bolton mopped at the stain. Something had upset her. What was it? Were they discussing Morgan Wycoff?

Foolish Morgan with her silly beliefs. She was a liability for St. Ursula's. Everybody knew that, but only she dared to act.

She remembered tightening the rope around that wet, white skin and felt a delicious shiver running through her. It was a secret vein of gold running like a beacon through the dark mine of her body, that pleasure. When she was little she'd thought that everyone thrummed to its internal pulse.

How old had she been that time in the park? She didn't know, only that she was young enough that the nanny had been there, sitting on a bench with the other foreign women, all of them twittering about their employers when she came running up with the dead bird hot in her small palm.

Her baby girl's voice high and bright with the wonder of it, trying to capture nanny's attention with the story of pressing her little thumbs against the fine bones of the thin neck hidden under that ruff of feathers.

She could still remember the horror on the woman's round face when she held the bird out to her, its small head twisted to one side, a film already forming on its bead-like eyes.

She'd learned from this that the gift must be kept secret. So many didn't understand and those that did lacked the strength to follow through if she wasn't there to push them forward. Even those closest to her didn't really understand. It was a strange power, this intense feeling. When the others hesitated, she was the one who acted, searching again and again for that exquisite sensation.

She looked up from her notebook and saw that Miss Kavanaugh had gotten up, tray in hand, preparing to leave the dining hall. She stood up as well, following at a discreet distance as the teacher wove her way through the throngs of students clustered outside the dining hall and along the walkways that led from classroom buildings to dormitories.

The wind pulled wisps of Miss Kavanaugh's blond hair free from the clip holding it tight against the back of her neck. It blew about her face and she pushed it back with an impatient hand. She walked with her shoulders slightly raised, as if expecting an attack at any moment. Where did all that anxiety come from? How could it be exploited?

She followed along behind the teacher, her own shoulders relaxed, her stride relaxed and even, a little smile playing on her lips. No one who looked at her knew what was going on in her mind. They couldn't know that she imagined placing her hands around that slim neck, feeling the marble column beat its nervous pulse against her fingertips. She imagined the skin cool to her touch, the fluttering of the heartbeat, the pressing of her fingers deeper and deeper into the flesh.

She smiled at Miss Kavanaugh's back and walked on.

Chapter Five

The annual start-of-the-academic-year chapel service became a memorial service for Morgan Wycoff.

The school chapel stood to the right of the main building toward the center of campus, a stone building in a Gothic style. Lauren directed the girls of Augustine House into the building, noticing the high, arching stained-glass windows that ran the length of the chapel on either side, casting faint red and blue shadows against the wooden pews.

The long center aisle ended in two wide steps that led to the altar, a stone table covered in white linen. To the right of it was a plaster statue of a serene-looking Virgin Mary, a golden halo circling the bowed head, her long, thin palms pressed together for all time in prayer. Under the statue was an iron stand with hundreds of flickering votive candles.

Lauren waited for the girls to file into their assigned pews and then took her seat at the end of the last row. Across the aisle Alice LaRue gave her a discreet wave.

Someone had found the time to enlarge a yearbook photo of Morgan and it was standing in front of the altar surrounded by huge arrangements of white roses. The picture wasn't particularly flattering. Morgan stared sullenly out at the congregation, the vivid hair the most striking feature of the photo.

High-pitched voices sang "A Mighty Fortress Is Our God" and the congregation rose en masse as two rows of girls wearing white satin robes and carrying open hymnals led a procession to the altar. They were followed by a single girl dressed in the simple cassock of an altar server; she held a pole with a gold crucifix mounted at the top. Sister Rose was next, dressed in a somber black suit with a satin arm-band fixed to one sleeve. She carried an arrangement of white lilies and was followed by two more altar servers. Bringing up the rear was an elderly priest, his shoulders hunched as if he carried some burden under his snowy white robes.

After some opening prayers, Sister Rose mounted the steps leading to a beautifully carved and polished lectern. She had to pull the microphone down so she could reach it. "Usually this is a happy occasion," she began, her voice carrying across the pews. "We gather today just as we gather every year at this time to celebrate the beginning of another academic year. Today, however, our joy has turned to sorrow because we've lost one of our own. Morgan Wycoff, one of our third-year students, died this morning."

There was a murmur across the congregation and Lauren wondered what the students were whispering to one another. Sister Rose waited for the noise to fade away before continuing.

"It is difficult to understand why the Lord would choose to remove Morgan from us in this, the flower of her youth, but we must accept the will of the Almighty."

It was the will of God that Morgan be tied to a tree and left to die? Lauren felt bile rise in her throat and had to swallow hard. She shifted on the hard pew.

"At times like this, when our community has been torn asunder by tragedy, we must heal by drawing closer together, finding strength, as we always have in times of crisis, in our community."

Lauren couldn't help noticing that the headmistress hadn't mentioned anything about how Morgan died. Did she really believe that what happened in the woods was an accident? Did the police think so, too? It was bizarre.

"We can honor Morgan's memory by doing our best this year, by approaching our classes with determination, our responsibilities with enthusiasm, our extracurricular activities with joy. We must not let this tragedy cast a pall over St. Ursula's. Morgan wouldn't want that."

The burnished gold of the candlesticks on either end of the altar caught a change of light from the windows and flickered as if they, too, were on fire. *"Ave, ave, ave Maria!"* Treble voices, some wavering girls marching along with white tapers dripping wax onto small hands.

Lauren pressed a hand discreetly against the side of her head. It was hot in the chapel, the cloying sweetness of the full-blown roses mixing with the faint scents of furniture polish and incense.

She needed to get out, but it wasn't over. Sister Rose stopped speaking, but before she stepped away from the lectern she signaled to someone in the front row. "We'll now hear from St. Ursula's head girl, senior prefect Elizabeth Lincoln."

Sister Rose stepped carefully back down the steps as a tall, slender girl with long blond hair rose to take her place. The girl made her way gracefully to the front, pausing to bow in front of the altar. It wasn't the quick bob that most Catholics gave, but a full, reverent bend from the waist that managed to look both dramatic and pious.

She mounted the steps to the lectern slowly, as if she were walking to some internal beat, and she paused in front of the microphone, waiting until everyone's attention was on her before she spoke.

"Morgan was our classmate," she said. Her voice was pure, dulcet-toned. "She was our housemate and our team-mate. Most of all, Morgan Wycoff was our friend."

The congregation sat rapt. All the girls' eyes were on her and Lauren, too, was drawn to that lovely face. The girl was reminiscent of a Botticelli angel, her lightly tanned skin gleaming under the lanterns hanging from the chapel ceiling. The boxy uniform, with its classic box-pleat uniform skirt and Peter Pan–collar blouse didn't look shapeless or bulky on her as it did on most of the girls.

"This tragic death cannot diminish Morgan's life. She will be remembered by all of us not just for the girl she was, but the woman she would have become. We are tempted at such times to ask why? Why Morgan? Why now? Why did she leave the safety of our campus at night to venture places out-of-bounds?"

There was another wave of murmurs at this, but it died away quickly as the girl held up one hand. "We are tempted to focus on these things, but we must not. Instead of asking why, we must ask ourselves, what now? What should we learn from Morgan's life that will help us in our own strug-gles? What can we take from this experience that will help us grow stronger as a community?"

It was quite an impressive speech and by the end most of the teachers and many of the girl's classmates were nodding their heads. When she finished speaking, Elizabeth Lincoln was greeted by a spontaneous round of applause. She smiled and bowed her head, the very picture of humility. For a mo-ment, her pose mimicked the statue of the Virgin near her.

Her speech was followed by a less inspired but still heart-felt address by the gym teacher, a square-shaped woman of indeterminate age looking uncomfortable in an ill-fitting black pantsuit. She was the only female not wearing a skirt, but Lauren suspected that being out of a tracksuit was prob-ably a big concession for her.

"Morgan was a natural at volleyball. She was a power hitter and the team will really miss her." She said more about Morgan's volleyball skills, none of which made sense to Lauren, and then the woman suddenly burst into tears, as if a dam had broken, blubbering into her callused hands until Sister Rose stepped forward with a handkerchief and led her away from the lectern.

When the service ended, the girls filed out of the chapel section by section. Lauren lingered on the steps, trying not to make it too obvious that she was taking deep breaths.

A girl with cascade of curling black hair and clear green eyes approached her. "Are you Ms. Kavanaugh?"

"Yes. And you?"

"Kristen Townson. Welcome to St. Ursula's." The girl offered a hand and Lauren shook it, returning the girl's easy smile.

"You're the one who found Morgan, right?" Kristen said.

Lauren's smile faded. "That's right."

"Was she conscious when you found her?"

"Excuse me?"

"I mean, did she say anything? Before she died, I mean."

"No, that is, not that I know of—" Lauren's struggle to respond was interrupted by a familiar voice.

"Kristen!" Elizabeth Lincoln appeared out of the crowd, frowning at the black-haired girl. "Don't put Ms. Kavanaugh on the spot like that."

She turned to Lauren and offered her a handshake and an apologetic smile. "I must apologize, I'm sure Kristen didn't mean to be rude." She shot another severe look at the other girl, who mumbled an apology and disappeared into the crowd of girls.

"I'm sorry that you've had such an upsetting beginning to your teaching experience," Elizabeth said. "I hope it hasn't negatively affected your feelings about our school."

Lauren smiled, touched and a little amused by the girl's unconscious imitation of the headmistress.

"No, not at all," she said. She glanced around at the other

girls milling about the entrance to the chapel and wondered how many of them were asking the same questions that Kristen had. "Were you friends with Morgan?"

"I knew her a little," Elizabeth said, her gaze moving away from Lauren's and resting on the woods where the body had been found. "I wouldn't say we were close."

Chapter Six

Half the pictures taken of Morgan Wycoff's body were fuzzy. "Idiot says the camera wasn't working," Oz said, slapping them down on the table in the squad room with disgust. "Guess what I bet we find if we check it out?"

"There's no problem?" Stephanie said.

"Bingo."

"He's a new CI, right?" Detective Sean Cone flicked one of the pictures with his finger.

"Yeah. Stupid kid. So freaked out he couldn't hold the camera straight."

Detective Joe Frangione shook his graying head. "Don't they have age requirements? Jesus, why is this place crawling with snot-nosed kids lately?"

He glanced meaningfully at Stephanie and Sean and she gave him an evil smile. "Didn't they offer you the retirement package already? Maybe they figure some of us need to be here to wipe your ass if you won't leave."

"Whoa, someone's sensitive!" He held up big hands, warding her off. "Warn me next time when you're on the rag."

"Sure thing, but I thought Depends would be a better choice for your problem."

Oz grinned as Joe muttered something about getting coffee and stalked away. "A little testy today?"

"Don't start with me. The guy's a dickhead." She looked at the pictures over and over again and went through them one by one, lining them up on the table and pulling out the case notes. She *was* a little testy. She'd been tense, tired, and in need of a drink by the time she'd left work last night and coming home to find Alex still sulking hadn't made her feel any better.

"Do you seriously think one interrupted fuck is worth all this?" she demanded after he'd answered her in monosyllables for ten minutes.

"One, I'd appreciate it if you wouldn't refer to our love-making as 'fucking' and two, you've got the mouth of a trucker. That's really attractive." He'd been standing with his back to her in the kitchen, chopping vegetables to throw into a stir-fry with some tofu. She hated tofu.

"One, I wish you wouldn't itemize everything and two, I hate tofu and you should know that by now."

His back went rigid, then he stalked past her to the silver-ware drawer, grabbed a spoon, and spent five minutes laboriously removing all the tofu and flinging it into the sink.

She should have laughed, she could laugh about it now, but at the time it just further pissed her off because it seemed so trivial compared with everything she'd dealt with that day.

So she'd called him a jackass and he'd responded by saying that he refused to talk to her when she cursed at him and she responded to that by calling him every foul name she could think of—and after seven years as a cop she knew quite a few—and he responded by shaking his head and giving her his patented disappointed look, at which point she slammed out of the house.

Cooling her temper over a beer at the nearest dive bar, conveniently located one short and fast drive around the corner, she pondered just how weird it was that she was in some sort of gender reversal with her soon-to-be-spouse. She was the cop, he was the gardener. Okay, landscape architect, but it was all about playing with plants. She loved action movies, he preferred comedies and could get misty at so-called chick flicks. She enjoyed cursing and resorted to it under stress, yet she'd never heard him say more than one muttered "shit" when he couldn't get something to work, and he'd never cursed at her.

All her girlfriends envied her. Alex was so kind and caring, so compassionate, so everything that their apparently Neanderthal boyfriends and husbands weren't. She might have wondered about his sexual orientation if it weren't for the fact that he obviously enjoyed sex with women and more importantly with her.

In fact, sex—making love—was the one area where they'd always been in complete agreement. Until lately. Until he'd gotten his license and a job with a great local firm and seemed to wake up to the fact that his girlfriend's job didn't come with such regular hours and never would. He'd been proud when she made detective a year ago, but he must've misunderstood the job because he seemed to think that she should be home with him at a regular time every night and spend her weekends with him.

And since they'd gotten engaged it was even worse. Snide comments every time the phone rang or her pager beeped. If they were in the middle of something and she answered the phone, he took it as a personal affront. It was as if she'd struck a blow to his manhood when she wasn't so blinded by his prowess as a lover that she could even hear a summons from the job.

After twenty minutes and two beers, she'd lost the anger she brought with her to the bar, but then she waited another twenty minutes before venturing out on the roads. She had seen enough DUIs to know it was never worth the risk.

The house was dark. Alex was sitting alone in the living

room watching a ball game on TV and drinking a beer. He didn't look up when she came in the room.

"I'm sorry."

He turned his gaze to her, but his face was cold. Even his eyes, and she loved his brown eyes, were cold.

"I shouldn't have cursed at you, I'm really sorry."

He nodded and turned his gaze back to the game. She stood there, feeling stupid for a moment, then went to take a shower.

The tears came when she was under the water and she tried to hold them back. Shitty, shitty day. She was a bad cop for taking it home with her. You weren't supposed to do that. Cops who did that imploded. You had to separate, find a place inside you that the violence couldn't touch, only she couldn't do that with death.

Kids were always the hardest. She didn't think any cop ever got past the kids. You tried not to think about what they'd suffered, you tried to be objective when you had to catalog bruises blossoming like flowers on a small body or write down which limbs were misshapen from a child being shaken or thrown. You swallowed your anger when you questioned the asshole sitting across from you who'd inflicted those injuries. You played the game because that's what you were sworn to do—uphold the law—even if the law seemed to protect the rights of useless fuckers while failing to protect their innocent victims.

This girl had been right on the brink. Not a girl anymore, but not a woman yet. Her body changing every day at that age. She'd been pretty, but she probably didn't know it. Not yet, not ever. Probably thought she was too fat or too thin or that her hair should've been straight or a different color. Skin that pale wouldn't tan. Had that been another part of her body that she'd grieved?

She heard the bathroom door click open while she was gulping back more tears and then the shower curtain slid back and Alex stepped in behind her and wrapped his arms around her.

"I'm so sorry," she said, turning in his arms so she could get her own around his neck. She wasn't apologizing to him this time as much as to the girl, but he didn't need to know that. He held her and kissed her head and bent to kiss her face and they stood there, rocking for a long minute before he said, "I'm sorry, too."

He'd brushed a hand across her breast and then bent to take her nipple in his mouth and she moaned against him, feeling herself respond the way she always did to his touch. She grabbed him with her hand because she didn't have much use for foreplay and he shifted her up against the wall so he could slip inside her and then they fucked, made love, whatever either of them wanted to call it, and afterward she'd fallen asleep in the safety of his arms.

So why was she testy again today? Because she knew they should've talked? Because he'd made another comment this morning when she'd left early, grabbing an apple for breakfast instead of the eggs he'd offered to make? They would have to talk, but that took energy and time and right now she needed both those things for this case.

Oz picked up the clearer photo of the pentagram and tapped it. "I think this is all the evidence we need to say this was some weird Wicci ritual gone bad."

"Wicca," Stephanie said. "I don't know. Look at the way she was tied. That rope was digging into her skin. I don't think she was voluntarily participating in this. This looks like a Matthew Shepard thing to me."

Detective George Wacker, known as Wackjob to his peers, groaned. "Christ Jesus, please don't go spreading some *Brokeback Mountain* theory around."

"Yeah, we don't need some faggot from the *Village Voice* up here." Joe "Fuck-off" Frangione was back with his coffee.

"Really sensitive," Sean said and then he flushed. He was the youngest next to Stephanie. Midthirties and baby-faced enough to look at least a decade younger.

Everyone paused to look at him for a moment and then Oz laughed and Wackjob said, "Shut up, Puff Daddy."

"I don't know why you keep calling me that—it's Sean Cone, not Sean Combs."

"Yeah, yeah, Puff Daddy."

"It's not like I even like rap."

"And you're pretty white, white boy," Wackjob, who was black and proud, said with an indulgent smile.

Sean flushed again, an embarrassing line of red climbing up his face from his collar. Stephanie's unsympathetic response was to be glad it wasn't her.

"Can we focus on the case?" Fuck-off said in between slurps of his coffee. Of the four other detectives in the department he was the only one Stephanie actually disliked. A big man, at least six-four and probably 250 on a doughnut-free day, he liked to throw his weight around with suspects and made no bones about the fact that he thought the only work suitable for women was domestic. He was an asshole, but he was an asshole with a gold badge and a gun and she had enough wisdom to know just how scary that was.

"I didn't say anything about gay, I just said it looked like harassment," she said. "Who would allow themselves to be tied up like that?"

"You're forgetting what we found around her." Oz tapped the faint circle visible in the photo. "Her own mother said she was into this whole Wicci thing. And let's not forget that she was drunk."

That had been one interesting find from the autopsy. Harriet Wembley found traces of alcohol in the girl's bloodstream.

"A trace amount," Stephanie said.

"It could have dissipated over time. She and her friends do some drinking and then they play this whole little witch game and then they leave her tied to the tree."

"They forgot her?" Fuck-off took a final gulp of coffee and then pitched the cup behind him into a metal trash can. "Hey, two points! Some friends."

Oz nodded. "Let's see if we can't find someone who can tell us exactly what that circle and those words mean."

Janice Wycoff had given Stephanie and Oz a short list of names of her daughter's friends and it was this list they had in hand when they made their way back into the main building of St. Ursula's.

They were met, almost immediately, by the headmistress. She exuded the same calm that she had the day before, moving almost soundlessly on her plain low-heeled shoes and wearing what looked like the same suit as the day before. Perhaps it was. The blouse this time had lace at the collar. It seemed incongruous.

"I'm sure you understand how upsetting this has been for all of us," she said, leaving the list untouched between them on her desk, a piece torn from a yellow legal pad, the words scrawled across it in black ballpoint. "I can't tell you if these girls are students here. That would violate their privacy."

She touched the list then, picking it up and offering it back to them. "Morgan's unfortunate death has already disrupted the beginning of the school year and we're trying very hard to keep things as normal as possible."

"We understand your concerns, Sister," Oz said and Stephanie squirmed slightly, thinking that there was something too placating in his tone. Where did this woman get off thinking that she could decide who they could question?

"But we really do need to talk to these girls," Oz continued. "It's essential for our investigation."

Sister Rose let the list hover a moment more and then, seemingly resigned to the fact that they wouldn't take it back, let it flutter back onto her clean desk surface. She sighed and pressed a hand to her throat for a moment in an absent-minded gesture that reminded Stephanie of someone choking.

"I'll need to secure parental permission," she said. "That could take a while."

Stephanie coughed and Oz glanced at her and gave an imperceptible nod. "Listen, Sister, we don't have a while," she said, trying to sound as sympathetic as Oz, but knowing that her impatience was probably not well hidden. "The first hours of an investigation into any crime are the most important."

"Crime? What crime?" Sister Rose's voice climbed and for a moment the placid mask cracked and the fear shone through, her pale eyes widening until Stephanie could see the veiny whites fully circling the pupils like variegated marble. "Morgan's death was an unfortunate accident," she said. "But it has nothing to do with the school. She made choices that were different from the ones offered here—"

She stopped short and the hand crept to her throat again and then down to fiddle with the edge of the leather blotter on which the list sat.

"Either I or our guidance counselor, Mr. Ryland Pierce, will need to be present," she said. "That's the only way I can allow it."

"Who does she think she is, the Pope?" Stephanie complained when the older woman left to find the counselor.

"She's just protective," Oz said. "She's been at the school a long time. Almost thirty years, I think."

Which had to make her what? Around seventy? She seemed younger than that, Stephanie thought, or maybe not younger but ageless. Timeless.

A short time later, as they walked through the halls to the library where they'd be conducting the interviews, Stephanie noticed the pictures on the walls of other girls, other classes, other years. There was a strange uniformity to it all even though time and hairstyles had changed. And habits. The nuns in the old pictures wore the scary-looking penguin costumes, their faces the only part of their bodies revealed, other than their hands, which always seemed to be folded as if in prayer.

It was clear within ten minutes of interviewing the girls that Janice Wycoff hadn't been as clued in to Morgan's life as she thought.

Several of the girls on the list denied being friends with Morgan at all.

"We had, like, one class together," one of the girls said, twirling a strand of straight brown hair around her finger. She looked at them with vapid eyes.

"What class?" Stephanie said.

"Religion. But we talked maybe once."

"What was that about?"

The girl shrugged with one shoulder as if she couldn't be bothered to raise both. "I don't know. I think it was something about there being no women priests. Something like that. Just how stupid it was, just bullshit—"

She covered her mouth, eyes widening with the first real interest they'd seen and an angry flush covered her pimply face. "Sorry."

Of the girls who conceded that yes, they had in fact been her friend, only one of them had anything of any significance to say.

She was short and dumpy, the boxy uniform skirt and kneesocks further shortening her body. Heather Lester, according to the list. She looked at them with suspicion, one pudgy hand fiddling with the strap of her messenger bag.

"Hey, Heather, come have a seat," Oz said, doing the whole fraternal thing, just one of the guys. He grinned, pointing to the chair at the table across from them, but while Heather took a seat, she didn't return his greeting or his smile. She had a pretty face, Stephanie thought, and then wondered how many times the girl might have heard that. Her features were small and even, her eyes round and outlined in heavy black liner. Her mouth was clearly and carefully outlined in a deep red shade of lipstick. Along with her short dark hair, which was pulled into little knots—sort of mini-ponytails—on either side of her head, it gave her the appearance of a child playing dress-up. Small silver earrings in a geometric shape hung from her ears. Around her short neck was another shape hanging from a leather cord.

"Morgan was fed up with the hypocrisy of this hellhole," she said. "All the rah-rah for St. Ursula's, one big happy family."

"It isn't one big happy family?" Oz said casually.

The girl rolled her eyes. "Hardly. All that school spirit is such shit."

Unlike the other student, she didn't seem concerned that she'd cursed. "Morgan was one of the few real people here."

Her eyes unexpectedly teared up, softening her harsh assessment of her fellow students.

"We've heard that Morgan believed in Wicca," Stephanie said. "Do you?"

The girl shook her head. "No way. I'm not into anything organized. It's all just one control system or another, isn't it?"

"But Morgan believed in it?"

Heather nodded. "Yeah. I don't know how serious she was. She liked the whole feminist thing, the goddess within us stuff. I think that's what appealed to her."

"Did the other girls accept her beliefs?" Oz asked.

The girl gave him a look that suggested she questioned his intelligence. "Hardly. They're all conformists. They made fun of her."

"How?" Stephanie asked.

"They called her 'witch,' 'satanist,' that sort of thing."

"Was it just name-calling?"

"No, sometimes it was more. Someone left a broom outside her door once, like it was her broomstick, and they used to leave nasty notes on her door, like 'You'll burn in hell,' that sort of thing. Just the kind, Christian response to a nonbeliever." The sarcasm was heavy in her voice.

Oz frowned. "Did she tell someone about it?"

"Like who?"

"The headmistress or the guidance counselor?"

Heather snorted. "No way."

"Why not?"

"Look, they don't listen to people like us."

Oz exchanged a look with Stephanie. She pulled her eyes back up from an examination of Heather's footwear. The shoes were dark leather, outlined with yellow stitching. Mary Janes on steroids. The soles looked rugged, different than the ones they'd found at the crime scene.

"People like us?" Stephanie prompted.

"Nonconformists. Me, Morgan, Beau Steuben. People who dare to ask questions about what these stupid rituals have to do with real life."

"What about Wiccan rituals? Were they stupid?" Oz asked.

The girl frowned at him. "Not to Morgan."

"Who's Beau Steuben?"

She shrugged. "Just this boy in town. He and Morgan went to school together when they were like five or something."

"Did you and Beau participate in any rituals with her?"

Heather shook her head. Stephanie studied her face closely, looking for a flicker of eyes or tilt of the head that could indicate lying. The girl was stolid, impassive.

"No. I told you—I don't do rituals."

"What about Beau?"

"How would I know?" She looked offended. "Do I look like his keeper?"

"Where were you two nights ago, Ms. Lester?"

She rolled her eyes. "My room. Where else would I be? There's nowhere else to go."

Stephanie suppressed a sigh and glanced down at the list of names. Next.

They wouldn't call *her* name; there was no reason. She passed by the library several times throughout the day just for the pleasure of catching a glimpse of the two detectives and their futile questioning.

Once the male detective came out to the hall to get a drink at the fountain and passed right by her. He was a large, lumbering man who gave her a goofy grin, pulling at his ugly pale blue tie as if it were choking his beefy neck.

He hardly looked competent enough to catch anyone. It was almost tempting to play with them, but she resisted the urge. Better to wait and watch and see what developed.

Later in the day she passed again and saw the female detective talking on a cell phone in the hall. She wore cheap shoes. They looked like they were hurting her feet. Her trousers were good quality but they needed to be pressed. She was young and attractive and her eyes were sharp.

They flicked over her while saying into the phone, "Nothing so far. I don't think we're going to get much." She resisted the urge to return the detective's gaze, walking down the hall at her same leisurely pace. Nothing, she thought. They had nothing and they would have nothing. She would use the detective's words when she told the others. It was the good news they needed. She hadn't doubted, but the others didn't have her strength or her gifts.

She had to lead them in all things. A minor irritant, this self-doubt. She'd never experienced such a disability herself. They looked to her as bleating sheep to a calm shepherd. And she would lead them, just like she always had.

The police would look, but they wouldn't find. She'd learned long ago that she could count on her own careful planning and the general principle that no one ever spotted anything hiding in plain sight.

Chapter Seven

Nicole Morel had been assigned as a roommate a quiet, plump girl who had the incongruously exciting name of Destiny. She'd gazed solemnly at Nicole behind owlish glasses upon her arrival and announced that since Nicole had gotten first pick of the beds, it was her choice as to which of the identical desks each would call their own. Nicole wasn't surprised when Destiny picked the one with the better view out the window.

They moved quietly around each other in the room, careful of personal space, careful not to touch each other's things. Nicole was nervous and wondered if Destiny felt the same. Would she have been happier rooming with another African American and not some half-French newcomer?

They set out their personal belongings quietly, both of them eyeing each other's things but with none of the chatter that Nicole heard coming from the other rooms.

Destiny put a series of framed photos on her dresser, all of them featuring her and a series of smiling people who had the same round faces and inquisitive eyes.

Nicole had two photos. The first was an aerial shot.

"What city is that?" Destiny had asked, moving closer to look at it. "Where did you take it?"

"Paris. From the Eiffel Tower."

The other photo was in a silver frame. Back home, her old home, its place had been on her bedside table. She found it wrapped in a sweater in her trunk. Her mother must have packed it because Nicole had left it behind.

There she was at ten, her smile so wide that the braces were visible on her teeth even though the picture had been taken from a distance. She was clutching her father's hand on one side and Paul's on the other. Her mother had her arm around Paul's shoulder. *Smile everybody, smile.*

They were standing by a fountain in Italy whose name she'd forgotten. Something famous. Something educational, Paul complained, and they didn't want to be educated on their holiday. Only he'd only said it to rile their mother and she'd laughed with him in the end. He'd always made her laugh.

"Is that your family?" Destiny had asked, her voice a jarring interruption.

"Yes." She placed the photo on the dresser next to the other picture. She put her clothes neatly away in the drawers and left her trunk in the hall to be taken down for storage.

Destiny was still unpacking. Nicole lay down on the bed, but from there she could see the photo. She got up and switched its place with the shot of Paris and stood back, assessing.

"Paul wouldn't want you to be this way." Her mother had said that to her so many times, but couldn't seem to take the advice herself. Her face had been so white and drawn. Not that her father had been any better since Paul's death; there had been circles under both her parents' eyes. They'd slept no better than she did, but the family meeting had focused on her.

They'd asked her to sit with them in the living room and

she was painfully aware of Paul's empty chair. They'd mentioned her falling grades, her truancy, her seeming lack of interest in everything she used to care about.

"You've given up ballet, riding, even going out with your friends," her mother said, ticking them off on her fingers.

How could she bear to explain to them that when she went to the ballet studio she saw Celeste, Paul's girlfriend? She didn't want to remind them of this and it hurt too much to reveal that most of her friends had really been Paul's. It was Paul everyone gravitated toward. He'd been so funny and full of life. She'd been included as his little sister, but once he was gone they were, too.

As for riding, it was easier to give up competing than to see the worry come back into her mother's eyes and feel her fear that she would lose another child.

"We are going back to the United States," her father had announced, stepping over her mother's concern, declaring his solution for whatever problem was at hand just as he always had.

"This isn't the time, Laurent!" Her mother hissed, her eyes flashing their annoyance. For a moment her father looked confused, but then his jaw hardened.

"We can't stay here now," he said, "there are too many ghosts here."

Were there other ghosts, Nicole wondered, or did he just mean Paul? Her grandmother had lived with them briefly, before she'd passed away. A sweet woman who was always pressing coins or foil-wrapped chocolates into their hands. They'd had the wake for her in Paris, too, but it had been different. Sighs and mournful faces, of course, but there had been laughter, too. Not like Paul's wake.

She'd taken the photo and angled it so that it couldn't be seen from the bed or from the desk. She would have put it in the drawer but her new roommate had seen it.

"You were talking in your sleep last night," Destiny an-

nounced as Nicole came into their room and dumped her
books on the desk. Nicole didn't respond.

"Don't you want to know what you were saying?" Destiny put aside the paperback she was reading and sat up on
her bed.

Nicole shrugged, trying to look unconcerned, and turned
from her roommate as if it didn't matter. She could feel her
face growing hot, though, and knew that the blush would
spread to the tips of her ears where Destiny could see it on
her pale skin. She pretended to be absorbed in arranging her
textbooks, but she was poised, listening.

"Well, I can't tell you because it was in French." Destiny
laughed. "And your French is a whole lot faster and better
than mine." She laughed again.

Nicole forced a smile, but her sense of relief wasn't
faked. She didn't want to embarrass herself. She didn't want
to scream Paul's name. She dreamed about him stepping off
the sidewalk, seeing it in slow motion, that slow step down,
his turning back with a smile on his face, the sound of the
truck's brakes squealing.

Stop. Stop thinking about it. She forced it back into the
box in her head and locked it tight.

"Are you going to lunch?" she said.

Destiny walked fast for someone with extra weight. She
didn't say anything until they spotted a tall, gangly white girl
with limp brown hair who had her head in a book but was
nonetheless walking in the direction of the dining hall. Carrie smiled at Nicole when Destiny introduced them and
stuck out a bony hand for her to shake.

"Do you like to read?" she asked and when Nicole nodded she gave another, wider smile.

She and Destiny chattered for the rest of the walk about
something called Runescape and some science fiction author
they were both addicted to. Nicole didn't bother to feign interest because they didn't seem to require it. She got into the

long line with them and slowly picked out food that looked unobjectionable, all the while wondering how to politely escape when the decision was suddenly taken out of her hands.

"Aren't you Nicole Morel?" a girl's voice, at once melodious and imperious, came from her left.

Nicole nodded, turning, and then stopped short. The head girl was standing there. Nicole recognized her; she'd seen her from afar during the assembly and she'd seen her clustered with other prefects in the halls.

"Hi," the older girl said with a wide, lovely smile. "I'm Elizabeth Lincoln."

"Nicole Morel," Nicole said and then blushed because the girl already knew that. Elizabeth laughed.

"I know," she said. "I've heard all about you."

She was tall and willowy with a small, yet defined bust and a waist that was somehow discernible even in the box-pleat uniform skirt. Her hair was long and that lustrous shade of golden blond that most people couldn't achieve without help. On her it looked natural. Her skin glowed, there was no other word for it. It wasn't as if it was tan, precisely, but it had a honeyed undertone that made her look healthy, as opposed to sallow, which was Nicole's own fate.

"Would you like to join us for lunch?" Elizabeth pointed one manicured finger in the direction of a small cluster of girls. One of them caught Elizabeth's eye and waved at her. Destiny looked from Nicole to Elizabeth and then whispered something to Carrie.

"Sure," Nicole said and followed her without thinking, only to turn back suddenly and wave at Destiny, who gave a little half-wave back.

"You looked like you needed to be rescued," Elizabeth said as she led the way through a maze of students to reach the table she'd indicated. Nicole laughed, noticing how they were being stared at by other girls.

"This is Tiffany," Elizabeth said, sliding in next to a pretty girl with long, caramel-colored curls and an infectious grin, "and this is Kristen." She nodded across the table at a super-skinny girl with long black hair and catlike green eyes. She surveyed Nicole coolly for a second before smiling and patting the seat beside her.

"Is it true you're from Paris?" she said.

Nicole nodded and Tiffany pronounced this "So cool!"

They bombarded her with questions about her life in France and why she'd come to the United States. Nicole noticed that whenever Elizabeth spoke the other two didn't interrupt her the way they did with each other.

"How long have you known each other?" she said.

"Kristen and I have known each other since grade school," Elizabeth said, "and Tiffany joined us her freshman year at St. Ursula's."

Tiffany nodded. "I was so glad to meet them," she said, picking at the food on her plate. "You have no idea how glad I was—my roommate was just such a loser, a complete geek!"

She made *geek* sound like a crime against nature. "You understand, though. Destiny Miller. Ugh!" She shuddered.

"Or Carrie Bonanon," Kristen added and they both gave a theatrical shudder that ended in laughter that was so infectious that Nicole couldn't help join in.

"You need to watch who you associate with," Elizabeth said. "If you hang out with the weak people, people will think you're weak."

"Don't worry," Kristen said. "We'll make sure that doesn't happen. It's too late to change your room assignment, but it doesn't matter."

"So, did you shop much in Paris?" Tiffany asked. "I bought the prettiest scarf at a little shop on the Ile Saint-Louis."

At one point, a hush fell over the lunchroom. Nicole looked up and saw the headmistress standing on the faculty dais near the rear of the room. She was holding up her hands like a bird about to take flight, but the girls seemed to understand her gesture, for the conversation died away to a smattering of voices and urgent "ssh's."

"This is just a reminder to our afternoon classes that the police are in the library and so it will remain closed for the rest of the day. If you are summoned to be questioned by the police, please leave your class promptly and report directly to the library. Likewise, when you are finished, you should return directly to class. There is nothing to be feared from the questioning—it is just routine. The inconvenience is unfortunate, but, as I told the police, St. Ursula girls can handle any challenge!"

Spontaneous applause broke out and Tiffany rolled her eyes. Nicole stifled a giggle. Elizabeth frowned at them both and Tiffany touched a hand to her lips as if she were locking a door.

"Do you think they're going to call us?" Kristen said once Sister Rose had stepped down. She was eating a salad, but Nicole had only seen one forkful actually enter her mouth. She stirred the leaves with her fork. It made Nicole feel funny about taking a big bite out of the pizza she'd chosen. It smelled good. She settled for nibbling.

"Of course they won't call us," Elizabeth said. "They want to talk to the witch's friends."

Tiffany giggled. "That isn't us!"

"Obviously." Elizabeth took a small bite from the grilled chicken breast she'd extricated from between two pieces of bread, lettuce, tomato, cheese, and mayonnaise.

"Who are you talking about?" Nicole asked. "The girl who died?"

"Morgan Wycoff," Elizabeth said.

"The campus witch," Kristen added.

"She was a loser," Tiffany said. "Nobody liked her."

"She shouldn't have been at St. Ursula's at all," Elizabeth said. "I personally gave her at least six demerits last semester. And she was suspended at least once. I mean, how many times does a person have to disrupt a place before someone puts a stop to it?"

Nicole nodded along with the others, but she wondered privately if Morgan had been unhappy. She was glad that they didn't know about how much trouble she'd gotten into during her last year of school in Paris. Maybe Morgan had lost someone in her family. Before Paul's death, she'd been a harsh judge of the girls who'd skipped school or slept in class. She hadn't understood that the root of apathy could often be depression.

"I'm not criticizing Sister Rose," Elizabeth said, "because she's practically an institution herself." The other girls nodded again.

"She's been here forever," Tiffany said to Nicole. "She was headmistress when my *mother* was at St. Ursula's."

"It's not her fault," Elizabeth said. "She had pressure from some of the teachers and from that girl's mother. That was the only reason she was allowed to stay. My mother told me."

Kristen put down her fork, pushing back her plate with a sigh as if she'd eaten a big meal. "I mean, if you think about it, her dying is a good thing for this school."

"Not that we're saying we wanted her to die," Elizabeth interjected. "Just that since no one found her up there I think we can all agree that it's good she died."

"Right," Tiffany said. She smiled at Nicole. "Believe me, if you'd known her you'd know what we're talking about. Ding dong the witch is dead."

The other girls burst out laughing and Nicole pushed her own plate of half-eaten pizza back and joined in.

The sun beat down on Lauren, she could smell her skin burning. The cobblestone street was melting under her feet. She ran toward the stone spires of an old church.

She pushed against its heavy wooden doors and plunged into the cool interior. The church was empty except for one figure sitting in the shadows near the altar. Her shoes clicked quietly against the stone floor. She slipped into a pew and bowed her head. She heard the sound of soft footsteps moving toward her and she started to shake.

"What have you done to Amanda?" a voice whispered.

She looked up and saw Michael standing before her, his laughing eyes somber. Water poured down his body, his blond hair brown with wet and plastered to his skull, the liquid forming a dark stain around him on the stone floor.

"Where is Amanda?" he repeated. She reached out her hand to touch him and his body burst into flames. "You killed me!" he shrieked.

Lauren woke with a scream. It was dark but she could feel something under her. Cotton sheets. She was in bed in Augustine House dressed in running clothes. Light shone through the blinds, but the clock glowed seven. It was moonlight. She sat up, breathing hard. She'd meant to lie down for ten minutes when she came back from her run, not sleep for three hours.

She got up, a familiar soreness in her calves as she padded down the hall to the small kitchen and put the kettle on to boil. Images from the dream replayed themselves over and over again and she pressed a hand against her forehead, kneading at the tension.

The kettle's shrieking startled her. She poured boiling water over a bag and carried the steeping mug out to the front room.

It was stupid, like feeding a fire or scratching an itch, but she couldn't help opening the bottom drawer of her desk and pulling out the photo album. She justified it as a desire to see Michael whole and well and not as he'd appeared in her dream.

There was a photo of Michael leaning against the doorframe in her flat in London. He wore jeans and a sardonic expression, his arms folded against his bare chest, one bare foot sliding against another. His *GQ* pose, she'd called it. His blond hair hung in his eyes, those blue eyes staring at her so intensely.

She ran a hand lightly over the photo and felt a deep ache that started in the base of her stomach and dipped down, between her legs. She'd wanted him then, she wanted him now. From the moment they'd met she'd felt the most basic physical attraction for him, a feverish longing that blocked any warning signals, that overcame any hesitation.

It helped that she was alone and lonely, on her own in a foreign country and still struggling to get comfortable with crowded streets. It helped that he was her first.

Amanda handled things differently. Tougher than Lauren, more confident with the opposite sex, aware too early of her physical attributes, even if she'd had no real idea of how to use them. She was strong to the point of brashness, where Lauren was shy, startled easily, didn't like making eye contact.

Michael called her soft and made it sound endearing, but he'd misunderstood her. It wasn't softness. Naiveté, certainly, but not softness. Had he ever really loved her or was it just what she represented?

Closing the album she slipped it back in the bottom drawer of the desk and slammed it shut. She should get rid of the thing, but she couldn't. So she kept it tucked away instead, hidden in a drawer along with a small stack of white letters all addressed by the same hand.

Her head hurt. She got some ibuprofen and swallowed it with the now-tepid tea. Being here wasn't good for her. The past came knocking here. In the city school the exhaustion of the daily commute, the constant need for vigilance in the school itself, had kept it at bay. Here, where she didn't have to worry about safety, surrounded by schoolgirls and the quiet of the woods, her past flooded back and she couldn't seem to stop it.

She would work here just long enough to pay off her debts and then she would start again somewhere else. There had to be somewhere to go where she could forget the past and no one could find her and remind her.

Chapter Eight

The same newbie investigator who'd botched the photographs managed redemption by coming up with a definite make on the sneaker print.

"Heelys," Mark Coleman said, slapping a photocopy of a black sneaker on the counter. "A perfect size seven."

"What the hell is a heelie?" Oz looked confused.

"I thought you had kids, Oz," Stephanie said. "They're the sneakers with a wheel in the back."

They'd called the crime scene unit to check on progress and raced straight over to the sheriff's office, which was more like a complex of offices, which included the crime lab.

"So it's some kind of roller skate?" Oz said, squinting at the picture.

"A tennis shoe combined with a roller skate," Mark Coleman said, "the best of both worlds. Your print is from The Atomic. Model 7145."

He pulled a Sharpie from his pocket and scrawled this on the back of the copy. "They're not just for kids, you know. I've got a pair."

Stephanie hid a smile and stepped in front of Oz to block

the look on his face from Coleman's view. "This is great. Thanks so much."

She slipped her sunglasses back on once they were outside. The weather had finally turned. It was a perfect fall day, high sun and blue sky, breezy enough for a light sweater, but not so crisp that they couldn't sit outside at the Java Joint for five minutes soaking up the sun.

"What kind of sorry excuse for a man buys a sneaker with a wheel in it?" Oz said, tapping the picture with his take-out cup. "That's just wrong."

"You've got latte on your mustache, He-Man," Stephanie said, handing him a napkin.

He took it, shaking his head at her. Mustache cleaned and manhood restored, he tapped the photocopy again. "At least doofus got us a make. Now we've just got to find the owner of these shoes."

"It's a guy's shoe. Didn't that girl, Heather what's-her-name—didn't she mention some boy?"

"Yeah, Brad or Rick something?" Oz reached inside the breast pocket of his blazer for his notebook. With her sunglasses on, the buffalo-check plaid was less objectionable. Stephanie wondered for the umpteenth time if Oz's wife, a seemingly pleasant woman who did all his shopping, was color-blind or just passive-aggressive.

Brad or Rick turned out to be Beau Steuben. "No wonder I didn't remember," Oz said as she punched the third number into her cell phone. "What the fuck kind of name is Beau?"

"Isn't there some soap opera hero with that name?" The phone rang and rang before an answering machine picked up. She left a message with her number and checked that one off the list.

"You give a kid a name like that, you're just inviting him to get picked on," Oz said as he drove back to the station. "What's wrong with old-fashioned names like Michael or John?"

"Isn't your youngest one named Jaspar?"

Oz scowled. "It's a family name." He drove for a few minutes in silence, making faces at the windshield. "There's nothing wrong with that name. What's wrong with it?"

Stephanie looked out the passenger window to hide her grin. "I don't know, just seems a little, well, girly to me."

"Girly?" Oz's already booming voice hit sonic levels.

"Ssh, it's ringing," Stephanie said, turning to show him the phone held to her ear, while she struggled to suppress laughter.

"Girly my ass," Oz muttered. "Jaspar is a fine name. He goes by Jas anyway."

"No answer," she hit the off button. "This might take time."

"It wasn't my choice," Oz said in a sulky voice. "I wanted Trevor, but Eileen insisted. It's someone on her side, General Jaspar."

Stephanie couldn't hold back the laughter and it burst forth in peals that were almost painful she'd been holding them back for so long.

In under a minute a multitude of expressions crossed Oz's wide face, running the gamut from insulted to puzzled, then back to insulted, before a grin finally slipped out and he guffawed.

"Okay, ballbuster, you got me."

"That's Miss Ballbuster," she said, wiping at her eyes. "There's nothing wrong with Jaspar. Trevor, on the other hand—"

"What's wrong with Trevor? That's a good masculine name."

"Reminds me of a dog. Here, Trevor, here, boy." Suddenly her cell phone rang. "Detective Land." She listened for a moment and then snapped her fingers at Oz and made a spinning motion with one hand.

He turned the car around, fishtailing with practiced ease, and smacked the siren on the dash.

Stephanie snapped her phone shut. "We got him."

* * *

The first thing Stephanie thought when she saw sixteen-year-old Beau Steuben was that this wasn't a kid who played football. He was small and slight, with spiky brown hair, a pug nose with a scattering of freckles, and big brown eyes.

He was dressed head to toe in black, the tight T-shirt and skinny jeans only serving to emphasize his diminutive size. While the black leather and silver-spiked dog collar around his neck and the silver barbell in one eyebrow were probably supposed to make him look tough, they had the opposite effect. He looked like someone's pet. If she'd been a drama teacher, Stephanie would have cast him as Puck in a production of *A Midsummer Night's Dream*.

He wasn't, unfortunately, wearing Heelys, but black Chuck Taylors; he fiddled absently with the laces on the left foot. He'd drawn that leg up when he sat down in the oversized armchair in the living room of the Steuben home.

"We're sorry about your friend Morgan's death," Oz said, and Stephanie was so ready to hear the boy disavow any connection to the girl that she wasn't at all prepared for the tears that welled in his eyes.

Stephanie looked at Oz, who blinked, clearly surprised, and she glanced at the boy's mother, Valerie Steuben, who'd been hovering in the arched entrance to the room since first summoning Beau. She vanished and came back with a tissue box, carrying it over to her son while shooting nervous looks at Oz and Stephanie as if she thought they might stop her.

"Thanks," he mumbled, taking one and swiping at his eyes.

"You were close?" Oz asked, recovering.

"Yeah."

"How did you two meet?"

His mother answered for him. "They went to school together all through elementary."

"But she didn't go on to the public high school with you?"

Beau shrugged, but Valerie Steuben seemed to take this

as an affront. "Gashford's school system is one of the best in the state," she said. "Our high school is top ranked."

"Why did Morgan choose St. Ursula's instead?"

"She didn't choose it, her mother did," Beau said with disdain.

Mrs. Steuben gave them a nervous smile. "I think Janice thought that same-sex education was beneficial for girls."

"How did you hear about her death, Beau?"

"A friend told me."

"Who? Heather Lester?"

The boy's eyes widened and his mouth fell open slightly, apparently a reaction to their incredible investigative powers. He nodded. "Yeah. How'd you know that?"

"We talked to Heather," Stephanie said. "Where were you three nights ago, Beau?"

His mouth closed and he stopped fiddling with his laces. "Home."

Valerie Steuben said quickly, "He was here all night." She sank down in the chair opposite his, one hand straying to her mouth as if she were going to bite her nails before she pulled it hastily down to her lap.

There was no sign of Mr. Steuben, who was probably out earning the paycheck that paid for this big house on one of Gashford's older, leafier streets, but if Beau owed anything to his dad in the looks department Stephanie would be surprised. Valerie Steuben was just an older, female version of her son. A tiny woman with big nervous eyes and small restless hands, she reminded Stephanie of some Disney-created, anthropomorphized woodland creature.

"Are you sure you weren't with Morgan that night?" Stephanie said to Beau.

"No, I mean, yeah, I'm sure."

"We know she wasn't alone," Oz said. "We also know that you used to visit her. How did you get up there? Did you drive?"

"I wasn't up on the Hill."

"C'mon, Beau. We know you hung out with her."

"Sure, I mean, she was my friend. But I wasn't up there." His right foot beat a silent tattoo on the carpet.

Oz glanced down at his notebook. "You're a self-proclaimed pagan?"

"Yeah." The small chin jutted forward as if the boy expected a fight. It came from his mother.

"It's just a phase," she said, shaking her head at him.

"Mom!"

She aimed her hand at him like a stop sign and looked from Oz to Stephanie, "We're Lutherans. This is just some idea that girl gave him."

"You mean Morgan?"

Mrs. Steuben nodded. "She was obviously rebelling—all teenagers do, right? Look, I don't blame Beau for going along with her—she's a pretty girl. Was, I mean."

"Shut up, Mom." It was muttered, but all of them heard it. Two spots of color appeared high on Valerie Steuben's cheekbones and the wide eyes grew wider still.

"How dare you!" she shrieked, standing up and over her son like a tiny bird of prey, her bony hands clenching like talons she longed to put around his neck.

"Okay, Mom, sorry—just chill." Beau held up his own hands in a placating manner, rolling his eyes at the behavior of adults.

Mrs. Steuben sat back down but appealed to the two detectives. "When I was a girl we didn't call boys, we waited for them to call us. Girls these days, they're just so forward."

"Yeah," Oz agreed. Stephanie shot him a dirty look and he hastily said, "What size shoes do you wear, Beau?"

"Seven."

"You own any Heelys?"

"No." The tattoo increased. His whole knee was shaking.

"Yes, you do, Beau—"

"Shut up, Mom!" Beau let his other foot drop to the ground.

"You shut up!" she shrieked back at him. "Yes, he owns Heelys. I paid a small fortune for them last year."

"They don't fit."

"Since when?"

"Since whenever they stopped fitting!"

"Don't be ridiculous. Your feet haven't grown."

"We need to see those shoes," Stephanie said.

Beau looked from her to his mother and back. "I gave them away."

"What do you mean you gave them away? Those things were expensive!"

"Who did you give them to?" Oz said, exchanging a look with Stephanie.

"Nobody. I put them in one of those Goodwill boxes."

"The one out by the Lowe's on Washington?"

"Yeah."

"How'd you get out there?"

"I drove."

Oz sighed. "There is no Goodwill box at the Lowe's, Beau. You're lying."

The boy's mouth fell open again and he pressed his back further into the chair. "I'm not!" he said, but it came out as a squeak.

Valerie Steuben looked like she might cry. "I don't understand? What do the shoes have to do with anything?"

"Your son was in the woods with Morgan Wycoff, weren't you, Beau?"

"Okay, okay, I was there, but not that night. The day before. I swear!"

"Were you drinking?" Stephanie asked.

"What? No way! If Heather told you that she's a liar."

"Was Heather with you and Morgan in the woods?"

Valerie Steuben closed her eyes, hands clasped on her knees as if bracing for the worst. "Beau, what have you done?"

"Nothing, Mom!" Beau sat up straight. "Look, we liked to hang out up there sometimes. It was private."

"A good place to perform witchcraft?" Oz asked.

The boy sighed. "It's not witchcraft," he said. "Wicca isn't like that."

"But you did some Wicca ritual in the woods?"

Valerie Steuben moaned and Beau rolled his eyes again. "Look, that was Morgan's thing, not mine. It's like, I support it, but I'm not that into it."

Stephanie pulled a crime scene photo of the pentagram out of her jacket pocket. There'd been no way to take a picture of the entire circle given the tree in the middle, but they'd put the photos of each half together and taken a photo of that. It wasn't a super-clean shot, but it worked.

She placed it on the coffee table and slid it over toward Beau. "You recognize this?"

The boy didn't touch the photo, just sat forward, elbows on knees, and stared at it. Stephanie watched his face looking for any sign of recognition, but he didn't react beyond absently twisting his eyebrow piercing.

"Yeah, it's a pentagram," he said, sitting back. "So?"

"Did Morgan draw this?"

"How should I know? If you're going to ask if I drew it the answer is no."

"What about any of Morgan's other friends? Do you know anyone who might have drawn it?"

"Morgan didn't have a lot of friends. Not at St. Ursula's, anyway."

"Did she have any enemies?"

He snorted. "Hell, yeah. The girls there are stuck-up bitches."

"Anybody in particular?"

"I don't know, I don't remember. It's not like we spent time talking about them. She wanted to forget them, forget that whole place."

"But you met her up in the woods?"

"Sometimes."

Stephanie said, "How'd you get past security, Beau?"

"You mean those old guys?" He laughed. "It's a big campus."

"So you were up there the day before. What time did you get there?"

"I don't know. Four maybe."

"And how long did you stay?"

The kid shrugged, avoiding her eyes. "I don't know. An hour." His foot began tapping again.

"C'mon, Beau, cut the crap," Oz said in a stern voice. "You're lying about this—"

"I'm not!"

"—just like you lied about your shoes. You'd better tell us the truth right now or I'm going to haul you down to the station and charge you with obstruction!" He stood up and slipped the cuffs from the back of his khakis. Stephanie stood up, too.

She knew this was mostly dramatics; they'd be hard pressed to make any charge against this kid stick without tangible evidence, but the Steubens didn't know that. Valerie gaped like a stranded fish and Beau leapt to his feet, waving his hands frantically at Oz to ward him off.

"No! Stop it!"

Oz took a step toward him. "Five seconds, Beau!"

"It's like I said—I was there the day before!"

"Four."

"You can't arrest me! I didn't do anything!"

"Three." The big detective took another step forward.

The boy turned wild eyes on his mother, who was now biting her nails. "Mom, please!"

Valerie Steuben looked at Stephanie as if she thought she might intervene. Stephanie stared her down and the mother turned on her son. "Tell them, Beau! Tell them what they want to know!"

"Two."

"Okay! Okay! Stop! I'll tell you."

Oz paused, but he didn't put away the cuffs.

"I was there that night, but just for a while."

"What time did you leave?"

"Eight."

"You're lying, Beau."

"No! It's the truth!"

Stephanie shook her head. "Why should we believe you now, Beau?"

"Because it's the truth!"

"You wouldn't know the truth if it smacked you in the face." Oz casually opened one handcuff.

"I can prove it!"

"How, Beau?"

"Just a sec." He sprinted from the room and came back carrying a sleek black laptop. He thrust it at Oz. "Here. Take it."

"What am I supposed to do with this?" Oz said.

"You can scan it or do some technical shit like that," Beau said breathlessly. He tapped the case. "It's all there, man. I couldn't have been in the woods with Morgan because I was in a chat room with some role-playing chick all night."

Chapter Nine

On Friday afternoon after her last class, Lauren laced up her running shoes for the first time since finding Morgan's body.

It had been five days since that morning, five long days, and it struck her as ironic that she felt less at ease after her first week of teaching than she had when she'd first arrived.

She'd learned a lot in five days, not the least of which was that she did not, under any circumstances, want to be resident faculty for longer than necessary.

All she'd been thinking about was the money she'd save. It hadn't occurred to her that this was some kind of surrogate parent position and she'd have to be available virtually round-the-clock for questions, complaints, and checking up on teenage girls whose only interest in her seemed to be in bypassing her authority.

Any illusions she'd had about bonding with the girls in Augustine House had evaporated by the evening of the third day. It was around nine-thirty and she'd taken a break from grading essays to go to the common room and talk with the girls. Hanging out with the girls was part of her job description and it embarrassed her to think that she'd actually envi-

sioned sing-alongs and s'mores, a boarding school variation
on *The Sound of Music*.

On Monday night it had gone reasonably well, but only
because the girls wanted to pepper her with questions about
finding Morgan. Tuesday night the girls lounging in the
common room seemed to want nothing more than for her to
wait on them, bringing snacks and drinks over to the wide-
screen TV. They were fixated on some teen drama that as far
as she could tell in ten short minutes of viewing concerned
uniformly good-looking boys and girls pouting at each other
in various glamorous settings while complaining about their
overprivileged lives. There was nothing particularly wrong
with the girls' request that she bring them food, but once she'd
made them a big bowl of microwave popcorn and some hot
chocolate they clearly wanted her to leave.

She'd stuck it out as long as she could, trying to strike up
a conversation with the only two girls in the room not watching TV, but Destiny and Hannah were engrossed in some sort
of fantasy board game and while they answered her questions, it was clear that they were just being polite. After a
few awkward minutes she'd left them in peace.

Wednesday night was the worst yet. She'd heard talking
and laughter as she came down the hall and as she rounded
the corner into the room she caught the end of a sentence,
"—hear her babbling in class this morning?" Loud laughter
greeted this and it wasn't until she'd stepped in the room and
the conversation abruptly ceased that she realized who they
were talking about.

She'd stood there, a stupid smile plastered on her face,
which felt swollen with heat. About ten girls were in the
room, lounging in comfy chairs or reclining on oversize pillows tossed on the plush carpet.

"Good evening, Ms. Kavanaugh," a girl named Tiffany
Bellam said, smiling politely from the armchair where she
lounged sideways, feet in fuzzy pink slippers hanging over
the arm. She wore baby-pink pajama bottoms detailed with

little red hearts and a tight baby-pink T-shirt with spaghetti straps that showcased her small round breasts. Her glossy light brown hair hung in a curling ponytail over one shoulder.

She looked like a Barbie doll, but there was nothing vapid in the expression in those brown eyes. They brimmed with suppressed laughter. Although she had a copy of *Vogue* in her lap, Lauren was sure that Tiffany was the one she'd heard speaking. Behind that polite veneer the girl was mocking her.

"Hello, Tiffany." Lauren stared into her eyes for a long minute, unblinking, before the other girl looked away. Then the other girls in the room chimed in with their greetings and just like Tiffany their faces reflected barely contained laughter.

She managed to say, "Half-hour until lights-out, girls," before fleeing for the safety of her bedroom. The lights in the dormitory halls dimmed at 10 P.M. That was the official curfew, though everyone knew and expected that many of the girls stayed awake, presumably studying, for at least another hour.

After Wednesday's fiasco, Lauren retreated to her rooms and went back to grading papers, trying to convince herself that she had work to do and wasn't just hiding. She said the same thing the next night when she didn't leave her rooms at all. No one came to her, either, though she could clearly hear girls laughing and watching TV down the hall.

If that had been all, if it was just a case of teenage girls not wanting to hang out with the teacher, she didn't think she'd feel so nervous about making this work. No, it was other things causing her anxiety.

Late Wednesday night she'd been nodding off over the essays she was grading when she heard the faint but unmistakable sound of footsteps in the hall. She got up and went to the door and looked out, but the long stretch of carpeted hallway was empty.

Girls were forbidden to visit each other's rooms after curfew and the lights in the halls were switched off with only two low-wattage nightlights left burning, casting the hallways in a dim orange haze. At night the doors on the houses were set to lock from the outside so that no one outside could enter. If residents tried to exit they couldn't get back in without a teacher's help.

She returned to her desk, trying to concentrate on the short essay she'd assigned to her sophomore class, when she heard whispering. This time she tiptoed to the door, pressing her ear against it and hearing the voices more clearly, but still too faintly to make out any words.

She opened the door as quietly as she could, but again, there was nobody.

Later, much later, when she'd finished grading and was heading to bed, she'd been startled by a thud and what sounded like a stifled giggle. This time she'd gone out in her pajamas, wrapping a robe around her as she went, only to find the hall completely empty again.

She was tempted to chalk it up to imagination and too many late nights, but she couldn't so easily dismiss the odd things she'd seen during the day.

The first thing had happened one morning in one of the newer classroom buildings, when she ducked into a second-floor bathroom mainly used by students and found a girl sobbing over one of the sinks as she swiped at her face with a paper towel.

She visibly jumped when she heard Lauren's footsteps, but seemed to relax when she saw who it was in the mirror and relaxed back over the sink.

"Are you okay?" Lauren asked, touching her lightly on the back. "Can I help?"

The girl flinched at her touch and pulled away. "I'm fine," she said in a voice rough from crying. She had a heavyset face and was scrubbing at it so hard that her skin was turning red in patches. Lauren suddenly realized that she was removing heavy makeup, not drying tears. Had the girl gotten in trouble for wearing such heavy makeup? She couldn't remember if there were guidelines in the student handbook about that.

"Maybe you'll feel better if you talk about it," she said gently, but the girl just shook her head. She looked strange with black mascara running from one eye and the other red and raw. Steam rose from the water pouring out of the faucet.

"Careful, you'll scald yourself," Lauren said, turning the hot tap down. The girl plunged another paper towel under the stream and Lauren noticed what looked like bruising on the girl's wrist. "How did you get those?" she asked, grabbing the girl's hand.

"It's nothing," the girl said, pulling away.

"It's not nothing—you're badly bruised. Tell me right now, who did this to you?"

"No one. I'm fine." The girl shrank back and then she suddenly darted around Lauren and ran from the room. Lauren ran after her, but the girl had the jump on her and was already far down the hall, running as fast as she could. Lauren watched until she was out of sight.

Later, when she checked the handbook, she found only the slightest mention of "modest makeup and jewelry" under the section on the uniform code. Had the girl been so harshly scolded by a teacher that she'd been reduced to sobbing? It was hard to imagine and harder still to imagine any teacher grabbing a student harshly enough to leave bruises, but she'd seen them clearly.

Then, the other afternoon, another strange occurrence. When she'd picked up her mail from the wall of slots in the main office, she'd gotten the drama teacher's mail along with hers. Lauren didn't realize the mistake until she was almost back to Augustine House, so instead of returning the mail to the main office she decided to drop it off in person.

The drama teacher, the lyrically named Margery Montgomery, was the resident faculty at Anselm House. She wasn't at home, however, so Lauren slipped the mail under her door. As she turned to leave, she saw a girl rubbing vigorously at a spot on one of the doors, pausing, and then rubbing again.

Curious, Lauren walked over to investigate, only to realize the girl was someone she knew, Chelsea Connor, a student from one of her advanced classes.

"Hi, Chelsea, what are you doing?"

The girl looked embarrassed, and when Lauren looked at the door, she saw why. The word "whore" was scrawled in red across the white paint.

"It's lipstick," Chelsea said in a small voice. "It smears when I try to get it off."

Lauren helped her find another cleaning product that would remove it, but when she asked Chelsea who'd written it, the girl was evasive. She claimed not to know, but Lauren didn't believe her, and her reaction when Lauren pressed was similar to that of the girl she'd seen in the bathroom.

Both incidents left her with the feeling that there was something wrong at the school that nobody was willing to acknowledge, but she didn't know the name of the student she'd seen in the bathroom, and when she mentioned reporting the door incident, Chelsea begged her not to with such a panicked expression that Lauren agreed to let it go.

The girl called it a prank and said she was sure it wouldn't happen again, but her eyes darted away from Lauren's. The two incidents combined to make Lauren feel a little wary when she entered a classroom or residential house alone.

It was absurd to think she was afraid of a group of teenagers, girls at that. Absurd and yet she was nervous enough about the impending weekend alone with them to head away from campus and the clusters of girls walking and whispering near buildings and paths. Everywhere she went there were girls and she imagined that they were talking about her and staring at her. She needed a break.

Lauren broke from a slow trot into a full-out run, cutting

across the front of campus and back into the woods. She headed away from the path she'd taken Monday, purposely going left where she'd gone right, trying not to think about that flash of color through the trees, that horrible moment when she'd found Morgan's body.

On impulse, she broke off the crushed limestone path and headed into the woods themselves. This was a challenge she liked. Rocketing hard between trees, skirting underbrush, focusing solely on avoiding collisions, running alone in the silence of the woods with only the crunch of pine needles and bracken and the sound of her own breathing in her ears.

Sunlight streamed in thin lines through the gaps between thin trunks, creating little spotlights on the forest floor, illuminating a red leaf or the gnarled black root of an ancient oak. The trees towered above her, stretching to heights of twenty or thirty feet, their branches reaching for some spot of heaven visible in the jagged pieces of sky she could see if she looked up.

In some ways it reminded her of the chapel. Here was another place of worship, and one of the few places she could feel totally comfortable with herself and with the universe.

She ran hard, jumping and twisting around and over obstacles, hurtling down small slopes and pumping up the other side. If she ran hard she wouldn't have to think about the girls or Michael or the growing pile of letters in their slim white envelopes.

She was moving fast across some level acreage when the trees suddenly got denser and she had to duck right and squeeze between two trunks to get past, her right elbow scraping against the bark of a tulip tree in the process.

Just past it the trees gave way and she stopped short and stared, breathing hard.

She was in a clearing, a small, almost perfectly cylindrical stretch of grass with trees forming a perimeter and a partial canopy over it. It was approximately fifteen feet across and at its center was a circle of large stones.

The clearing looked natural, but not the stones. Someone had to have placed them like that. Lauren walked closer, wobbly-legged, with her muscles twitching and aching from the sudden stop. The stones were large, gray, and smooth, with little bits of moss and lichen clinging to them, as if they'd been there for a long time. They formed the perimeter of a fire pit.

Inside the circle, the ground dipped sharply before rising slightly and leveling out. A pile of half-burned wood sat at the center, layers of ash a testament to years of use.

Needle-thin tendrils of gray smoke rose from between the logs. She stepped over the stones and slid the short distance into the pit, putting out a hand tentatively, but the wood was cool. No fire, just cigarette butts, freshly smoked, the tips still warm to the touch and one of them still smoldering. Another was stained with pink lipstick. There were three in all.

Something snapped behind her and Lauren jumped up and whirled around, scanning the trees.

"Who's there?" she called, her voice sounding loud and higher than usual and full of fear. She heard something else, a faint, breathy snicker, but she couldn't see anyone.

Clutching the butts in her hand, she climbed back out of the pit. Who'd been meeting up here? Were they students or kids who'd climbed up the hillside from the back? Were they in the woods watching her even now? Shading her eyes with her hand, she moved closer to the edge of the clearing, trying to peer between the trees, but the sunlight cast shadows. She couldn't tell what she was looking at.

Suddenly she caught a glimpse of something white slipping between the trees, but when she got back into the woods she saw nothing but trees and underbrush and heard nothing but a slight breeze rustling the leaves high above her.

A series of soft thuds—footfalls—sounded to her left, and she whipped that way in time to catch a glimpse of white, the back of uniform shirts, darting away. Students then, running from their secret meeting spot deep in the woods. They were too far away to identify.

She started after them, but stopped after realizing they were long gone. They knew the woods better than she did and she'd never catch them.

Looking down at the cigarette butts cradled in her right palm, she carried them back toward the pit. Should she report this to the school? Girls were meeting here, but so what? Classes were over for the day, so they weren't truant. The only thing they were guilty of was smoking. Unless this area was out-of-bounds? She'd have to check on that.

She kicked at the ashes, wondering how often they came up here. Part of her understood that need to have a private place. Hadn't she done this, too, as a girl? A corner of something glossy slid through the ashes. She let the cigarette butts drop and bent down, sifting with her fingers until she pulled out a partially burned Polaroid. It was a fuzzy, out-of-focus picture of a girl swimming. Long white arms churning some dark water, the rest of her hidden in its black depths, but it was the hair Lauren recognized. That red hair hanging wet and heavy just like it had been on Monday.

The acid taste of bile rose in her throat. Lauren scrambled out of the pit and struggled to hold down her stomach. What the hell was this? Her hand shook as she looked at the picture again. It was definitely Morgan Wycoff. Was this the lake where she'd been swimming? It was hard to say. The picture was out of focus and charred along the right side. Somebody had taken this photo and then they'd brought it here to burn it. Had the girls who'd run away been the ones who tied Morgan to the tree?

Suddenly, she wanted to be away. The tension of the school was back on her, making it hard to breathe. She felt the eyes of watchers in the woods, though she was sure that they were probably long gone.

She ran, sticking the photo in the pocket of her shorts, leaving the clearing and running through the woods as fast as she could, aware of her heartbeat pounding in her chest, of her breathing loud in her ears. She didn't know how to get back to the path; the trees all looked the same.

Blind panic grabbed her. She felt as if she were being pursued, though there was no one behind her when she whirled around to check. The land dipped slightly and she hurried down the slope, her feet slipping on the underbrush in her haste.

She could see something different, a black strip ahead of her through the trees and a blur of blue with yellow underneath, but just as she had processed that it was road and a cyclist she came flying out of the woods onto the strip of asphalt and crashed full-on into the rider.

The next few seconds were a blur of movement and sound. The crunch of metal against road, someone yelling, and then she was scraping the asphalt with her palms and right knee. Her chin thudded on the ground and she bit her tongue and her mouth filled with the tangy taste of blood.

"What the hell do you think you're doing?"

The voice was behind her. She turned her head to the side, but she couldn't see anything beyond a pair of sneakers. Pushing off her raw palms, she got slowly and painfully to her feet, wincing as every part of her body screamed in protest.

A tall, athletic-looking, short-haired woman was standing opposite, glaring at her, blood smeared across one cheek and dripping from the opposite arm. She was wearing jeans, but one knee had a small gash and the denim was darker around it as if it were being soaked by her blood. The gray T-shirt she wore was spotted with something that might have been blood. "You could have killed us both!"

"Sorry," Lauren said, breathing heavily.

"Yeah, well, that doesn't really cut it." The woman wore a helmet that looked none the worse for wear, and her eyes bored in on Lauren, dark, cold and angry. She took a step back and then did a funny hop sideways to avoid tripping over the front wheel of her bike.

"Why don't you look where you're going?" she complained, leaning forward to grab the handlebars of her bike. The frame was black with slashes of yellow.

"I couldn't stop." Lauren moved closer, warily eyeing the other woman, and then helping her right the bike.

"You shouldn't be running out here." The woman sank back on her knees immediately, examining the bike for damage. Lauren watched her, trying to stop her hands from shaking. Leftover adrenaline.

"I've got some bent spokes here," the woman said. She tried to straighten them and Lauren knelt beside her to help, but the metal burned against her cut palms and she pulled back. There was a small tear on the seat cover and some scratches. Otherwise the bike looked good to go.

"At least a dozen scratches." The other woman sounded like she was tallying. She took off her helmet and ran her hand through her cropped brown hair. Her forehead looked whiter near her hairline, as if she spent a lot of time on her bike.

She caught Lauren's eye and frowned again. "You're not allowed to be running out here—I'm reporting you." She stood up and dug a cell phone out of her jeans pocket. "What's your name?"

"Lauren," she said. "Who are you calling?"

"Lauren what?"

"Lauren Kavanaugh. You're calling the police?"

The older woman gave a short bark of unamused laughter. "No, though you might prefer that. I'm calling the headmistress. I'm sure you can count on losing some privileges for the term."

"Look, I don't think you—"

"I don't want to hear it," the woman silenced Lauren with one raised hand. "You know perfectly well what the rules are—I'm sure it's all laid out in your student handbook."

Lauren laughed, feeling slightly hysterical. "I'm not a student."

The other woman flipped the phone shut. "You're not a student at St. Ursula's?"

Lauren shook her head and opened her mouth to explain, but the woman was off and running hers again.

"Then you've got no business being on this property at all. What's your parents' number? C'mon, you'd better tell me. It's either your parents or the police, and you know that your parents will find out, anyway."

"I'm a teacher," Lauren said.

Now it was the other woman's turn to laugh, though she sounded no more amused. "Very funny. Number please, right now." She snapped her fingers and Lauren's tight control over her own emotions slipped.

"My name is Lauren Kavanaugh. I'm a teacher at St. Ursula's. I have no number to give you unless it's the number for Augustine House, where I'm resident faculty. Call the school if you don't believe me."

The tall woman made no move to call anyone, staring at Lauren stupidly for a long moment, her mouth gaping like a frog's.

"I suppose I should ask what you're doing here," Lauren said in the silence. "Are *you* trespassing?"

That snapped her mouth shut, but only long enough to form an answer. "Of course not," she blustered. "I'm a teacher, too."

They stared at each other for a long, baleful moment and then the other woman seemed to collect herself and stuck out a bloody hand for Lauren to shake. "Candace Huston."

"Lauren Kavanaugh." She recognized the name. This was the teacher Alice LaRue had mentioned at lunch.

They gingerly shook hands. "Sorry," Candace said, "it's just you look so young."

"I'm sorry about crashing into you," Lauren said.

"Yes, well, it was pretty stupid thing to do."

"It's not like I planned it. I lost control coming down the hill."

"If you aren't used to running cross-country you probably shouldn't be doing it."

Lauren bristled. "I'm more than used to it, I just miscalculated the pitch of the hill." She suddenly remembered what she'd been running from that had ended up with her sprawled on the road and checked her pocket. The photo was gone. Panicked for no good reason, she looked left and right, searching the ground.

"What? Did you lose something?" Candace sounded grumpy.

"A photo." Lauren couldn't see the charred Polaroid anywhere. Had she dropped it in the woods? She looked back at the hillside and spotted it along the verge where dirt met asphalt.

Candace wheeled her bike closer. "What is it?" She tried to look over Lauren's shoulder.

"Nothing, it's just a photo I found."

The other woman reached to pluck it from her hand, but ended up examining Lauren's palm instead. "You're bleeding."

"I'm okay."

"No, you're not." Candace grabbed Lauren's other hand before she could pull away. "These look bad—you've got to wash them out or you'll get an infection." She looked down at her own torn knee. "This needs to be treated, too. C'mon, let's get back to the main campus."

She started walking her bicycle as if expecting Lauren to follow. It irked Lauren and she was tempted to take off into the woods again. Screw this woman and her bitchy, highhanded manner. Except that Lauren *was* responsible for the accident.

"So you teach history, right?" Candace said, looking over her shoulder. Lauren shoved the photo back in her pocket and hustled to catch up.

"Yeah."

"Another popular subject." She laughed and, seeing the

confusion on Lauren's face, added, "No one likes science, either."

Lauren felt defensive. "I try to capture their interest."

"Oh, so do I!" Candace laughed again. It was quite a change from her nasty attitude of a few minutes ago. As if reading her mind, Candace said, "Look, I'm sorry about before. It was just a surprise. I've never seen anyone out here when I bike, much less have anyone crash into me."

"Do you bike out here often?"

"In good weather, sure. It's nasty in the winter, so I tend to use the campus gym. There's a nice new pool—have you seen it?"

Lauren shook her head. She found she had to hurry to keep up with the woman's longer stride. "How long have you been at St. Ursula's?"

"Too long." Candace breathed heavily as she pushed the bike slowly up the hill. "Six years. And I've been a resident faculty for every one of those years."

"Really? How can you stand it?" The words tumbled out without thought and Lauren immediately wished them back, but Candace burst out laughing.

"Having a hard time?" She gave Lauren a knowing look. "It gets easier—you get used to it and the girls get used to you."

They'd reached the edge of campus and the path that led to the entrance to Augustine House. Candace paused.

"Do you have first-aid supplies?" she said. "There's probably a box somewhere in the common room."

Lauren nodded. "Thanks. Again, I'm sorry about crashing into you. If you need to get the bike repaired, just let me know and I'll pay." She started down the path.

"Hey!"

Lauren turned and saw Candace beckoning her back. "Listen, if you can't find any Band-Aids, you can always go to the infirmary."

"Which building is that?"

"Just past the dining hall—oh, hell, I've got plenty of Band-Aids and Neosporin, too. Just come with me."

Lauren hesitated and Candace waved at her. "C'mon, it's no problem. I'll play nurse and you can tell me all about your troubles with the beasts—I mean the sweet little angels—at Augustine House."

Lauren trotted after her. It turned out that Candace's house was the next dormitory over—Ambrose House—and that her apartment was the mirror image of Lauren's.

"Don't mind the mess," Candace said, after she'd locked her bike to one of the racks out front and Lauren was standing in her tiny front hall. "I'm afraid I'm not very domestic."

The layout of the apartment was the same, except it opened to the left, not the right. Even the furniture looked similar, but it was obvious that Candace had been in this apartment long enough to stamp it with her own personality. A large stack of newspapers was piled haphazardly next to the armchair and the desk, which was in the opposite corner as Lauren's, was cluttered with various papers, magazines, textbooks, and mugs of half-drunk tea.

A large poster of Albert Einstein dominated one wall and on the opposite was a framed painting of the periodic table done in bold colors. Candace shifted a pile of books off the sofa onto the floor and gestured at it. "Have a seat and I'll fetch the first-aid kit."

Lauren sat down gingerly, wincing at the pain in her cut knee. She glanced at the overflowing bookshelves, noticing a predominance of books about science and female scientists.

"Here we are." Candace came clattering back, first-aid kit in hand. "But you've got to wash those cuts out. Come in the kitchen." Lauren followed her. There were white daisies in a blue vase on the small table in the kitchen; otherwise, it looked exactly like Lauren's.

Candace left the first-aid kit open on the table, tore some paper towels off the rack mounted under the sink, and ran them under warm water, adding soap. "Sit down," she said, kicking out a chair for Lauren, who promptly plopped into the seat. Candace examined her injuries.

"All right, knee first," she said at last. "That looks like the worst."

She knelt down and with a tenderness that surprised Lauren, she cleaned out the wound with the paper towel, gripping the back of Lauren's knee as the pain caused a reflexive kick.

"All done," she said in a soothing tone. "Now some Neosporin and a Band-Aid—better make it a big one." She rummaged in the box and brought forth a square self-adhesive pad. "There you go. That should do the trick."

She stood up and snapped her fingers. "Okay, hands."

Lauren held out her palms and Candace repeated the process. Next she examined the scrape on Lauren's chin, cleaned it, and pronounced it okay.

"So what's going on in Augustine House?"

Lauren began, haltingly, to explain what was going on with the girls. Candace listened, nodding and at times uttering agreement, her presence so calm and inviting that before she realized it, Lauren began describing her own insecurities about teaching and second thoughts about being resident faculty.

Finally she ground to a halt. "I'm sorry, I didn't mean to vent. It's just that, I didn't think it was going to be this hard."

"It takes time," Candace said. "The first semester I was here I thought about quitting every single day."

"Great, I've only got another three months of hell to go."

Candace chuckled. "I'm sure it feels like that. If it's any consolation, your predecessor, Sister Agnes, apparently wasn't any more popular."

"Why? What was she like?"

Candace glanced down at her own knee. "Let me just change out of these clothes and I'll tell you." She headed down the hallway to the bedroom, calling over her shoulder.

"Help yourself to a drink. There's diet Coke in the fridge, or I think there's some iced tea."

Lauren got out two diet Cokes and poured them over ice. She sipped her drink, staring at the pictures magneted to the front of Candace's small fridge. Most of them were shots of a beach paradise: a stretch of sand on a sunny day with waves curling perfectly against its edge; Candace perched on a rocky groin with waves crashing in great gusts of foam; Candace bobbing in aquamarine water, a snorkeling mask pushed up on her forehead. Only one shot had other people: Candace with her arms around a gray-haired couple who shared her features.

"The parents," her voice suddenly said. Lauren jumped. Candace was standing right behind her, the torn jeans and stained shirt replaced by butter-yellow shorts and a V-neck white T-shirt that clung to her. She'd shed the sneakers and her footsteps were muffled by short white socks.

"Sorry, didn't mean to startle you," she said reaching past Lauren and pointing at the couple. "Mom and Dad looking happy because I was paying for dinner." Her skin smelled pleasantly sweet. She smiled, stepping back and picking up the drink from the counter. "Thanks for pouring," she said.

Lauren nodded. "Do they live on a beach?"

"No. White Plains. Though they're threatening to retire to Florida. I'm doing nothing to discourage them."

She sat down in the chair Lauren had vacated and rummaged in the first-aid kit for a Band-Aid.

"Here, let me," Lauren said. She got a paper towel and wet and soaped it. When she knelt to touch the other woman's knee, Candace drew back. Lauren looked up at her.

"Sorry." The knee edged forward and Lauren dabbed gently at it. She finished with the Neosporin and a Band-Aid, trying to keep her touch gentle. Candace's leg quivered, but she didn't say anything. Her cheeks were flushed when Lauren finished.

"Thanks." The other woman busied herself packing up

the first-aid kit, avoiding Lauren's eye. Had Lauren done a
clumsy job or was Candace embarrassed that someone else
had helped her? Lauren sat down in the other chair and
picked up her drink, hurriedly taking a few sips.

"You were going to tell me about Sister Agnes?" she said
after a minute.

"Oh, right." Candace looked up, meeting Lauren's eyes.
For just a moment there was something in them, some need
that startled Lauren, but then the other woman picked up her
drink and her eyes slid away. "Basically, she was a stereo-
typical nun—no nonsense, strict disciplinarian. She had certain expectations and she was quick to reprimand the girls
for relatively minor infractions."

"And the girls disliked her?"

"Yes. Some did. Some girls loved her—I guess they responded well to her style. And she definitely loved the girls.
Tough love, perhaps, and out of fashion now, but she'd been
at St. Ursula's for many, many years. I think she was hoping
to die in the job."

"What happened?"

Candace shrugged. "Not entirely sure, but it sounded like
Alzheimer's. She began acting paranoid—claimed there
were students out to get her."

Lauren thought of the whispers and footsteps she thought
she'd heard in the hallway late at night and was glad she hadn't
mentioned them. "So what happened? She retired?"

The other woman nodded. "Forced to, I heard. I think
she's in a nursing home."

"That's sad."

"Sure is. Sad way to go out after so many years here." She
gave a little laugh. "I hope I don't stay that long."

Lauren imagined waking up every morning to the same
view, turning the key in the same door, walking to the same
classroom. She shuddered. "Me, too."

*   *   *

She watched Lauren Kavanaugh leave the apartment all bandaged up and smiled. They'd scared her away and with any luck for good. The woman had no business snooping in the woods and it had been a pleasure watching her flee their cover.

She laughed a little as she remembered that shaky voice calling "Who's there?" Lauren Kavanaugh was easily frightened. It would be fun to play with that and easy to keep her off balance. If she ventured back in the woods things would intensify. Miss Kavanaugh thought she'd experienced fear in the woods, but that was just a tiny sample. Things would get much worse for Miss Kavanaugh if she didn't back off.

Inventing ways to frighten people was enjoyable, not nearly as much as doing these things, of course, but it was fun nonetheless. It was something that required careful thought if she wanted to do it right, and she always wanted to do it right. A perfectionist by nature, she abhorred doing anything in a slipshod fashion.

She thought of the gardening crew her family had employed one summer and how one ugly man had felt comfortable leering at her whenever she sunbathed poolside. He found reasons to linger around the fence surrounding the pool or made sure he was the one assigned to watering the many planters surrounding the pool itself.

He must have thought he was subtle or, worse, that she found him attractive with sweat staining his armpits and glistening under his porcine nose.

She spied on him, taking her time, watching and waiting for the nugget of personal information that would prove useful. Most people were too jumpy to do this, had to have instant gratification, but that internal throbbing pulse hummed along, steadying her. She had infinite patience.

It was rewarded the afternoon another landscaper brought his fishing gear to work with him, talking about hitting some lake after work, showing off his rod for everyone to see. She ignored the discussion of casting and flies. It was the bait can she noticed, and the way her stalker wouldn't go near it. She overheard him telling them that he couldn't be near worms, they just scared him, no bullshit, it was like some kind of phobia.

A few calls to area bait shops and she had three large buckets delivered. Heaped worms in the planters, scattered them over the lawn and the flowers, and filled the cab of his battered pickup truck with them. And when he jumped out of the truck screaming she made sure he saw her standing at the top of the front steps smiling sweetly down at him.

He never came back. Some people were better opponents than others, of course. Miss Kavanaugh seemed pretty weak, but first impressions could be wrong. She might prove more persistent than was desirable. That was okay. She liked a challenge.

It was close to dinnertime by the time Lauren got back to Augustine House, but she didn't bother to go to the dining hall. She didn't feel like being on display, especially when all she really wanted was a hot shower.

The photo fell out of her shorts when she slipped them off and she picked it up from the bathroom floor, staring at the charred edges and the fuzzy image of the girl in the water.

Should she take it to Sister Rose? Give it to the police? But what did it really show besides a girl swimming? There was no evidence that whoever took this photo had tied Morgan Wycoff to that tree.

Lauren threw the photo in the wastebasket and then had second thoughts and bent to retrieve it. Standing under the hot spray of the shower she tried to make sense of what she'd seen in the woods, wondering if she might have imagined the girls running away through the trees. She thought again about the fire pit and finding the photo in the ashes.

Suddenly she remembered the cigarette butts. She'd let

them drop when she'd found the photo, but they would have been something tangible. They could get DNA from cigarette butts, couldn't they?

She should have taken them. Lauren cursed her stupidity as she hobbled around her bedroom, gingerly slipping on some soft pajamas. All of the cuts and scrapes were starting to ache. She swallowed some Advil and carried the photo she'd left on the vanity back into the bedroom, propping it up on her nightstand.

She crawled under the covers, thinking about what she had to do. She didn't want to go back in the woods, not to that spot, anyway, but she had to. She had to get the butts and then she would take both those and the photo to the police.

Chapter Ten

On Saturday morning, Nicole packed recklessly for the weekend, throwing more clothes than she needed into the open bag on her bed while Tiffany lounged on the unoccupied section.

"You're so lucky that your parents live in Manhattan," she said. "I mean, at least it's somewhere close and fun to visit." Her parents lived in New Hampshire, which she'd declared to be boring.

"I don't know about that. I'll probably be dragged to the opera by my mother."

Nicole made it sound like a chore, but it was really a secret hope. Not that she liked opera, but at one point it had been a passion of her mother's and one that she'd insisted on sharing with her children. To have her mother want to go out, to want to instill some culture in her—this was something Nicole wanted. These were the things that had been missing since Paul's death.

"Will they take you to Planet Hollywood? I love that place."

"Probably not. My father doesn't like restaurants like that."

Nicole had a sudden memory of the last time she'd eaten in Manhattan. Two years before. A summer trip abroad, her mother excited because the family got to accompany her father on his business trip.

They'd done all the touristy things again, things they hadn't done since she was little, like going to the top of the Empire State Building and riding a carriage through Central Park. One warm afternoon stood out in her memory, a long, languorous day that they'd spent shopping and lounging in Central Park, her mother relaxing with a book on a bench while she and Paul raced model sailboats.

Their father met them at six for drinks and then they walked a few blocks east for dinner. He'd been jovial, a good day of deals making him relaxed and happy and able to concentrate on the story that Paul told. She couldn't remember it now, but it had been something funny, something they'd observed during their day, and Nicole could recall how her parents laughed at what he was saying and how her father's hand stole across the table to clasp her mother's.

She could see the glow of the wineglasses on the white linen cloth and the way Paul's hands, a boy's hands, rough and unwieldy, circled the air with their own puppyish grace while he described something. She recalled breathing in the scent of the two gardenia blossoms resting in a low bowl on their table and watching how the candlelight smoothed the lines from her mother's face and made her smile look like a girl's.

If someone had asked her to define happiness, this was the moment she would describe.

Tiffany helped her carry her bags out of Augustine House and over to the main building, where she had to sign out. Her taxi arrived at nine, another one pulling up behind it. Weekends were a busy time at the school. Girls were allowed visits home on weekends, provided that parents had requested them.

Nicole waved good-bye to Sister Roberta, the elderly nun

whose sole job was to monitor the large black book that recorded the comings and goings of the girls, and rolled her overnight bag down to the taxi.

On the long train ride into Manhattan she did her homework with her iPod providing a soundtrack and tried not to think about what it was going to be like being at a new home without Paul.

There was no one to meet her at Grand Central. Her father was probably at his office, but once her mother would have been there to greet her. In Paris she'd always been at the station, hustling between one train and the next, gathering her children like chicks, clucking about how ill-fed they looked and how they needed her good cooking to fatten them up.

Nicole hefted her backpack, pulled the carry-on behind her, and waited in a queue in the rain for a taxi. She gave the address to the driver and stared out the window at the rain-splattered streets of the city as the taxi darted between cars and sped through traffic to the Upper East Side.

She'd seen the building once. Gray limestone, Art Deco detailing, a maroon awning sheltering the entrance.

A portly doorman hurried to open the taxi door and greeted her by name with a gap-toothed smile. She couldn't remember his. And then there was her mother, standing in the lobby, looking anxious despite the smile that crossed her face.

"Darling," she said, pulling Nicole to her in a firm embrace. She felt bony and it wasn't disguised by the thin cream-colored sweater set, camel skirt, and the brown-and-cream Hermès scarf knotted casually around her neck. She smelled of Chanel No. 5 and beneath it the faint scent of the lavender soap she loved. Her black hair was tied back in a loose chignon and there were a few more gray strands streaking it.

"Are you hungry?" she asked. "I've got lunch ready."

It felt strange, this hesitancy, and Nicole didn't know

what to say to fill the void. She allowed her mother to take her carry-on and followed her onto an elevator. "It's on the fifteenth floor, did you remember?" her mother said as she pressed the button. Nicole shook her head. They were silent as the elevator whirred upward.

The apartment was slightly smaller than their apartment in Paris, but the kitchen and baths were newer. Nicole followed her mother through the space, feeling as if she was at a hotel and not her home, even though the furniture had been shipped from France and her mother had decorated the place remarkably like their old home.

"Here's your room, darling." Sabine Morel paused at a bedroom down the hall from the master. Inside was the bed Nicole had had since childhood, a full-size four-poster in walnut, painted a creamy color with flowers in muted shades edging the headboard and foot rail. There was the matching dresser and the desk with flowers painted along its drawers and a pink cushion secured with crisp bows to its back spindles.

Everything was the same. Except it wasn't. There were no pictures on top of the dresser or on the wall.

"I left some things for you to do," her mother said. "The rest of the boxes are over there." She nodded at a corner near the desk where two boxes were stacked neatly.

They ate lunch in the large empty kitchen. Soup and some bread and cheese. Her mother served Nicole and drank coffee herself, sitting across from her and taking occasional sips of her own bowl of tomato bisque.

"It's good," Nicole said to fill the void.

"Yes, the housekeeper is really very good." Nicole's mother hesitated. Was she thinking of Marie, their taciturn housekeeper in Paris? Was she remembering that the only person who'd been able to coax a smile out of her was Paul?

"Where is she?" Nicole asked.

"I gave her the afternoon off. I wanted it to be just you and me." Sabine Morel smiled, looking for just a moment like she had throughout Nicole's early childhood, as if she were a coconspirator in her children's play.

"So, how are you liking school?" The smile faded and she got up to fetch more coffee from the elaborate machine on the wide stone counter.

"It's good. I have some friends."

"I'm so glad, darling." Her mother sat back down and smiled at Nicole. Her soup sat untouched. Nicole was painfully aware of the sound of her own spoon scraping against the porcelain bowl. She tried to swallow quietly.

"What would you like to do? The Met has a nice Manet exhibit?"

"Okay, sure."

"But we don't have to. We could just stay here, cuddled up on this rainy day?"

Nicole could tell that this was what her mother wanted, but she had to get out. She couldn't stay in the silent apartment all day.

She felt better in the museum and also worse. Seeing her mother out among others made it even more clear that Sabine wasn't well. She'd definitely lost weight; her collarbone was visible through the thin weight of the sweater set, and her anklebones looked like they'd snap if something grazed them. There were hollows at her wrists and a crease between her eyes that Nicole had never noticed before.

Her behavior in the museum was different, too. She seemed to shrink in on herself, pressing close to Nicole as if she were afraid of being contaminated by the other people around them. The confident woman who used to lead the way, gaily pointing out portraits to her children or grilling them about what they'd learned about this painter or that sculptor was gone.

In contrast, Nicole felt as if she must make up for this and found herself trying to get her mother's attention in a way that she hadn't done since she was little. Calling to her to look at a particular painting, pulling her along to another gallery when her mother seemed lost in thought, telling stupid stories to coax a smile from her.

At the end of the day she felt as if she'd run a marathon. It was dusk when they got back to the apartment, the evenings coming sooner because it was fall. The rooms were dark and Sabine Morel walked around turning on lights all over the apartment while Nicole stood helplessly in the foyer feeling like a stranger in her own home.

"Look, it's a gas fireplace," her mother said, flipping a switch on the side of a stone mantel so that flames leapt up in the grate. "It's nice, isn't it?" She took a seat on the couch and beckoned Nicole to her. "I'm too tired to cook or to go out. Why don't we have something delivered?"

She let Nicole choose food from a Chinese menu she found in a drawer by the phone. They sat across from each other in the living room while they waited for the delivery, her mother falling asleep on the couch. Nicole covered her with an afghan and huddled into an armchair.

"Isn't Dad coming home?" she asked later, when the food had been delivered and her mother was dishing it out onto plates in the wide, empty kitchen.

"He has a late meeting," her mother said, pausing with a carton of sesame chicken in her hand. She looked from Nicole back to the food. "He'll be home later, darling. I know he's looking forward to your visit."

They ate in the kitchen again and again her mother simply picked at the food, this time drinking wine, while Nicole ate too much because of nerves. Her stomach hurt afterward, while they sat in the living room and watched a flat-screen TV that was cleverly hidden in a wall unit.

Her mother fell asleep shortly after eight and Nicole covered her with a throw. Just before nine, her father unlocked the door.

"Nicky, my little Nickel," he said when he saw her and she ran to him and he spun her around in the air.

"You're so late, Laurent," her mother said behind them. She was sitting up on the couch, blinking. Laurent Morel released his daughter and Nicole slid to her feet and looked at her mother. Sleeping had pushed Sabine's hair oddly to one side so that it looked like she was wearing a wig.

"I told you I would be. I had a meeting," Laurent said in a terse voice. "Did my girls have a good day?" he asked more cheerfully, addressing the question to Nicole.

She started to tell him, but her mother interrupted. "Do you want something to eat?"

"No, I'm fine."

"But when was the last time you ate? Don't tell me you made a meal out of those dreadful snack machines." Sabine rose from the couch and came to her husband's side. He caught one of her hands as she was about to lay it against his head.

"Sabine," he said and Nicole tensed at the coldness of his voice. "I'm fine. We had dinner brought in."

Her mother subsided, went back to the sofa, and sat quietly while Laurent Morel sat down in an overstuffed armchair and pulled Nicole down onto his lap.

"Are you being mistreated by those dreadful nuns?" he asked, tickling her side.

"Stop it!" She giggled, batting at his hands. "They don't have many, Dad. Just a couple."

"And they're ogres? They beat you?" He made a face and she laughed.

"No, you're ridiculous."

"What? What am I paying all of this money for if not to have you whipped into shape? What's the world coming to, Sabine? They don't even beat schoolchildren anymore."

Her mother smiled, but didn't say anything. Nicole hugged her father, pressing her face against his chest and breathing in that familiar mixture of aftershave and the faint scent of his single daily cigar. He felt solid, whole, the same.

"Have you missed me, little girl?" he murmured, cupping her head with one of his large hands. "I've missed you very much."

Later, they both tucked her into bed, just like they'd done when she was small. Only then Paul had been in the room across from hers and when their parents had gone back into the other section of the apartment, he'd steal out of bed and into her room and they'd giggle together.

She drifted off to sleep, remembering spying on her parents' parties with Paul. He would come to get her, a finger to his lips, and they'd tiptoe down the dark hallway, tile cold against their bare feet, the two of them clad in cotton pajamas, hair cut in almost identical bobs. They stayed in the shadows, going just far enough to see the lights in the living room and hear the sound of adults in conversation.

In the twilight between awake and asleep, she conjured up the magic of those parties: the scents of sweet bourbon, of spicy perfume, of warm Brie, Turkish cigarettes, and dark chocolate. The rustle of silk, the clink of ice stirring against glass, the faint pop of a cork sliding free from a present of wine. The slow rise and fall of pleasant conversation, the occasional swell of laughter, and in the background the low, melodious voice of a sad jazz singer.

She woke to loud voices. Her father yelling and her mother telling him to be quiet, but her own voice just as loud.

"No, I won't be quiet, Sabine. This has gone on long enough, you can't keep acting like this—"

"Don't tell me how to grieve! Don't you, of all people, tell me how to handle losing my only son!"

"He was my son, too!"

Nicole pulled the covers over her head and covered her ears. She closed her eyes tightly, but she couldn't stop the tears. They spilled out onto her pillow and she gulped as quietly as she could, feeling the relief of their release hot on her cheeks.

Chapter Eleven

The squad room was virtually deserted on Sunday, except for a couple of uniforms filling out traffic-stop reports. Except for a few salient details, the police station in Gashford resembled almost any other office building, complete with cubicles, stained carpeting, and the smell of microwave popcorn.

Of course, the average citizen paying a visit couldn't fail to notice the Wall of Honor for officers killed in the line of duty and anyone who got beyond the main desk was probably going to see the photos of blood spatter from a recent murder-suicide pinned up in preparation for an upcoming inquest.

Now there was a big whiteboard taking up one corner, allocated for the Wycoff case. The prevailing theory was that Morgan Wycoff, Beau Steuben, and Heather Lester had been performing some sort of pagan ritual in the woods—maybe some others as well—that they'd tied Morgan to the tree, perhaps in a moment of drunken revelry, and they'd left her there.

Only Stephanie seemed to think that theory was crap. For starters, she believed that the dark fibers found under Morgan's fingernails were from the clothing of whoever had tied her to that tree and that those and the bruising on her forearm were evidence of defensive wounds.

Oz thought she'd gotten that bruise and the wound on the back of her head from struggling to untie herself once she realized her friends weren't coming back. The captain seemed to support this theory, especially after learning that several of the older sisters regularly visited the Stations of the Cross early in the morning. Morgan was supposed to shock these old religious women; she might even have wanted this herself, but they hadn't anticipated the temperature dropping so far on a summer night.

Stephanie was studying the crime scene photos again, staring at them until her eyes glazed over as if they were like those hidden pictures where you had to relax your eyes to reveal the image hidden among the pixels.

Of the detectives, Oz was at a funeral for his wife's aunt, Wackjob and Puff Daddy were out following a lead on the origin of the rope, and Stephanie had no idea where Frangione was and she didn't want to know.

Something about the crime scene had been niggling at her, but she didn't know what it was, so she'd come back into the office to take a look at the photos and see if actually staring at them again could pull forth from her subconscious whatever it was trying to tell her. So far, it wasn't working.

At least she didn't have pressure to be anywhere else. Alex had gone to his parents' to help set up for the big engagement party they'd insisted on throwing for their son and his fiancée. Knowing he wouldn't approve, she'd waited until he was gone before heading in to work.

She had mixed feelings about this party. Mixed feelings about the whole marriage thing, if she was honest. Suddenly there was all this pressure that hadn't been there before. Apparently getting married had to involve an elaborate and expensive ceremony and everyone assumed that by virtue of being female she had been consumed by dreams of the perfect wedding since birth.

The truth was that she had almost no interest in most of the details and that went double for gown shopping. So far she'd been to two bridal shops, both at the behest and in the company of her very excited mother. Stephanie had been itchy, uncomfortable, and felt very much like Gulliver being trussed by the Lilliputians who seemed to operate these businesses. Armed with measuring tapes and clicking tongues, the shrunken old women buzzed around her as if she were a flower and they were the bees.

Shaking that memory from her mind, she stood up and got a diet Pepsi from the machine in the front hall and stood staring out the dirty window that gave a partial view of Gashford's main street. There were carefully pruned young trees planted at intervals along the sidewalk, alternating with Victorian-style lampposts, a project spearheaded by a former mayor. All part of Gashford's upwardly mobile climb. It might not have quite the wealth of Summit or Short Hills, and granted the train took longer going in and out of Manhattan, but more and more moneyed people had discovered Gashford.

Staring at the thin designer trees staked in their small squares of dirt, Stephanie felt that niggling sense again. Whatever was bothering her had to do with the tree. She returned to her desk and looked at the crime scene photos yet again. Here was that enormous oak tree up close, the places where the rope had rubbed the bark clearly visible. And here was the tree from a distance with the vic still tied to it. She shuffled through them and stopped when she came to the shots of the pentagram at the base of the tree. There were seven of these, one of each side of the circle, then close-ups of the writing within each point of the star. She laid the five photos out to form the star and that's when she spotted it.

*   *   *

It rained on Saturday, a steady downpour that persuaded Lauren to wait to return to the woods. Sunday dawned clear and sunny and she sat in the hard wooden pew in the chapel with the girls of Augustine House listening to an elderly priest named Father Dominic mumble his way through Mass.

She stood and knelt and stood again and recited the prayers in unison with the young, high voices all around her and she didn't hear a word of it. All she could think about was the fire pit and having let the cigarette butts drop from her hand. She pictured them slowly uncurling, the lipstick fading, the tobacco scattering under the force of the rain.

As soon as Mass ended, while they were still singing the final hymn, she slipped out the chapel doors, bypassing a handshake with the doddering and smiling Father Dominic and pushing past a surprised Sister Rose with a fast "excuse me" in her haste to get back to her apartment.

She unstrapped her high-heeled sandals as she went, peeling one and then the other from her feet as she ran, clutching her pearls to her neck so they wouldn't bounce off. Inside her apartment she dropped the shoes and flung everything else on her bed, racing to get into shorts and a sports bra, pulling a Lycra top over her head. She jammed her feet in her running shoes and remembered at the last moment to take off her pearl earrings and slip on her sports watch.

Her confidence that she could find the spot slipped once she was actually back in the woods. She was sure she'd chosen the same path as before, veering left away from the direction of the pond, but after forty minutes she was no closer to finding the fire pit than she had been when she started.

Several times Lauren veered off onto a satellite path, just as she had last time, sure that the dense clumping of trees she saw ahead would give way to the clearing, but each time she was disappointed.

She was hot at this point, tired and feeling confused. She paused and pulled up her shirt to wipe the sweat from her forehead, wishing she'd thought to bring a water bottle. Sweat crawled over her scalp, tickled the back of her neck. A slight breeze barely stirred the leaves and the loudest sound was her own heavy breathing.

A sharp snap, like a tree branch splitting, jerked her head left. She scanned the trees there, but saw nothing. The slightest movement in her peripheral vision brought her eyes right. Again, nothing, but Lauren felt her skin prickling with nervous anticipation. Suddenly, a figure in black stepped out from behind the thick trunk of a hemlock tree and stared at Lauren.

Shock held her rooted. The figure was only about thirty feet away, but she couldn't tell if it was male or female because it was covered completely, black pants and a black hooded sweatshirt pulled tight around the face so only the smallest oval of pale skin was visible.

All at once the figure turned and ran.

"Wait!" Lauren called. She sprinted after him or her, darting around trees and scrambling over brush, trying to keep the figure in sight. She could see glimpses through the trees, a moment of perfect sight when the figure passed through a pool of sunshine, but then they'd vanish again.

Lauren was lost now, she could feel it, disoriented by the unrelenting maze of green and brown. She thought she'd circled once, but she wasn't sure, and the figure was gone again. She stopped short, panting, dropping her hands to her knees and ducking her head, trying to get steady.

The faint, high-pitched giggle brought her head up fast. There was the figure again, closer this time, no more than twenty feet away. Lauren chased after it, slipping in a soft carpet of pine needles and using her arms to block branches whipping at her cheeks.

She was gaining on him or her. She made a harder push, her head throbbing and chest sore from the effort. The figure dashed between two trees and Lauren reached out her hand as she followed, so close her fingers whispered over the sweatshirt fabric and then there was a sharp jerk against her right foot and she fell forward through space.

Oz didn't care for computers. He'd told Stephanie on more than one occasion that good police work didn't depend on technology but instinct. Well, she'd had the instinct to look up Wiccan practices on the Internet and the technology had helped her identify something they'd missed.

She took her own car out to the crime scene. It was a black Ford Focus and she loved it even though she put up with a lot of razzing from the other detectives. Wackjob drove an Esplanade that always looked as if the chrome had been spit-polished and Frangione was on his second Hummer. Even Oz, who owned a minivan, lusted after designer pickup trucks and gave her grief.

"You've got no kids, how come you're not in a better ride?"

Well, cost for one thing. She and Alex were saving so they could afford to buy a home before they reached retirement age. Plus, even if she had the extra cash she wasn't sure she'd spend a dime on another car. Nothing beat the combination of great price and great design. And the Focus was a sweet little car. It hugged the road just like a pricier sports car and it had great pickup.

It needed it to make it up the hill. She parked in the same lot where she'd been the first time and flashed her badge at the older rent-a-cop, who got off his can to wander out of the small booth and see who was paying St. Ursula's a visit. He retreated after giving her a nod, one professional to another, and she headed into the woods.

It was strange being alone where last time there'd been a crowd. She'd made fun of Oz for protesting the long walk, but this time she was feeling it, too. The marble statues gave her the creeps. The one where Christ was nailed to the Cross was particularly gruesome, what with the wild eyes rolling back in their stone sockets.

Every few feet she'd check over her shoulder and several times she pulled her left arm in tight against her side just to feel the reassuring weight of her weapon.

She was relieved to find the crime scene tape intact. Ducking under it, she headed straight for the tree and the pentagram at its base. The rain had softened its edges, but had not erased it. She exhaled in relief, the sound loud in the stillness. A crow cawed somewhere overhead and a slight breeze carried the smell of pine and damp earth.

What she thought she'd seen in the photos was confirmed. The pentagram was inverted. It was clear from the way the words were written, so they could be read if you were standing in the center of the circle, that it was inverted. Furthermore, the words in each point were in the wrong spot. Spirit should have been in the center point, but it wasn't, and earth and air were confused.

A little time on the Internet had been very useful. She's learned, for instance, that Wicca and satanism were two distinct religions with very different beliefs. Wiccans used a five-pointed star, but it was not inverted. Satanists used the inverted pentagram.

If Beau and Heather were right about Morgan, she'd taken her religion seriously and wouldn't have made this kind of mistake. Someone else had drawn the pentagram who didn't know the difference between the two. The words had been put on to emphasize the ritual aspect, but whoever had written them had gotten it wrong.

The question was, had Morgan been forced to go for a swim or was she already in the water? Her roommate said she'd liked to go up here, but the headmistress had been quick to point out that swimming in the pond was against the rules.

Stephanie walked over to the edge of the pond, trying to

picture what had happened. She imagined the girl going for a swim. It would have been a cool night, but if she was into the whole nature thing then she'd probably done it anyway. If they'd confronted her when she got out of the pond, that could explain the bruises on her arms.

She stared out across the murky greenish water, an occasional breeze rippling its smooth surface. The sun danced across it, highlighting a skim coat of bright green algae on the far side. She wouldn't want to swim here during the day, much less at night. Closer to shore the water was marginally clearer and something sparkled.

At first she thought it was just the light glinting off the water, but then it happened again. She stepped nearer, the tips of her sneakers breaking the water's surface, her heels squelching in the mud. Shading her eyes, she leaned forward and there, yes, there it was. Something sparkling underneath the surface.

Stepping back, she looked around for a long stick. She extended it as far as she could and slid the tip under the water's surface gently, but the minute she tried to move whatever was there, the silt from the bottom stirred up and she had a big, brown mess.

Oh, hell. She was going to have to go in. She took off her jacket and slipped off her shoes, rolled down her socks and stuffed them in the toes, and rolled her jeans up to her knees.

"Shit!" The water was cold and she flinched, stirring up silt. She waited for it to settle, trying to ignore the unpleasant squishing between her toes. She remembered going crayfish hunting as a kid with the little boy who'd lived up the block and thought of the pincers on those miniature lobsters, pushing the thought of one scuttling toward her far from her mind.

She waded out slowly, keeping an eye on the spot where she'd seen the sparkle. When the sun vanished behind some clouds she had to stand there with the gloomy water surrounding her and resist the urge to run screaming for the shore.

The clouds shifted and the sun peeked through, skipping along the water's surface. A sudden shimmer. She took two more slow steps, waited for the surface to settle, and looked down. There it was! Something small and gold.

She pushed up the sleeve of her T-shirt, leaned forward, and reached down in the water. Not far enough. She bent her knees, water soaking through the edges of her cuffed jeans, and pushed down, her chin grazing the surface of the water, her arm in danger of separating from its socket. Her fingers grazed something, then closed on it.

She yanked her arm up in triumph and carefully uncurled her fingers. A small gold five-pointed star lay on her damp palm, its delicate chain interwoven with slimy algae. The clasp was broken.

Splashing back to the bank, Stephanie used her socks to dry her legs and feet, shoved her shoes back on, and headed to her car.

On the drive back to town she kept the necklace nestled in tissue on the passenger seat. She drove fast, beating her hand on the steering wheel in time with an old Springsteen song blasting from her radio.

She dropped the necklace off at the crime scene unit and tried to emphasize just how important it was that they check it for prints. Could they tell how long it had been in the water? Maybe. Always a maybe with those guys. The investigators didn't know squat until they handed it over for analysis, and the scientists didn't want to commit.

Still, she was feeling pretty good when she checked back in at the station. Morgan had been wearing that necklace and whoever had tied her to that tree had ripped it off her. That explained the raw spot on the back of her neck. She pictured Morgan struggling to defend herself and someone grabbing her by that chain, pulling her along by it until they tore it off her neck and tossed it away.

Rebecca Drake

She was scribbling a note to talk to Harriet Wembley about the source of the marks on the vic's neck when the desk sergeant, Mabel Gery, wandered back from the break room with a cup of coffee in her hand and stopped by Stephanie's desk.

"I thought you were supposed to be at a party?" Stephanie's head flew up, looking past Mabel to see the clock. It was five fifty-five. The party started at six.

"Tell me that clock is wrong," she said jumping up so fast her chair fell over.

"I'd do that, honey," Mabel said, "but I'd be lying."

Stephanie grabbed her jacket and took off running.

Chapter Twelve

Falling headfirst, Lauren just had time to bring her arms up around her head before she landed hard on her right ankle. She immediately rolled again, slamming her left hip against rock-strewn earth before skidding to a stop at the bottom of a narrow gully. A small shower of wine-red maple leaves glided to rest on her prone body.

For a moment, she couldn't move. She couldn't breathe. Her lungs hurt too much to gather air and her head was spinning. When the world came back into focus, she got carefully to her feet, only to collapse again, writhing in pain. She couldn't walk on her right ankle. Already she could see it swelling. Besides that, and a raw patch on her left side, the rest of her seemed intact. Her arms had protected her head and while she was scratched up and the scrapes from two days ago had reopened, nothing but her ankle seemed badly hurt.

Only how was she going to get out? She was at the bottom of a steep embankment and could see the trees she'd dashed between high on the hill above her. The figure in black was gone.

"Help!" Lauren called, only to hear her voice echoing

back at her. No one would hear her. She was alone and in the evening it would grow colder. She shuddered, remembering Morgan's body tied to the tree.

It was enough incentive to push her into inching her way up the hill on her backside, using her good leg to push off with. It was slow going and far too soon it felt as if she were poking holes through her posterior with all the rocks and twigs. She used her hands to push off the ground and for the rest of the climb scuttled like a disabled crab, pausing every few seconds to get her bearings and check that the path behind her was clear. Her left foot slipped occasionally in the crumbly earth, so that she would slide back down the few feet she'd managed to climb, but eventually she was at the summit and panting against the base of one of the trees.

Once she'd caught her breath, she shifted on the hard ground and looked around. How the hell had she fallen off the side of this hill but the hooded figure hadn't? There was little more than a foot across between the trees and the sudden downward plunge. Had he or she simply turned suddenly, thus avoiding the drop?

The sunlight shifted and she saw something glisten. Lauren leaned toward it until she was close enough to reach out a hand and confirm what her eyes refused to believe. A thin wire was strung between the two tree trunks. She hadn't tripped, her foot had caught on this wire and sent her sprawling headfirst over the embankment.

Lauren sat back, reeling. It was a beautiful day; the sky was a shade of blue so bright that it hurt the eyes, and the few clouds dotting it looked like puffs of spun sugar. It seemed impossible that something so hideous could happen on such a beautiful day, but she knew better. It wasn't an accident that she'd plunged over the hillside and the hooded figure hadn't. She'd been lured here.

The stillness of the woods was ominous. She scrambled around the trees with the wire strung between them, oblivious to the dirt and debris digging into her knees, and used another trunk to pull herself upright. Hopping on one foot and moving slowly from tree to tree, she searched for a path out.

Every strange sound—the far-off call of a bird, the burrowing of a small animal through the leaves—startled her. She looked behind her repeatedly and jerked her head right and left at every juncture. Once she thought she spotted the hooded figure standing in shadows a few feet away, but the light shifted and where the figure had been standing was nothing but empty space.

By the time she saw the edge of the trees and the asphalt road that led back down to the school, she was damp with sweat and her damaged ankle had swollen to twice its normal size.

Without an injury the walk back to school would be trivial, but every time she put any pressure on her right foot the subsequent shrieking pain convinced her that she really couldn't walk on it.

She inched along the edge of the woods, continuing to use the trunks of trees and their outstretched branches as support. When she heard the car engine behind her, Lauren's first reaction was relief, followed instantly by panic when she realized how fast it was coming. There was little shoulder on this section of road, the trees pressing against the verge on either side.

She turned her head just as a small dark blue car sped into view. Lauren's good foot slipped in some gravel and she fell backward this time, the car horn blaring and brakes squealing as her feet went up and she landed with a *whump* on her back, blinking up at the sky.

A car door slammed and she sat up as rapid footsteps approached.

"Are you okay?"

The voice brought her head up fast. Candace Huston loomed over her, looking equally surprised. "You certainly seem to have a death wish, girl."

"I'm not the one with a death wish—someone else is!" Lauren struggled to stand and Candace helped her up.

"Hey, I saw you in plenty of time," Candace said.

"Not you. In the woods. Someone was trying to kill me. As it is, I think they broke my ankle." She hovered flamingo-like on one leg.

"*What* happened?" Candace looked down at Lauren's swollen ankle and shook her head. "Never mind. Can you walk if you lean on me? C'mon."

Lauren hobbled toward the car with her left arm flung over Candace's shoulder and Candace's right arm wrapped around her waist. Candace helped Lauren get in the passenger side of the small Toyota, both of them wincing as her injured leg bumped against the door.

"You're going to have to get that x-rayed."

"There was a wire strung between two trees—that's how I fell into the ravine."

"What are you talking about?"

"Someone tried to kill me, that's what I'm talking about."

Candace glanced at her with an incredulous expression. "Who? And why?"

"Would you watch the road?"

She looked back in time to turn the car left and Lauren fell against the side door.

"Sorry," Candace said, "but you seem, well, delusional. Did you hit your head?"

"No, but I've got a headache." Lauren's temple throbbed in time with her ankle and she didn't want to think about how she was going to get around with a cast.

"You need to get that x-rayed," Candace said again.

"It's probably just a sprain."

"Still, you've got to get it checked out."

"Isn't there an infirmary on campus?"

"Yeah, but the nurse will tell you the same thing I did—you've got to go to the hospital to get an X-ray."

* * *

She watched from the woods as that bitch Huston loaded Lauren Kavanaugh into the car and drove away. There appeared to be nothing wrong with her other than the leg. It was infuriating. How could she have survived that fall?

When the car vanished, she ran back through the woods to the spot where she'd strung the wire and, pulling out a pair of wire cutters, snipped it from the tree. Then she rubbed dirt around the bark to conceal any sign that it had been there.

At least that part had worked perfectly. Miss Kavanaugh fell just like she was supposed to, but somehow, miraculously, landed without breaking her neck. It just didn't seem possible.

Clutching the wire in one hand and the cutters in the other, she peered over the edge down into the rock-strewn ravine far below. The sweet, satisfying rush she'd gotten when this snoopy teacher went over the side had been as intense as the disappointment she felt moments later hearing the first grunt that indicated her target had survived.

It had been tempting to kick Miss Kavanaugh back down as she scaled the hillside, but that was too risky. She might have been pulled down herself or had her identity revealed. She cursed her failure to bring a knife—she might have made swift work of an exposed neck as Kavanaugh climbed the hillside.

Instead, she had to watch, impotent and inwardly raging, as this surprisingly strong woman inched her skinny self from the woods to the road. She had a moment of hope when the teacher faltered on the road, but despite the fact that people got hit and killed by cars every damn day, it didn't happen here. She could have screamed with frustration when the car slammed on its brakes just shy of hitting Miss Kavanaugh.

Now what? She'd have to try again, that was clear, but how and where? Maybe it was time to try something closer to home? She considered this while she wound the wire into a tight little ball and stuffed it in her pocket. It was a large campus and there were many possibilities.

One thing she knew for sure, she thought while striding back out of the woods. Whatever method she chose, it would have to be soon.

Candace drove like she was in Le Mans, ignoring the brake pedal and simply easing off the accelerator for tight turns. They turned in at the entrance for Gashford Community Hospital, a maze of matching red brick buildings, in just over eleven minutes.

The building housing the emergency room was in the process of being remodeled. Candace pulled the car into the driveway, narrowly avoiding some traffic cones set up by construction workers, and pulled to a stop in front of the double glass doors, putting on her blinkers.

Lauren hobbled through the doors with Candace's help. The nurse at the front desk looked harried, but took her information and pointed toward the waiting area.

Most of the seats were empty. A few older, neatly dressed women sat staring at a TV mounted high on one wall where a far too cheery broadcaster was discussing the weekend forecast. Nearby a little boy knelt on the floor running a tiny car over the seat of the chair next to the one holding his listless mother. He kept repeating, "Vroom, vroom, vroom," getting progressively louder with each, and then his mother would look up from her magazine and say, "Hush," and he'd be quiet for a moment before starting again.

A large, middle-aged man sat wedged in a chair, elbows on knees, head in hands, while a middle-aged woman with gray streaking her black hair patted him gently on the back.

"What did you mean about a wire?" Candace asked in a low voice once they were seated.

Lauren poured out the story, with Candace interrupting

periodically to tell her to slow down or telling her to back up
and explain something again.

"Who the hell would string a wire between two trees?"
she said when Lauren was finished.

"I have no clue. Someone who didn't want me snooping?"

Candace shrugged. "It's very strange. You have to report
it."

"I was going to take the cigarette butts to the police."

Candace looked thoughtful. "I'd tell Sister Rose first. She
doesn't like people going outside of the school."

"What do you mean? Don't you think the police would
want to test them?"

"Of course." Candace sighed and glanced around the
waiting room before leaning toward Lauren and lowering
her voice even further. "Look, I know you've only been at
the school for a week, but hasn't your experience with finding Morgan Wycoff's body taught you the meaning of tight
knit? It's very much St. Ursula's against the world."

Lauren pictured Sister Rose speaking from the burnished
lectern at the welcoming cum memorial service in the
chapel. *"St. Ursula's offers a place to resist the social evils
celebrated by much of the world."*

The headmistress had immediately placed Morgan's
death in a context that had nothing to do with the school.
The subtle message underneath the sentiments for the death
of *"one of our own"*? If Morgan hadn't resisted St. Ursula's
and its values, she would still be alive.

Stephanie ran a red light and barely paused at two stop
signs on the way to her future in-laws' home. The dress she'd
been going to wear hung in the closet back at the town
house. In the opposite direction. She wavered for a minute,
thinking of how nice she'd planned on looking, but the fear
of being any later drove her toward the Greenbergs'.

She discovered her cell phone was shut off, which was just as well because there were probably a dozen frantic calls from Alex. Better that she claimed not to know. Better that they thought she'd gotten called away on a case.

The Greenbergs' house was in one of Gashford's newer developments, outside of town in an area that had been hotly contested wetland. Long before Stephanie joined the force there had been protests along this stretch of road with earnest environmentalists waving placards at surveyors. That was then. Now it was an area called Windsor Park, which was to an English country village what Busch Gardens was to Europe.

Lots of stucco, stone, and half-timber aged to look as if it had stood there forever—in sharp and disconcerting contrast to the two-car attached garages. The scraps of lawn were neatly trimmed and the roads perfectly paved. The houses all had dramatic entrance halls and massive kitchens and they were built close enough together that neighbors could keep tabs on each other's latest toys, but far enough away that no one would overhear arguing about overextended credit cards or failed dot-coms.

The Greenbergs' faux Tudor was the dream home they'd built when their boys were in their early teens. Whenever Stephanie visited she couldn't help comparing this place to the postage stamp Cape Cod on the poorer side of Gashford, where she grew up and her mother still lived. Owning a house like one of these had been her dad's dream. A dream that died along with him.

The sweeping driveway in front of the Greenbergs' was full of cars when Stephanie arrived. Shit, shit, shit. She was twenty-five minutes late to her own engagement party.

She parked on the side of the road and pulled down the visor to check her face in the mirror. A quick swipe of lipstick, a fast brush through her hair. That was all she had time for. Stephanie hoped it compensated in some way for the mud-stained jeans and shoes. She brushed at the beige spots left by the pond water on her white T-shirt and donned her crimson blazer. At least that was clean.

She hurried to the front door of the two-story home, realizing only as she rang the bell that she was still carrying her weapon. Just then, her future mother-in-law opened the door. It was too late to retreat.

"There you are!" Lois Greenberg squealed, waving her inside with a bejeweled hand. "We were worried about you!" Proud of her slim figure, Lois Greenberg was showing it off in a figure-hugging black dress with three-quarter-length sleeves. She was one of those women who weren't conventionally pretty, but had learned to highlight their best features—in her case her large brown eyes and an engaging smile—so that the overall effect was of great beauty and style.

She kissed the air near Stephanie's cheek, the crystal glass in her hand tipping precariously, but Lois easily righted it before red wine splashed onto the tile in her foyer. A large chandelier twinkled above their heads, competing with the diamonds at her neck, wrists, and fingers.

The Greenbergs' house teemed with people, many of whom Stephanie had never seen before. Lois grabbed her hand and tugged her past some of them, pausing at the entrance to the massive two-story living room complete with floor-to-ceiling stone fireplace. "Look, everybody, here's the bride-to-be!"

An entire room full of people turned en masse to look and Stephanie managed to smile, resisting the urge to bolt back out the door. Lois disappeared into the crowd, but not before giving Stephanie's outfit a quick once-over.

Lots of the people in the room were older friends of the Greenbergs and everybody was nicely dressed. Silk, linen, and cashmere abounded. Nobody else was wearing jeans and a T-shirt. She tugged at her corduroy blazer.

Lois emerged from the sea of bodies leading a small,

nervous-looking woman with a distinctly disapproving look on her face. Stephanie stifled a groan as her mother made it through the crowd to her side.

"What on earth are you wearing?" Debbie Land hissed as she pecked Stephanie on the cheek. "I thought you'd decided on that print dress?" Her own dress was silk, ill-fitting and the wrong color of peach for her skin, making her cheeks look ruddy. Stephanie complimented her anyway, trying to placate her.

"I came straight from work," she muttered searching the crowd for Alex.

"Your sister and I were worried. I tried your cell phone six times. God only knows how often Alex tried."

"I guess I was out of range." Stephanie lied without compunction. She spotted her heavily pregnant younger sister waddling across the plush cream carpet and pulled away from her mother to greet her.

"Hi, Sam." She patted her sister's tummy, which was the closest thing to her.

"Are your hands clean?" Samantha said, drawing back. "What's that crap on your jeans?"

"Pond scum," Stephanie said. "Latest fashion, it's in the new issue of *Vogue*."

"Ha, ha." Her sister blew a curl of damp brown hair off her shiny forehead. She was wearing a red maternity pantsuit. "Don't bother telling me I look good—I look like a fucking side of beef."

"Can't the baby hear you?" Stephanie feigned shock.

Sam snorted. "Two guesses who bought this outfit for me."

"Better you than me. Why on earth did she pick that peach dress?"

"It was on sale, of course." They both laughed. "Thank God you're finally here. If I had to listen to Mom bitching anymore I was going to keel over."

"Where's the liquor?"

"Gee, thanks, rub it in." Sam took a savage swallow of what looked like a glass of seltzer. "Dan is on his fourth beer and making jokes about drinking for two. Please go shoot him."

"Sure, just as soon as I've had a drink."

"Here, this way." Her sister pulled Stephanie along in the direction of the equally spacious family room where she could see her future father-in-law tending bar.

"What'll you have, sweetie?" Fred Greenberg said, coming around the bar to engulf her in a big hug. If he felt the gun under her jacket she didn't notice it in his expression.

"Cabernet," she said, pointing to one of several bottles of wine arrayed on the cherrywood bar. He poured her a glass with nimble fingers that spoke of his favorite retirement hobby—building model boats. A former electrical engineer, he seemed to have spent most of his married life content to let Lois take the limelight. His suits were expertly cut because Lois saw to his wardrobe. She also made sure that he got his short iron-gray hair and matching mustache groomed every three weeks.

"Alex is out back," he told her with his usual gentle smile. "Go on, I'll catch up with you later."

"Out back" was how the Greenbergs referred to the multitiered deck overlooking an in-ground pool. Alex sat at a wrought iron and glass-topped table along with Sam's husband, Dan, and some other friends.

He'd obviously made it home in time to change. His beautifully pressed blue shirt, freshly knotted deep yellow tie, and knife-pleat brown trousers were a sharp contrast to her rumpled appearance. Even his wing tips looked polished.

He was as devastatingly handsome as ever and she smiled at him just as he looked up and spotted her. She didn't get a smile in return.

Rising slowly, laughing in response to something a friend said, he made his way around the table and slipped an arm around her waist, his squeeze a little more than greeting.

"Nice of you to show up," he said in a low voice.

"I'm sorry I'm late."

"Sure." He looked anything but understanding. "What was it this time?"

"I had to go out to a crime scene."

"And that couldn't have waited until tomorrow?"

"I'm one of the lead investigators on a case, Alex."

"And you just got engaged to me. Is that important to you at all?"

Stephanie winced and tried to embrace him. "Of course it is."

He pulled back. "You couldn't even dress?"

"If I'd gone home, I would have been another thirty minutes at least."

He nodded tersely and turned his back on her, resuming his seat at the table. She pulled up a chair and sat down next to him.

"Let me see your ring!" one of the women, Garlin or something, said, snatching at her hand and cooing over the diamond as if it were a fuzzy creature.

"Are you excited?" another woman asked. "Have you picked out a dress yet?"

Lois appeared with a plate piled high with various elaborately prepared finger foods that she placed in front of Stephanie. "Here, honey, I wanted to make sure that you got some before it's all gone."

Stephanie smiled and smiled and all the while she was aware of Alex's disapproval next to her.

"Aren't you sweating in that jacket?" one of her friends asked. "I'm glad the weather cooperated and you got sun today, but it's actually humid out here now."

Stephanie shook her head and took another sip of wine.

"Really, Stephanie, why don't you take it off? Don't worry about your T-shirt." Jenny Newhouse tugged at a sleeve.

"I'd rather not," Stephanie said.

"She can't take off her jacket without shocking the old folks," Alex said with smirk.

"You're not wearing a bra?" This from Barry, one of Alex's friends whom she'd always despised. He gave her a lascivious grin.

One of the women groaned and Jenny slapped Barry. "You are so gross!"

"It's nothing like that, is it honey?" Alex said to Stephanie, a fake smile plastered on his face. His eyes were hard. "Why can't you take off your jacket? These are our friends, you can tell them."

Stephanie stared back at him, trying to convey a four-letter word with her eyes. "Better yet," she said, "let me show you."

She stood up and slowly slipped off her jacket, lifting her arms and pivoting slowly so everyone could see her shoulder holster and gun. "I'm packing, people. So don't anybody piss me off."

Leaving her jacket on the chair, she stalked away.

"What on earth are you doing?" Debbie London caught up with her daughter as Stephanie stalked across the living room. "Take that thing off!"

"I can't, Mom, I've got nowhere safe to put it."

"Well, then, put your jacket back on."

"Why? People know I'm a cop."

"Well, you don't have to advertise it."

The words were like a slap, but she'd heard them before. "I'm sorry that I didn't pick some other profession, Mom, but I'm not going to hide who I am."

"Oh please. Nobody's asking you to hide anything. Just have a little sensitivity. This is an engagement party, not some Fraternal Order of Police gathering at the bowling alley."

"Mom, you're a snob."

"Fine, I'm a snob. Now please put your jacket on."

Stephanie was suddenly aware of the stares she was attracting. She headed back outside and plucked the jacket

off the chair, deliberately ignoring Alex, who seemed engaged in the same game. Great. We'll see who wins, buddy.
Match set.

She ducked through another set of French doors and back
to the bar.

"Bad day?" Fred said with sympathy as she took a seat.

"Long."

"You're investigating that death up at the school, right?"

Of all her relatives, now and soon-to-be, Fred was the
only one besides her Uncle Mike, may he rest in peace, who
seemed to genuinely enjoy discussing her line of work.

She told him a little about it, avoiding anything specific.
He listened, asked questions. Shook his head with sympathy
at the thought of the poor mother and how the school was
going to manage once the media really got hold of the story.

She could feel the tension dissipate, her shoulders moving down from her ears, her stomach uncurling. The weight
of her holster became a comfort again, not some scarlet letter. This unwinding was what she did with Alex when he
wasn't too busy resenting her work or expressing surprise
that she should have chosen it.

It was ironic, really, because she'd met Alex exactly one
month after graduating from the academy. He'd thought it
was pretty funny then and loved to tell people that he was
dating a cop.

All police officers were used to doughnut jokes and other
slurs. They were also used to being unappreciated and underpaid. Still, sometimes it wore you down. Sometimes it
wore relationships down.

Oz's marriage survived because he'd gone to AA and
Wackjob was on marriage number two. Frangione was divorced, but that probably had more to do with the guy's antisocial personality than with being a police officer. As Mabel
Gery, the sweet, grandmotherly looking desk sergeant, had
told her more than once, "You can have the job or the man,
honey, but most of the time you can't have both."

She'd met Alex during happy hour at Doc Holliday's Bar, which was owned and operated by a fifty-some-year-old man named Buddy who was neither a doctor nor a Holliday. Buddy was born Goldstein, but he'd changed it to Gold because he thought that went better with his interest in all things Western. He'd opened the business during an urban cowboy craze and behind the bar kept a framed photo of himself wearing a ten-gallon and sitting astride a mean-looking horse on a dude ranch in Wyoming.

Doc Holliday's was where most of the cops went because Buddy was partial to the police after they'd caught the guy who smashed his front window and ran off with $500 from the cash register back in 1983. He still told the story to anyone who'd listen and because he offered them all discount drinks, every cop did listen, politely, at least once.

Stephanie had been celebrating with three other women who'd been through the academy with her, the four of them laughing and talking at a table in the corner. She'd spotted Alex across the room, dressed in jeans and a snug-fitting T-shirt, workman's boots on his feet.

She'd pegged him for a construction worker, or a member of a landscape crew, and he'd pegged her for a secretary or a teacher out with the girls from work.

She'd been wearing a blue sundress with little spaghetti straps because it was a hot May, the temperature already climbing to the mid-80s and the humidity making the hair lie heavy on the back of her neck.

He noticed the bruise on her right shoulder and asked how she'd gotten that and she guessed that he was thinking possessive, abusive boyfriend the way his eyes darted anxiously around the bar, and she caught the eyes of the other women and they all burst out laughing.

"It's from shooting an assault rifle," she said. When she'd explained that they were all police officers he'd been genuinely shocked and then delighted. He and his three buddies, another landscape architect and two lawyers, spent a couple of hours teasing the girls and making bad jokes about arresting them.

She and Alex went from dates at the bar to dates alone at a nice restaurant, to moving in together in her cramped apartment, to buying the town house.

Her mother had been leery of the relationship from the beginning. "You're doing it backward," she said. "You're playing house together without making a commitment."

Alex's mother had similar reservations, which only seemed to increase when she learned about Stephanie's job.

"It's not that there's anything wrong with being a cop," Lois had said to her son one Sunday when she'd had them over for brunch. "But what kind of life is that? Crazy hours, crazy people. It's dangerous work."

Stephanie had dressed nicely for that. She'd overheard the remark on her way back from searching for a bathroom in that maze of a house. Lois's high-pitched voice carried through the window.

"It's not dangerous in Gashford," Alex had replied. "We don't have crime. Traffic stops, a little theft. Someone steals a slurpee from the 7-Eleven—that's not dangerous."

Only he was wrong. He'd found that out soon enough. Even in suburbia there was crime. It was just better hidden.

The first time she'd come home with a bruise from being slugged by a drunk stockbroker beating the shit out of his trophy wife he'd been shocked. Soon after he started talking about other lines of work, trying to gauge her interest in other professions.

"I read an article that said that lots of former police officers end up going to law school. Some of them even become judges."

Once he said, "If you don't think you have enough money to go back to school, I'd be happy to help pay for it."

She'd tried to explain it to him, how the desire had been in her for a long time. How the people who went into police work were either really interested in law and order or into helping people or just adrenaline junkies. Sometimes all three. She tried to tell him that she'd chosen this profession and worked hard to get where she was and wasn't about to retire before she'd even had a chance to try for the gold shield.

It was the major disagreement between them. Other couples fought over things like money or sex. Those things were good with them, so they had to have conflict somewhere, right?

When she'd made detective last year, Alex had been grudgingly supportive. He'd brought her lovely pink roses, but they were barely withered before he was complaining about the new responsibilities that came with her job.

Fred put a hand on top of hers, interrupting her musing. "Go talk to him," he said though she hadn't said a word to him about his son. "You talk and you can work it out."

He was quiet man, but he understood a lot. Stephanie smiled at him and went in search of the man she was going to marry. Why did just the mere thought of that word make her insides tighten like a cork being squeezed into a bottle?

Chapter Thirteen

After forty-five minutes had ticked slowly by on the large industrial clock above the nurse's station, Lauren's name was finally called.

Candace helped her into the examination room, but when the nurse discovered that she wasn't family she was asked to leave.

A tall, stoop-shouldered resident with bags under his eyes and a bad haircut asked about her accident and prodded her ankle for several minutes, seemingly oblivious to Lauren's discomfort.

"It's probably a strain, but you never know," he said cheerfully. The small nameplate pinned to his lab coat said Dr. Buttons and she felt absurdly like laughing. "We'll get it x-rayed." He briefly examined the rest of her scrapes, checking her body with long white fingers and an air of professional detachment. He looked into both eyes with a penlight and felt her skull and neck and then he paused and she knew what he was staring at before she felt his fingers running a second time over the two-inch jagged scar near her collarbone.

"Interesting," he said. "Is this from a burn?"

"Yes." She felt her throat tighten and drew back from his touch.

He moved his fingers away but continued to stare. She felt burned by his eyes. "What caused it?"

"An ember."

"Goodness. Painful." He said it the same way one would say good morning. "You didn't consider skin grafting?"

"No." There hadn't been that opportunity. It wasn't a priority, there had been other injuries. There were many different ways to answer that question, but she didn't elaborate.

"I'm interested in plastic surgery," Dr. Buttons said, pulling his gaze away to look at her face. "I'm sure you could have it minimized if you wanted."

She smiled a little at his word choice. Nothing would minimize it. "How do I get an X-ray for my ankle?"

Another twenty minutes passed while she sat in a wheelchair in the hallway and then an orderly whisked her down to radiology. Three pictures later and they whisked her back. Fifteen minutes of staring up at the drop ceiling of the examination room while listening to the faint sound of Muzak coming from the front desk.

"Well, Ms. Kavanaugh, let's see what we have," Dr. Buttons said as he slouched back into the room with some large X-rays under his arm. He turned on the light board on one wall and slipped them in place. There were the bones of her lower right leg, but she couldn't see much because he blocked her way, tapping at the X-ray and then his upper lip with a pen, all the while make strange little sucking sounds.

"Good news!" he declared at last. "You have a severe sprain but no break. You'll need a soft cast and we'll get you some crutches. You'll have to stay off it for a week or two, but otherwise you should be fine."

"Crutches?" She couldn't hide her dismay.

"Oh, you'll soon get used to them," he said with the sort of false cheeriness that seemed to be reserved for professionals about to deliver bad news.

Another forty minutes of getting a cast, some crutches, and a prescription for painkillers and then she and Candace were finally on their way back to St. Ursula's.

Candace dropped her off outside the main building and Lauren managed the walk at a halting pace, but without falling. She thought she might find the central doors closed and locked on a Saturday, but they opened at her push and she made her way slowly down the gloomy hallway toward the headmistress's office.

She was surprised to see Sister Rose's secretary behind her desk, packing up to leave for the day.

"I'm afraid Sister Rose is busy right now," Pamela Jones said with an apologetic shrug. She was wearing a pale pink sweater and a pencil-line gray skirt that hit just below the knee and the same string of pearls around her neck. She fiddled with them nervously. "Is there something I can help you with?"

"When will she be free?"

"I'll have to check her calendar for next week," the secretary said with reluctance, sitting slowly back down at her desk.

"I need to see her today," Lauren said. "It's urgent."

"I'm afraid I can't interrupt her—" the secretary began only to be interrupted by Sister Rose in person, who suddenly emerged from the inner office.

"Never mind, Pamela," she said in her usual gentle voice, though her eyes widened at the sight of Lauren's cast and crutches. She didn't say anything, though, simply ushering Lauren into her office and closing the door behind them.

"How did you injure yourself?" she asked, offering an arm to steady Lauren as she sank into a seat in front of the desk.

Lauren explained going for a run and following the figure in the woods. Sister Rose listened, her eyebrows rising and going still higher when Lauren described finding wire strung between the trees.

The headmistress leaned forward in her chair, though her voice didn't change tone or timbre. "Where, exactly, did this accident happen?"

"Up in the woods."

"You weren't on one of main hiking trails, then?"

"No," Lauren said. "I mean, I started on one of them and then I went onto one of the smaller trails."

"Do you think that's wise?" Sister Rose commented. Before Lauren could reply the older woman pushed a button on the black box on her desk. "Have Mr. Macklin bring the golf cart around to the front of the school."

She stood up. "Let's see if we can find that spot."

Waiting on the circular drive was a beefy man in his fifties with sun-burnished skin and a salt-and-pepper buzz cut. He offered a broad, freckled hand to Lauren and said in a voice that reminded her of old wood and whiskey, "C. E. Macklin. Everyone calls me Mac."

"Lauren Kavanaugh. Everyone calls me Lauren."

He blinked and then gave her a quick sideways grin before nodding at her foot. "You best ride up front with that."

Sister Rose accepted the backseat in the small cart without comment, while Lauren sat on the front seat with her crutches at her side, gripping the seat so she wouldn't slide into Mac.

He drove where directed without asking any questions, showing no particular interest in the destination, but he listened carefully and stopped when Lauren said to, pulling the cart off to the side of the path. He helped both women out and waited, arms crossed over his chest, to be told what to do next.

"This is the path I followed in," Lauren said. "I'm sure of that, but it's confusing once you're off the main path. The wire was on two trees back that way." She pointed in the general direction.

"Well, let's find it then," Sister Rose said. "You have wire cutters, Mr. Macklin?"

Apparently not *everyone* called him Mac. He nodded and unearthed them from a toolbox in the back of the cart. Navigating the woods on crutches was almost as difficult as it had been without them and the use of one leg.

Lauren made halting progress, stumbling several times. In contrast, Sister Rose walked briskly and nimbly, showing no evidence of her advanced age as she tramped along. She also showed no signs of impatience with Lauren's slow progress, simply waiting periodically for her to catch up. Mac brought up the rear, almost as if he believed that this was his place.

It was just as confusing as before. Lauren wasn't sure if she was following the same path she'd taken, relying on the memory of certain trees or places where the forest floor wasn't covered in pine needles or rotting leaves. Several times she was sure she'd found the spot, only to be disappointed when they got closer.

At last, though, they passed around a section of scrub that seemed familiar and ahead of her she spotted the identical trunks that she'd followed the figure through, only to be thrown.

"That's it," she said, pointing. "Those trees right there."

She picked up her pace, but Sister Rose reached the trees before Lauren, peering and then bending over and running her hands over the lower trunk of each tree.

When Lauren reached her she understood why. There was no wire.

"It was here," she said. "I'm sure of it." She recognized the base of the trees, where she'd clung after climbing out of the ravine, yet nothing was tied to either trunk and there was no sign that anything had ever been tied to them.

"Perhaps you're confused about the trees?" Sister Rose suggested mildly, but Lauren felt her face flush. She looked to her left. There was another stand of trees that looked similar.

She moved in that direction and this time Sister Rose followed. As soon as she got closer, Lauren knew it wasn't the spot. She'd been right the first time.

"No, this isn't it," she said. "I know it was this spot." She backtracked to the maples and passed cautiously between them, almost expecting to feel the wire against her leg, but of course there was nothing. She could see over the side of the hill, though, and it showed clearly where she'd fallen.

"Yes, this is it," she said excitedly, signaling Sister Rose to take a look. "You see where the leaves have been disturbed? That's where I tumbled down the hill. And look here," she pointed to a gouge in the dirt near their feet. "This is from climbing out."

Sister Rose nodded her head and looked back at the trunks and then at Lauren. "I believe that this is where you fell, Ms. Kavanaugh, but are you sure you weren't imagining the wire?"

"No!" Lauren was surprised. "No, of course not. I saw it with my own eyes. I touched it. It was here." She stepped back and touched the spot on the tree trunk where she'd seen it. "It was tied right here. Whoever put it there must have taken it down."

"But why would someone do that?" Sister Rose asked.

"So you wouldn't find it!"

"No, I mean why would they tie it between the trees to begin with? It just doesn't make sense."

"They knew I'd come through here. They didn't want me back at the fire pit. I found a fire pit the other day and I'm sure there were students here—"

Sister Rose held up her hand and Lauren tried to stop the words that seemed to be flowing, uncontrolled, from her mouth.

"Please, Ms. Kavanaugh, you aren't making any sense. You were here before and found a fire pit?"

"Yes, well, not here but somewhere close to here."

"Mr. Macklin," Sister Rose called, signaling the groundskeeper who was standing back waiting to be given his next orders. He stepped forward with the same bland expression on his face.

"Is there a fire pit in these woods?" Sister Rose demanded. He nodded slowly.

"Probably more than one," he said, "seeing as this was an estate back before it was a school. I think they used to have bonfires up here in the fall."

Sister Rose turned to Lauren. "These are just relics of the past," she said. "Nothing that anyone uses now."

Lauren thought of the cigarette butts and the photograph. "But I'm sure students had been using it."

"Why? Did you see any students?" Sister Rose's voice was sharp.

"Yes, well, no, not exactly, I thought I caught a glimpse of some, but I'm not sure"

"And this other person you saw, this figure in black. You couldn't tell whether this person was a girl, right? You said it might have been male?"

Lauren hesitated, seeing where this was going, but she could do nothing but nod.

The headmistress sighed. "I'm sorry, Ms. Kavanaugh, but I think your mind's been playing tricks on you. You had an accident and you probably weren't thinking straight afterward."

"There was a wire here," Lauren insisted. "I touched it with my own hand."

"Even if that were true," Sister Rose said, "and I'm not saying it isn't, there's no wire here now."

"They must have taken it down." Even as she said it, Lauren realized just how ridiculous it sounded. "Look, let's find the fire pit. There were girls up here smoking—I found cigarette butts."

Sister Rose looked at her intently for a moment without saying anything and then she sighed. "All right, Ms. Kavanaugh."

It took another eight minutes of tramping back and forth several twisting, narrow paths before they came upon the clearing. The fire pit looked exactly as she'd remembered it and Lauren lurched toward it excitedly, anxious to find the cigarette butts. Only there weren't any.

"You said you found them in the pit?" Mac reached the circle of large fieldstones before she did, stepping over the side and into the pit, squatting down to sift through the ashes. "I don't see nothing here."

Sister Rose stayed on the outside and steadied Lauren as she stepped in next to Mac. "They were right here," she said, pointing to the small pile of charred, desiccated wood. "One of them was still lit—that's how I spotted them."

Mac carefully sifted through the pile with his broad, freckled hands, the burned wood crumbling in his fingers. Ashes and leaves. She could smell the wood mold underneath it all. "Nothing in here but old firewood," he said, his eyes sliding her way for a moment before looking up to Sister Rose.

Above them the headmistress clicked her tongue. "Okay, then, Mr. Macklin. Thank you."

It wasn't until they were back in the golf cart that Lauren remembered the photo.

They didn't believe Miss Kavanaugh's story. Of course they didn't, she hadn't really thought they would, but it was still satisfying to see it in the headmistress's expression.

She adjusted the lens of her telescope and zeroed in on the handyman. He was turning the cart in the direction of campus, which was a good sign. Clearly, he wasn't arguing that they should pursue this hunt. Only Miss Kavanaugh looked angry. She swung the scope back to see the dark expression on the teacher's face as she labored to get into the cart.

"Let me look," one of the others begged for the third time. She ignored her, focused on her own internal thrum of excitement.

They were stationed at least two hundred yards away from the golf cart, hidden in the woods on the other side of the path, camouflaged by dark clothing and the sure knowledge that what Miss Kavanaugh wanted to find was not to be found here.

The telescope had been a birthday gift from her father, who assumed she wanted it to study the stars.

"Must be beautiful up on that hill at night," he said when she thanked him for it.

She'd nodded, thinking of the play of moonlight on Morgan's dripping skin. "Yes," she said. "Beautiful."

They'd also given her a lovely knife, a single-blade switch, ostensibly for camping. She could feel the cold steel through her jeans pocket, the shape imprinting itself on her thigh.

Her parents seemed to accept the explanations she offered for the tools she wanted. Or maybe they just didn't think too hard about what she did. It had been easy enough to explain the small skeletons she kept in her room as the gifts of a friend who was also interested in science. They didn't need to know that she used the guesthouse kitchen to boil the bodies of the small mice and moles she killed so she could save their clean, white bones.

One of the benefits of coming from a family with wealth was the privacy it afforded. She wouldn't have been able to conduct any experiments if they'd lived in some horrible little tract home or subdivision, but in the five-bedroom, six-bath home on two private acres that her family called home, there was plenty of space to explore.

There had been a few disruptions, such as the time the housekeeper told her parents that she'd seen her take the steak from the fridge. She'd denied this, of course, and in any case there had been no way to prove that the steak in question was the beef that had been injected with rat poison and fed to their closest neighbors' annoying little schnauzer.

Her parents had chosen to believe her tearful denial, believed her and not the housekeeper. In any case, the death of the dog had been too sudden to provide much satisfaction. It twitched and moaned for a few minutes, foaming at the mouth, but it died very quickly after that and because he was too big for her pot, she had to load him into her backpack and spirit his corpse back onto the neighbors' property without seeing his bones.

She would like to see Miss Kavanaugh's bones. They looked so thin. So easy to snap. Poor little injured teacher, all alone in her suspicions. She almost felt sorry for her.

She adjusted the scope again so only Miss Kavanaugh's eyes were visible. Were those angry tears glistening? It just kept getting better and better. She liked watching eyes, they really did mirror the soul of some people. Miss Kavanaugh's emotions were delightfully transparent.

Her own contented purr must have been overheard because the tugging at her sweatshirt sleeve started again.

"Let me look, I want to see."

This time she handed the telescope over. Her companion peered through it eagerly, only to declare, "They're gone!"

"Are they?" she said, taking the telescope gently back. She collapsed it and tucked it inside the front pocket of her hoodie.

"But I didn't get to see anything," her companion protested. "What did I miss?"

"Very little," she said. "And yet, more than enough."

She hummed a little song as they moved quietly through the woods toward home.

Chapter Fourteen

It was dusk when they dropped Lauren off in front of Augustine House. The hallway was empty and the building quiet except for the faint thump of rock music coming from some room down the hall. She fumbled with the key to her apartment, balancing precariously on the crutches, hands trembling with fatigue.

Her ankle throbbed and she realized that she'd left the pain medication from the hospital in Candace's car. Ignoring the pain, she moved as quickly as she could down the hall to the bedroom where she'd left the photo propped on the nightstand.

It was gone. There was nothing on the nightstand but a lamp and her alarm clock. Lauren cried out, a small sound of shock. It had been right there!

The crutches clattered to the floor and she sat down heavily on the bed. It had been on the nightstand. She'd propped it against her clock the night before and it had been there this morning. She could remember seeing it, touching it.

She slid down to the floor and scrambled along its wood surface searching for the photo. Maybe it had slipped off and come to rest under the nightstand or the bed. She ran her hands under both, peered into the dimness. Nothing but small clumps of dust. Frantic, she searched behind the night-stand and dragged herself to a kneeling position to jerk open its single drawer, trying to believe it had fallen inside when she opened it that morning.

Except she hadn't opened the drawer this morning or at all. The only thing in it was a small New Testament, as if this were a hotel room, the scripture in tiny black type on cheap paper.

The sickening realization that the photo was gone was followed immediately by fear. Someone had been in the apartment. That was the only explanation. The photo didn't vanish, it couldn't walk away.

She reached for the crutches and lurched back out to the front door. The lock seemed to be intact. There was no sign it had been forced. Leaving the crutches in the kitchen, she hobbled around the small apartment checking the few win-dows. All were shut, all locked. She even checked the small one over the kitchen sink, absurd as it was to think of anyone crawling through that small space.

How then? How had someone gotten in here? She could feel the presence of another person, paranoia creeping along her spine like a bug. A dishtowel lay on the kitchen floor—had she dropped it? The books on her desk looked like they'd moved, but maybe she'd shifted them.

She suddenly remembered what was in the desk, and limped over to it, pulling open the bottom right drawer with trembling hands. There in the back, behind a ream of paper, was the neatly piled stack of hand-addressed white en-velopes. The neat printing was always the same; only the ad-dresses changed. They looked untouched.

A sharp rap on the door startled her. She slammed the drawer shut and called loudly, "Who's there?"

"It's Candace. You don't have to yell, I'm not deaf."

Lauren hobbled to the door and swung it open. Candace stood there grinning, dressed in jeans and a jacket zipped to her neck, holding up a large paper bag with a grease stain in one hand and Lauren's medication in the other.

"Special delivery," she said. "I thought you might not feel up to the dining hall tonight so I ordered takeout. Hope you like Mediterranean."

She pushed past Lauren into the apartment and slapped the bottle of pills into her hand on the way. "Here, you should probably take one of those."

"You remember the photo, right?" Lauren limped after her, tossing the bottle of pills on the sofa.

"What photo?" Candace set the bag on the kitchen counter and unzipped her jacket. She pulled out a bottle of red wine. "Surprise! I just assumed you wouldn't have any and I do like a nice glass of wine with dinner."

"The photo I had when we crashed into each other on Friday—"

"You crashed into me, remember?" Candace pulled out several containers from the bag, peeking under the lids. "I didn't know what you liked or whether you're one of those vegan freaks, so I got a little of everything. You do have plates, right?"

"Yes, I crashed into you and I was carrying a photo, remember?"

Candace pulled a corkscrew out of her jacket pocket. "Voilà! I wasn't sure you had one, so I just brought my own." She expertly uncorked the wine. "C'mon, the food's going to get cold and I don't like eating cold lamb. Glasses? Plates?"

"Behind you," Lauren said automatically, nodding at the cupboards. "Left of the sink. I dropped the photo when we crashed, but then I found it."

"Yeah, I remember. So?" Candace glanced over her shoulder. "Aren't you getting sore standing there? You should elevate your leg."

She put the plates down and crossed the room to the where Lauren stood. "Why don't you have a seat?" she said, nodding toward the sofa. "I'll serve." She picked up the bottle of pills Lauren had tossed. "Hmm . . . maybe you should wait until after dinner for one of these."

Lauren grabbed her arm. "I'm not hungry," she said. "Will you stop and listen to me? I need to know—do you remember the photo?"

Candace threw up her hands. "I already told you—yes, I remember the photo. A Polaroid, right?"

"Yes, exactly." Lauren felt almost light-headed. Not that she'd really believed it, but confirmation that she wasn't crazy came as a relief.

"Okay, I've answered you," Candace said. "Now please sit down."

Suddenly aware she was shaking with the effort to keep weight off her bad leg, Lauren let go of Candace's arm and sank onto the sofa with a sigh. Candace gently lifted her legs and swung them up onto the couch before Lauren could say more than "oomph" in surprise. Then she propped a throw pillow under Lauren's bad leg.

"There, that should do you some good."

She turned back to the kitchen and began spooning food onto plates. It smelled good and Lauren's stomach suddenly rumbled.

Candace laughed again. "Yeah, I can tell just how not hungry you are," she said. "Silverware?"

"Drawer on the right of the sink." Lauren stared at the ceiling without seeing it, trying to figure out who could have taken the photo and how. "Does anyone else have keys to our apartments?"

"I suppose they've got copies at the main office. Why?"

"Who has access to them?"

"I don't know—I'm not even sure they do exist, but it makes sense. My guess is that Sister Rose would have access, and Mac."

Candace came over with a plate of food and a glass of wine and Lauren struggled to a sitting position, wincing when her injured foot bumped against the floor.

"What you need is a little table," Candace said, "but this will do." She pulled Lauren's desk chair over to the couch and sat the plate on it along with a rolled bundle of napkin and silverware. She handed the wine to Lauren before grabbing her own plate and glass and sitting down in the armchair across from her.

"Bon appetit," she said, raising her glass.

Lauren raised hers and took a tentative sip. It tasted dry and complex and felt warm in her stomach. She looked at the plate of food and couldn't really identify anything but rice. Still, it smelled good. She picked up her fork. "So you've never seen extra keys or know if Mac has a master set?"

Candace shook her head. "No to both. Why all the questions about photos and keys? I thought you were going to talk to Sister Rose about what happened in the woods."

"I did."

"And?" Candace ate fast, obviously enjoying it. When some sauce spilled down her wrist, she applied her tongue to it first, rather than a napkin.

"Apparently I imagined it." Lauren told her about the fruitless search for the wire. Candace listened quietly, eating with an appetite that Lauren envied.

When Lauren was finished talking she looked thoughtful for a moment before saying, "Look, don't get annoyed."

"Doesn't that always mean the person's going to be annoyed?" Lauren said lightly, feeling her shoulders tense because she knew what was coming.

"You said you'd been running for a while and you were tired and sweaty. It's possible you were dehydrated—"

"And imagined it?" Lauren finished for her. She took another swallow of wine. "I was thirsty—not hallucinatory. I didn't imagine it."

"You obviously tripped over something, but maybe it wasn't a wire. Maybe you thought you saw a wire and it was just a trick of the light."

"I felt it with my own hands." Lauren put down her glass

and held them up, palms out. "Just like I touched that photo. And you saw the photo, too, but now it's gone."

"Oh, that's why you were asking about keys." Candace put her empty plate down on the floor beside the chair and settled back in her seat with her wineglass. "So you think someone broke in here and took the photo? Why? What was it of?"

"Morgan Wycoff swimming in what looked like the pond."

"I don't see why someone would steal that."

"It was partially burned." Lauren described finding it in the fire pit and the cigarettes with it. "There were girls in the woods, they were burning a photo of this girl who died—doesn't that make you the least bit suspicious that whoever was doing that is in some way connected to what happened to Morgan Wycoff?"

Candace looked skeptical, but she said, "Where did you have the picture?"

"It was on my nightstand this morning and it was gone when I got back this afternoon. It didn't just walk away."

"Maybe it fell—"

Lauren sighed. "I checked everywhere. It didn't fall—it's gone. And I didn't imagine it. You said you remember seeing it."

"Do you want me to look?"

"You don't believe me?"

"That's not what I said. Isn't it a good idea to double-check?"

So Candace went back into the bedroom to do her own search, only to emerge less than six minutes later shaking her head.

Any feeling of satisfaction Lauren had about being proved right was immediately squelched by the reality that the photo was truly gone.

"You had Morgan as a student, right?" she asked Candace as the other woman got up to refill their wine.

Candace nodded. "She was a good student, if a little un-conventional."

"Did she get along with the other girls?"

"Not all of them. She made a point of telling people she believed in Wicca. Maybe she was trying to convert people, I'm not really sure, but this is a Catholic school."

She laughed and took a sip of wine. "It's not like she was subtle about it. Picture a class full of all these uniformed girls wearing cross necklaces and there's Morgan, wearing a big gold pentagram around her neck."

"Did the other girls tease her about it?"

"Yes, but I never heard about anything more than that. Actually, some of the teachers were more annoyed than the students. I know she was ordered not to wear it by at least one teacher and some others gave her demerits."

Lauren lay back against the sofa cushions, feeling the wine slowly relaxing her. "But you didn't?"

Candace shrugged. "I didn't see any harm in what she was expressing. It wasn't anything evil, just normal adolescent behavior. I think she just wanted to be different."

"But some people didn't accept that?"

"Exactly." The science teacher sighed and looked down into her wineglass before responding. "Look, I can't blame them either—if someone is very into the school traditions and school spirit they'd find Morgan's views threatening. Even insulting."

"Enough to hurt her?"

Candace shook her head. "It's a far cry from accusing her of being a witch to tying her up and leaving her to die."

"Maybe they didn't mean to kill her." Lauren's wineglass was almost empty. She had a pleasant buzz going, could feel it slowing down her speech a little.

The last time she'd had this much to drink was Valentine's Day in that pub in London. A place they'd never been before, a little upscale compared to their usual student haunts. What had Michael called it? A treat. *"I've got a treat for you to-*

night." His eyes holding some hidden joke like they always did. Laughing eyes—that's what Michael had. Eyes to get lost in.

He'd dressed with uncharacteristic finesse, eschewing the T-shirt, jeans, and trainers for a proper shirt and tie. Trousers so new they squeaked and a pair of dress shoes she didn't know he owned.

She'd worn a little black dress that she'd found in a second-hand shop and high heels borrowed from a friend that pinched her feet just a little, just if she stood too long.

She'd been happy, truly happy. Sappy happy, willing to believe in those maxims from positive thinkers—maybe things did happen for a reason and all the awful things that had happened in her life before had some greater purpose preparing her for this moment. She'd actually thought he was going to pop the question, he'd been so nervous, glancing over his shoulder enough times that she feared some embarrassing public declaration of love. And then the truth of that night arrived in a camera flash.

"You mean it was bullying?"

For a moment Lauren thought Candace was asking about Michael. No, not Michael. They were discussing Morgan. "Yes," she said slowly, rewinding back to the conversation. "Maybe someone tied her to the tree, but thought she'd be found."

"Maybe," Candace said. She was slouched in her seat, her legs crossed comfortably.

It occurred to Lauren that Candace was probably gay and she giggled a little, wondering if this was supposed to be some kind of seduction. If it was, she wasn't biting.

"I dated a man in England," she said out loud.

"Did you?" Candace didn't sound heartbroken. She glanced around the blank walls. "Do you have his photo or did that get taken, too?"

They both laughed at that and when Candace sat up with the bottle Lauren held out her glass for a refill.

"What was his name?"

"Michael."

"Nice, if a little standard. Are you still dating?"

"No, most definitely not."

"Why?"

Lauren considered how to answer. "He was a treat," she said at last and giggled.

Candace smiled. "I don't understand."

"He didn't, either," Lauren said and they both burst out laughing.

Candace shook the last drops of the bottle into their glasses. "Whatever happened, that's the end of it."

"The wine?" Lauren said.

Candace was taking a sip and she snorted, wine rolling down her chin. She wiped it off with the back of her hand. "No, you idiot. The end of trouble. Whatever happened with Morgan, it's over."

Chapter Fifteen

The hallways are loud at night even if they tiptoe, even if they wear expensive athletic shoes with whisper soles, even if they glide across the quadrangle as quiet as ghosts.

They don't talk until they're safely in the woods, among the trees, one with the other creatures of the night, the rest of their world asleep.

The moon is a sliver short of full. When they're past the security lights, once they've adjusted to the sudden blackness, they can see each other's hooded faces in the moon's strange glow.

When they reach the fire pit there's a short discussion about who brought the lighter. It's a few minutes before the flames really catch and even then they have to be careful. The pit is deep enough that they can have a fire if it doesn't get too large. They keep it small and brief.

When flames lick the wood they join hands around the circle, cold palm in cold palm, someone's ring digging into the skin, someone's watch catching on another's sweatshirt. They are quiet for a moment, breathing in the wood smoke, reflecting on the evening ahead. Then she speaks. She's always the one to offer the prayer. No one else has volunteered, nor does she ask.

It is the first time they've met since it happened and things have changed. There is a weird mixture of exultation and anger, fear and excitement.

"I can't believe she died."

"It's her own fault for going swimming in that weather."

"You said they'd find her."

This last directed at their leader. She is, as always, calm and unconcerned. Her smile is enigmatic. "They did find her—just a little late."

She is the one who unites them. Without her they are just talk, one of them prone to giggling, another worried about getting mud on her new shoes. Individually they wouldn't do this; it's together that they are strong. Still, it's one thing to talk, it's another to do.

They aren't sure now, they need to blame the girl for her own death, they need to find a way to justify it.

"Morgan was a blight on our school," the leader says, getting to the heart of things quickly, daring to say the name out loud. One of them giggles, the other sucks nervously on a cigarette. This time they'll take the butts out with them.

"What if they find something?" the cautious one asks. "That teacher's been up here twice."

The excitable one giggles. "We took care of that."

Their leader smiles. She calmly lights her own cigarette before commenting. "She shouldn't have been snooping."

"She took the photo. What if she showed it to the police?"

"Stop." The leader's voice is hard, commanding. "The photo isn't a problem. I got it back. You need to be strong, we need to be strong."

She tells them they're chosen. Of those to whom much is given, much is expected. And the hardest part is that no one else must know. She tells them that every time they meet. No one must know. No one must know about them, about what they do. Other people aren't as strong and what the strong must do isn't always appreciated by the weak.

"Morgan worshipped the dark side. That's what killed her. She was meant to die."

If she had heeded the warnings they'd given her, if she'd turned away from sin. She didn't and she paid the price. Standing in front of the fire, they admit what they've all been thinking.

"It's better without her."

"Yeah, I mean, it's like people are glad she's gone."

The leader nods. It is better without her. Only they dare to say this, but it's as if the school is breathing a collective sigh of relief. The girl who questioned everything, who made them uncomfortable with their traditions, who insisted on fighting every single rule—this girl is gone.

She waits until the others have finished discussing this, until they have rationalized the death, become comfortable with it. When they really think about it, isn't the death a service to the community? They have done a good thing, performed a good deed. They are like anonymous saints.

"We have a problem," the leader says, taking a long draw on her cigarette, the ash glowing red as she waits for the others to respond.

"What problem?"

"Someone saw us that night."

"What do you mean? When?"

"When we were coming back from dealing with Morgan."

"But we were careful—I know we were!"

"Who saw us?"

The leader takes a photo out of the pocket of her sweatshirt. She passes it around.

"How did she see us?"

"She was out again with that boy."

"But I thought we warned her."

The leader gives a small smile. She stubs her cigarette out. "Apparently the warning didn't take."

"What are we going to do?"

"Do you think she'll tell?"

"Maybe we can tell her we were somewhere else."

"Or bribe her."

"And so what if she saw us? That doesn't mean we had anything to do with Morgan."

"We must take care of the problem," the leader says. "She is a blight, just like Morgan."

"No!" the cautious one says. "No way! Morgan was an accident, but this—"

"Would be a deliberate act," the leader finishes for her. "She has left us no choice."

"What if she's already told someone?" the one prone to giggles isn't laughing anymore.

"I won't do this." The cautious one steps back from the fire. "I won't be a part of this."

The leader takes her by the arm and jerks her back in the circle. "You already are a part of this."

Chapter Sixteen

The partial fingerprint investigators lifted from the rope proved too smudged to produce any match. Stephanie and Oz had done slightly better with the rope itself. It was Chinese made, a particular brand of nylon fiber that met minimum outdoors standards and was available at discount chains nationwide.

Only it wasn't carried by the Wal-Mart closest to Gashford and it became obvious pretty early in their trips to all the discount kings in the surrounding area that they weren't going to get far unless they wanted to view literally thousands of hours of surveillance tape from the sporting goods departments and only then if one blue-smocked employee or another had managed to remember to turn on the security cameras that day.

They collected the tapes anyway, had a couple of uniforms assigned to watch them. They were still watching them. So far nothing. The rope wasn't likely to yield them a name. For all they knew it had been moldering in someone's basement for more than a year. They had to go with what distinguished this case and that, Stephanie thought, was the necklace she'd found.

The tiny gold star had yet to yield any prints, but the lab rats weren't done with it and for now she had a photo to show around.

"I say we take this to school and see if anyone recognizes it," she said to Oz.

"The necklace doesn't prove anything," Oz said. "Someone could have lost that anytime."

"What about the pentagram?" She tapped the crime scene photos laid out on the table between them. "It was drawn upside down and we know that wasn't Wicca."

Oz was eating an Italian hoagie with obvious relish, apparently unperturbed by the photo of the rope digging into that milky and purple-tinged skin. He paused to take a swig of diet Coke. "Do you really think this was a well-thought-out religion?"

"Her friends say she took it seriously. Plus, there's nothing about being tied to a tree in anything I read."

"I think we've got to stick with the obvious—Beau and that Goth girl. You got these two kids who admit they'd been with her earlier in the day. I think they all thought this was some sort of game and they didn't mean to kill her."

"Beau was in a chat room, remember?"

"Computers can be tampered with."

"Yeah, and the computer *experts* who examined it would have told us if it was."

Oz shrugged, his beefy shoulders rolling up like small boulders. "Maybe they missed something."

"And maybe Beau told the truth and he has an airtight alibi for the time of Morgan's death."

"Yeah, well, let's talk to the girl again. Or find out if there's anyone else. Did we forget any names on the list?"

Stephanie found the list from Morgan Wycoff's mother and looked over the names. "We've got one we haven't checked out, but she's a former student, she's in college in the city and she hasn't returned our calls. It seems like a long shot."

"Yeah, well, a shot in the dark is still a shot."

Steph stood up and stretched until her back cracked. "A shot in the hand is worth two in the bush?"

"A shot in time saves nine." Oz settled back in his seat with a pleased look on his face and reached for a Snickers bar he claimed as health food.

"A shot a day keeps the doctor away."

"A shot by any other name would smell as sweet."

Stephanie was searching for another cliché when Wack-job came around the cubicle with a frown on his face and his arms crossed over his chest. She was about to apologize when he said, "Remember, two shots are better than one."

By the end of the day on Wednesday, Lauren's ankle was aching and she wanted nothing more than to swallow some painkillers, lie down, and sleep.

She'd hobbled to and from classes for three days. Three days complete with whispers and giggles and blank faces when she tried to confront the girls. Why had she thought she could teach? It seemed like a tremendous mistake now, any job had to be better than this, and she thought longingly of the waitressing job she'd had at a diner in Hoboken briefly when she first came back to the States. People had smiled at her there, talked in other than monosyllables, been genuinely glad to see her show up, albeit to deliver their hot turkey sandwiches and tuna melts.

She lurched along toward the dormitories, glad that at least she didn't have to face any more inquiries about how she'd gotten hurt. Part of her longed to tell the truth, to say to at least one person that someone had strung a wire between two trees so that she fell over a hillside, but then she'd remember the look on Sister Rose's face after the fruitless search in the woods and all she could say was that she'd tripped while running.

It wasn't so much that she no longer believed that a wire

had been strung between the trees, but that she couldn't disbelieve that her mind might have been playing a trick on her. What if Candace was right and she thought she'd seen the wire? What if her estimation of her own skills was too high and she'd been thrown not by a wire that she hadn't been able to find, but by a root or a fallen branch?

She was so deep in thought that she didn't notice that something was pinned to her door until she was almost in front of it. It was a cartoon drawing of a blond-haired woman falling headfirst over a hillside. Superimposed over the woman's face was a grinning skull.

Lauren gave a little cry of shock and a girl's voice behind her said, "Is something wrong, Ms. Kavanaugh?"

She turned and saw the head prefect, Elizabeth Lincoln, standing in the hall with an open textbook in her hand and a questioning look on her pretty face.

"Nothing," Lauren said quickly. She ripped the picture down before the girl could see it. "I'm fine, thank you, Elizabeth." She turned the key in the lock and pushed the door open, feeling her pulse beating in the heat radiating from her skin.

When she was safely alone, Lauren turned the paper over and examined it more closely. The picture had obviously been done on a computer and the image of the skull was some sort of clip art dropped in place on top of the anime face. There was no signature, no way to tell who had done it, but the raw anger she felt propelled Lauren back out the door and straight to the main office.

Sister Rose smoothed the drawing out on her desk and looked it over very carefully without speaking. Lauren was aware of the distant sound of running feet and an adult voice calling, "Slow down, girls!"

The headmistress made a faint clicking sound with her teeth, but otherwise she was perfectly still, her fingertips resting lightly on the edges of the paper.

"It's fairly common for students to give new teachers a

hard time," Sister Rose said after a few minutes. "Especially teachers who don't make the effort to get to know the girls." She paused and looked up at Lauren.

"I am getting to know them," Lauren said. "And I don't think that this"—she tapped the picture—"is a good example of a 'hard time.' This goes way beyond that."

"I'll concede that it's a distasteful prank," Sister Rose said and Lauren nodded. "But it is nothing more than a prank."

"Whoever posted this on my door is the same person who strung the wire between the trees."

Sister Rose sighed. "Ms. Kavanaugh, we didn't find any wire or evidence of wire in the woods."

"Then explain this drawing—how did whoever drew this know I fell over a hillside unless they were responsible?"

"You must have told somebody."

"I've told no one. Not one single person." Except Candace, she thought suddenly, but immediately pushed that idea out of her mind. Candace wouldn't have drawn this and she doubted she'd told anyone. "Someone tried to kill me and then they pasted their death wish on my door!"

Sister Rose winced. "I think you're overreacting because you had an accident."

"I'm reacting because I could have been killed on Sunday," Lauren said. "And it was no accident."

"The girls aren't allowed off the main paths in the woods without adult supervision," Sister Rose said. "The rules are very clear on that and the consequences very clearly spelled out. I seriously doubt that any St. Ursula's girl would risk that and certainly not to harm a teacher."

She must have seen the disbelief that Lauren made no effort to hide because she held up one soft hand as if to ward off a protest Lauren hadn't uttered.

"But we'll look into this—pranks like this mustn't be tolerated. I'll have Mr. Pierce investigate."

She stood up. Clearly Lauren was being dismissed.

"I don't think this was a prank," she said helplessly, struggling to her feet and thrusting the crutches back under her arms.

"But you have no evidence otherwise," Sister Rose said gently. "And without knowing who did this I don't think we can speak to their motivation. That's just not a Christian thing to do."

"I don't think it's particularly Christian to string a wire between two trees," Lauren said.

"Well, yes, that certainly wouldn't be." Sister Rose said in her gentle voice, but Lauren didn't miss her meaning. The headmistress didn't believe her.

They walked out of the office together, Lauren struggling to accept that this was really all that the headmistress had to say on the subject. Almost all. As she turned off the lights in the office, Sister Rose paused.

"I understand that you are adapting to a new environment," the nun said, "but I feel that I must remind you that it is in your own best interest to make every effort to get along with the girls."

"I believe I've been trying to do just that," Lauren said, unable to hide the bitterness she felt.

Sister Rose nodded. "Remember, your position at St. Ursula's is contingent upon a glowing midterm review."

And with that she bid Lauren good night in that same gentle voice and departed in the direction of the stairwell to the second floor.

Lauren looked after her, stunned into a silence that gave way to rage. She clumped back to her rooms, ignoring the looks she got from the swarm of girls crossing to the cafeteria, and when she was safely locked inside, she vented her anger by hurling her crutches across the room. One of them hit the potted jade plant on the bookcase and it fell with a crash to the floor.

"Great, just great," she muttered, hopping and hobbling into the kitchen to fetch a dustpan from under the sink.

She swept up the dirt and shards of terra-cotta, balancing on her good leg and trying not to lean any weight on her bad foot. Two slow trips back and forth to the trash bin under the sink and the floor was clean. She looked up along the shelves and saw that a smattering of soil had fallen along the edges of some books. She swept away what she could see and then took the books out one by one and wiped them down.

Lauren brushed off a book on Elizabethan poetry and then a volume of Shakespeare's sonnets. She carefully pulled out the next book, a large volume with a tooled leather cover and gilt edges. It was heavy and her hand slipped on the wide spine so the book pitched toward the floor, its cover opening. Something white slipped from between its pages and fluttered onto the floor.

Lauren pulled the book up with her other hand and brushed it free of soil and dust. *New American Catholic Bible* was written in gold script on its cover. She returned it to the shelf and then sank back down to the floor to sweep up the crumbs and paper. She plucked the folded sheets of paper from the dustpan and opened them. They were pages torn from a notebook, with jagged edges and line upon line of elegant, if old-fashioned, script.

Dumping the rest of the soil, Lauren returned the broom and dustpan to their storage spots and sank down in the armchair, propping her foot up with a sigh of relief. She smoothed out the folded sheets of paper and started to read. The month and day were listed at the top of every sheet, but no year.

October 12—Candles left burning in the chapel and Sister Rose has blamed me for not checking. She thinks it's sweet that the girls want to pray after hours. I'm from the old school if I complain. What can I do?

December 3—They are at it again. I woke to the sound of voices, but of course no one was there when I opened the door. I checked all the rooms, but the girls complained to Sister Rose that I'd woken them and now she's expressing concern about my health. What can I do?

January 10—I found mud tracked in on the soles of their shoes. They've been in the woods again. I scraped some up and put it in a bottle to have proof, but then thought, what does this really prove? I know who they are now, each and every one, but what does it matter? They are so innocent looking, these demons. No one else realizes what they're doing. I'm all alone in this knowledge.

January 23—A girl has been hurt. She tripped on the landing and fell down a flight of stairs or at least that's what they say happened. I know better. She was pushed by one of them, maybe by all of them. They don't like her for some reason, why I couldn't say. She was outspoken before, one of those girls who needs to fight the church on everything. I sympathize, but I've grown too old for those battles. Still, she was like that and she isn't anymore. She's gone. They drove her away.

February 2—I can feel them gearing up for something, whatever it is. L. laughed when I tried to talk to her. She is the worst of them, I think. There is nothing she won't do. The others, I'm not sure. They follow her, with their whispers and laughter and that cruelty masquerading as kindness.

That was the end of the first two pages. Lauren looked at the third page.

February 14—I'm having trouble thinking clearly and I'm beginning to wonder if Sister Rose isn't right and it's stress. It's Valentine's Day and instead of the card I was expecting from my niece I got a nasty little note telling me to mind my own business. I planned to show the note to that fool Pierce, but it was gone. My head aches. I'll write more later.

February 28—*They've locked me in again. I know they did it because I set my alarm and when it went off I got up and checked the door and it wouldn't open. It was open again this morning and the carpet outside was soaked from snow.*

March 1—*The headaches are getting worse and I couldn't teach today. I have an appointment next week, so we'll see. I almost hope they do find something because I dread hearing that it's all in my head. Sister Rose thinks that. She says I'm stressing myself with these thoughts about the girls. It isn't my thinking that's causing the stress, I've told her. Is everyone blind?*

March 15—*Beware the Ides of March. This time I was ready for them. I waited by the door when the lights went out and when I heard the footsteps, I opened the door really fast. There they all were, L., B., and T. The latter had the decency to look embarrassed, but L. just laughed. She insisted they were going to the chapel to pray and stuck to that story this morning when I had them called before the headmistress. Nothing happened, of course, beyond their being restricted for one week.*

April 5—*I know they are doing something to me, but I don't know how. Yesterday I couldn't recall how to spell my own name. I have the shakes now. It's so cold that I've taken to turning up the heat on the little stove for extra warmth.*

April 10—*I can't eat much anymore, food doesn't taste the same, though I force myself to have green things. No wine anymore, that's been gone for months, and meat just doesn't taste of anything so what's the point. I've lost weight and one of them dared to comment on it. 'You're looking thin, Sister,' with a little smirk. Of course no one else heard her.*

April 20—*Today I didn't know who I was. I woke up disoriented and it lasted most of the morning. I'm feeling worse again. I'm being poisoned, why does no one else see this?*

May 3—Toxicology scans came back negative. I'm not being poisoned, but that can't be. Someone is tampering with my records. I'm sure it's L.

May 10—Where are the girls? I know they're here somewhere, but I've misplaced them. I try to keep them with me because I don't want things to be worse.

May 15—I can't think straight anymore. No one would tell me what day it was, except L. She told me and I thought how nice she is, but then I remembered that she isn't. How could I have forgotten? I'm becoming addled.

May 23—I'm to have a brain scan again, but they won't find anything, just like last time. If I knew how to use the computer, I could find out what is wrong, I suppose, but I don't and I can't trust anyone. Not anymore.

That was the end of it. Lauren turned the pages over and then read them through a second time. She assumed they'd been written by Sister Agnes. It fit what she'd heard.

Lauren flipped through the pages of the Bible, then held the large book open by the covers and shook, but there was nothing else hidden in its pages. She scanned the bookshelves, searching for a journal, but couldn't find one. She even checked several books near the Bible without success and soon the throbbing in her ankle forced her to stop.

Why had Sister Agnes torn out these notes and put them in the Bible? What had Sister Agnes seen? Who were the girls she was referring to and what had they done? Were these the ones she thought she'd seen in the woods? And what had happened to her that she'd suddenly left little more than two months after the last entry was written?

Amanda is holding a key in her hand, a small copper key, and she is wearing a school uniform. She holds the key out to Lauren, but there are flames licking around her hands, swallowing her feet, singeing her legs. Lauren can't touch her, it's too hot. She's afraid.

Michael's voice says, "Where's the key?"

Lauren points to Amanda but then the scene changes and she's alone in a room with a scratched metal table and a large clock on the wall. It is ticking the time slowly and loudly, but the hands move backward. Her throat hurts, she's thirsty but no one brings her water. Someone is sitting in the corner of the room, but she won't look at them, she won't.

Then she hears a noise and goes outside. The streets are gray and filled with a crowd of people moving slowly toward a tall church she can just see in the distance. Someone is carrying a cross at the front of the procession; it looks black against the sky, bobbing along in the air. She follows it. People are weeping on either side of her, but when she asks why no one will answer.

The crowd pours in through the doors of the church, but when Lauren finally enters the pews are empty. Then she sees Amanda, a lone figure dressed for First Communion, with a short white dress and a veil, her hands pressed palm to palm in prayer.

"Amanda!" Lauren calls, but the girl walks up the aisle and vanishes behind the altar. Her steps are slow and measured, but even so Lauren can't catch up with her.

Lauren turns back and where Amanda first stood is a white coffin piled high with flowers.

"Do you want to see?" Michael asks. He is standing beside the coffin, grinning at her. "Let's open it and see what's inside."

She shakes her head no, but he is reaching for the lid, the flowers spilling at her feet. The lid is rising, rising—

Lauren woke up in a cold sweat with her injured ankle burning with pain. She untangled the sheets and hobbled to the bathroom to swallow a couple of pain pills.

She resisted going back to the bed right after, afraid of

falling back into the same dream. Instead she limped out to the living room and sat down with the journal notes.

Maybe it was perusing them that made her sensitive to strange noises, but her head shot up when she heard the click. Reaching for her crutches, she swung as fast as she could over to the door. Heart pounding, she cracked it open and peered out. Again, the hallway was empty.

Shaking her head at her own paranoia, Lauren started to shut the door when another noise stopped her short. Something rustling. Far down the hall. It sounded like it came from the common room.

Lauren looked back out the door and down the long hallway. She couldn't see anything, but she heard another noise, a single step.

Fear made her stomach contract at the same time that it loosened the muscles in her arms and legs. She gripped the crutches more tightly to keep from falling and tried to think straight.

She had to know what was going on. If there were students sneaking around at night that was her responsibility and even if wasn't so late at night she couldn't very easily call the headmistress for help. Not after everything else that had happened. If Sister Rose didn't think she was crazy, she certainly would if Lauren woke her up because she was afraid to investigate strange noises she heard in the hall.

Being left with no other option made it surprisingly easy to venture out in the hall. Lauren tried to swing her crutches quietly, wanting the element of surprise on her side if she could possibly manage it.

As she drew closer to the common room she could hear another faint and somehow familiar sound, but she didn't know what it was. Not until she sprang around the corner and startled the small girl tucked in an armchair reading a book. She and Lauren both cried out.

"It's okay," Lauren said immediately, wondering if the

fright on the girl's face mirrored her own. "You're Nicole, right?"

The girl nodded sinking back down in the chair. "Yes," she said. She had the slightest hint of an accent.

"I didn't mean to scare you, Nicole, but I'm afraid you scared me."

"I'm sorry," the girl whispered.

"What are you doing here?"

"Reading," the girl said, but Lauren sensed that wasn't the whole story.

"What's wrong? Couldn't you sleep?"

The girl stared at her for a moment and then shook her head. "I don't sleep well," she confessed.

"Me, either." Lauren tried to remember what she knew about the girl. She had some vague recollection of a dead sibling, but she wasn't sure. Was it grief that kept the girl awake?

"I had a bad dream," Nicole said as if she could hear her thoughts. "I'm sorry I disturbed you. I'll go back to bed now."

She got up from the armchair, but Lauren stopped her. "Wait. Why don't you tell me about your dream and we can have some warm milk to help us get to sleep."

The girl made a face. "I hate warm milk."

"Me, too," Lauren confessed. She smiled. "All right, we'll skip the milk and just talk."

The girl sat back down in her chair but she looked uncomfortable. Lauren nudged her with a gesture. "Go on, you might feel better if you talk about it."

"I don't think so," the girl said. Her voice wavered just the littlest bit and that decided it for Lauren, who'd wondered whether pushing like this was a mistake.

She sat down in the chair across from Nicole and leaned forward. "Is it something personal? Something about family?"

The girl looked down at her lap. She wore pajamas that

looked too big on her. "It's always the same dream," she said. "We're on the corner and then Paul steps into the street. I try to tell him the truck is coming, but he doesn't hear me. I can't get to him before the truck hits him."

She looked up and Lauren saw tears tracking slowly down her face. She handed the girl a box of tissues. "Who's Paul?"

"He was my brother." Her voice broke on the last word and then she started to cry. "I'm sorry," she said, "this is so stupid."

"I don't think it's stupid," Lauren said. "Tell me about Paul."

Little by little the story poured out. Who Paul was, how he'd been killed. How the accident had changed everything. How she was at the school because of those changes. Once she started talking, the girl couldn't seem to stop and Lauren let her go on, realizing that she'd probably had everything bottled up for a long, long time. Maybe since the accident.

"If I hadn't called to Paul, if I hadn't distracted him, he would have seen the truck."

"But the driver still wouldn't have stopped in time, right?" Lauren said. "Didn't you say that the driver lost his license because he'd been speeding?"

The girl slowly nodded. "Paul wasn't watching because of me."

"Even if he had been watching, it sounds like nothing could have been done. The driver was going too fast, he didn't stop in time. It was just an accident, Nicole. You are not to blame."

When the clock in the common room softly chimed midnight, both teacher and student were startled.

"I didn't realize it was so late," Nicole said, standing up. "I have a class first thing in the morning."

"Me, too." Lauren stood up, struggling to reach her crutches. Nicole handed them to her.

"Thanks," Lauren said. She smiled at the girl. "Do you think you'll be able to sleep now?"

The girl nodded, giving her a lopsided smile. "Thanks," she said.

"No problem. Anytime you need to talk you know where to find me." Lauren gestured toward her room with one crutch. She walked Nicole to her room, where the girl gave her a shy little wave before slipping inside.

Later, once she was back under the covers of her own bed, Lauren thought about how odd it was that this was the first moment she'd felt like a real teacher and all she'd done was listen.

Chapter Seventeen

There was a faculty meeting on Thursday afternoon and Lauren was the last to leave the building afterward, hampered by her crutches and the messenger bag she'd slung over her shoulder.

The hallways were empty, deserted by students and teachers equally eager to get away for what promised to be a beautiful fall evening.

She passed through the hallways lined with portraits of graduating classes through the years. The girls wore white dresses, the length and cut of their gowns and of their hair the only things that appeared to change through the years. They carried white roses in their arms like brides and their happy, eager smiles stood in stark contrast to the dour expressions worn by the habited sisters who flanked either side of every graduating class.

Black robes touched the ground and a white wimple covered up all but the smallest circle around their faces. It was impossible to tell how old they were, Lauren realized, but their somber faces made them look years older than they probably were.

Her footsteps dragged down the hall and she thought she

heard a soft clicking noise, like the sound of wooden beads, behind her, but when she turned no one was there.

As she passed through one hall and into the next, Lauren felt the weight of the school's history pressing on her. Here were other photos, sepia-tinted pictures of winning basketball teams and the debate society from 1932. Trophies tarnishing in glass cases. Faded rosettes attesting to some championship or another. All that glory gone. All those students gone God knows where. Many of them were probably dead.

A faint click, click sounded again behind her. She turned fully this time, pausing to look back at the hallway receding into shadow.

"Hello?" she called, feeling foolish when her own voice echoed slightly. There was no one. It was silly. She hurried on as fast as she could toward the main exit and suddenly ran into Ryland Pierce.

"Well, this is a pleasant surprise!" He shifted his briefcase to his left hand and dug a set of keys with a leather BMW fob out of his overcoat pocket. "I was just leaving for the day, but Sister Rose said you wanted to talk to me, so no time like the present."

He led the way to his office and unlocked the door, holding it open with exaggerated courtesy. "Please, after you."

Lauren moved past him, pushing away the unsettling thought that he was checking out her ass, and sat down awkwardly in one of the leather armchairs in front of the glossy desk.

The counselor's office was overtly masculine. Leather. Wood. Nautical paintings on the wall. An autographed baseball and football prominently displayed on the built-in shelves behind the desk. It was as if he had purposely stamped it with everything masculine in order to offset all the feminine energy elsewhere in the building. It even smelled masculine—the smell of leather mixing with a woodsy, spicy scent that was his cologne.

He set his briefcase next to his desk, hung up his full-length black wool overcoat on a coatrack, and adjusted the jacket of his charcoal suit before making a great fuss about putting her leg up on a small leather hassock and moving her crutches to one side. Finally, he sat down behind his large mahogany desk.

"Let's see, let's see," he said in a cheerful voice, picking up a notepad from his otherwise immaculate desktop. "Hmm . . . you saw something in the woods and you've been having problems with the students." He looked up at Lauren. "That's what I hear from Sister Rose. What's your version of things?"

His smile was disarming. She could see why he made a good counselor. "I had an accident in the woods that wasn't an accident," she said and then she explained it as simply as she could, including finding the fire pit the day before.

Leaning his chiseled chin on his hand he gave her his full and undivided attention, making appropriate "hmm" sounds whenever she paused, his brow furrowed in concentration.

"Well, that does sound strange," he said. "But you said that Mac couldn't find this wire, is that right?"

"It had been taken down," Lauren spoke firmly.

He nodded. "Right. Okay. Well, Ms. Kavanaugh, all I can say is that St. Ursula's certainly doesn't support or condone girls doing things against school policy, much less harming teachers."

She hadn't expected him to say anything different. What could he say? "Why did Sister Agnes leave?" she asked. His surprise at the change of subjects was evident in the way his finely shaped eyebrows rose, but he didn't object.

"She retired," he said. "She'd been teaching for quite a few years." He shifted in his chair and flashed his trademark affable smile. "A new teacher always feels a bit vulnerable. You'll probably feel uneasy until you have that first year under your belt."

He was good at steering the conversation away from uncomfortable topics. It probably worked to dissuade parents from asking for too much financial aid or students from requesting a room change, but she wasn't going to be sidetracked.

"I understand that Sister Agnes had more than thirty years under her belt," she said.

"Yes," he spoke slowly as if considering where she was going with this. "Yes, she had a long and distinguished career with St. Ursula's."

"Was she ill?"

"Ill? Yes, yes, I think she was. She was an older woman and the strain—"

"Did she complain about problems with the students?"

This time a look of annoyance flashed across his handsome features before the bland mask slipped back into place. "I'm not at liberty to discuss another teacher's complaints with you, Ms. Kavanaugh."

"Was there anything to her complaints?"

"Excuse me?"

"Did you investigate her complaints? Were they valid?"

"Why are you so interested in Sister Agnes, Ms. Kavanaugh?"

"I'm staying in her rooms, I'm the teacher who replaced her."

"Yes, well, I'm afraid that whatever Sister Agnes complained about—if she complained—is confidential information and the fact that you're her replacement doesn't change that."

He straightened in his seat and selected a green enameled pen from a silver cup on his desk. "Now, I think we should focus on your complaints. Have you had other problems with the students?"

What could she say? That the girls were whispering behind her back and giggling in the classroom? She would come across as incompetent and if she mentioned the noises she heard at night, the suspicions so like those Sister Agnes recorded in her journal, she'd be labeled crazy.

She shook her head. "Just what happened in the woods."

"I wonder if finding Morgan Wycoff might have caused some undue stress?" His tone of patronizing concern made her skin crawl. "Perhaps you should drop by the infirmary and talk to Linda Whipple about being checked for stress."

She had no intention of getting a checkup, but dropping by the infirmary did give her an idea. "Yes," she said standing up and flashing her own version of the Pierce smile. "I think maybe I'll do that."

Nicole found the invitation slipped under her door. Afterward she would realize that the moment it arrived had nothing to do with chance and that they'd picked a time when Destiny would be at choir practice, but at that moment she just thought it was lucky that she'd been there to get it and not her roommate.

Heavy white card stock was the first thing Nicole noticed, with her name written in elegant black letters on the front and a red wax seal covering the back. The seal was the shape of an open eye. She slipped her nail under the flap, breaking the seal, and pulled out the single card inside.

It contained the following: "You've been selected for consideration to become a member of Oculus. Details to follow. Tell no one."

She had no idea what it meant. What was Oculus? She checked the envelope carefully, sure that she'd missed something that divulged the sender, but there was no return address, no signature, nothing that revealed the identity of the sender. The name Oculus sounded familiar. Hadn't she heard some girls whispering about it one morning in the bathroom? Something secretive, that was clear, but what was it?

In the end, she put the card back in the envelope and tucked it in a desk drawer.

Three days later she sat down in math class, opened her book, and found another envelope. It was exactly like the first, complete with red wax seal. She wanted to open it, but there were too many other girls around. She tucked it between some other pages and looked around the classroom. No one was watching her.

During class she opened the book to that page and stared down at the card. Did she want to join a club? She hadn't belonged to anything like that, ever. It wasn't so much that she wasn't a joiner, as that other girls had never asked her. Paul had done Scouting, but that hadn't interested her. There had been dance class and gymnastics and horseback riding, but nothing like this.

She'd enjoyed riding the most, but even that had been mainly solitary, and she hadn't been able to continue after Paul's death. Her mother was afraid of another accident, too nervous to sit by quietly while her only surviving child went riding. She didn't make Nicole quit, but her anxiety before each lesson was so palpable that eventually Nicole stopped going rather than deal with it.

She felt something akin to anxiety now, her stomach fluttering with excitement and dread. Did she want to join? What would be required of her? Not that the invitation had said anything about that, but that was the way clubs operated, wasn't it? Wasn't there always some kind of initiation?

During the rest of class she fantasized about being asked to perform some kind of test and impressing the other girls with how well she passed it.

As soon as class ended, Nicole ducked into one of the bathrooms and hid in a stall. Then she opened the envelope, surprised at how eager she felt as she sliced the seal in half.

"Midnight. One week and a day. Wear dark clothing. Be ready and someone will come for you. Tell no one."

For the rest of the day, Nicole watched other students, trying to catch someone watching her. What if it wasn't a club
at all, what if it was a joke? She desperately wanted someone
else's opinion and thought of discussing it with Destiny, but
both cards had been explicit. Tell no one.

Part of her wanted to go, wanted to perform well at whatever Herculean task was set for her, wanted to be accepted
by this group, whatever it was. Another part of her was
scared by the thought. Whoever had sent the invitation knew
her—of that she was sure—and the thought of being watched
concerned her.

Every private conversation, the whispers between friends,
became suspect. She was sure she saw people talking about
her, but then something would make it clear that this wasn't
the case and instead of chalking it all up to her imagination,
she'd immediately focus her attention on another cluster of
girls. By the end of the day, she was driving herself mad.

When Destiny was out of the room, Nicole took the second card and placed it with the first in the back of her desk.
One week and a day. She sighed. It seemed like such a long
time to wait.

Chapter Eighteen

Her jeans were too tight. Chelsea Connor pressed back on the bed and sucked in again, willing that extra little bit of stomach to flatten itself against her spine while she worked the zipper with both hands. It snicked reluctantly into place, straining at the seams, and she slowly exhaled before sitting up and slipping on the hot red patent-leather open-toed and cork-soled heels she'd bought last weekend.

"Can you even breathe?" her roommate asked, looking up from her chemistry text to peruse the other girl.

"I don't need to breathe. I just need a tight-fitting pair of jeans that won't make me look like I have a saggy ass." She stood up and pivoted. "So, what do you think?" She addressed this to the mirror where she patted the ass in question, admiring the view and picking imaginary lint from the sleeves of the black, clinging, long-sleeve silky shirt she was wearing.

"I hope this is worth being suspended."

"God, Brooke, you're such a downer!" Chelsea wheeled on her roommate. "Just say what I told you and everything will be fine."

She sashayed back over to the bed and gave the pillows she'd tucked under the covers a few more squeezes, hoping they'd look less like an enormous sausage and more like a body. Satisfied, she adjusted the mannequin head with blond wig, turning it so that one cheek was on the pillow and the other artfully covered by strands of hair. She stepped back and considered the effect. If she didn't get too close it definitely looked like a girl lying on her side, fast asleep.

"Remember, switch off the lights if anyone comes to the door. Ms. Huston isn't going to look closely if you're already sleeping."

"And how, exactly, are you planning to get back in? You know they lock the doors."

"That's for me to worry about." Chelsea giggled and admired herself once more in the mirror before reluctantly slipping out of the heels and into a pair of Adidas. She'd change back into the pumps once she reached her destination.

That was the most exciting part of all of this. She didn't know her destination. Not yet. He'd promised to text that to her once she was on her way.

She shoveled through a dresser drawer and emerged with an impossibly small red satin handbag in which she managed to shove a cell phone, lipstick, ten-dollar bill, cigarettes with lighter, and a condom.

"I can't believe you carry those," Brooke said, pert nose wrinkling at the sight of the bright foil-wrapped package.

"Safe sex, girlfriend. I don't depend on guys."

"There is another way."

"Yeah?" Chelsea flipped her hair once more in the mirror. "What's that?"

"Abstinence."

Chelsea snorted. "R-r-right. C'mon, Brooke, even you aren't that repressed."

Brooke didn't answer; she just watched as her roommate

slowly opened the door, peeking out a crack before opening it wider and waving a silent good-bye.

"Just be careful," Brooke whispered.

Chelsea laughed quietly. "I always am."

Once she was clear of Ambrose House, she dug her cell phone back out of the purse and checked the screen. The first text message had arrived a few days ago, two simple lines that appeared while she was in study hall: "CU F2F? Cory." What she loved about text messaging was that none of the teachers knew how to translate. Not even all the students knew that it meant, "See you face-to-face?"

She'd been surprised to hear from Cory. He'd been her date to last spring's dance, but they hadn't spoken since. His prep school was in Morristown, but he had cousins in town. One of them had set her up with Cory, figuring she'd go for his swimmer's build: tall, lean, and muscular with big shoulders. He'd been good looking if a little unimaginative. She was surprised he was texting her, but maybe he'd started to develop a bit more personality.

She typed back "fbm" for "fine by me."

The next day she'd gotten this: "tpm 10? cys" which meant, "Tomorrow night at 10? See you soon."

Getting out to meet him at ten was too difficult so she responded: "cu 10:45"

His answer came quickly: "Cul8r sxci"

That made her smile. Being sexy was an important part of her self-definition. She hoped this outfit delivered.

Now her screen showed one word, "Chpl" for chapel.

She headed in that direction, smiling at his choice of rendezvous. This was definitely an improvement on the old Cory. The big excitement after last year's dance had been making out in the backseat of his parents' Mercedes, where he'd been more concerned about spilling vodka on the leather upholstery than about her. Fortunately, she was good at bringing attention back where it belonged.

The chapel looked dark and forbidding from the back of Augustine House and she shivered. This was delicious! She crept around the side of that dorm, moving stealthily along the shadows cast by the stone, before darting the last few feet across open lawn up to the chapel entrance.

She knew from experience a side door would be open and she wasn't disappointed. Her footfalls made a whispery, sandpaper sound on the slate floor. There was a second set of doors that led into the chapel itself and she opened one, holding her breath at its creak, searching the pews for a familiar face under the flicker of dozens of votives vying for space in metal racks.

A sound behind her and she let the chapel door swing closed. Her eyes searched the outer room. "Cory?" she whispered, clutching her purse tightly, her heart pumping a little faster.

Then she noticed one of the wooden doors against the far wall standing ajar. A thin sliver of light split the space between frame and door and spilled onto the stone floor. Had it been there before? Surely she would have seen it.

"Cory?" she called again, a little louder this time, walking slowly toward the light. "Is that you?"

Again, no answer. "This isn't funny, Cory." Annoyance overtook apprehension just a little, just enough to get her moving She was at the light now, reaching for the brass doorknob.

"Hello, Chelsea."

The voice came behind her and it wasn't Cory's. She whirled around and saw a hooded figure sweeping out of the shadows. She reared back and from behind felt gloved hands slip something over her head. It settled against her throat and jerked tight, cutting off her cry of terror.

Her hands went to her throat, clawing helplessly at the rope choking her, staring wild-eyed at the hooded figure now looming over her.

"Ssh, Chelsea, ssh," the figure said in a calm voice. "We can't have that noise. Can you be quiet?"

She tried to nod, tried to say yes, though it came out garbled. Anything at all, anything, just let her breathe.

Suddenly she could. The rope still circled her neck, but it was slack, resting near her collarbone. She clasped it with her hand, taking rasping breaths. She stared at the hooded figure. The sweatshirt swaddled the figure, the hood pulled so far forward that it was impossible to see the face.

"Turn around, Chelsea."

"W-why? What do you want—"

The rope jerked from her hand and tightened around her neck again.

"Now, now, Chelsea. No noise, remember?"

Again, she tried to nod against the rope. The pressure on her neck and in her chest brought burning tears. She blinked them back, trying to see the person pulling the rope, but all she caught was a glimpse of another hooded figure.

"Turn around, Chelsea." The first figure spoke again, the voice still calm. A gloved hand reached out to direct her and Chelsea turned this time, turned willingly, but the rope was still taut around her neck.

"Stairs, Chelsea, step down and we'll loosen the rope. You hesitate and we'll drag you. Blink if you understand."

Blink, yes, okay. She could do that. Blink, blink. Anything to get the rope off. Her fingers couldn't get under it. She was going to die.

The sudden rush of oxygen blinded her and she took the first few steps down in darkness, a hand in the small of her back, another hand gripping her right arm just above the elbow.

She knew they were in the tunnel that connected the chapel to the main building, but why? What did they want? The desire to ask was so strong that she had to bite her lip to keep from begging for some explanation or her release.

Down, down they went. It was such a long way down. She'd never realized that before. She stumbled once and the rope immediately tightened against her neck. She couldn't get away on the steps.

Wait for the bottom of the steps and then maybe she could catch them by surprise and run forward fast enough to pull the rope from the other's hands. She couldn't think of another way. Get ready, she chanted silently in her head, get ready.

On the second-to-last step she surged forward, taking two down instead of one. It worked! Her arm jerked free of the captor next to her and she could feel the rope fly through the fingers of the stranger behind her.

She ran flat out, screaming for help, throat burning, her ragged cries echoing off the walls, fully expecting to be caught from behind.

The dimly lit tunnel curved left and as she came around the bend she screamed again as she slammed into yet another hooded figure, knocking them both to the ground.

Gloved hands fell on her shoulders and pulled her up with the help of the noose that tightened again.

There were three now leading her deeper into the tunnel, the first figure talking quietly as they variously pushed and pulled her along. "Bad Chelsea, very bad. You can't escape the judgment."

That calm voice seeped through Chelsea's fading consciousness like a poisonous gas, weakening the muscles in her legs and loosing her bladder. A sudden stream of heat down her leg and someone giggled. She felt ashamed.

They stopped and the first figure moved around her. "You are a whore, Chelsea," that frightening voice said.

She tried to shake her head, but the rope wouldn't let her. Tears streamed down her face. She could smell the pungent scent of her own urine and another voice said, "She stinks."

"Do you know what they used to do with whores?" the first voice inquired. "They used to stone them."

The word penetrated. Through streaming eyes Chelsea looked down at the gloved hands, but they were empty.

A soft chuckle brought her gaze back up to the dark faceless hood. "No, no, we're not going to stone you."

A tiny bit of hope, like salve on a bleeding wound, but then a gloved hand jerked Chelsea's head back and she saw the iron hook jutting from the wall.

Chapter Nineteen

Elsa Klossner woke up early just like always. She remained snuggled under the covers for another five minutes, listening to the soft snores of her roommate, but her feelings of discontent with her body pushed her out of bed.

Lying prone, clad only in thin pajamas, she was aware of her large breasts bobbing gently against her chest and of her plump thighs rubbing against one another. She didn't like her body and she liked it even less unfettered. Grabbing a large robe, she trudged off to the showers, a process she endured by making sure that the mirrors were sufficiently steamed before she so much as glanced in their direction.

Once she'd finished washing and wiggled on a pair of contouring panties, a control-top bra, and her boxy uniform, she could focus on the one part of her body that wasn't a disappointment—her hair.

It was a lustrous, rich shade of brown and hung in glorious straightness halfway down her back. People always commented on it. "You have such lovely hair, Elsa," was something she heard at least once a week. Knowing that sometimes they were saying it because there was nothing else on her lumpy body to compliment didn't make it any less true. She did have lovely hair and she lavished attention on it.

After brushing and stroking and fashioning it into a variety of different styles, she finally settled on wearing it loose and pushed back with a wide headband. With a small sigh, she put the brush away and slipped on her school shoes. Chunky like the rest of her. She posed in the mirror, turning to one side, then the other, wondering if she could see any effect at all from the diet she'd started a few days ago. She wouldn't know for sure if it was working until she weighed herself later in the locker room, and that was iffy because she didn't like to use the scale unless the room was completely empty.

She could get over there before class if she went now. The locker rooms were probably open early and if she encountered Miss Tinston, the skinny-minny gym teacher who seemed to think that Elsa wanted to look the way she did, Elsa could always describe her new eating regimen. Maybe it would even bring a smile to that otherwise sunken, sour-lemon face.

Grabbing her backpack off her desk, Elsa looked out the window and was startled to see in the gray light of dawn that it was snowing. She cranked open the casement and stretched out a hand. A snowflake, perfectly formed and the size of a dime, landed on her palm and melted before she could get a close look at it. September flurries. That had to be a first. They were gone as soon as they touched the warmer ground, but the air was frigid. She quickly closed the window, watching steam form on the glass. It was going to be a cold hike across campus; maybe she should just wait until tomorrow to check the scale.

Unless there was a different way to get there. Staring at the snow blowing across the chapel bell tower had given her an idea. She could take the tunnel that linked the chapel with the main building and from there all she had to do was cut through two more buildings and cross a small strip of lawn to get to the athletic center. Minimal time in the cold, which would probably save time in the long run and certainly be a lot more comfortable.

Strictly speaking, this wasn't allowed. The tunnel was used when there was a snowfall and only when escorting girls from the main building to the chapel for Mass. It had been designed to keep the chapel relatively clean in what Sister Rose always referred to as "inclement weather."

It was snowing, even though the flakes were vanishing as fast as they fell. If she left now, no one needed to know about it. As quietly as she could, Elsa left her room and Augustine House and headed out the door in the direction of the chapel. The flurries blew against her face, little bites of cold that further convinced her she was doing the right thing.

The main doors to the chapel were locked, but then she thought to try a side door and it inched open when she tugged on the giant iron ring. She slipped in out of the cold and paused for a moment, listening in case Father Dominic or, worse, that other priest, Father Dombrowski—whom lots of the girls referred to as Father Dogface—were around. The chapel itself was through another set of doors. This was the anteroom, though it was lined with the same slate floor.

The building seemed vacant and when she peeked through the door into the chapel the only light and movement visible came from the votive candles softly flickering at the slippered feet of a stone virgin.

The door to the tunnel was the third of three dark-stained solid oak doors. It was kept locked, but the key was easy enough to find if you knew where to look, and Elsa did. She'd seen Mr. Macklin open it last year, reaching into the utility room, the second oak door, to take a small brass key from a nail high on the wall.

Sure enough, when she opened the utility door there was the small key dangling from the nail. She unlocked the tunnel door and then propped it open with her backpack so she could return the key to its hook and no one would ever be the wiser.

She hefted her backpack onto her shoulder and peered into the open doorway. There was a set of concrete steps disappearing down into darkness. It looked forbidding. She ran her hand lightly around the interior plaster wall and felt a switch. With a hum, a dim yellow light came on above her head at the entrance to the steps.

Swallowing hard, she took one step down, then another. She'd never been in this tunnel alone before and she was beginning to think it was a bad idea. Still, she'd gone and pulled the door shut behind her. There was nothing to be afraid of, especially since she could see another light mounted at ceiling level a few steps down.

Five more steep steps descended and there seemed no end to them. What if this wasn't the door to the tunnel at all, but some entrance to a basement or a sewer system? What if she couldn't get back up? Who would hear her cries for help? Would someone come looking when she didn't show up for class?

Four more steps. Another light. Three more steps and then she could see it, the tunnel opening up and stretching ahead of her. The same yellow lights were mounted at regular intervals in the curved ceiling. She sighed with relief and adjusted her satchel. Her wristwatch said 7:00. She still had an hour before class started. Plenty of time to get over to the locker room scale and then back to class.

Only the tunnel seemed endless. She began by counting lights, but soon lost track of how many. It was easier to look at the walls on either side of the tunnel to mark her progress, for this was where some ingenious educator had decided to store extra supplies. Industrial shelving had been erected to hold reams of office paper and cartons of chalk, boxes piled high with blue exam books and plastic bags brimming with name-tag stickers and ballpoint pens.

She passed row upon row of crammed shelves, the only

thing that changed along the ancient rounded walls. In places the plaster had chipped and she could see the faint outline of stone. The lights were old and some of them buzzed faintly and flickered as she passed beneath them. They gave the off-white walls a yellow cast and beneath the musty smell of things too long without air was the faintest scent of something damp and loamy.

A slight panicky feeling took hold in Elsa's gut and crawled up her spine. What if she were wrong about this tunnel? What if it didn't connect to the main building but was leading her far astray? Maybe there wasn't one tunnel but a maze of tunnels crisscrossing the campus.

It was just about this time that she heard the noise. A single, repetitive sound that grew stronger the farther she went. The sound of something dripping. A drip of what? Water?

She fought back visions of a crack spreading in the stone, breaking through the plaster and a hidden reservoir of water flooding the tunnel and washing her away. It was nothing, she told herself as the noise grew louder. The nothing grew more distinct, the definite sound of liquid falling from a distance onto a hard surface.

The tunnel took another slight turn and she turned with it and then she stopped dead because the source of that dripping suddenly came into view. Elsa felt the hair rise all over her body like a cat's and the scream that came forth from deep within her could also have come from an animal.

Elsa screamed and screamed again, the noise echoing loudly in the space. She scrambled back, forgetting about the weight of her backpack, and it pulled her down. She screamed again because she couldn't stop it, just as she couldn't stop staring at the body hanging in front of her.

Chapter Twenty

A girl's body dangled from an iron hook in the side wall, the toe of one of her red pumps scraping against the side of an overturned plastic crate, a bright silk scarf twisted around her neck. Her face was purple, her eyes bulging like those of a dead fish at Elsa, and her tongue was sticking out from her mouth as if she were hissing. The repetitive dripping came from large droplets of wax spilling over the side of a tall pillar and hitting the base of the even taller candlestick.

"Oh my God," Elsa said once she'd stopped screaming. "Oh my God, oh my God, oh my God." It was both prayer and blasphemy and she scrabbled against the floor with her hands and her feet, like a crab trying to scuttle back and out of the way. Only there was no escape.

The girl wore jeans and they were unzipped and gaping open just enough to reveal a thin, sharply jutting and shaved pubic bone. A thin white hand was sticking into her pants in an obscene way. The other hand hung at her side, the nails painted a garish red that matched the shiny shoes.

The drip, drip, drip from the candle seemed increasingly loud in Elsa's ears. She stared at the hot yellowish wax pooling around the flaming wick before it overflowed, rolling down the side of the taper before falling the last foot and landing with a tiny splash on the candle base.

The toe of the girl's right shoe dangled perilously close to the flame and the shiny red leather was sooty in that one spot. Elsa's eyes followed the jeans-clad leg up to the hand jammed against the genitals. The skin appeared as waxen as the candle, as if all the blood in the girl's body had gone straight to her contorted, red face.

Elsa swallowed the bile that rose in her throat and struggled to her feet, leaving her backpack behind. She wanted out, but she'd come too far to go back. She moved to the other side of the wall and pressed herself against it to move past the girl. Her foot bumped against something small and she screamed again, but it was a cell phone.

Elsa scooped it up and flipped it open, rapidly hitting 9-1-1, but nothing happened. There was no signal in the tunnel. She kept it anyway, jamming it in her pocket and screaming instead.

"Help!" The word echoed, coming back to mock her. There was no help in here. She was trapped. No one would hear her. She ran as fast as she could, stumbling in her haste, catching herself against the wall and then running again. She needed help. The hanging girl needed help. She had to get out.

She became aware of another, desperate rush of noise and realized it was her own keening. The steps came into view and she wept at seeing them, flinging her body against the banister, struggling to get up them. Four steps. Five. It was just as long as the set in the chapel. Finally she saw the door.

The brass knob was cold in her hands and she turned and pushed but nothing happened. She tried again and again before realizing with a sudden, sickening clarity that it was locked. She was trapped in the tunnel.

Elsa flailed at the door with her fists, screaming, "Help! Let me out!" Her knuckles were raw and her voice hoarse when she heard the sound of metal scraping and then suddenly she fell forward into the bright light of the hall.

"What are you doing?" A woman's voice shrieked above Elsa. She rolled to her side and sat up, blinking in the brighter light, trying to focus.

"Police," she gasped, clutching the woman's sturdy black shoe, then her stocking-clad ankle. The woman pulled back out of her grasp.

"What's going on? What were you doing down there?"

Elsa struggled to her feet, but it was hard to find purchase against the marble floor when she felt as if whatever had held her together as a whole body had disintegrated. Her bones and muscles were mush.

There were rapid footsteps and she got her legs under her just as Mr. Pierce and Sister Rose came running around the corner.

"What's happened? Ms. Klossner?" Sister Rose was out of breath and that was definitely a first for Elsa. She'd never seen the headmistress like this and the surprise of it did nothing to calm her down.

"There's a body in the tunnel," she cried. "Call the police."

"A body?" Mr. Pierce's tone suggested that Elsa was dramatizing.

"A dead body," she corrected him. "At least I think she's dead. Oh God. You've got to call the police."

But Sister Rose had her cell phone in hand already. "Ms. Klossner, you're sure you're not imagining things?"

Elsa laughed then, a hysterical laugh that turned into a sob. "Oh yes, I'm quite sure."

The guidance counselor walked briskly down the steps with a set look to his face. Sister Rose watched him go while talking rapidly to a 911 operator. She demanded police and an ambulance while Elsa stood shaking under the fierce gaze of Sister Bernice.

Elsa took deep breaths, trying to remember things that she'd learned about handling stress from the therapist at the weight-loss camp her parents had sent her to last summer. She'd learned lots of strategies for using things other than Doritos and Hershey Bars to manage anxiety, but they hadn't covered seeing violent death.

She shoved her hands in the pockets of her coat and found the cell phone she stuffed in there earlier. She pulled it out and looked at it. It was one of the newer camera phones. She'd wanted one of these for her birthday, but she'd been given a subscription to *Shape* magazine and a gym membership instead.

This phone must belong to that girl. Until that moment Elsa hadn't given any thought to who the girl actually was—she'd been too concerned with escaping from what the girl had become in the tunnel.

An image of that protruding tongue came to mind and Elsa swallowed hard and flipped open the phone. She gave a little gasp when she saw the picture on the screen. Sister Bernice looked over and Elsa quickly flipped the phone shut and slipped it back in her pocket.

It couldn't be, could it? Surely she would have recognized her? But it had to be. This was her phone. Elsa knew this phone, she'd seen it before when they were texting each other in the cafeteria. She'd fantasized sometimes about being one of the girls texted. It seemed impossible that she could be dead. Elsa felt tears spring to her eyes.

Mr. Pierce came huffing back out of the tunnel. His face was pale and the lips that had been compressed were open. His eyes were huge.

"Are the police coming?" he croaked.

Sister Rose nodded. "Is it a student?"

He nodded and pulled a neatly folded triangle of white linen from the breast pocket of his blazer and patted it against his face and neck. "It's Chelsea Connor," he said in a muted voice, but Elsa heard him and gasped again. Chelsea Connor?

"Are you sure?" she asked.

The guidance counselor looked her way. "Yes, I'm sure."

Sister Rose headed for the stairs. "Don't," Pierce said loudly and grabbed her arm. "You don't need to see. Don't."

"I've got a responsibility," she said, but trailed off at the look on his face. "I guess I can wait for the police."

"We need to lock down the school," he said.

"Yes, but we don't want to disrupt classes."

He nodded and patted his face again before returning the handkerchief to his pocket. "I'll guard the front door and look out for the police."

He strode past Elsa, sparing her a glance that told her he was trying to recall her name. She was still in shock. It was Chelsea Connor in the tunnel. But this wasn't Chelsea's phone in her pocket.

She was just about to show it to Sister Rose when the full implications of finding that particular phone in that particular place at that particular time finally reached through the shock and smacked her metaphorically across the head.

No, don't show Sister Rose. Don't show anyone. In any case, Sister Rose didn't look like she could handle anything more.

Two little spots of color had shown up on the headmistress's cheeks. She clasped her hands together once, then again, the palms striking loudly in the empty hall. Whether this was in thought or in prayer Elsa couldn't say, but she could see that Sister Rose's usually calm, unflappable exterior was cracking.

"Alert the teachers that we're in lockdown," she said to Sister Bernice, "but not a word as to why."

"What if someone asks?" the other woman stared dumbly at the headmistress, waiting to be told what to do. It might have been comical under other circumstances, but not now.

"Just say it's an emergency. Don't mention a body."

Sister Bernice nodded, practically bowing in deference, and scurried away toward the main offices. Sister Rose turned her wild-eyed focus on Elsa. "How did you get into the tunnel?"

She didn't think about lying. "With the key."

"The key? What key?"

"The one in the chapel."

Sister Rose's right hand flew to her throat, fluttering against the skin like a bird. "How did you know where to find the key?"

"I-I saw Mr. Macklin take it from the utility closet." For a moment Elsa thought the headmistress might faint—her face went very pale and she squeezed her eyes shut. Almost immediately, though, her face flooded with color again and her eyes popped open.

"Why did you go down there? What were you doing?" The question sounded accusing and Elsa couldn't help the color rising in her own cheeks.

"I thought it would be easier to get to the gym that way," she said, "because it's snowing."

"Snowing?" Disdain was evident in the headmistress's voice. "I'd hardly call a few flurries snow, Elsa." It was clear that unlike the guidance counselor, she knew exactly who Elsa was and found her lacking. The girl sniffled.

"What does it say in the handbook about the tunnel?" Sister Rose demanded in her most pedantic manner.

"It's to be used from November through January," Elsa mumbled, swiping at her eyes with the sleeve of her wool coat.

"Is it November?"

"No, Sister."

"So you were breaking the rules by being in that tunnel, weren't you?"

"Yes, Sister."

Sister Rose nodded, satisfied. "Were you in that tunnel with Chelsea Connor?"

"Oh no, Sister!" Elsa was startled by that question. It hadn't occurred to her that they'd think she and Chelsea were together. She barely knew the girl.

"Did you let Chelsea Connor into the tunnel?"

"No!" Elsa was genuinely shocked.

"Then how did she get down there? Students don't have access to the tunnels."

"I don't know."

"You weren't supposed to be in that tunnel," Sister Rose repeated as if Elsa's being in the tunnel was somehow responsible for Chelsea Connor's death. "I'll have to call the parents," she murmured, more to herself than to Elsa. "They'll have to know before the press gets wind—they'll be all over this."

She tapped the silver cross at the center of the circle pin affixed to her navy blazer. "I don't know why this is happening," she said. "St. Ursula's is such a good school."

It was an odd thing to say, Elsa thought, as if death should only come to bad schools.

Across the hall from the door to the tunnel was a wall of leaded glass windows looking out on the main entrance. Elsa stood there and watched a line of police cars climbing the hill, their lights a faint glow at first, then full beacons flashing against the grayness of the day.

An ambulance crew came with them and suddenly the halls of the school were filled with people, boots clattering on marble, loud voices, and the static of radios clipped to equipment belts. Two uniformed cops headed into the tunnel followed by a pair of paramedics. One of them was calmly sipping from a Starbucks cup. They looked at Sister Rose and Elsa, but didn't say anything. That was for officer number three, an older man straining the seams of his uniform, his belt covered by his belly. He took a notebook out of his back pocket and looked around.

"Who found the victim?" he demanded, looking from Sister Rose to Elsa and then past them to Miss Jones, the office secretary, and Sister Bernice, who'd come out of the main office and were hovering in the hall.

"I did," Elsa said. She recounted what had happened, trying to follow his questions and putting up with his interruptions. He wanted the story clarified many times and in many different ways.

It felt like it took forever, but when she glanced at her watch Elsa was surprised to see that only twenty-five minutes had passed since she'd been freed from the tunnel. While she was answering questions, one of the police officers emerged from the tunnel, muttering "Jesus Christ" under his breath.

His face sallow, he signaled to the beefy older officer. They conferred privately for two minutes, the younger officer using his hands to describe the scene. When he mimed someone hanging, Elsa looked away.

The older cop coughed and hacked, sounding like he was about to spit out some phlegm but, remembering where he was, he held it back. "Call homicide," he ordered the young guy. "And don't forget to alert the desk."

He turned back to Elsa. "So this girl was a classmate of yours?"

Elsa nodded, cupping her hand gently around the phone in her pocket. She was glad that she'd found it. Just think of the trouble that could have come if Mr. Pierce had seen it. Or the police.

Chapter Twenty-one

When the phone rang in the dark of the morning in Stephanie and Alex's apartment, it wasn't another case of coitus interruptus. More like coitus possibilitus interruptus. They'd been making moves in that direction, but it was early enough, and the evening before had been late enough, that they was having more of a silent discussion about who had the energy to initiate any serious action.

She lifted her hand from the languid stroking of his clothed penis, which had been responding favorably to the faint pressure, and reached for the phone.

"Leave it," Alex said, his hand slipping from the breast he'd been caressing as she rolled to the side.

She ignored him. "Detective Land." This time it was Oz calling and he spelled things out in a frenzied burst that had her up and out of bed in one swift movement. "Okay, right. Jesus. Okay, okay. In five."

Jeans and a T-shirt were fastest. Throw a jacket over it and she'd look semiprofessional. She switched on the light to check her holster and suddenly remembered Alex as he groaned loudly behind her.

"Sorry." She flicked the light off.

"Just once you could leave it," he said, voice muffled from the pillow he'd thrown over his face.

"No, I couldn't." She slipped the harness on, stepped into the closet, and switched on the light to check the Glock's safety before slipping it in the holster.

Black corduroy jacket and small silver hoops. She moved on to the bathroom to wash her face and brush her teeth. Alex said something else but she couldn't hear him above the rushing water.

"Waz?" she garbled, stepping to the doorway while she continued to scrub her teeth. He threw the pillow to one side and sat up.

"I said, is this what it's going to be like on our wedding night? Are you going to answer the phone then, too?"

"Azzole," she muttered as she ducked back over the sink to spit.

"Don't curse at me." The bed creaked and then he stood in the doorway, arms crossed. "I don't deserve that."

"What? I didn't say anything?" She rinsed and spit, but could feel her face flushing.

"You are such a terrible liar," he said and his voice was softer so she risked a look at his face. He was smiling and she smiled back.

"Sorry, but you could stop hassling me about my job."

"I'm not trying to hassle you, I just want you to set up some boundaries."

Stephanie sighed and ran a boar-bristle brush roughly through her hair, trying to pull her bed head into something resembling a style. In the end she gave up and just pulled it back in a ponytail.

"It doesn't work that way, Alex," she said as gently as she could. "I can't just shut the phone off. It's my responsibility to be available."

"I'm your fiancé, it's your responsibility to be available to me."

She stepped toward the door and for a moment she thought he might not move. Then he stepped to one side and she walked past, feeling her heart clenching with the stress she could feel emanating from him. As always, his anger provoked the same in her. She didn't feel sorry, she just felt pissed that he was being totally unreasonable.

"I am available to you," she said as politely as she could. "But I also have to be available to the job. And this is one of those times."

She leaned in for a kiss and he turned his face to the side so it landed against the roughness of his unshaven cheek. "I'll call you," she said.

"Yeah."

She hurried to the kitchen and grabbed a PowerBar and a bottle of water from the fridge to shove in her purse. A car horn sounded and she grabbed her keys and headed out the door. It was closing behind her when Alex's voice stopped her.

"Hey, wait," he said. He was wearing only his boxers, but that didn't stop him from stepping after her onto the stoop. One of his strong arms encircled her waist, pulling her back into an embrace, and he cupped the back of her head gently with his other hand before pressing his mouth against hers and his tongue down her throat.

The kiss was long, brutal, and passionate. When he let go she was panting.

"Have a good one," he said, grinning at her like a madman.

She nodded, dazed into silence, wiping moisture from her lips with the back of one hand.

Oz was watching them from the car, and he raised one hand to Alex, but didn't say anything until Stephanie was buckled up and they'd peeled out.

She was taking a swig of water when he said, "Why doesn't he just piss on you while he's at it?"

Stephanie sprayed the windshield and Oz started laughing, a low infectious rumble.

"Bastard," she said when she'd got her breath. "You're just jealous."

"Yeah," he said and then he said in a falsetto. "Alex is so-o hot, I really want him."

They laughed some more, but she could feel her face flaming. She offered him some of her PowerBar to shut him up.

The first time she'd had sex with Alex had been after they'd dated for six weeks. She'd known from about the third week that he was the one and that had made her strangely reticent. Not that she'd been in the habit of sleeping around, because she certainly hadn't, but she'd had one longer relationship before him and one rebound romance that also failed and those had left her gun-shy of men in general and of bedding men in particular.

She knew she liked sex and she had a vague sense that it was another one of those things, just like her interest in crime, that made her different than a lot of women.

"Wow," was Alex's first coherent word when they were lying side by side after the first time and she was staring at a watermark on the ceiling without focusing on anything beyond that lingering internal hum.

"Yeah," she'd agreed. "Wow." She knew then that it would last. They were beyond good together in that one respect and that helped to quell any doubts she had about just how good they might be in other areas, like understanding what each other really wanted in a mate.

By the time she thought to ask that question, she owned a town house with him and was wearing his ring on her finger. Only now, post saying yes, post beginning to plan what was fast becoming a much bigger deal of a wedding than she'd ever wanted, post the meeting with both sets of parents and hearing the dreaded talk of grandkids, she'd started to ask herself exactly what else they had in common. Sometimes the answer scared her.

Stephanie shivered and fiddled with the knob for the heating.

"Colder than a witch's tit," Oz commented as he ran the wiper blades again to brush away the flurries clouding the windshield. It was a gray day, the line dividing sky from land vanishing into nothingness. Even the grass was gray, a morning frost silvering large swaths of lawn on the houses they passed.

Once they turned into the main entrance and began climbing the hill, the temperature seemed to drop another five degrees.

"I hope this one isn't in the woods," Stephanie said as they got closer.

"No, for which I am damned grateful. This one's in the main building, some basement or something."

"Or something" turned out to be a tunnel. "Holy shit," Oz muttered when he saw the steps leading down to where they were heading and then he turned a bilious shade of red and apologized three times to the headmistress. Stephanie eventually took his arm and tugged him along.

"I'm an idiot," he said as they headed down into what could only be described as subterranean.

"No, you're not, just a loudmouth. Watch your head."

"Gee, thanks." He ducked to avoid the light fixtures. They trotted along the narrow passageway and Stephanie began to feel like she was going to be traveling this same route forever. She tried not to think claustrophobia, but of course the minute she tried not to think of something the word began hammering in her brain. Sweat beaded along her forehead, though it wasn't overly hot in the tunnel.

They had some warning of the body because Patrolman Brian Mooney was standing guard.

"Hey," he greeted them with a look of frank relief and Stephanie figured he was probably feeling the claustrophobia thing, too.

"Got to warn you," he said, but he looked straight at Stephanie. "It's pretty brutal."

"Yeah, well you can run along, then," she said, looking him straight in the eyes and trying to inject as much of a motherly, patronizing tone in her voice as she could.

He had the decency to flush, turning his rather pointy ears a brighter shade of red, and he stepped aside with a sour look on his face.

"Now, now, don't scare the children," Oz said in her ear, handing over a pair of latex gloves.

She laughed and slipped on one of the gloves before pausing and sniffing the air. "Getting ripe in here. You want some Vicks?"

He nodded looking ahead. She followed his gaze and saw the basics. Body. Female. Hanging. Look away fast. Deep swallow and the PowerBar stayed down. She fished the tube of Vicks VapoRub out of her pocket with her free hand and smeared some below her nostrils before handing it over to Oz. "Second death in two weeks. Still think that necklace just came off?"

Oz shrugged, handing back the tube. He had a shuttered look on his broad face and she could tell he was working hard not to personalize what he saw.

She slipped on the other glove and followed him to the body. The other patrolman, a brighter fish with the pop-star name of Lance, looked up from his perusal of the ground around the victim's dangling feet.

"I don't think she wore these shoes in here," he said, standing up. He looked a little green around the gills, but he hadn't thrown up and he wasn't averting his gaze like Moonface Mooney.

"Why?" Stephanie took in the gestalt first: the iron hook in the wall, the ruby-colored silk scarf knotted around it and then around the victim's neck. The victim herself: female, approximately 5'2", small build, blond hair, apparently gray

eyes, though those were bloodshot so it was hard to say. Face
dark red from blood congestion, bruising evident around the
neck.

"No wear on the soles," Lance said. "There's a store sticker
on the bottom of one shoe—they look like new—and it doesn't
have scuffs."

"Yes, good." Stephanie nodded and Lance beamed at her.
She had to resist the sudden urge to pat his towhead. There
was a royal blue backpack lying on the floor a few feet from
the body. "Who does the bag belong to?"

"The girl who found her. She says she dropped it when
she was hurrying to get help."

"What was she doing down here?" Oz asked, leaning in
for a closer look at the girl's neck.

"I don't know, something about this being a shortcut to
another building."

Oz used a ballpoint pen to carefully lift the girl's hanging
hand, closely examining the painted nails for signs of break-
age or for skin.

"Make sure she stays so we can talk to her," Stephanie
said. She felt the internal ping that said game on. Something
was going on here—you didn't have two student deaths this
close together without someone knowing something.

"No signs of struggle," Oz said. "And this hand is in her
pants. You think it's that sex thing?"

"You mean the choking game? Or the sex version, what's
it called—erotic something?"

"Autoerotic asphyxiation," Lance said. They both turned
to stare at him. "I read an article about it," he said defensively.

"Sure," Oz said easily, turning back to the vic. "You think
this is consistent with what you read, Lance?"

Lance looked happy to be consulted. "Maybe," he said,
standing up. "Yeah, I think so. The scarf certainly fits."

Stephanie shook her head. "But why here? That doesn't fit."

"Sure it does," Oz argued. "It's private and this hook is just about the perfect height."

Stephanie couldn't argue with that, but she also couldn't shake the feeling that there was more going on. She looked around the tunnel. Shelving filled with school supplies on either side of the vic, with an overturned plastic crate next to her. Private, yes, but not exactly erotic.

"Not sexy to you or me," Oz said, reading her thoughts as he frequently seemed to, "but she's a teenager and this place is forbidden. That makes it exciting."

"Yeah, okay, I'll grant you that, but why the clothes? This isn't the outfit a girl wears alone. Those jeans are practically painted on."

"Maybe it made her feel sexy."

"And maybe she wasn't alone." Stephanie stared at the candle near the girl's feet. Wax had congealed along the candle base and some had splashed onto the tile floor surrounding it, but across from the single candle she could see other opaque blots on the tile. She knelt to look more closely.

"See something?" Oz glanced her way and then back to his perusal of the vic's neck.

"Maybe." Tiny, perfectly formed circles and teardrops of pearly white. She nudged one gently with a pen and it didn't move. "It's wax."

"What's that from?"

"I don't know, but I don't see any other candles, do you?"

Lance immediately turned his attention to that, sniffing around the shelves and walking in both directions for a few feet. "No other candles anywhere," he announced.

Stephanie suddenly wondered what he was like in bed, this eager-to-please puppy of a boy who was probably twenty if he was a day. She had a sudden mental picture of him beaming as she praised him for his massage technique, followed immediately by revulsion at her own mind for conjuring up this image.

Jesus, what was happening to her? Was she already so jaded by this line of work that she could find sexual innuendo in the worst of circumstances? That was just like the older guys with their stupid remarks about women's bodies and the not-so-subtle jabs at gender differences. She was twenty-eight years old, not forty-eight, but she already knew what it was like to become detached from the most heinous reality, to compartmentalize it so that you could see the worst of humanity and come out the other side without screaming.

"We need to get that wax photographed and scraped," she said to Lance, "where's the crime scene unit?"

"I'll go check." He was off, marching briskly back the way they'd come in.

Oz chuckled and Stephanie glanced at him. "What?"

"Let me do it, teacher, let me," he said in sing-song.

She laughed. "Now who's being mean to the kids?"

"Was I ever that young? I think I was older than that at birth."

A series of rapid footsteps thundered down the tunnel and the crime scene photographer showed up with Lance and the medical examiner in tow. Harriet Wembley always managed to look slightly pissed off, as if they were in some way responsible for the crime scene. Stephanie didn't take it personally. Everyone had their own way of dealing with the gross unfairness of violent death.

"When was she found?" the medical examiner asked as the photographer quietly snapped pictures from every possible angle and then some that Oz or Stephanie asked for.

"Seven o'clock or close to it."

"Hmm." Harriet slipped on her own gloves and pressed against the underside of the dangling arm. It shifted slightly and then settled back into place as she stepped back. "Beginnings of rigor," she said. "Petechiae consistent with hanging." She stared at the scene for several moments, her eyes darting between the scarf knotted around the girl's neck to the unbuttoned jeans and the hand cupped over the pubic bone. "I've never seen this before," she said, "never with a female, that is."

Oz shifted. "You've seen it with a male?"

The medical examiner nodded. "The percentage of males practicing autoerotic asphyxiation is far greater than for females."

Stephanie waited until the body was bagged and she saw the wax droplets scraped and bagged before she left the basement in search of the girl who'd found the body. The hallway was crowded with students and some adults she assumed were teachers, all of them being kept at bay by crime scene tape. On a bench underneath some windows sat a pudgy girl with eyes red from crying.

It became apparent fairly quickly that the girl had moved past shock at finding the body and was now far more concerned about what trouble she was going to be in for having ventured into the tunnel.

"It was snowing," she repeated more than once, her voice plaintive. "I just didn't feel like walking through the cold."

She barely knew the victim and didn't have much to say about her except for a cryptic remark about Chelsea Connor "going out with a lot of guys." When pressed, Elsa Klossner admitted that she had only heard this around school, not witnessed it.

That interview ended quickly. Given permission to leave, the girl scuttled off to class with the backpack Oz returned to her. Stephanie was headed back toward the tunnel when she heard someone call her name. She was startled to see the same young teacher from the first crime scene.

Stephanie walked quickly to the crime scene tape boundary where the woman stood.

"I'm surprised to see you again," Stephanie said. There was no need to be coy and she didn't feel like she could handle anything less than direct communication after what she'd seen in the tunnel.

"Yes." The woman's face was pale. She had the tight-lipped look of someone enduring.

"You wanted to talk to me?"

Lauren Kavanaugh nodded and brushed at a strand of curly hair that had come loose from the barrette holding it back. She looked thinner, though that couldn't really be possible, could it, in such a short time? Maybe it was just that the A-line black skirt and black-and-white fitted blouse she wore emphasized it. There was a bulky temporary cast buckled around one ankle.

"What did you do to your leg, Ms. Kavanaugh?"

"I tripped when I was running and sprained my ankle." There was something too quick about that answer, but before Stephanie could pursue it the woman was talking rapidly in a voice so low that Stephanie had to lean closer to hear her.

"I saw what was written on her door—it said 'whore'—but she wouldn't tell me who'd put it there."

Stephanie tried to make sense of this. "You're saying someone wrote 'whore' on Chelsea Connor's door?"

The teacher nodded. "She was being bullied, I'm sure of it, but she wouldn't tell me who was doing it."

"Do you have any ideas?"

Before she could answer, the headmistress suddenly stepped in front of Stephanie and laid a small hand on her arm.

"May I help you, detective?" Sister Rose said in a deceptively soft voice.

"I'm speaking with Ms. Kavanaugh."

"This has been a very a very difficult morning for our community, as I'm sure you can imagine, so it's important that we keep things flowing as smoothly as possible. Ms. Kavanaugh has a class to teach, but if you need to answer some questions I'd be happy to talk with you."

"Thanks, Sister, but I really need to talk to her." Stephanie took a step forward, but instead of moving out of her way, the older woman tightened her grip. Stephanie had a sudden memory of listening to Catholic friends telling stories about tough-as-nails nuns who didn't take crap from anyone and certainly not kids in their care. She shook free from her grasp, but the headmistress didn't step back.

"I'm in charge here, Ms. Land," the older woman said. "I'd really prefer it if you talked to me instead."

The smile never wavered and the voice never rose, but there was a challenge in that statement all the same and Stephanie had to choke back the immediate anger it provoked. Who the hell did this woman think she was? This was a police investigation and she'd better, by God, not impede it.

"I need to do my job, Sister," she said, smiling down at the small woman and being careful to keep her voice equally modulated. "You need to let me."

Sister Rose blinked, though whether or not she was intimidated was hard to say. She did let go of Stephanie's arm and stepped quietly to the side.

It was too late, she'd already done her damage—the teacher was gone.

She stood unnoticed and untouched in the jostling crowd that had gathered in the main hall. A jarringly yellow strip of police tape blocked anyone from getting too close to the scene of the crime. The girls pushed against it and a young police officer, wearing an ill-fitting uniform and a self-important expression, ushered them back whenever it looked like the tape was in danger of breaking.

"Chelsea Connor killed herself." The whisper reached her but she didn't respond to it. Her eyes were on the black body bag being hauled out of the tunnel on a stretcher.

Someone was crying and she heard a mournful voice say, "Poor Chelsea." As if they'd actually cared for the whore. The whole school knew what she was, but no one else acted. Only she was strong enough to do what needed to be done.

It had all gone remarkably well. The fear when she'd seen the hook had made Chelsea struggle hard, but the three of them easily overpowered her, hoisted her up. She'd had the knife as backup, but it hadn't been necessary.

She felt strangely at ease after this second death. Of course, Morgan's had been a happy surprise and this killing had been planned, but it was more than that. When she was younger she'd read a book about some indigenous warrior tribe who believed that they absorbed strength from eating their victims after they killed them. Perhaps this was what was happening to her without tasting their flesh.

Whatever caused it, she could feel a shift had occurred. It was if an invisible shield surrounded her, protecting her from being caught. She knew that she could do anything she wanted if it was to girls like Morgan and Chelsea. Not that anyone else would acknowledge this truth. Oh no, the school would enter into mourning Chelsea just like they had Morgan as if anyone really believed that St. Ursula's was worse for their deaths.

Only they would celebrate and she knew she'd have to prod the others. They simply weren't naturals, but she didn't let it deter her. They were learning and that was all that mattered, really.

She was old enough now to understand that very few people had the visions she did. It was like having the stigmata, only her marks from the divine were internal. Even if others could see that strong internal pulse, the way it hummed along inside her, directing her to make flesh bone, they wouldn't have believed.

She didn't attempt to explain it to the others; it was enough that they understood and accepted why these girls had to die. So they would celebrate Chelsea's death while the rest of the school distorted the truth about her and lots of girls rose to claim her as their "best friend." Status through a connection with the dead. It was both morbid and amusing.

She hid her smile, schooling her own features into an appropriate mixture of grief and confusion. "I thought we were safe here," she said and several girls nodded in somber agreement.

Chapter Twenty-two

Everything else on Harriet Wembley's docket got pushed to the side to deal with this case. Fortunately, the only other autopsies waiting to be performed were on an eighty-year-old woman who'd probably died, just as the nursing home aides had said, by slipping as she stepped from shower to bathroom floor, and on a twenty-two-year-old college student killed by his own stupidity in an unfortunate DUI.

"Cause of death is hypoxia, but there's something strange," she announced when Stephanie and Oz showed up at the medical examiner's office Monday evening. Dr. Wembley led the way to Chelsea Connor's body, which was lying on a stainless-steel examining table.

As many deaths as Stephanie had seen in her eight years on the job, nothing ever took away the shock of seeing a body laid out for an autopsy. It seemed strange given the many violent deaths she'd seen that it was here that her nerves threatened to overwhelm her. She had to fight the urge to flee the room. Maybe it was the intensity of the chemical smells along with the usual smells of death and decay, or maybe it was because in this setting, where her investigative skills weren't called for, she could see the victim as a whole person.

In death Chelsea Connor looked especially young, her face and hands still rounded, lacking the angularity that came with aging. Her body was free of wrinkles and scars and the other records of life experience. In contrast to her smooth body, the marks on her neck stood out boldly, deep horizontal lines of reddish purple bruising from where the scarf had choked her. It was here that Dr. Wembley focused.

"There are two lines," she said, "one is slightly higher and lacking the inverted 'V' that is apparent when death comes from hanging."

"What are you saying?" Oz said. "She died twice?"

"I'm saying that there is a second line that indicates she was strangled first, then hanged."

Stephanie looked where she was pointing. She wasn't sure she would have noticed the second line if it hadn't been pointed out. "You're sure the scarf didn't just shift?"

"Positive."

"Maybe she played the game once without suspending her body from the hook and the second time she used the hook."

Dr. Wembley looked thoughtful. "It's possible, but given the degree of compression I don't think it's likely."

"What do you mean?" Oz absently fingered his own neck while he stared at the girl's.

"Let's say she was playing this game alone, choking herself for sexual gratification—I don't think she could pull the knot that tightly against the back of her own neck. That's why people usually suspend themselves from something."

"So we're looking for someone else who played the game with her," Oz said.

Stephanie shook her head. "I'd say we're looking for the person who strangled her and tried to make it look like she died accidentally."

"Well, I'll leave that to you to investigate," Dr. Wembley

said. "She was a healthy girl otherwise. She was sexually active and she'd had an abortion."

"Recently?" Stephanie wondered if this could have been the motivation for killing her, or maybe it was really a suicide and the first time she'd chickened out. But the coroner shook her head.

"No, not recent. Probably a year ago. Perhaps you could subpoena her medical records."

"Were there any other marks consistent with a struggle?"

"She had fibers under her fingernails, but they match the scarf and they're consistent with clawing at it. It's silk, by the way."

She passed over a tray with the knotted scarf on it. Stephanie knotted and then donned gloves before carefully undoing the knot. She unfolded the scarf and she and Oz examined it. Approximately two feet long, the silk rectangle featured black flowers on a ruby background.

"It doesn't look like something a teenage girl would wear," Stephanie said.

"She wasn't exactly wearing it," Oz said.

"Still, don't people usually use something at hand?" she asked the medical examiner.

Harriet Wembley nodded. "You see a lot of belts and ties. But that might be because the typical person who tries autoerotic asphyxiation is male."

"There's nothing to say a female couldn't do it though, right?" Oz looked up from his examination of the scarf.

"Right."

By the time they left the medical examiner's it was dark. Stephanie got behind the wheel and took a swig of coffee, grimacing at its tepid temperature while Oz settled into the passenger seat.

"That poor kid," he said. "I'm just glad we didn't have to tell the parents on this one."

"Ditto." Stephanie pulled out of the parking lot and headed back toward the station. Sister Rose had broken the news over the phone and the parents were flying in tomorrow from, of all places, Brazil. Apparently the father's business was international, which explained why their child was in boarding school.

"I think we need to get back out to the school before they arrive and see if we can find a link between Morgan Wycoff and Chelsea Connor."

"Why do you think there's a link?"

"Two deaths in three weeks at the same place? What else could it be?"

"A coincidence."

Stephanie gave him a look. "Give me a break."

"Would you watch the road?"

She swerved in time to miss a car parked illegally on the shoulder. "I am."

Oz grunted. "If you're going to clip something make sure it's on your side."

Stephanie grinned. "Stop worrying, Grandpa."

"God forbid." Oz crossed himself. "Just wait till you have teenagers—it's a real fear. You think her parents knew about the abortion?"

"Hard to say. Could be they helped arrange it or it could be that she didn't tell anyone. I don't know if we should bring it up or not."

"Unless we think there's some link between the abortion and her death, I don't see why we need to."

"Which brings me back to the link between both vics."

"Okay, I'll admit it's possible, but sometimes weird things happen. Besides, I'm not seeing the connection. One girl dies from exposure, the other from asphyxiation. Those are two totally different causes of death."

"Two unusual deaths just a few weeks apart."

"Fine, I agree they're unusual, but that's all I'm agreeing to."

"You up for some more interviews? We've got the scarf

and the necklace to pursue. I say we head back to the school."

"Okay, let me call home first."

"Better yet, you drop me off, we freshen up, grab some food, and we could be back at the school within an hour and a half?"

Alex was in the kitchen when Stephanie got home, humming along to a song on the radio while tossing together a salad.

"Hey!" He greeted Stephanie with a hug and kiss and she could smell fresh air and earth on him. It was a relief after all the other odors in her day and she held on for longer than necessary, breathing him in.

"What's this? You miss me?"

"Yeah." She didn't want to say that she'd spent the day smelling blood and death and the chemicals used to preserve a body after death.

"I'm making flank steak. Medium rare, right?"

She swallowed. "Um, I'm not very hungry, I think I'll just have a salad."

"But it's already on the grill," he said, looking disappointed. "C'mon, I can't eat it all myself."

"Okay, sure."

"Wow, you're easy," he said and pulled her into his arms again. "You easy in any other ways?"

"Hmm, maybe," she said, kissing him and enjoying the taste of beer on his lips.

"So maybe you can show me later."

"Maybe—oh, shit, no I can't."

He stiffened and pulled back. "What? Don't tell me you're leaving again?"

"We had another death at St. Ursula's today. I've got to get back up there and question some people."

"And that can't wait until tomorrow?"

"No. It's important to move fast. Besides, tomorrow we have to deal with other things."

His face darkened and he slipped his hands off her, turning back to snag his beer from the counter. "You sure you got enough time for dinner?"

"Yes. That's why I came home. So we could eat together."

"That's not all we're supposed to do tonight. We have an appointment with that caterer we heard about from Linda, remember?"

"Oh, shit. I totally forgot. Should we cancel? No, you know what, you go without me. You're better at food than I am, anyway."

He took an angry swig from the bottle and smacked it down on the counter behind him. "Do you really think I want to go to that appointment alone? Jesus Christ, Stephanie, most of the time it's the bride taking care of these things."

"Okay, fine, we'll reschedule."

"You mean I'll reschedule."

"If you could call and cancel that would be great. Otherwise, I'll do it now. Where's the number?"

He gave a short bark of laughter that was far from amused and stalked out of the small kitchen into the combined living room and dining room.

"C'mon, Alex, I only have an hour. Let's not spend it fighting." She reached for his hand, but he pulled it away.

"You have no idea, do you?" he said.

"About what?"

"You have no idea where we keep the planner for our wedding."

"Of course I do!"

He gave her a thin smile and crossed his arms across his chest. "Fine. I'll just wait here while you get it, then."

Stephanie blinked at him. Shit. She stalked toward their bedroom trying to look as if she did know where they kept the damn thing. She could only vaguely recall what it looked like. A blue binder, maybe? She had a dim recollection of watching Alex gathering papers and brochures into an organized pile, but that was as far as it went.

In the bedroom, she looked around and settled on the small oak desk tucked in an alcove next to the closet. They both used it since there wasn't room in their place for more than one desk, but because Alex had brought it with him from his apartment she still thought of it as his.

On the desk's surface was a neatly stacked pile of bills—more of Alex's work—and some of his work in a manila folder, but nothing that hinted of wedding. She was still fruitlessly searching through the drawers when Alex interrupted her.

"It's not there," he said from the doorway.

"Okay, fine," Stephanie said, kicking the bottom drawer closed with such force that the pencil cup on the desktop fell over, pens and pencils rolling over the surface and dropping onto the floor at her feet. "I admit it, okay? I have no idea where it is. Happy now?"

He walked away without a word and she took a deep breath before following him. He opened a drawer in the coffee table in the living room and extracted a blue binder. At least she'd been right about the color.

"Here," he said, handing it over. "Everything's in there—the places we've been considering for our reception, the caterers we've talked to, the florists we liked."

Stephanie took the binder from him and flipped through its contents. "Where's the number for tonight's caterer?"

He grabbed the folder back and whipped out a sheet of paper. "Here. Willow Creek Catering. Remember?"

"Of course!" She snatched the paper from him and took the cordless phone from an end table. "What do you want to do? Reschedule?"

"I want you to take some interest in this process."

"That's what I'm trying to do!"

All at once he bolted toward the back of the room and she

turned to see flames shooting up from the grill. He jerked open the sliding glass door so hard that it bounced back and then closed itself, rattling in its frame. She watched for a few seconds as Alex fiddled with the grill and fought back the flames. At least there wasn't much to catch fire back there. A cement patio with some potted plants they both forgot to water.

Once she was sure he wasn't going to catch fire himself, she canceled the catering appointment, bracing for the blame she was sure he would assign to her for the overdone meat.

The door opened again, but when Stephanie chanced a glance at his face, Alex was smiling. "Just in time," he said. "They're perfect."

So dinner was salvaged and with it his mood. They talked about other things during the meal, his day and the eccentric millionaire client who wanted to re-create the gardens at Versailles on his property. The way the weather had turned cold so early and what that meant for winter and whether they should try to get to Vermont this year for a ski weekend.

Any time they came close to discussing scheduling or the wedding one or the other would steer the conversation carefully in another direction.

For an hour she pretended it was like before, before they got engaged, before she'd gotten her gold shield, before every conversation seemed to end up in a fight over whether she was more committed to him or her career.

At the end of the meal, as they were clearing the plates, she dared to reopen the previous discussion and apologized again for screwing up the evening's meeting.

"It's okay," he said, but his eyes slid from her to the plates in his hand. "We'll reschedule."

"Yeah." She let that go, but picked up the binder and flipped through it. "How about I take care of the next big thing," she offered. "Don't we have to send in the deposit on that hall?"

"You sure you want to go with that one? We liked the place on Orchard, too."

She struggled to remember the difference. "Didn't it have a smaller dance floor?"

"Yeah, but we thought it looked nicer."

He was looking at her now, completely intent on this decision as if it made a huge difference. She swallowed the urge to ask him to go with whatever he wanted and tried to appear just as interested. All the while she was aware of the clock ticking and Oz waiting for her.

"Let's go with the place on Orchard," she said. "I think ambience matters a little more than the dance floor, don't you?"

He nodded, smiling. "Yeah, and it'll be good to have that decision taken care of."

She slipped her shoulder holster back on and adjusted her jacket over it. "So, I'll send them a deposit check."

"I'll take care of it," Alex said.

"No need, I can do it."

He looked skeptical and she felt a flash of anger. "I said I'll do it, Alex."

"All right," he held up his hands in surrender. "I just think we should let them know this week or we might not get the date."

She silenced him with a kiss, pressing him back against the kitchen counter. "This week," she repeated when they came up for air.

He walked with her to the door, one arm wrapped lightly around her waist. "Be careful. I worry about you out there, you know."

"You don't have to."

"But I do."

She nodded and snatched another kiss. "I'll call if I'm going to be super late."

"Don't make promises you can't keep, babe," he said lightly, but she carried that comment with her into the car.

"What are you so quiet about?" Oz asked as they drove along Gashford's dark streets, in and out of the yellow pools created by streetlights.

"Nothing. Just got a lot to do."

"Aah. Wedding, right?"

She nodded, but when she switched the radio on, he took the hint and they drove without speaking.

Chapter Twenty-three

The infirmary was a wing of the original building that had been converted several times since the school's inception, but still owed its primary interior design to the late 1940s. It consisted of one long, large room with numerous twin-size metal bed frames and hospital track curtains that could be pulled around each to form private cubicles. Each bed was made up with white sheets that looked like they'd been boiled and starched, and the pillowcases all had neat little cross-shaped creases in them where they'd been precisely folded and unfolded.

A large black-and-silver crucifix hung above each bed and the place smelled like lemon floor polish, rubbing alcohol, and hydrogen peroxide.

A girl sat on a vinyl-covered examining table just inside the door, whimpering while Linda Whipple, the school nurse, a thin, whey-faced woman with a disposition somewhere between Nurse Ratched and a robot, daubed a cotton pad over cuts on her leg with a dispassion that bordered on cruelty.

"Can I help you?" She turned to Lauren with a harried

expression that seemed strangely incongruous given the vast, empty room.

"I can wait," Lauren said.

"Then have a seat out there." She gestured toward some chairs surrounding a low table in the hall and Lauren dutifully sat down. There were no magazines, just some brochures with graphic and bold-colored illustrations of diseases of the liver, heart, and kidneys, and resting alongside these gruesome informational pamphlets were a pile of devotional tracts with illustrations of a Northern European–looking Jesus with the strangely vacant eyes of a drug addict. It was like a Scared Straight program for hypochondriacs.

Lauren flipped through one nervously while the girl's whimpers turned to moans.

"Hold still, Carrie. You're not one of those crybabies, are you?"

So much for a bedside manner. Lauren was having second thoughts when the girl suddenly appeared in the hall, several large bandages across both knees.

"Okay, back to gym class, but no more running today." The nurse gave the girl a tight smile as she left and glanced at Lauren. "Come on, you're next."

Lauren followed her back into the room and the nurse sat down next to a sharply angular desk complete with a flat-screen computer and a lamp that resembled a praying mantis. Everything, including the gleaming file cabinets to one side, was shiny gunmetal grey. "Now, what's wrong with you?"

"Nothing." Lauren shifted, taking a step back toward the door. "I mean, I just wanted to ask you a few questions, but if this isn't a good time—"

"About what?"

"Sister Agnes."

Linda Whipple looked puzzled for a minute and then her face cleared. "Oh, you're the new teacher, aren't you?" She shook Lauren's hand. "What is it you want to know?"

The nurse gestured for her to sit down and for a brief second Lauren thought that meant the examining table, but then the other woman pushed over a chair.

"I wondered why she had to retire."

"I'm not really at liberty to tell you much, just that Sister Agnes was ill."

"I heard she exhibited signs of Alzheimer's."

"Yes, eventually." The nurse tucked strands of her short, steel gray hair behind her ears. "It was puzzling. She had something that looked like stomach flu, but it didn't clear up."

"I heard from others that she was having hallucinations."

"I really couldn't comment on that." The nurse's voice was neutral. "Why are you so interested, anyway?"

"It's just that she left some books behind and I wanted to send them to her." She'd prepared this story ahead of time and it slipped effortlessly from her lips. "I wasn't sure if she'd be able to enjoy them and I don't have her address."

"I'm sure if you take the books to the main office the headmistress can see that they're sent on to her."

"Oh, I'm happy to do it if I could just have her address."

Nurse Whipple's eyes were a shade of blue so pale that they reflected everything around them. The pupils reminded Lauren of BBs. They fixed on Lauren's face like a bull's-eye. "I can't give you that. My patient records are confidential." She stood up in a gesture that was clearly a dismissal. "I'd try at the main office."

As Lauren exited the building a teacher entered with an arm around a small girl coughing with great vigor. Lauren looked back as they disappeared into the infirmary. On impulse, she followed them back in.

Hovering beside the door and out of sight, she listened to Linda Whipple talking with both teacher and student. "Breathe in," she heard the nurse say and then there was more discussion. At one point she heard what sounded like a drawer opening and then the nurse said something about "history of colds?" The student murmured something between coughing spasms and then Lauren heard "bug going around" and "rest and lots of liquids" and then there were footsteps retreating.

She risked a glance around the corner and saw that the nurse and the teacher were walking the girl toward one of the beds on the same side of the room as the nurse's own desk. They helped the girl sit down and Lauren ducked quickly back out of sight as Linda Whipple suddenly turned and reached up for the curtain.

A ratcheting sound and then Lauren looked again. They were hidden from view behind the white curtain. It was now or never.

She darted into the office area and saw that a key stood in the file cabinet. The drawer opened soundlessly, but it took a minute of fumbling to extract Sister Agnes Crowley's file from the other C's. Lauren lifted it out with slippery fingers and soundlessly shut the drawer.

Just as she was about to step out, she heard the sound of footsteps coming back. Shit, shit. She stepped behind the screen that stood beside the examination table. The teacher walked past, never looking in her direction.

Lauren risked a glance out, saw that the curtain was still drawn around the cubicle, and darted out of the office. She took the emergency exit, out the back door and away from the other teacher, and then cut across the grass verge holding the folder tightly against her chest, the name hidden from view.

"Ms. Kavanaugh?" The voice came from a distance behind her and Lauren picked up the pace, hoping the brisk wind provided her with an excuse. She would have broken into a run, but that wasn't possible. No crutches anymore, but her ankle was still sore, still weak, would still betray her if she moved any faster.

"Miss Kavanaugh!"

She couldn't pretend anymore. She stopped, turned with a

smile on her face, clutching the folder tightly against her coat, using the excuse of the cold to hold it pressed against her chest.

Leonard Whitecliff came forward with a smile, his cheeks slapped red from the cold. "I'm glad I caught you," he said, making her start until he continued, "We signed up for AV equipment on the same morning and I'm wondering if you'd mind switching to another day?"

"I'm sure we can resolve it," she smiled, trying to move on, but he fell in step beside her, prattling on about this scheduling conflict and she nodded her head, kept nodding, yes, yes, they would have to work that out.

"Let me check my schedule and I'll get back to you," she said at last, anxious to get away.

Inside her room, with the doors locked, she opened the folder. There was the medical history of Sister Agnes Crowley, fewer pages than she would have thought for a woman sick enough to leave the school.

Only when she looked closer was it clear that most of the information dealt with the last two years and that five sheets alone dealt with the six months before Sister Agnes summarily left St. Ursula's.

"Complaining of chest pain," read one report, "disoriented and tired."

There were reports of a physical that she otherwise passed and blood tests that were normal. On one of the last sheets, a month before Agnes Crowley had left St. Ursula's, a note had been scrawled at the bottom: "Early symptoms of Alzheimer's?"

The date on the page corresponded with the date on the second journal page Lauren had found.

And nowhere in the medical records was any mention of girls or trouble or anything tangible that Lauren could take to the police. It did, however, reveal one very substantial piece of information: Sister Agnes's new address.

A sharp knock on the door interrupted her reading. Lauren quickly closed the file and slipped it into a desk drawer before responding. What if it was Linda Whipple? She schooled her features into blandness in anticipation of fielding the nurse's accusation, but it was Candace at the door.

"A *New York Times* reporter is coming to do a story on the school and Sister Rose has handpicked students for him to interview. There are two from our houses, Elizabeth Lincoln and Stacy Chin. We've got to make sure they're neat and tidy and deliver them to the main office ASAP."

"There's no need to be nervous, girls," Sister Rose said at the same time that she flicked lint off one girl's sleeve and adjusted the Peter Pan collar on another's blouse.

Lauren didn't know how the girls felt, but that sort of statement just made her feel more nervous. She stood to one side and watched them taking turns checking their faces and hair in the gold-framed mirror that hung above an antique refectory table in the school's meeting room. This was where the interview with the *New York Times* reporter would be conducted, Sister Rose had decided, and it was easy to see why.

It was a room dedicated to preserving the past and it exemplified everything traditional about the school. This was a room where prospective families met with the headmistress or school counselor; this was the room where alumnae with deep pockets were treated to high tea.

A long sofa upholstered in crimson velvet faced two wing chairs in a subdued print, all of which flanked a log-burning fireplace with an imposing stone mantel that had the school's crest carved in its center.

There were heavy draperies at the windows and glass-encased bookcases framed one wall while an enormous landscape of what looked like a fog-covered sea graced the other.

"You'll answer his questions," Sister Rose said. "Don't volunteer anything beyond the questions. If you don't know how to answer a question, don't say anything. Mr. Pierce or I will handle it."

"Yes, Sister," the girls recited. Lauren wondered if they knew that they'd been picked as much for the differences in their ethnicities as for their sterling records. There was Tasha, African American and a budding Shakespearean actress; Maria, both parents from Spain; Stacy, Chinese American; and Elizabeth, the All-American blond beauty.

They were all attractive, all smart, all intended to show the world that this awful thing that had happened was just an aberration. Except, of course, that it wasn't. This was the second death at St. Ursula's in a month.

That Sister Rose herself was nervous was also obvious to everyone in the room, except perhaps the headmistress herself. She even reached up a hand to touch her short gray hair, startling Lauren, who'd always assumed that nuns had no personal vanity at all.

"Remember, girls," Ryland Pierce chimed in, "we want to make sure that we give the message that St. Ursula's is a safe place and a good school."

Sister Rose added, "Do not volunteer details about what happened. He won't know much and that's just how we want to keep it."

"But what if asks us something specific?" Stacy said. "You don't want us to lie?"

"Of course not!" Sister Rose looked offended. "Just don't offer more information. If you can keep your answers to yes and no that would be even better."

A buzz from the intercom interrupted her. It was the signal from the office that the reporter had arrived. Sister Rose clapped her hands. "All right, girls, places."

The girls dutifully filed over to sit close to one another on the long sofa. Lauren and Candace sat down in chairs pulled to either side. Ryland pulled another chair uncomfortably close to Lauren. "Ready for the show?" he whispered, his breath tickling her ear and then he chuckled. She moved her

head, feeling sweat beading against the back of her neck.
The girls chattered quietly, all of them looking relaxed.
Stacy actually looked bored.

Sister Rose nodded at the guidance counselor and swept
out of the room, managing to look much taller than her small
5'3" stature.

When she walked back into the room with the reporter,
the first thought that crossed Lauren's mind was that a man
so small couldn't possibly be a threat to anyone. Daniel
Stein introduced himself with a surprisingly firm handshake.
He seemed positively elfin, small-boned and standing maybe
5'1", but he was also extremely beautiful, as if someone had
taken a male model and given him a shrinking potion.

He had short-cropped, shiny black hair, an aquiline nose,
and a nicely shaped mouth. He wore clothes obviously hand
tailored since they hung on his diminutive frame so well.
The navy blazer, fawn trousers, and button-down blue shirt
gave him a casual yet preppy look that somehow managed to
be elegant as well, in the way that quality clothing always did.
But it was his eyes that made him so distinct, Lauren thought.
They were large and a startlingly shade of clear blue, and he
turned them on each person in turn, a small smile tugging at
the corner of his lips.

Sister Rose gestured to the wing chair, though he probably would have fit better on the ottoman, but Lauren noticed
that he perched on the edge of the seat, so his feet didn't
dangle. "I'm so sorry for your loss," he began, the corners of
his mouth quirking downward, eyes shifting to include
everyone in this gesture of sympathy.

"Thank you, Mr. Stein." Sister Rose murmured.

"Please, call me Daniel." Another smile for everyone and
he pulled an equally elegant black notebook out of his
pocket, flipping it open and slipping a hand into an inside
jacket pocket to retrieve a beautiful black pen. "Tell me
about what happened to Chelsea Connor."

Sister Rose quietly cleared her throat. "Miss Connor died

as a result of a game gone wrong," she said. "I'm sure you've heard of the choking game?"

Daniel Stein nodded sagely and she continued. "Yes, well, this was clearly a case of that dangerous game, only it proved to be fatal."

"She died while playing the game?"

"Yes."

"You mean she strangled herself?"

The words sounded harsh and one of the girls quietly gasped. Two spots of color darkened Sister Rose's cheeks.

"Yes, though I wouldn't describe it that way. Obviously, Chelsea did not want to die—it was an unfortunate accident."

"Have you had other incidents like this at the school?"

Ryland took that one. "No, not at all."

Daniel Stein's beautiful eyes widened. "Oh?" he glanced down at his notebook and flipped back a few pages. "But I thought I understood that you had another tragic death at the school just last month?"

Unlike Sister Rose, when Ryland Pierce was embarrassed his skin turned an unfortunate shade best described as puce. "Yes, well, not by the choking game is what I meant," he blustered.

"These two tragic accidents are not related," Sister Rose said.

"How did the other student die?"

"Exposure," Sister Rose said. "Again, an unfortunate accident."

"Are the rumors about satanic rituals true?"

"Absolutely not," Sister Rose said.

Daniel Stein scribbled something, nodding, but Lauren suspected that he already knew everything about the death and just wanted to get the official reaction.

"What was Chelsea Connor like?" he asked next, turning to the girls. Stacy blinked in surprise and all of them sat up straighter.

Tasha said, "She was a nice enough girl."

"Did you know her well?"

"Everybody knows everybody at St. Ursula's," Elizabeth Lincoln said. "We're a small, close-knit school."

This answer had Sister Rose beaming and Ryland's skin returning to normal. "We consider our community a family," she added.

"But even within families, some members are closer than others," Stein said with a slight smile. "Were any of you close friends with Chelsea?"

Most of the girls shook their heads. Candace said, "She lived in my dorm, but I couldn't say that we'd grown particularly close."

"Did you know of her interest in the choking game?"

Candace shook her head. "Absolutely not. If I'd known I would have tried to talk her out of it."

"It's stupid," Tasha said. "Obviously it's dangerous. There are safer ways to get a high."

"Chelsea's behavior wasn't typical of St. Ursula's students," Elizabeth said. "At St. Ursula's we're taught that our bodies are temples."

The other girls offered similar platitudes about the school's values and Daniel Stein nodded and scribbled. All at once he turned to Lauren. "You were Chelsea's teacher?"

She nodded, trying not to look away, but his eyes seemed to bore through her.

"You look familiar. Have we met before?"

Her legs tensed and she pushed back in her seat. "I don't think so."

"Really? I was sure I knew you. What's your name?"

Sweat was prickling on her scalp. "Lauren Kavanaugh."

"K-A-?"

She spelled it for him and watched as he wrote it down, resisting the impulse to grab the book and pen from him and hurl them across the room.

"Did you know Miss Connor?"

"Not well. I'm a new teacher."

"But you'd taught her and talked with her?"

Had she talked to her before she'd seen the bruises? Probably not, aside from any brief exchange in class. That had been the extent of their contact. Lauren felt suddenly ashamed that she hadn't pushed harder at Chelsea, hadn't demanded to know what was going on.

But even Ryland Pierce had said that the girls managed to work most things out and that disagreements between teenage girls was common and not necessarily anything to worry about. Chelsea was a girl prone to wearing her uniform skirt too high and her blouses too tight, but there were a lot of teenage girls like that, desperate to show the world their sexuality. It didn't mean that they all played the choking game. If you could even call it that. It looked a lot more like autoerotic asphyxiation, but either no one had told Sister Rose the difference or she'd decided to adopt this sanitized version of the death.

"Did any of you see any signs that Chelsea played or was interested in playing the choking game?" Daniel Stein asked of the girls.

Tasha and Maria shook their heads, but Stacy said that she'd heard some girls were interested in it because their boyfriends told them about it.

"Chelsea was always like that," Elizabeth added. "She wasn't really like the other girls at St. Ursula's. She was more interested in boys than in the school."

Sister Rose interjected, "Now, now Elizabeth, we mustn't speak ill of the dead."

"Sorry, Sister," Elizabeth said, ducking her head a little.

"That's all right, dear, you're just telling Mr. Stein what you observed."

Sister Rose's voice didn't change but Lauren sensed that she was really glad to hear Chelsea Connor's reputation called into question, rather than the school's.

Daniel Stein asked some difficult questions about security at the school and access to the tunnel, which Ryland Pierce fielded with a degree of aplomb worthy of a politician. Lauren wondered just how often he'd had to do this kind of damage control.

The sound of the bell chiming ended the interview. Sister Rose stood up and everyone else did, too. At her nod, the girls said their good-byes, accepted Mr. Stein's thanks, and left to go to their respective classes. Sister Rose walked them to the door, speaking quietly with them before they departed.

Lauren stretched, not realizing how stiffly she'd held her body, and along with Candace moved their straight-backed chairs back against one wall. She looked out one of the large arched windows.

Students were crossing the campus singly and in groups, identical figures dressed in navy blue and white, their hair and skin color the only major differences between them. Tiny flakes of snow floated through the air and Lauren watched as the girls from the interview suddenly appeared below her. They looked like they were in an intense discussion.

"Excuse me, Ms. Kavanaugh."

Daniel Stein stood at her shoulder. She hadn't heard him approach. He smiled at her and shook his head.

"I'm trying to figure out where I know you from. You aren't a Dartmouth alum, are you?"

She shook her head.

"No? Too bad, I thought maybe that was it."

She tried to return the smile, but it stuck in her throat. "I don't think we've met," she said.

Sweat trickled down her back, between her shoulder blades. Why was the heat turned so high in this room? It was like being in a sauna.

"Maybe not. I'm not going to be arrogant enough to stand here and argue otherwise, but I just have a feeling. Maybe

I've just seen you or met you through someone else. You know, the whole six degrees of separation thing."

She nodded, her head feeling leaden. "Maybe."

"Don't worry, it'll come to me. I'm really good at faces, never forget someone once I've seen them."

Chapter Twenty-four

It was practically the first time since classes began that Lauren was actually happy to go teach. Anything to escape from that strange little reporter with his penetrating gaze.

She thought she'd handled him poorly, not at all like Amanda. She would have lied with ease, but Lauren wasn't Amanda. She was sure Daniel Stein knew when he first looked at her, certain he was just being polite when he tried to place where they'd met, but she'd been lucky. He didn't know. With any luck he would go back to the city, publish his story about St. Ursula's, and that would be the end of it.

The classroom where she taught American History was in one of the older buildings, which seemed appropriate. At some point the wooden desks and chairs had probably been state of the art, but that time was at least fifty years earlier and now they were older than the parents of the children who sat in them.

The class full of sophomore girls were chattering loudly when she entered five minutes before the bell rang, the girls huddled together, some perched on desktops and others straddling chairs. The room smelled faintly of chalk dust and lemon oil and more sharply of competing perfumes liberally applied.

Lauren took her time setting up, noting how hyper the girls looked and sounded. One by one, they noticed her presence and gradually the crowd dispersed into orderly rows of students. They submitted to her roll call without taking issue, but as soon as it was over one of the girls waved her hand.

"Yes, Natalie?"

"Is it true that Chelsea Connor killed herself?"

Lauren hesitated for a moment before saying, "I don't know." This was a lie. She'd heard the details from Ryland Pierce.

"I heard she hanged herself," the girl said and someone gasped at the word. Another girl with a long face that reminded Lauren of a greyhound vehemently denied it, others chiming in.

"Chelsea wouldn't do that," they said.

Then some others defended the first girl and then they were interrupting each other in their eagerness to talk about what had happened.

The words scrambled in Lauren's head—suicide, killing, police, blood—she didn't want to talk about it, think about it. Her legs felt heavy and she thought of Sister Agnes's notes and what had happened to her. There was the faint smell of something burning. She sat down heavily in the teacher's chair.

She couldn't blame them for wanting to discuss Chelsea Connor's death instead of what happened in American history more than three hundred years ago, but she had to control this, this wasn't teaching. If the headmistress happened by or Pierce with his smarmy smile—she didn't know which would be worse, she only knew she had to stop this. With the flat of her hand she rapped sharply once and again on the desk. They fell quiet then, their heads swiveling front, their eyes fixed on her with resignation or boredom or barely concealed insolence.

Swallowing hard, pushing away the feeling that she was being stripped by them, the layers of her self peeled away and each found wanting, she looked down at her notes and began.

"We were talking last time about the Salem witch trials," she said in her teacher's voice, poised and professional. She hoped that the prospect of someone else's hanging would distract them from Chelsea's death. "We began by reviewing the history of the Puritans and what came before the events in Salem. Today, we'll discuss the trials themselves and the victims of the hysteria that seized one town. If you'll turn to page one hundred twenty in your textbooks."

The students soon settled down, engrossed in the story of how a group of girls of about their age could have convinced an entire town that they were being possessed by demons sent by witches.

She wondered if any of them saw the parallels to Morgan's death or Chelsea's. Were there girls in this room who'd called Morgan a witch or written "whore" in lipstick on Chelsea's door? They all looked so young, so innocent, so incapable of anything so cruel, but then so had the girls in Salem.

"Maybe some of the girls really believed it," a student said toward the end of class. "Maybe they got caught up in the hysteria and really thought they were possessed."

"Okay," Lauren said. "Let's talk about that. How many think the girls were simply lying? Raise your hands."

Less than half the class raised their hands and when she called for more comment, one of the girls said, "Well, some of these accused witches were really outsiders, right? If they didn't share the faith of the town doesn't it seem natural that the other residents would blame them for any problems?"

Lauren glanced down at her class list for the name. "Is that natural, Tiffany?" She tried to keep her voice neutral. "Is it natural to ostracize people because they're different or accuse them of things just because they're different?"

The girl shrugged, tossing long, caramel-colored curls over one shoulder. "I don't know, maybe. I think it's just human nature to blame the people that won't fit in."

Lauren was so shocked she didn't know how to reply, but was saved when another student jumped in to disagree. The two students debated and other students joined in. All in all it was a successful and lively class discussion, but Lauren was still shaken by some of the girl's callous comments when she headed to the main office after class to pick up her mail.

Alice LaRue was standing next to the wooden slots where each employee's mail was placed upon delivery.

"I heard you know the *New York Times* reporter," she said, eyes wide with interest. She was draped in various shades of blue, giving her the appearance of a fabric store.

"He thinks we've met before."

"Probably trying to pick you up," the other teacher said. "Though I also heard that he'd be a little short for you."

"More than a little," Lauren said acidly. There was an exceptionally big pile of letters in her slot that day. She had to wrestle it out. "And how come you're so well informed, anyway?"

Alice laughed. "Don't look at me like that—you know how schools are. Everyone's in each other's business desperate to have something new to talk about."

"Yes, well, there's nothing to this story. Just a case of mistaken identity." She kept her face averted and sifted through the mail as it were the most fascinating thing in the world. Junk, junk, bill, bill. The third notice from the credit card company made her heart sink. She was going to have to send them something. At this rate, she'd be lucky if she paid off everything by the time she was forty.

"Hey, this got in my box by mistake." Alice held out a white envelope printed with Lauren's name and the school's address.

Lauren stood stock still staring at it. She recognized that penmanship, the careful, printed script.

"You're the lucky one, getting personal mail. C'mon don't you want it?"

"Of course." Lauren forced herself to take it, but she didn't open it, sticking it between the books she carried. She thought she could feel its added weight.

It hadn't even been forwarded. He'd found her just like he always did. She couldn't hide.

The question of the teacher's identity niggled at Daniel all through the long drive back to Manhattan. He wove deftly back and forth in lanes of increasingly congested traffic and darted in front of an enormous SUV near the entrance to the Lincoln Tunnel. The driver flashed him the finger and Daniel grinned, resisting the urge to wave. He'd done that once and an irate trucker had crunched the bumper on his Prius.

Given his small stature, he had to have the front seat ratcheted as far forward as possible, and when the airbag deployed it smacked him in the face with such force that his nose bled and his face was badly bruised. His limited height had ceased to matter to him years ago, but he was justifiably vain about his features. Now he let such insults go. Let the other guy think he'd won, it didn't matter to Daniel Stein.

In the middle of the stalled traffic in the tunnel he had a flash of recognition, a moment's surety darting through his mind like a fast-swimming fish, vanishing in the depths before he could catch hold.

"I do know you," he said out loud, slapping the steering wheel with satisfaction. "It'll come back, it always does. I never forget a face."

He let it go then, slipping in a CD of classic Sarah Vaughan and letting his mind wander with the music. It would come to him in time, he just had to let it go.

Letting things go was something Daniel Stein did well. As the only height-challenged member in an average-sized family he'd learned early that life held extra challenges for him. Challenges were how his mother described it. Nobody spoke about his height as if it were a disability, though in his early years his parents had taken him to specialist after specialist trying to find out the cause and possible cure for his short stature.

There were uncomfortable exams and a series of X-rays, MRIs, brain scans, and every test the medical profession could possibly think of to measure both his physical and intellectual abilities.

He distinctly remembered the doctor who'd examined him as if he were a creature and announced to his parents, "He's a midget."

His mother, dressed as if it were the high holidays as she did for each and every doctor visit, had stiffened at the word. Daniel remembered watching his father's hand rest lightly on her arm, a gentle restraint.

"It's a genetic anomaly," the doctor, a tall, heavy orthopedist with yellow teeth and bad breath, said. "It's not your fault and there is no cure. It's just a fluke. Midgets are freaks of nature."

"My son is not a freak," his mother said in a voice very close to a growl.

That had been the last of the doctor visits and the last time anybody in Daniel's family ever mentioned his height, at least in his presence. In their home outside of Philadelphia there were extra stepstools for Daniel and his father took him to his own tailor, teaching him early to value made-to-order suits.

It worked. He never felt that he had to compensate professionally for his height. Adjustments in a taller world were so much a part of his life that he made them unconsciously and there'd actually been a few times when he was some-times surprised when other people mentioned it.

If asked, he would have answered that being small had ac-tually benefited his life. It had certainly affected his choice of career. Being small and unobtrusive had given him access to news far earlier than his friends and he was often asked to eavesdrop on adult conversations. From this he learned how to recount stories in a quick and interesting way.

It was natural for him to choose journalism and after a se-ries of positions at lesser publications he'd finally reached the nexus of his professional ambitions: the *New York Times*.

Three years later he was still excited by the job but his ambition had shifted. He didn't just want to be a *Times* re-porter. He wanted to win a Pulitzer and become known for his byline as much as for the institution backing his work. He hadn't found the story yet that was going to get him there, but he knew he would. And the strange deaths at the Jersey prep school might just be the one. The familiar-looking teacher just added to his conviction that this was a story worth pursuing.

His desire to get a story written while it was still fresh in his mind kept him from Googling Lauren Kavanaugh until he'd finished a rough draft. That done, he sat back in his comfortable chair in the newsroom and began an Internet search with all the self-satisfaction of a man used to finding his prey.

Only his hunt yielded nothing. He couldn't find Lauren Kavanaugh, at least not one that matched her description. There was an seventy-year-old woman with the same name in Kansas who'd earned her fifteen minutes of fame by stop-ping a would-be burglar with a round from her very own AK-47. Other than that, nobody of that name had garnered much attention.

On a whim and because he couldn't stand not knowing,

Daniel next checked the alumni records of his schools, Dartmouth and Northwestern, but again found nothing.

At that point, one of the editors stopped by his desk to ask about another story he was covering and Daniel put the search for Lauren Kavanaugh back into the corner of his mind where it would continue to prick him.

Chapter Twenty-five

One of them was crying for Chelsea, a small trickle of tears freezing on her face in the cold night air. It was sad that she'd died, the girl said when questioned by the others, but then their leader asked, "Do you think that whore deserves your tears?" And that stopped the crying.

They prayed first, linking hands like they always did, though now their hands were gloved, asking the Lord to guide their work because it was hard work and they wanted to do God's will.

"What we've been chosen to do is hard," the leader said as she lit the sacred fire. "Only the chosen can do this work. Only the chosen can do what God commands and help rid the world of evil."

The fire started, but the flames licking the wood were low because snow had been falling steadily all day.

"To every thing there is a season, and every time a purpose under heaven," the leader intoned. "A time to be born and a time to die."

She took the lock of hair and the photo out of her pocket. "We consign our sister Chelsea to the dust from whence she came." She dropped the photo and the lock of hair on top of the wood and they sizzled and burned, the photo curling in on itself, the lock of blond hair sparking.

Someone sniffled and the leader whipped her head from the fire to fix them all with a stern look. "If it was easy, you wouldn't be chosen! Do you think it was easy for Christ? Do you think God wants us to take the easy path?"

The hoods covering their heads cast shadows over their faces, so the leader couldn't see their eyes, but the lips of one were trembling. "Walking in the path of the righteous is hard," the leader said, speaking softly now. "Evil must be stamped out. Whores are evil. If they are allowed to exist they'll contaminate everyone around them."

The photo burned upward until only Chelsea Connor's eyes remained to stare at them.

After the others were gone, the leader stood alone in the woods stirring the flecks of the photo in the dying fire, absorbing the power from Chelsea.

She'd imagined it was Chelsea's bones being consigned to flame, not just her photo. Transubstantiation. She smiled and sniffed the fresh, cold air mingled with wood smoke.

There was more to do, much more and it became clearer with each step she took. There would be others now. Morgan and Chelsea were only the first. She couldn't tell the group that. They didn't understand, just like Christ's disciples. She understood Him better now, knew what it felt like to be alone in the world, secure in the knowledge of one's own power but with no one else who truly understood.

She had learned early the necessity of keeping it quiet, of hiding the truth from a world not ready to face it. Even her own parents, as much as they loved her, didn't know what it was like to see the beauty of the bones beneath the flesh, to see death as a natural part of life.

To see fear in the eyes of another, to see the surprise of life slipping away—this was the pinnacle of the human experience! Even small creatures felt that fear, but the sensations had been more intense with Morgan's death and now Chelsea. She'd watched Chelsea's eyes while she was hanging, seen the fear slipping away, watched that moment between life and death, absorbing it, becoming part of the transcendence.

Soon there would be another death, she could feel it coming, the internal pulse humming happily along. She wanted it to be Lauren Kavanaugh, but not yet. There were still things to learn about the teacher, a new method to decide. She enjoyed the planning, too, but it was the death she needed.

Someone else then before Miss Kavanaugh. She didn't know who, but she would wait and it would be revealed. Looking up at the great expanse of black sky, she thought of how she was becoming stronger, more powerful. It seemed to her that the gift had never been clearer, that she moved as someone invisible, soaring through space without fear of detection. She was like an angel, the angel of death.

Chapter Twenty-six

The earliest train on Saturday was at 7 A.M., but the local taxi service didn't begin operating until 7:30 and Lauren certainly couldn't hike all the way into town even if her ankle hadn't been sprained.

She made the 8 o'clock train just before it left the station and then spent the hour ride north fretting that she wouldn't be able to find the address that she'd written on the small piece of paper clutched in her hand.

Blessed Sacrament Retirement Home, Lauren read for the umpteenth time. Woodshire Boulevard, Union, New Jersey.

At the station in Union, Lauren had to wait a half-hour for a cab and then the foreign-born driver had to call in to dispatch for directions.

"This place is in the countryside," he said to Lauren as he drove, but it turned out he was wrong, unless a highway littered with strip malls counted as country. She'd pictured rolling fields and a Colonial-style redbrick building. Instead, there was a long parking lot, short strip of lawn, and several low-slung buildings, putty-colored with olive-green trim, scattered about like children's blocks.

The inside of the building seemed as depressing as the outside, part hospital, part cheap hotel with the same bad art hanging on the walls and the same bad smells lingering in the hallways.

"Are you on the list?" the woman at the front desk said when Lauren said that she was there to visit Sister Agnes Crowley.

"What list?"

The woman produced a clipboard from below and slapped it down on the countertop. "The list of approved visitors. You just can't walk in here, you got to be on the list."

"I'm a colleague of hers," Lauren said. "I'm sure she'd like to see me."

The woman wore a medical smock in primary colors with smiling bears on it. Her own face was grouchy. "So you're not on the list?"

"No, no, I'm not."

The woman, whose nameplate read, "Glory," took the clipboard back very slowly, rolling her eyes. "Well, you can have a seat then, because I'm going to have to call."

There was no one else in the waiting room and the magazines on the cheap pine coffee table were at least four months old. Lauren flipped through an ancient copy of *People* and tried not to think about what would happen if the person at the end of the phone wouldn't let her in. Or what if they were calling the school? That would be even worse— what on earth would she say to Sister Rose? *I felt bad about my predecessor's abrupt departure and thought I'd visit her?*

"You can go ahead," Glory interrupted her thoughts. She waved Lauren over to her. "Here, you got to wear this pass." She handed over a clip-on pass with Lauren's name printed in crooked letters under the red, preprinted VISITOR. "And you can't go alone. Someone's got to take you over to the Spring Lark Wing."

That someone turned out to be a girl of about eighteen

with bad skin and purple glasses, who smiled when she heard who Lauren was visiting.

"She'll be so happy," she said of Sister Agnes, leading the way down hallways dotted with old women in wheelchairs. Lauren's eyes stung from the heavy scent of antibacterial cleaner and the underlying aroma of urine.

A shrunken woman in a pink housecoat propelled a wheelchair slowly down the hall with her slippered feet. Pinned carefully to her thin white hair was the black veil from a modified habit that had gone out of fashion some thirty years earlier.

She reached out and pulled on the girl's baby-blue smock. "I need a doctor," she croaked. "I need to see one real bad."

"I know, Sister Clara," the girl said soothingly. "They think they're not getting medical care," she said to Lauren after they were past. "And it's better just to agree with them sometimes."

They passed a woman with rheumy blue eyes who stared at Lauren, drool running in a thin stream from the corner of her open mouth.

"These places scare me," Lauren confided. The girl just laughed and Lauren didn't know if that constituted agreement or not. She wondered what it was like to end up like this at the end of a lifetime of service. Certainly most of the women in the hall didn't seem to know any better, but they passed some rooms where women were reading or tending small potted plants lining their respective windowsills.

They paused outside room number 512 and the girl tapped on the door. "Sister Agnes?" she called. There was no answer, but Lauren thought she heard someone moving inside.

"You've got a visitor, Sister," the girl said in a louder voice and she winked at Lauren, an inane grin in place. Lauren forced a smile in return.

The girl pushed open the door and Lauren saw a woman

in a plain brown dress sitting in a chair by a window that looked out on one corner of scraggly lawn and the farthest section of the parking lot.

"Sister Agnes," the girl began in a louder voice and the woman held up a hand.

"I heard you the first time, Alison, thanks." She appeared to be absorbed in something. "I'm just finishing the crossword."

"Of course you are," the girl said in a cheery voice that set Lauren's teeth on edge. She winked again at Lauren. "Just go ahead and sit down," she said in a lower, normal voice and nodded at the other chair in the room.

"Ms. Kavanaugh is here to talk with you, Sister," she said again in a louder voice. "I'm sure you'll have plenty to talk about, since she's from St. Ursula's."

At this the woman's head lifted from the newspaper in her lap. She was short and old and her dress, which was thirty years out of date with its zip front and wide, pointy collar, looked like it was made from 100 percent polyester. The way she held the newspaper had pushed up the skirt so the doughy skin of her kneecaps was exposed, contrasting strangely with the tan support knee-highs that ended in a pair of fuzzy green slippers.

"I don't recognize you," she said with a frown. "What do you teach?"

"History," Lauren said, perching on a plastic-and-metal chair opposite the old woman's armchair. Besides the two chairs the only other furniture in the room was the complicated looking hospital bed and a pasteboard dresser, its top carefully lined with photographs.

"That's my subject, was my subject." Sister Agnes looked puzzled. "I am a teacher, or was a teacher. No one will tell me what my status is."

Her silver hair was cut very short and Lauren could see lines of shiny pink scalp. Her hands reminded Lauren of pastry, soft and fine and crisscrossed with hundreds of tiny lines.

"I'm teaching your classes for now," Lauren said.

"Oh? Well, I hope you're remembering to make the girls take notes. They won't learn anything if they don't take good notes."

"Yes, I'll remember that."

Sister Agnes nodded at her before turning her attention back to the newspaper.

"I'm staying in your rooms," Lauren pushed on, "and I found these." She took the papers out of her purse and Sister Agnes reached out a small hand and snatched them.

"Thank you," she said in a prim voice and without looking at them placed them carefully on the bookshelf underneath the windowsill.

"You wrote about having troubles with some students." Lauren looked from the elderly woman to the bookshelf and back again. "Do you remember what you were writing about?"

Sister Agnes frowned, looking as if she were concentrating, and then shook her head with a slight smile. "No. Not really."

"Maybe if you read the papers again," Lauren said. She stood up and reached for them, but the small woman got a hand on them first.

"These are mine," she said. "You can't have them."

"I brought them to you," Lauren said, struggling to take them back.

"Let go! Let go or I'll call the nurse!"

Lauren immediately let go of the papers and the nun settled back in her chair staring balefully at her. She looked out the window while stroking the papers and then seemed to forget that Lauren was there at all, staring out the window again.

"Sister Agnes?" Lauren said softly after a few minutes.

The woman turned slowly to look at her with a beatific smile that made the hair rise on the back of Lauren's neck. "Yes, dear? Do I know you?"

"I'm Lauren Kavanaugh. A teacher at St. Ursula's."

The woman's smile broadened. "Why that's where I teach," she said with delight. "What do you teach?"

"History."

"Me, too!"

"Please take a look at the papers in your lap," Lauren said. "We need your comments on them for the department."

"Of course, dear."

She unfolded the papers and then looked up helplessly. "I'm afraid I can't see anything without my glasses."

Lauren found the thin silver wire-rims on the dresser and handed them to the nun. Sister Agnes put them on carefully and then blinked several times before finally, painstakingly, unfolding the papers in her lap.

She appeared to be reading the pages, but Lauren wasn't really sure until she saw the old woman's hands begin to shake. Then the woman began muttering something, rocking back and forth, her head bent over the shaking pages.

Lauren leaned forward and strained to hear her say, "I tried to tell her, but she wouldn't listen."

"Who, Sister Agnes?" she said softly, afraid that interrupting would make her stop talking. "Who did you tell?"

"Sister Rose." The rocking increased.

"What did you tell her?"

"I tried, I went three times! Three is a special number you know." She looked up at Lauren. "The Trinity, of course, and the Lord's ministry began in his thirty-third year. And his death." Her face clouded. "I told her there was evil in the school. I told her, but she wouldn't listen."

"Why was the school evil, Sister Agnes?"

"Not the school," Sister Agnes said. "Not the school, though maybe it helped it along. I don't know, but I tried. It was the girls."

"Which girls?"
"The bad ones. Oculus."

Daniel Stein lived in a loft on the top floor of a Lower East Side building in an old industrial neighborhood whose more recent inhabitants had been junkies and squatters. What a difference a few years made. With property in the West Village and SoHo beyond reach, ambitious but cash-poor urbanites looked elsewhere for housing. "Gentrification" was used so often to describe his neighborhood that sometimes Daniel thought of that as its name.

He was lucky to get his loft before housing skyrocketed. It helped that he found it when it was still in its holes-in-the-roof, pigeon-crap and broken-glass phase, before some ambitious real estate investor flipped it. It helped that his parents offered to give him the down payment.

It had taken just over six months, but at the end of the renovation he had a completely new, modern space with lots of sleek wood and stainless steel. He had skylights installed and hung the freshly painted walls with the better pieces from emerging artists. It was his place, designed by him and for him. It was the first time in his life that he could reach the kitchen and bathroom sinks without standing on a stepstool.

At the end of a long day, he liked nothing better than to take the short subway ride from midtown, make the brisk walk two blocks from the station toward the river, turn left at the laundromat, go one block up and arrive at his personal oasis. If a man's home was his castle, than Daniel Stein's was that in miniature.

Tall friends felt as if they'd arrived in Lilliput. He was not above enjoying their awkwardness in his space, experiencing a guilty pleasure at watching them stoop to reach drinks left on the coffee table or sit kneecaps to nose on his small-scale furniture.

He'd come home early today, having worked late the

evening before covering the mayor's press conference, but he didn't let the early hour deter him from his usual ritual of preparing a drink at the small teak bar in the living room.

Two fingers of good vodka, a shot of tonic, and a lime slice over ice in a club glass. He carried the drink with him over to the windows and looked out at the rooftops of the buildings across from his and down at the bustling streets below.

There was a faint hum of traffic and the distant whine of a siren, but the sounds were softer than the ice clinking in his glass because he'd paid the extra money for triple-pane windows.

He sucked vodka off an ice cube and thought about his search. It had been more than a week since his interview at the school and that second death was already old news. Other events rose to take the media's time and attention.

A released mental patient somehow purchased a gun and got off a lucky round at the mayor, shattering a window at Barney's and wounding a bodyguard.

An aging socialite was murdered by her young lover, who argued that the fall he'd helped her take down a flight of marble steps had been assisted suicide.

A sweatshop raid in the garment district yielded more than fifty illegals and at least half that number were children.

Every story had potential and he covered each one with due diligence, but each day he felt a persistent pricking in his brain, his desire to follow up on the school story becoming more need than want.

He took his drink with him to the small office partitioned off from the living room by frosted glass panels and sat down in a padded Eames chair at the mid-century modern desk he'd had cut down to size.

A legal pad next to his keyboard had the list of every source he'd tried and eliminated in his search for Lauren Kavanaugh. A few phone calls to St. Ursula's and a little verbal manipulation yielded a few tidbits of information: This was

Lauren Kavanaugh's first year at the school and her first teaching job. She'd been a substitute in the public schools the year before.

Since learning this, he'd been engaged in the search for the public school where she'd taught. This involved phoning school districts and he needed to do that during working hours. It was only half-past three. With any luck he'd manage to get through another five to ten schools. Maybe he'd be lucky and hit the one he needed.

It wasn't clear to him yet what he hoped to find with this information, but that was the way it was with reporting, you gathered things and laid them out, like shells on a beach, and gradually some sense, like a pattern, would be revealed.

Each phone call took time and a patience he'd never mastered. When they put him on hold he'd drum the edge of his desk or get up and walk the length of his loft, calling it exercise.

"No? You're sure? Thank you for your time."

Another name crossed off the list and he punched in the next number, resisting the urge to make another vodka tonic. A nasal-voiced secretary picked up the phone at the next school and in a few minutes he was back on hold, overly cheerful Muzak blaring.

His reporter's instincts told him that the deaths at the school were not accidents. The police wouldn't go on record with that, but if they were halfway good at their jobs they thought so, too. So he had the puzzle of these deaths and then there was the teacher. The flash of recognition hadn't returned and he knew he was going to have to dig for it, like prying a splinter from his subconscious.

He held the phone away from his ear and rapped a pen against the pad, thinking about Lauren Kavanaugh. He remembered how her eyes slipped away from his face and how she looked like she wanted to flee the room. She knew something, of that he was sure, and it was only a matter of time before he knew it, too.

Chapter Twenty-seven

Stephanie had finally tracked down the extra name on the list from Morgan's mother, the former student at St. Ursula's who was now a freshman at New York University. She'd agreed to talk, but only if they met in the city.

"Forty-five bucks to park," Oz said wonderingly as they walked out of the garage down near Washington Square Park. "We should arrest that scam artist."

"At least it's not our dime." Stephanie scanned the crowd as they approached the park. Kathy Rice had described herself as medium height with straight black hair and said she'd be wearing a green shirt and black pants. Not that she would stand out in that. For that matter, she could probably wear a clown suit and blend in with this crowd. Stephanie moved around the group of people surrounding a juggler and covered her ears as they passed a screeching soapbox preacher.

"You better hope we get something useful out of this or it could easily be our dime," Oz grumbled. "Just wait and see, the captain's going to want to know why we didn't just call her."

"And we'll just explain to him that we need to talk to her in person to be able to assess whether what she tells us is the truth. For all we know she could have been in the woods with Morgan Wycoff that night."

It was a nice day so the park was crowded with chess players and tourists, street performers and families with young children. It smelled like the city always smelled to Stephanie: fried food, gasoline fumes, hot asphalt, and the sweat of millions of people living too close together. Under all of it, and varying only in intensity, was the smell of urine. It was strongest in the subway, but even here, in one of the greener sections of the city, it smelled as if junkies and alcoholics had chosen the base of everything—bench, tree, trash can—as their personal piss pot.

She tried to ignore the smell, trying instead to concentrate on the extra scents of dirt and fresh grass and the chlorinated water bubbling up out of the fountain. And ice cream. A small boy ran by with a drippy cone and narrowly missed dropping it on her.

"Green shirt, black pants," Oz muttered, shading his eyes. "You want to get a hot dog?"

"No, and neither do you. Keep looking."

Oz grumbled under his breath, but looked back toward the Arch. Stephanie did her third visual circle of the crowd. Plenty of people wearing green and black, even a little poodle in a green and black sweater. Nobody wearing both with black hair. And then there was one. Stephanie spotted a young woman with black hair, green shirt, and black pants standing on the far side of the fountain scanning the crowd just like they were.

"I found her, c'mon." Stephanie walked rapidly toward the girl while Oz huffed along behind her.

"Kathy Rice?" Stephanie called as they got closer and the girl jumped. Literally. Down from the bench she'd climbed upon.

"I was trying to find you," she said, looking nervously from Stephanie to Oz and back. "You the detectives?"

The black hair was dyed, cut in a pageboy that framed a

pale face that was unremarkable despite multiple piercings. The thrift-store green polo shirt was at least clean, which couldn't be said for the paint-stained black jeans and Doc Martens. The whole ensemble just screamed art student, which was how Kathy Rice described herself.

"How well did you know Morgan Wycoff?" Stephanie asked.

"We were good friends last year," she said. "Hey, I didn't eat lunch, do you mind if we get something?"

Oz perked up. "Sure, no problem." Stephanie shot him a look and he mimed "What?" with a big shrug. They followed the girl to the perimeter of the park, where she joined a line of people at the dosa cart.

"You graduated from St. Ursula's last year?" Stephanie asked.

"No, I left St. Ursula's. I graduated from the public high school in Gashford."

"What's a dosa?" Oz asked, perusing the menu. He and Kathy had an animated discussion of Indian cuisine that ended with both of them placing orders while Stephanie paced.

Their orders were already in when the girl suddenly dug in her jeans pocket and came up empty. "Oh, wow, I forgot my money. I'll have to go back to my place to get it."

She paused and Stephanie rolled her eyes. The girl would be inviting them to play three-card monte next. She took a five from her purse and handed it over. "Here."

The girl beamed. In a few minutes she and Oz were happily sprawled on a bench munching away while Stephanie stood in front of them feeding the girl questions. The first thing she established was the girl's alibi for the night of Morgan's death. They'd have to verify it, of course, but that would be pretty easy since she'd freely given them the specifics of the gallery opening where she'd been part of the waitstaff serving champagne and canapés to guests.

"When was the last time you talked to Morgan?"

"A month or so." Kathy Rice seemed embarrassed by this admission. Her voice was defensive when she said, "I was really busy with college starting."

"Why did you leave St. Ursula's?"

"I didn't like it there."

"Is that something you and Morgan shared? Your dislike of the school?"

She nodded. "Yeah, I guess."

"Were you into Wicca as well?"

She shook her head and dabbed at the sauce spilling down her chin. "Not really. That was Morgan's thing."

Stephanie pulled the evidence bag with the pentagram charm and chain out of her jacket pocket. She extended it to the girl. "Was this Morgan's?"

Kathy Rice put down her food and took the bag. She fingered the necklace through the plastic and stared at it for a long minute without speaking. "Yes," she said at last.

"You're sure it didn't belong to you?"

"No, I told you, Wicca's not my thing."

"How do you know it was Morgan's?"

The girl hesitated, then said, "I gave it to her."

"That's quite an expensive gift for a friend," Oz said.

The girl's chin went up in a defensive gesture Stephanie recognized from her own poor childhood. "You save up for it?"

"Yeah." The girl handed the bag back. "I spent a whole paycheck on it. I liked her. I wanted her to have something special."

"Why didn't you like St. Ursula's?"

"You mean, why leave if I wasn't being picked on for being a witch?" She got up and dumped her trash in a nearby can. "You didn't have to be into alternate spirituality to get picked on."

"What were you picked on for?"

The girl sighed and plopped back down on the bench. "I don't know—lots of things. Not fitting in, not being interested in being the poster child for St. Ursula's. I mean, some of those girls are like fifth generation at the school. It was like the big status thing was how much you were into the school."

Oz said, "And you weren't that into it?"

"No. And my mom didn't go there, so I didn't have that status. And I wasn't a boarder, that definitely made me a lower rung on the status ladder."

"But you stayed for three years. What happened that last year that made you leave?"

There was a pause and finally the girl said, "I just got sick of it, okay?"

Stephanie and Oz exchanged looks. "I'll bet it was hard for someone creative like you," Stephanie said. "It sounds like they really didn't understand the artistic spirit."

"Yeah, exactly," Kathy said. She picked at a sliver of dried yellow paint on her forearm.

"So what was the final straw for you?" Oz said.

Instead of answering, she said, "What does any of this have to do with Morgan?"

"If someone hurt you, maybe they're the same person who hurt Morgan," Stephanie said.

"I don't know who did it," she said, "so I can't help you with that."

"Did what?"

The girl abruptly stood up. "Look, I've got to finish some work before class tomorrow, so if you don't mind?" She kept picking at her forearm and Stephanie's eyes went there and then back to her face.

"C'mon, Kathy," she said. "We really need to know."

"I already told you!" the girl said with obvious anguish. "Why do I have to go over it again?"

"Told us?" Oz said. He shot Stephanie a bewildered look. "When did you tell us?"

"Not you," the girl said angrily. She kept scraping her

forearm with a fingernail; the skin was turning red. "The police. We told the police. We filed a report back then, not that
it made a damn bit of difference."

"Okay, we'll look that up. I'm sorry we don't know about
the report, so tell us."

"I kept getting these notes. Always telling me how worth-
less I was—how I didn't deserve to be going to school there,
that I was taking up space and scholarship money for someone more deserving."

"So you called the police about the notes?"

Kathy Rice grimaced and gave a little laugh. "Are you kidding me? No, no I did not call the police because I received
some fucking notes."

"Why did you call the police?"

"You know, I didn't even tell my mother about the notes,
not for a long time." She glared at them, angry tears in her
eyes. "I mean, she was so proud that her daughter was going
to prep school. She didn't even mind that I was on scholarship. I think she thought it was great—my daughter's smart
enough that she got an academic scholarship."

"What happened, Kathy?" Oz said in a soft voice.

"While I was in gym class they filled my locker with shit.
Excrement. Feces. Dog shit." She screamed the words. Some
people turned and stared. A woman frowned and pulled her
toddler away.

"Top to bottom with shit," the girl said. "My uniform,
every piece of it smeared, my backpack, and every single
thing in it. All my books, all my supplies. Every single fucking thing." She took a long shuddering breath. "Look, it's all
in the report. If you want to know more, just read it." She
stalked away, but not before Stephanie saw a thin line of
blood ooze from the scratches along her forearm.

"What is Oculus?" Lauren asked. "What does that mean?"
"Didn't they teach you Latin?" Sister Agnes looked up at

her with surprise. "When I was a postulant we had to study Latin. The Eye—that's what it means." All at once her face turned a mottled red and she shouted, "Blasphemy! Blasphemy!"

Startled, Lauren jerked back and the chair scraped against the linoleum floor. A nurse suddenly appeared in the doorway. "Now, now Sister Agnes, what's all this about?" she said in the tone of voice a mother uses talking to a recalcitrant toddler. "There's no need to shout."

"Heretics and blasphemers! No one would listen to me, but that's what they were!"

"Yes, yes, of course they were," the nurse took Sister Agnes' wrist to check her pulse and gave Lauren the once-over. "I don't know what you're talking about, but it's best if you keep her calm. She gets very disoriented."

"I'm fine," Sister Agnes said, trying to swipe the nurse away. The nurse gently fended her off.

"Just taking your pulse, Sister. It's all part of the job."

Satisfied with the reading, the nurse poured Sister Agnes a glass of water from a plastic pitcher and hectored her into taking a few sips.

When she was gone, the nun promptly put the plastic cup aside. "They don't know," she said seeming more lucid than at any other time. "They think I've got dementia, but it isn't true."

"You referred to girls in your writing," Lauren said, gently tapping the sheets still clutched in Sister Agnes's lap. "Are these girls members of Oculus?"

"They thought I didn't know," Sister Agnes said. "But I knew. I always knew."

"What did you know?"

"I heard their footsteps in the halls. I saw the marks they left in the snow. They thought they moved like ghosts, but I knew." She looked triumphant for a moment and then her face clouded.

"Who are the girls?"

If Sister Agnes heard, she didn't answer. But what she said next startled Lauren. "They thought I didn't know about the pills, but I knew what she was doing."

"Who?" Lauren begged. "What pills?"

But Sister Agnes seemed to be gone again, looking off into the distance out the window. The sun was starting to sink. Soon they would come to wheel Sister Agnes off to a meal with the rest of the elderly nuns.

"Who are the members of Oculus? I need to stop them, Sister Agnes, but I can't if I don't know who they are."

"Sister Rose says there aren't any bad girls in the bunch." Sister Agnes turned from the window and Lauren suppressed the cry that rose in her throat at the death's-head grin on the other woman's face.

"Sister Rose is wrong, isn't she?"

"They are there," Sister Agnes said and she reached one hand out to clutch Lauren's. "Don't be fooled, my dear. They are there and they will hurt you if you get in their way."

The clock was ticking closer to four. Visiting hours would be over soon. Desperate, Lauren grabbed at the papers in Sister Agnes's lap. "You used initials," she said. "Are these members of the group? Who is T.? Who is B.?"

"T.B.?" Sister Agnes looked like she was concentrating, but she shook her head. "I don't know. T.B.?"

"They're two separate names, I think. T. and B. What about L.? You mention L. several times."

"L is for love," Sister Agnes sang and laughed. "That was a song when I was a girl."

Lauren wanted to shake her. She could hear footsteps in the hall. "You know who L. is, don't you?"

The nun made the sign of the cross and started to rock again. "Get thee behind me, Satan," she muttered. "I reject Satan, prince of evil and father of darkness."

"Who is L., Sister?"

Sister Agnes began to moan, rocking back and forth in her seat, shaking her head.

"You have to tell me, Sister! You can't keep it a secret anymore. Who is L.?"

"Lincoln," she said. "Elizabeth Lincoln."

Chapter Twenty-eight

When the soft knock came at the door Nicole was ready. She wore dark jeans, a black jacket over a dark T-shirt, and a pair of dark sneakers. She'd followed the instructions to the letter, even choosing dark-colored socks. She opened the door cautiously in case it was Ms. Kavanaugh.

The hooded figure on the other side made her draw back and she slapped a hand over her mouth to stifle the gasp. The figure quickly pushed the hood back and she saw Kristen Townson grinning at her. She gave Nicole a silent but obviously approving once-over, nodding her head, and then pointed toward the hall.

Destiny stirred in her sleep at the soft knock on the door and again when Nicole moved from the bed where she'd been resting, waiting, but Kristen was careful not to let more than a flicker of hall light into the room and that fell in a thin pie-shaped wedge across the floor, far short of the sleeping girl.

Nicole stepped into the hall with Kristen and pulled the door ever so carefully closed behind her, but the lock clicked a little anyway, a noise that seemed to resonate in the stillness of the house. It was midnight.

Kristen placed a finger against her lips and led the way toward the exit, glowing a spooky red under the neon light mounted above the door. Nicole swallowed the gasp as the cold air hit her and followed Kristen mutely across grass crisp with frost. She didn't speak until they'd skirted the dormitory buildings and were safely against the far side of the closed chapel.

"What if my roommate wakes up?" Her greatest fear at that moment was that Destiny would wake up and find her gone and then alert Ms. Kavanaugh, who would alert Sister Rose, who would alert her parents. She could be suspended.

"She won't," Kristen said, with a confidence that Nicole would only think to question later. Kristen pulled a small flashlight from the pocket of her hooded sweatshirt and turned it on with the beam carefully pointed at the ground. It was cloudy, the moon slipping in and out of view, the woods awash in charcoal shadows. Nicole could see her breath, little puffs of silver air. She stuck her gloved hands in the pockets of her jacket.

It was too cold to be out and she wondered peevishly why the club couldn't find an indoor meeting place. She was about to ask Kristen this when the other girl suddenly dimmed the light and pulled Nicole down with her to huddle flush against the stone wall.

Nicole heard the faint crunch of approaching footsteps seconds before a beam of light blinded her. Then the light shifted and she could see two other hooded figures. Kristen stood, pulling Nicole up with her.

The taller of the two girls pushed back her hood and Nicole saw with relief that it was Elizabeth Lincoln. She smiled and shifted the flashlight so Tiffany Bellam was revealed standing next to her.

"Did you bring it?" Elizabeth said to Kristen.

Kristen nodded and pulled something from a sweatshirt pocket and handed it to Elizabeth. Nicole didn't know what it was even when Elizabeth held it up so she could see a strip of black cloth. "Where you are going cannot be revealed until you've joined the group," she intoned, folding the cloth neatly. Then Nicole realized it was a blindfold.

"But I need to see or I'll run into something," she said, feeling suddenly unsure about all of it. "I don't want to wear that. Please."

Elizabeth shook her head and stepped forward. "It's one of the rules. If you're going to join the circle you have to do this. You do want to join, don't you?"

Did she? Now Nicole wasn't so sure. She opened her mouth to say so, but instead uttered a tiny, "Yes."

She was rewarded by Elizabeth's smile. When they placed the cloth over Nicole's eyes, she swallowed several times and fought the urge to panic and run. They tied the scarf tightly against the back of her head, the knot pressing painfully against her scalp. A hand grabbed one of hers.

"Kristen will lead you," Elizabeth said. "You won't fall."

They walked for some time, or it could have been that the blindfold and the cold made her think it was long. She knew they'd crossed into the woods because sometimes her arm brushed against a trunk or a pine branch brushed lightly against her face. Her feet slipped in the leaves and bracken that carpeted her steps, but Kristen did keep her up, one hand firmly gripping Nicole's, the other pressed lightly against her side to help direct her path.

Nicole was breathing hard and was relieved when they came over a dip in the hill. Kristen let go of her hand and pulled the blindfold free.

They were standing in a clearing surrounded by trees. By the beam of Kristen's flashlight, Nicole could see Elizabeth and Tiffany standing with their backs to her, obviously engaged in something. At a touch on her shoulder, she moved forward and saw that they were in front of a fire pit, a deep bowl cut in the earth heaped with logs and encircled by large, smooth stones. Elizabeth and Tiffany were trying to start a fire.

Nicole didn't know which one was Elizabeth until the girl slipped her hood back and smiled at her, blond hair a ghostly white in the darkness, those mesmerizing blue eyes glistening like gray glass. "Welcome," she said in a formal voice, the voice she used for speeches before the student body. "We are honored you have chosen to join this circle."

She bowed her head slightly at Kristen, who bobbed her own in acknowledgment and then they both looked expectantly at Nicole, who hastily did the same.

Tiffany turned her head and looked up at them from her position by the fire ring, shoving the hood back so she could see, and greeting them with a chipper "Hi" that brought a slight frown to Elizabeth's face. Elizabeth liked formality and ritual, Nicole knew, but Tiffany seemed oblivious to her gaffe.

"Are you any good at setting fires?" she asked Nicole. "I suck."

"Push more kindling underneath the bigger logs," Elizabeth instructed, tapping her foot against a pile of brush next to the stone ring. The low flames that had been licking several bigger logs at the center of the pit climbed higher as Tiffany dutifully shoved thin sticks and bark in their path.

For a moment everyone stood still, watching the flames, and Nicole shivered from the cold and anticipation. Then Elizabeth bent down and reaching into a black backpack that she must have carried with her, she pulled out four white tapers.

Tiffany stood and accepted a candle from Elizabeth. Another one went to Kristen. Without speaking, the girls circled the fire pit and Nicole moved where she was silently directed, so that the girls were compass points around the circle and she was standing catty-corner to Elizabeth.

"Tonight we add a new member to our group," Elizabeth said in that same dramatic voice. "She comes because she has been chosen, just as all of us were chosen. She comes to complete our circle."

She knelt in a graceful movement and extended her taper over the flames until the wick caught and then stood quickly and just as fluidly. A drop of hot wax spilled over the candle and splashed against her bare hand. It must have burned, but Elizabeth didn't so much as wince. She stood with the candle extended in front of her and aloft. "Behold the light of Christ that burns in all of us like a fever, wiping out anything that separates us from the Lord."

"Amen," Tiffany and Kristen said in solemn whispers and then Elizabeth extended her taper first to Kristen and then to Tiffany and all three of them held their burning candles and looked at Nicole.

"Nicole Morel," Elizabeth said. "Do you wish to join Oculus?"

"Yes."

Elizabeth lit the last taper and passed it around the circle until it came to Nicole, who took it with hands that trembled slightly as much from nervousness as from the cold.

"Many are willing," Elizabeth said, "but few are chosen."

The hoods obscured their faces. All Nicole could see were the glowing candles. "Repeat after me," Elizabeth intoned. "I will accept the challenge of being one of the chosen."

Nicole repeated the words, her voice faint at first, but then carrying across the crackling fire to the others.

"I will accept the responsibilities that come with being one of the elect."

This time, Nicole's voice was stronger, surer.

"And I will never tell another living soul about the group or my remaining days at the school shall be filled with misery, my nights haunted, my days restless, my nerves shattered by fear of retribution for my betrayal."

Nicole felt her voice shake slightly. What would happen if she slipped and accidentally told someone?

"Those who wish to be members of the elect must prove their worthiness. Are you willing to prove yourself?"

"Yes."

"You must carry out the task assigned to you without delay, without complaint, and without support. Are you willing to undertake this challenge?"

Nicole nodded, then forced a "Yes" from her throat. Trembling, she watched Elizabeth pull out a small envelope sealed with wax and stamped with an eye, just like the invitation. She handed it to Nicole.

"You will not open it in our presence, only once you are alone. When you have completed the challenge, you will write the word 'finished' on a slip of paper and slide it under my door. Remember, The Eye is watching you."

Kristen took the candle from Nicole's hand and handed it to Tiffany, who blew it out. Then she put the blindfold around Nicole's eyes again.

Nicole trailed Kristen back down the hillside, clutching the letter in her hand. It seemed faster this time, but maybe it was because she was eager to know what was in the letter.

After they were back on the edge of campus and the blindfold had been removed, Elizabeth put a hand on Nicole's arm. "Don't forget," she said in a low voice. "We will know if you tell anyone else. We will know if you show the letter to anyone else. The Eye is watching."

Nicole didn't open the letter until she was alone in Augustine House, Destiny still sleeping peacefully in her bed. She waited until she'd undressed and slipped between the cold sheets of her bed. Holding the covers up to block the flashlight, she broke the seal and unfolded the thick, ivory stationery.

"Who is Lauren Kavanaugh? Why would a *New York Times* reporter know her, but she deny knowing him? You must get into her rooms and discover the truth. Find the secret she's been keeping from the school."

She read the letter through twice and then a third time. How on earth was she going to get into Ms. Kavanaugh's apartment? There were no suggestions for how to accomplish this or any mention of the consequences if she were caught. Nicole read it a fourth time, wondering what, exactly, she was supposed to find out about the teacher. She liked Ms. Kavanaugh. Did they know that? Was that why they'd asked her to do this? Folding the invitation into a small square, she tucked it and the flashlight between the mattress and the box spring.

Lying in the darkness, she kept replaying what had happened in the woods. It was different than what she'd expected, but in some ways more exciting, too. She'd tried to think of things they might ask her to do, but none of them had come close to this.

Paul had belonged to a club once. Something he'd formed with other boys during a winter holiday when it was too cold to play football and they gathered in his room instead, door closed and no entrance for a younger sister. She'd tried to weasel her way in, taking the lunch tray for the housekeeper, but the door had only opened a crack and Paul snatched the food with barely a thank-you and an emphatic "No!" when she asked if she could be included.

Nothing they'd done had come close to this. What would happen if she couldn't complete the task? She drew her cold feet up and tucked them under her nightgown, lying curled like a cat. The faint scent from the burning candle clung to her fingers. If she accomplished the task, she would be a full-fledged member of the most coveted group. It was funny to picture other girls looking to her, shy little Nicole, as their role model. She laughed a little at the thought and Destiny stirred. Nicole tensed, but the other girl rolled over without waking.

The digital clock silently blinked 1:00 A.M. The sheets were finally warming from her body heat. Nicole yawned and burrowed deeper under the covers. She fell asleep pondering ways she could get inside the teacher's room without getting caught.

Chapter Twenty-nine

By the time Stephanie and Oz made it back from Manhattan and had discovered that yes, Kathy Rice's mother had made a complaint, it was past dinnertime.

"Okay, that's enough for one day," Oz said once they'd found that the officer who'd followed up on the complaint, an older patrolman named Bob Franklin, was off for a few days on his annual vacation.

"Maybe we should call him back in," Stephanie suggested when they'd checked Franklin's schedule with the front desk.

"Maybe. But we have to clear that with the captain and I for one do not want to have that conversation at this hour. Do you? I am too wiped to explain today's adventure. I'm going home to bed and so should you."

Stephanie opened her mouth to argue and yawned instead. She walked with Oz out to the parking lot and then drove slowly back to the town house fantasizing about the shower she was going to take once she got there. She wanted to wash off the grit from the city and then she wanted to sleep.

It had been so many hours since her last meal that she

couldn't even remember what she'd eaten, but she had no appetite now, she was too tired.

The door opened as she turned her key in the lock. Alex stood on the other side and he looked crazed. "Did you send the check?" he said.

"What?" She stepped past him, kicking off her shoes.

"The check—the deposit check." He slammed the door so hard it shook in its frame.

Stephanie blinked at him for a moment, the words penetrating the fog. Check. Deposit check. "Oh, shit!"

"You didn't send it, did you?" Alex sounded almost satisfied, like he was pleased to discover she was a complete screwup.

"I'm sorry, it fell off the list, I'll send it tomorrow."

"Tomorrow is too late! They've already given our date away."

"But we asked them to hold it," Stephanie said, feeling stupid. She slid down onto a chair. "I'll just call them and explain."

"I already called them. I called to double-check on restrictions about bringing in outside caterers and they couldn't find our information."

"I'm sorry, Alex, I'll write the check now—"

"It's too late! What part of that don't you understand? We can't get that date anymore and there are no other dates available!"

Stephanie rubbed her eyes and tried to think. "All right, so we'll call that other place. Our second choice. I'll do it first thing in the morning."

"You just don't get it, do you?" Alex said and his voice was quiet this time, the sort of calm that worried her more than his yelling. "I'm sick of it, Steph, I'm sick of your job being the only thing you think about morning, noon, and night."

"That's not true. It's just this case right now, these killings—"

"And then it'll be the next killing and the one after that," Alex said. "You just don't get it—it's not just this case, it's every case. It's what it does to you."

Stephanie's temple pulsed. She could feel a migraine coming on and wondered if she could interrupt things long enough to get some ibuprofen.

"You know, I work with things that are alive," Alex said. "Everything I do is about making things more beautiful, pleasing to the eye, pleasant to smell and touch. Everything about your job is the opposite."

"That's not true."

He sat down across from her and stared at her. "Everything you do is about dealing with the ugliness of the world. You see and smell and experience ugliness every single moment on that job and I just don't understand why you'd want that."

"I help people," Stephanie said. "It's not just about ugliness."

"You help drug addicts? How? By arresting them? You're not a doctor. You're not a psychologist."

"We take bad people off the streets," Stephanie said. "That is helping. And we help people who've gotten hurt."

"You could do that in so many other ways," Alex said. "I'm tired of wondering every time you walk out that door what experience you're going to bring home with you. Not to mention worrying that you won't make it home. I'm tired of playing second fiddle to your job."

"I love what I do," Stephanie said, struggling to find the words. "I've wanted to be a detective since I was a little kid, you know that."

"I know about your father, Steph—"

"When he was killed I can remember feeling totally lost," she said. "I can remember being in a store with my mom after his funeral and wondering how everybody around us could be laughing and buying food and going on with their lives because my dad was dead.

"And then my uncle arrested the drunk who hit his car. I can still remember the night he came to tell my mom. I can remember the way he looked in the glare of the outside light. And I knew right then that I wanted to be him. I wanted to be the person who could make some things right."

"How are you going to make things right with us, Steph?" Alex said. "How are you going to make that right?"

She saw it clearly then, the one choice that had been looming on the horizon and that she'd ignored. She got to her feet, feeling the pounding in her head increase with the movement.

"This is how," she said. She lifted her left hand and slid off her engagement ring. She put it down gently on the coffee table. "Good-bye, Alex."

Chapter Thirty

Lauren caught up with Candace as she was crossing the quad to the cafeteria, hands jammed in the pocket of an old navy pea coat.

"I've been trying to find you," Lauren said, breathless from running all the way from the classroom in the main building. Her ankle ached and she was limping again.

"Oh?" Candace, as always, had an amused and somewhat tolerant smile on her face. "What's up?"

"I found her."

"Who?"

"Sister Agnes."

Candace's eyes widened and she glanced from side to side. "What do you mean you found her?" she said in a low voice.

"She's in a nursing home in Union," Lauren said. "And everything she told me confirms what I thought."

"You went to see her?" Candace sounded incredulous.

"Of course." Lauren shrugged, feeling her own mood shifting in response to Candace's surprise.

"How did you find out where she was?"

"It was in her medical file."

The other teacher's eyes narrowed. "Nurse Ratched let you look at it?"

"No," Lauren admitted. "I took it."

The expression on Candace's face was one of disbelief. She darted glances both ways again and gripping Lauren's upper arm steered her off the central path, leading them rapidly down a path that led away from the central flow of traffic. There was a bench under a tree. She sat down, pulling Lauren down next to her.

"Are you crazy?" she said. "Do you want to get fired?"

Lauren pulled her arm free. "What are you talking about? Of course not."

"You stole her file—"

"I didn't steal it, I borrowed it."

"Oh for heaven's sake, Lauren—you took a private file without permission!"

"All right! Fine! I stole the file, but if I hadn't I wouldn't have found out the truth. Does that matter to you at all?"

Candace sighed. "What did you find out?"

Lauren told her everything she could remember about her meeting with Sister Agnes and what she'd said.

Candace didn't react until Lauren got to the part about the students' names.

"Elizabeth Lincoln?" she repeated. "You have got to be kidding me."

Lauren shook her head. "Nope. She definitely said her name. She said it twice."

The other teacher simply stared at her for a moment, mouth hanging open, and then Candace shook her head and stood up.

"It must have been a mistake."

"No way. It was no mistake."

Candace looked down at Lauren. "I agree that it sounds incriminating, but think, Lauren. Isn't it possible—more like probable—that she does have dementia? And isn't it possible that she said Elizabeth Lincoln's name because that's the name that came most easily to mind?"

"I don't think so," Lauren said, "not the way she said it. And it makes sense if you think about it—who are you least likely to suspect but the head girl?"

Candace shook her head. "You are concocting this fantasy in your head."

"There are two girls dead, Candace. I didn't fantasize that."

"And you think that Elizabeth Lincoln, the head girl, the perfect student, someone in the running for valedictorian, had something to do with their deaths."

"I know it sounds crazy."

The other woman laughed, but she wasn't smiling. "Yeah, crazy just about covers it."

"Fine. Don't believe me. Maybe you will when I develop dementia."

"Are you suggesting they're poisoning you?"

"No. Not yet. I'm sure they would if they could get away with it."

Candace was giving her a look that Lauren had seen before. She sighed wondering if she'd made a mistake in telling her friend. "You don't believe a bit of this, do you?"

The other woman hesitated and then slowly shook her head. "I'm sorry, but I don't."

"So how do you explain it? You think Sister Agnes imagined it all?"

"I think she's an old woman who got dementia and that illness made her imagine that certain things were going on."

"And what about the deaths? How do you explain those?"

Candace sighed. "I don't know, Lauren, but unless she told you something concrete we have nothing to go on. The deaths could just be unfortunate accidents. You have no evidence that Elizabeth Lincoln had anything to do with them, right?"

"You said yourself that you had suspicions."

"About bullying among the girls, yes! But not at this level—I would never have imagined it could be Elizabeth."

"Just think about it," Lauren said. She held up a hand as

Candace opened her mouth to protest. "I know, I know, but really think about it: What if you wanted to get away with something? What better way than to be the best student, the very best, in the school?"

To her credit, Candace did stop and think about that for a moment, fingering a loose button on her coat. The breeze was chilling and Lauren could feel the cold of the stone seat through her slacks, but neither woman moved.

"You have no proof," the other woman said at last.

Lauren waited until Candace's eyes met hers before uttering a one-word answer: "Yet."

"I can't believe I agreed to this," Candace hissed. She was standing in the doorway of Elizabeth Lincoln's room in Ambrose House, acting as a guard while Lauren pivoted slowly inside the room itself, trying to decide where to focus her attention.

It had taken the better part of an hour to convince Candace that the best way to eliminate Elizabeth Lincoln as a suspect was to find proof one way or another. And when Lauren proposed searching Elizabeth's room—the best idea she'd come up with on the long train ride back from seeing Sister Agnes—she thought Candace was going to have a fit.

"You'll get us fired!" the other woman said. "No! Absolutely not!"

But here they were, three hours later, standing in the empty dormitory while the girls in Ambrose House were at gym.

"Hurry up," Candace hissed. "Look for whatever it is you think you're going to find and let's get out."

"I'm trying," Lauren said. The room was just like all the others, only because of Elizabeth's status as head girl it was a single—a bed, a dresser, a desk, and the ultimate luxury of the single rooms, her own bath. Just like all the other rooms, this one was dominated by the tenant's personality.

Elizabeth's bed was neatly made and everything was in its place. This was a girl obsessed with organization, Lauren thought, running a finger lightly over the alphabetized rows of books, neatly lined up on a narrow bookshelf next to the desk. Framed photos hung in an invisible grid on the wall. She glanced at them. Elizabeth skiing with a man and woman who seemed vaguely familiar. Probably the parents. Elizabeth posing on a beach with a tall boy who looked remarkably similar. Probably an older brother. The last photo, and the one that captured Lauren's attention, was of Elizabeth in profile sitting alone in a garden. Her face without the forced smile seemed remarkably composed for a young girl, but in this obviously caught-off-guard moment there was something else. It took Lauren a moment to realize that what had caught her attention was the utter coldness—a dead, animal-looking blankness—in the eyes.

Lauren forced her attention on the rest of the room. There was a computer monitor with a paper-thin screen on the desktop. She slid open the four drawers, checking one after the other, but there was nothing out of the ordinary—school supplies, old writing assignments, the draft of an essay for English class on the poet Gerald Manley Hopkins.

"Hurry up," Candace whispered.

"I'm doing the best I can," Lauren hissed. She turned to the closet, folding back the slatted door as quietly as possible and surveying a perfectly aligned row of clothes. What was she going to find here beyond the evidence that Elizabeth had expensive clothes that were far different from the puritanical skirts and blouses worn by all St. Ursula students?

There was nothing here that indicated anything more than a teenage girl's interest in fashion and the money to indulge it. Lauren unconsciously fingered a green velvet jacket and snatched her hand away as Candace hissed her name again.

"There's nothing here," Candace said. "Let's go before one of the students gets back."

"Not yet," Lauren said. She closed the closet door and headed into the small bathroom. Only two single rooms had their own baths and Elizabeth was lucky enough to live in one of the two. Only in here was there any indication of a teenager living in the space—an array of cosmetics were spread across the vanity counter and tissues dabbed with lipstick kisses had missed the trash can and were lying around the tile floor.

Lauren opened the medicine cabinet and was surprised to see a variety of pill bottles crammed on the thin shelves. She examined them quickly one by one. Several were out of date, some by more than a year, and it was one of these that caught her attention because the prescription was for a Beverly Lincoln, not Elizabeth. The rest of the label had been ripped off.

"Someone's coming!"

On impulse, Lauren stuck the bottle in her pocket and quickly closed the cabinet door. She ran out of the bathroom and smack into Candace, who clutched her arms so tightly that Lauren would find marks later.

"There's someone in the hall!" Candace's voice sounded high pitched and panicked. She looked around Lauren as if searching for a place to hide.

"Was it Elizabeth?" Lauren held her in place, prying Candace's arms off in the process.

"No, I don't know. I just heard voices."

Lauren strained to hear above the sound of their own heavy breathing. She could hear two girls talking at a distance. The sound of their voices and footsteps grew louder. They were coming closer.

She and Candace could pretend they'd been conducting an inspection, but there was no way that would hold up to scrutiny. Violating another's privacy was against the rules, even for teachers. There was an honor code at St. Ursula's, and inspection of student property was conducted within that code. To violate a student's privacy, a teacher had to have some direct evidence of wrongdoing or justified suspicion that the student was harboring illegal substances. Two teachers caught in a student's room without that student's permission and without any reasonable explanation for what they were doing—Lauren would lose her job.

The voices grew louder and the footsteps closer. Lauren felt her throat tighten and her own breath came in shallow gasps. Then the footsteps stopped.

She heard a key in a door and her eyes flew to the handle, watching, horrified, as it slowly turned.

Then, all at once, the voices were on the other side of the wall. It was the room next door! No one had been turning this handle; she'd imagined it. Lauren pointed and Candace nodded her understanding and stepped back. Loud music suddenly came on in the other room and Lauren breathed deeply for the first time.

"We've got to go," Candace whispered. Lauren nodded. They slipped out the door without incident and made it down the hall to Candace's room.

"There was nothing there, right?" she said to Lauren as she fumbled for her own keys.

"No," Lauren said, feeling her face flush as her hand closed around the pill bottle in her pocket. Except this, she thought of saying, fighting the impulse to take the bottle out and show Candace. She couldn't tell her she'd taken it. Candace would just insist she take it back and if Lauren did that she'd never know the truth.

"I knew you wouldn't find anything," Candace said. "I'm just glad we didn't get caught proving that."

In the safety of her own rooms, Lauren pulled the bottle out of her jacket and examined it.

Something in a fairly high dosage prescribed to one Beverly Lincoln, not Elizabeth, a year ago. Lauren sat down with the bottle in front of her laptop, but without the name of the drug she could find nothing.

She looked again at the bottle. This was it. It had to be. Elizabeth had been doping Sister Agnes with these pills.

The shock of the realization was enough to propel her out the door and halfway across the lawn toward Sister Rose's office before common sense caught up with her. She paused, jiggling the bottle of pills tucked in her coat pocket, and thought through what, exactly, she could say.

How would she explain getting the pills? And more important, couldn't Elizabeth simply claim that her mother had left them behind while visiting?

The cold air seeped through her jacket, chilling her and reviving the lingering ache in her ankle. With it came a sense of futility. She couldn't prove anything, she had nothing but one more little piece in a puzzle that nobody else believed existed.

Chapter Thirty-one

Nicole stood at the window and watched Ms. Kavanaugh head toward the main building for the first class.

"I'm sick," she said turning to Destiny. "Can you tell Mr. Whitecliff?"

"What's wrong? You seemed okay at breakfast." Destiny stopped packing her book satchel and stared at her roommate with frank curiosity.

"Stomachache," Nicole said, sinking down onto her bed and rubbing her lower abdomen. "Maybe it was something I ate. Or my period." She got back under the covers and rolled onto her side, moaning.

She counted to ten once Destiny had gone and then climbed softly back out of bed and watched out the window as her roommate and the rest of the residents of Augustine House crossed the campus heading to class. She waited five more minutes and then she sprang into action.

Grabbing her digital camera and a credit card, she quietly exited her room and headed down the hall to Ms. Kavanaugh's door.

It had taken a little experimentation and a few hours of

watching and waiting, but she'd figured out how to get in the teacher's apartment.

The locks on all the old doors were the same and through tinkering with her own, she'd discovered, much to her surprise, that it could be bypassed with a credit card pushed against the lock in that narrow slit between door and jamb.

The TV was playing in the common room and she could hear some girls talking, but there was no one in the hall. With a quick look right and left, she pushed the card in and turned the knob. The door opened with a tiny click. She slipped inside and shut the door just as quietly behind her.

Once she was in, Nicole wasn't sure where to begin. She'd estimated a maximum of thirty minutes to get in and out before anyone might make it back to the house. It wasn't a lot of time when she had no idea what she was even looking for.

The secret, the letter had said. Find out Ms. Kavanaugh's secret. She decided to start in the bedroom. On the bedside table were several books but nothing unusual. She slid open the single drawer but found nothing beyond a small New Testament. The closet was equally barren. If she'd expected a box piled high with mementos of Ms. Kavanaugh's former life she was disappointed.

The strangest thing about the apartment was how little of Ms. Kavanaugh's life was revealed. Nicole had seen the apartments of two other resident faculty members and both of them had been bursting with family photos and personal mementos, but other than several pairs of running shoes and an abundance of athletic wear, there was nothing else that revealed any hobbies or anything personal. It was odd.

At first she bypassed the kitchen, sure that Oculus wasn't interested in what type of jam Ms. Kavanaugh preferred or whether she was used margarine or butter. Then she thought of medication, remembering that she'd had a cousin who kept his diabetic supplies in the refrigerator, so she did a quick search of all the cupboards, drawers, and appliances and a quick search of the medicine cabinet in the bathroom before declaring that a bust.

Ms. Kavanaugh didn't have any secret medical condition or addiction, unless a daily multivitamin could be considered incriminating. There was nothing beyond those pills and a bottle of ibuprofen.

She started in the living room, quickly eliminating the bookcases and moving toward Ms. Kavanaugh's desk. Again, there was little there. Pens, paper, and pencils in the top drawer. Copies of the syllabus for every class. Notes about future lesson plans and the outline for a final exam. Her pencil cup was a mug with a picture of Trafalgar Square. It was by far the most personal thing in the apartment and Nicole began to consider the possibility that there was simply nothing else to find.

Then she found the photo album. It was a small black leather-bound book tucked in one of the bottom drawers. Nicole eagerly laid it on the desktop and turned the pages. They were all fairly recent photos of Ms. Kavanaugh in Europe. Some of them were typical tourist photos—Ms. Kavanaugh in front of various monuments, including the Eiffel Tower.

Nicole looked quickly past these, but she lingered on the photos of a fine-boned blond man who smiled out of several photos. He was good looking and from the way he preened for the camera he obviously knew it. European, Nicole thought, not American. She wasn't sure how she could tell, but it had less to do with fashion and more with facial structure. He just didn't look American.

Who was he? She searched cover to cover, but there was no writing anywhere in the album. Then she searched the rest of the desk, expecting to find a cache of love letters, but again she came up short. Who was this man? Was this enough of a secret? Nicole slipped the album back in the

drawer and glanced at her watch. Damn! She had less than
ten minutes left.

She closed the drawer and then, anxious that she'd put it
back wrong, jerked the drawer back open too far so it fell
out. It fell with a loud thud onto the floor. Nicole froze, waiting for someone to come and hammer on the door, but there
was no other sound. She bent down to pick up the drawer
and that's when she saw the letters.

They were in a little pile tucked in the very back of the
drawer, which was why she'd missed them the first time. A
series of identical white envelopes neatly printed with Ms.
Kavanaugh's name and address. Nicole carefully opened the
envelope on top of the pile and unfolded the single sheet of
paper within. The letter was short and it didn't make a lot of
sense, but it took Nicole less than five minutes to realize that
she'd found what she was looking for.

Candace wasn't in the cafeteria when Lauren arrived for
lunch on Tuesday, so she went ahead and picked a table, certain that she'd just been delayed by a student.

She pulled out the lesson plan for that afternoon's class
and began tinkering with it, thinking through what she
wanted the students to learn about the American Revolution
and what was interesting, but might sidetrack the class too
much.

Elizabeth had been in class that morning as usual, the
same smile on her face that she always wore, but now it gave
Lauren chills.

She'd had trouble meeting her eyes as she led the class
through a discussion of the crusades.

At one point Elizabeth raised her hand and Lauren was
forced to call on her.

"Isn't it our job as Christians to defend our faith against
infidels?"

A supposedly innocent question, but Lauren was watching for it and saw the flicker of something else—was it amusement?—in those cold blue eyes.

"A good question, Elizabeth," Lauren said easily looking away then, though she could feel an internal tremor. "Let's see what your classmates think?" And she deftly turned it into a class discussion.

Deep in thought, Lauren didn't realize how much time had passed until someone tapped the table.

"Do you mind if I join you?" Ryland Pierce smiled down at her, bearing a tray piled high with that day's pasta special.

"Actually, I'm having lunch with someone," she said, trying to return the smile though she felt her lips freeze in an insincere curve.

"Are you sure they're coming?" he said, looking around. "The lunch hour's almost over."

Lauren realized with a start that a half-hour had passed. Where was Candace? Before she had time to reply, Ryland Pierce was pulling up the chair across from her.

"I'll leave if they show," he said. "But tell me how things are going? How's the teaching?" He gave her an expectant look while taking a large bite of pasta.

"Great, the classes are going well," she said, summoning an enthusiasm she didn't begin to feel. She had no desire to confide in this man and she certainly wasn't going to say anything that he could use against her.

"And how are things with the girls? Any more problems there?"

For a few seconds she was tempted to tell him about the pills, but common sense took hold and didn't let go.

"Pretty good," she said at last. "No recent problems." Beyond a secret group of students killing their classmates.

"I knew you'd settle in," he said. "It always takes a little while at the beginning, but that's to be expected. Once the girls know that you're there for the long haul they won't give you any more grief."

She endured his pabulum for another ten minutes, wondering how much of it he really believed, before excusing herself to head for class.

Just before she left, it occurred to her that she could ask him something without revealing too much.

"Are you familiar with Oculus?" She watched his face, but if he knew what the word meant he was hiding it well. His face was blank.

"No, what's that?"

"Nothing. Just Latin."

That started him talking about how he'd endured, but hadn't retained, several years of Latin when still a boy. She nodded, smiling politely, waiting for him to wind down.

She didn't think about Candace again until the end of afternoon classes, when she wanted to discuss the minor success she'd had with the last class with someone who could admit that teaching wasn't always an effortless and joyful experience and discuss their own failures without considering it a liability.

Candace wasn't in the science room; another teacher was standing at the front table gathering papers into a neat pile. She gave Lauren an inquiring look.

"Sorry, wrong class." Lauren stepped back out and double-checked the room number. No, this was room 204. There must have been a room switch. She stepped back inside the door. The other teacher, a heavyset woman whose name Lauren couldn't remember, was erasing formulas from the blackboard.

"Isn't this Candace Huston's classroom?"

"It was." The woman gave Lauren a long once-over before turning back to the board. "It's my classroom now."

"Oh. Where's Ms. Huston?"

"Ms. Huston doesn't work here anymore."

"Where's her new classroom?" Lauren said, feeling as if she was having to spell things out.

The other woman shook her head. "She doesn't work at the school anymore."

"What? Since when?"

The other woman shrugged. "Since today, I think."

"But why? Did she quit?"

Another shrug, the stooped shoulders rolling back slightly under the shapeless flowered dress. The older woman had a look of complete indifference on her moon face.

Lauren headed across campus, puzzled, but not unduly alarmed. Not yet. She was sure it was some sort of mistake and she imagined laughing with Candace about it.

Classical music could be heard faintly through the door to Candace's apartment. She answered just as Lauren had her hand raised to knock a second time.

"I'm sorry about lunch," she said in greeting.

"No problem." Lauren followed her in. "You'll never believe what I was told," she said and then the words died in her mouth. There were cardboard boxes lining the floor of Candace's front room. One box was brimming with books, another had things wrapped in newspaper.

"What did you hear?" Candace asked.

"What is this?" Lauren looked around. "I don't understand, why are you packing?"

"I was fired."

The words were so quiet that Lauren barely heard her. "Fired?" she whispered, her own voice unconsciously echoing Candace's muted tone. "Why?"

Candace looked at her and then away. "Elizabeth Lincoln had a photo of me looking around her room," she said. "Apparently her computer is set up with a webcam that takes pictures automatically every ten minutes." She removed some more books from one of the built-in shelves and stacked them in the box at her feet.

"So what?"

"So she went to Sister Rose and showed her the photo and said that I'd been in her room. And then she told her that I was interested in her and that I'd probably been in her room more than once and I was probably the person who'd stolen some of her things."

"What? Sister Rose can't have believed that!"

Candace gave her a slight smile. "I'm not sure if she did at first. She wanted to give me the benefit of the doubt, those were her words. But this was a serious accusation and she had an obligation to follow through on what this 'exemplary' student had said."

"So why were you fired? They can't have found anything?"

Candace spoke as if Lauren wasn't in the room. "I didn't think to refuse the search," she said as if reconsidering. "Why would I? I had nothing to hide and I said so. She went with Mac while I waited in her office. They were gone for half-an-hour all told. Barely thirty minutes and then she came back and told me she was sorry to report that everything the student had said was true and that under the circumstances she had no choice but to immediately remove me from my position and ask me to vacate the premises because I posed a danger to the students."

She said it all in a flat tone. "But that's ridiculous!" Lauren said. "What could they have possibly found?"

Candace suddenly blushed, a dull brick red that suffused the pale skin like blood across a field of snow, climbing up from her neck to her forehead and painting the tips of her ears a darker cherry color that blended with her short dark hair.

"Lingerie," she said and her voice shook, for the first time expressing any emotion. "They found several pairs of her panties in my dresser."

Lauren didn't know what to say. "How did you, I mean, did you have—"

"I don't know how it got there!" Candace shouted back at her. "I didn't take it, but it was in my dresser!"

"She must have put it there—the little bitch."

Candace nodded once, sharply. "Yes, that's the most likely explanation. Proving it, however, is an entirely different matter."

"I'll go to Sister Rose. I'll tell her I was there and show her what I found—"

"What are you going to tell her? That you broke in and stole medical files for the teacher who was forced to retire because of mental illness?"

"There's more to it than that—I can show her the pills I found—"

"While you were snooping in a student's room," Candace finished for her. "You'll only get yourself fired." She paused. "I thought you said you didn't find anything?"

"There was a bottle of pills prescribed to someone else. I think those are probably the pills."

Candace looked thoughtful, but then she turned back to the shelves, lifting down books and stacking them in the box at her feet.

"I can't believe you're just packing up without a fight," Lauren said. "There's got to be something we can do."

Candace smiled. "There's no 'we' here," she said with bitterness. "I'm the one who's been fired. This has nothing to do with you."

She grabbed more books off the shelf, shoving them into the box. Feeling helpless, Lauren simply watched for a minute before joining her.

"You don't have to help," Candace said, trying to block her.

"I want to," Lauren pushed past her and put the books in the box.

"Well, then, you do this and I'll move on to my desk," Candace said. This was the same as the one in Lauren's rooms, a large and ancient wooden office desk, but flanking the personal computer on Candace's desktop were small plants in brightly colored pots.

"There's just so much stuff." She sat down and pulled open the top drawer. "Six years is a long time."

"I'm so sorry, Candace, it's my fault."

"No, it isn't," Candace said. "It's Elizabeth Lincoln's fault, hers and whoever else she has working with her."

"But if I hadn't convinced you to search her room—"

"Stop," Candace interrupted her. "It doesn't matter."

"How can you say that?"

"I should have left a long time ago. This just forces the issue."

"But not this way. You can't let them push you out, not over some lies."

"I'm gay, Lauren, that part wasn't a lie." Candace gave her a small smile.

"I know," Lauren said, surprised at her own admission. She did know. She had known what she saw in Candace's eyes when the woman looked at her, but she hadn't wanted to admit it. "So what? That isn't a crime."

"This is a Catholic school," Candace said. "There are plenty of rules regarding the conduct of straight teachers. Can you imagine the reaction by some of the parents if they knew their daughters' science teacher was gay? They'd think I was corrupting their children."

Lauren opened her mouth to protest, but promptly closed it again. Candace was right.

She helped her pack, loading the contents of the small apartment into boxes that they trundled out to Candace's car on a trolley provided by Mac. He hefted them into the car for her, looking as taciturn as ever, though his obvious willingness to help signaled his distress better than any words.

"Hard to believe that six years can be packed up like this," Candace said when they'd finished and were standing in the stripped living room.

"I'm so sorry," Lauren said again. She could feel tears pricking against the back of her eyes.

316   *Rebecca Drake*

"Don't be," Candace said. "I meant what I said about staying too long. I've hidden myself here because it was easy, but it isn't healthy."

She picked up the last thing left, a small spider plant in a ceramic pot, from the windowsill. "I've got the chance to lead a fuller life than I could here. That's a good thing."

They walked slowly out the door and down the path toward the car. Candace anchored the plant on the floor of the passenger side and then leaned back against the car, hands jammed in the pockets of her pea coat. "Look, Lauren, you haven't asked for my advice, but I'll give it to you anyway."

Lauren smiled, but she was shaking and she knew it wasn't only the breeze.

"You're doing the same thing I was—hiding out I mean," Candace said. Then she smiled. "I know it's not for the same reason. I know you're not gay, you don't have to worry."

"I'm not worried," Lauren said, shifting defensively.

"Yeah, okay, but let's not forget you dated a man in London."

She laughed and Lauren joined in, but tears sprang to her eyes. "I'm so sorry, Candace."

"Ssh." Candace touched her cheek. "Take care of yourself." She looked deep into Lauren's eyes, that same amused smile playing on her face. "You're a beautiful girl," she said. "I hope you find the peace you're looking for."

She leaned forward and brushed her lips quickly over Lauren's before getting briskly into the car and pulling away from the school. Then she was gone and Lauren was alone.

Elizabeth watched from the far side of the chapel as Miss Kavanaugh and Miss Huston said their good-byes. She grimaced at the kiss. How touching to see the lesbian take her leave.

She leaned comfortably against the stone wall, immune to the cold seeping through her wool coat. All her focus was on the young teacher standing on the sidewalk little more than a hundred feet away, completely oblivious to the fact that she was being watched.

Miss Kavanaugh was completely alone now. The science teacher had been her only friend and now she was gone. Elizabeth felt a cold delight in the game she was playing, imagining that she was a cat watching a bird that doesn't know it's cornered.

It had been a shock seeing the pictures taken by her webcam. She hadn't anticipated that they'd break into her room, and in the initial fog of anger she'd fixed on accusing both of them of trying to seduce her. But then she'd had a better idea.

Elizabeth had realized it wasn't necessary to get rid of both of them, not yet. Miss Kavanaugh's accusations were only powerful because they were bolstered by her friend. With Candace Huston gone, nobody was left who believed Lauren Kavanaugh.

If the teacher didn't know that now, she'd learn it soon enough. She'd been foolish to think that she had any power over Elizabeth and like a child snatching burnt fingers from a hot stove, Miss Kavanaugh would learn soon enough that there were some things better left untouched.

In the meantime, it would be fun to toy with her, batting her around a bit, enjoying the game. She was eager to see what Nicole would find in the teacher's room. The midget reporter's surety that he knew her had piqued Elizabeth's interest. What was Miss Kavanaugh hiding?

Elizabeth wished she could search the space herself, in part to repay the violation of her space, yes, but also because of the heady power that came from touching another's things and inhaling their scent. She wanted to leave her own mark on Miss Kavanaugh's space, but it was important not to take unnecessary risks.

The cell phone in her pocket vibrated. Elizabeth flipped it open. "Yes?"

She listened and her smile grew wider. "Very interesting. No, don't do anything. I'll be there soon. Definitely do not turn it in at the office—I have something better to do with it."

Miss Kavanaugh turned from the road and Elizabeth stepped back into the shadows cast by the juncture of two chapel walls. She watched her walk past, passing close enough that Elizabeth could see the wavy lines in the tortoiseshell barrette restraining her hair.

"Someone has a secret," Elizabeth whispered in a sing-song. She watched the teacher disappear from view resisting the urge to follow. "Soon, very soon." Her fingers traced the cool steel of the knife hidden in her coat pocket.

Chapter Thirty-two

Elsa fingered the cell phone with a touch that bordered on reverent. It was amazing that one small object could come to have such importance in a person's life. If she hadn't gone in the tunnel that morning, if someone else had gotten there first, then they would have found the cell phone instead of her.

"Aren't you going to lunch?" Elsa's roommate, Stacy Chin, was buttoning up her coat.

"No. I've got something else to do."

"But it's free ice cream day."

"So?" Elsa rolled away from Stacy on her bed. "I'm on a diet, remember?"

Skinny people never took diets seriously. They didn't understand the tremendous effort it took to resist food. How every bite was the enemy, every pound shed something to celebrate. Stacy was one of those naturally thin people. She calmly drank can after can of Coke when they were pulling late-nighters and polished off candy bars and bags of M&Ms, all without seeming to show any effect. Meanwhile, if Elsa deviated even once from her diet soda the calories seemed to jump directly to her stomach and butt.

"Suit yourself."

Elsa heard the jingle of keys and then Stacy was gone with a bang of the door.

As soon as she'd left, Elsa sat up and slipped on her shoes. She didn't have much time if she was going to meet them.

It was getting colder. She dug her hands in the pockets of her red toggle coat and ran as fast as she could, which wasn't very fast, across the campus toward the woods.

They were allowed to leave campus during the day only with special permission, but Elsa knew that none of the other girls had this permission and she certainly hadn't been stupid enough to try and secure it.

She climbed the path as fast as she could, huffing with the effort, slipping in places on the piles of leaves carpeting the ground. The first time she'd been this way was late last spring, when the trees had been in bloom and the predominant color was green. Now it smelled like rotting vegetation and everything was brown.

At a certain point she thought she'd taken a wrong turn, following the path down another offshoot because she was confused by the myriad tree trunks that surrounded her. All at once a figure stepped out from behind the massive oak tree directly in front of her.

Elsa screamed and stepped back, losing her footing in the leaves and falling hard.

"Be quiet." The tone was harsh, but the familiar voice made Elsa happy.

"Elizabeth!" she cried as she scrambled to her feet without any help from the other girl, who stood watching her, arms crossed and a sour expression on her pretty face.

"What are you doing here, Elsa?"

"I came to see you." Elsa brushed the dirt from her knees. It wasn't quite the reception she was hoping to get, but that was okay. Once she saw her cell phone, she'd be happy. Only she wasn't.

"I came to bring you this," Elsa said, holding out the phone. Elizabeth's expression further darkened and she snatched it from Elsa's hand.

"Where did you get this?"

"I found it," Elsa said, faltering a little when the phone was taken from her. Elizabeth didn't look happy, she didn't understand the favor Elsa had done for her, for her and the club.

"Found it?" The word was imbued with sarcasm. "Found as in stole?"

"No! No, I wouldn't do that." Elsa felt confused. She hadn't envisioned Elizabeth being angry. In all her scenarios Elizabeth thanked her with tears in her eyes for saving her. "I would never—" Elsa started than stopped as Elizabeth held up a hand.

"Never mind," she said, flashing her trademark megawatt smile. How did she get her teeth so white? That was one of the things Elsa wanted to know. "Thank you for finding it."

It wasn't until she'd actually taken a few steps down the path that Elsa realized she was being dismissed. That was it? A simple thank-you? She hadn't skipped lunch for this.

"I want to come to the meeting," she said, following after Elizabeth. "That's why I'm here."

"There is no club."

"Yes there is." Elsa felt desperate. "Everyone knows there's a club."

Elizabeth only smiled. "Hmm, well maybe you should ask everyone about joining because I don't know anything about it."

"I know you meet here!"

The smile vanished from Elizabeth's face. "I don't like people spying on me, Elsa," she said. "I think you need to go back to school now."

And just like that she disappeared up the path. Elsa jogged after her, conscious of her body as an impediment as she ran, her large breasts bouncing against her chest, her stomach jiggling like molded Jell-O, her thighs rubbing against one another. No matter how hard she ran, she couldn't keep up with Elizabeth. Who wasn't even running. Who seemed to glide up the path with that long, graceful stride of hers.

"I found it in the tunnel," Elsa called out, desperate and breathless with the exertion.

That got Elizabeth's attention. She stopped short and then turned slowly back. "What did you say?"

"The phone," Elsa said. "I found it in the tunnel."

"What tunnel?"

"The tunnel. You know, the one connecting the chapel to the main building."

Now she had her interest. Elizabeth came back down the path. "When?"

"The morning I found Chelsea. I could have left it for the police, but I knew that would have made things hard for you." The words spilled out of her in a rush, but she couldn't hold them back any longer. Elizabeth had to know how she'd helped. "I knew the police would have questioned you."

"Why would you think that? We didn't have anything to do with Chelsea." Elizabeth's voice was harsh.

"I know that. But they wouldn't know that. You must have dropped your cell phone in the tunnel."

Elizabeth stared at her for a long moment and then she smiled again. Her smile reminded Elsa of a warm fire. "You are so right," Elizabeth said. "I'm so glad you're the one who found it."

"I'm good at details," Elsa said. "I could be an asset to the group."

"I think you're right," Elizabeth said. "But you understand that I can't make that decision alone."

"Oh, of course."

"I have to talk to the other girls first."

"Sure, I understand."

"But I know when they see this"—she held up the phone—"they'll be eager to have you join us."

Elsa went back down the path feeling great. This was a new beginning. She could feel it. She was going to stick to her diet. Maybe Elizabeth would even help her with it. Then she was going to buy a bikini just like the other girls wore, not that ugly black one-piece that was supposed to make her look like she'd lost ten pounds but just squeezed her middle so that the extra flesh seemed to pop out from her arms and thighs.

She wouldn't be the fat girl anymore, she'd be a member of the club. The rush of excitement was a new experience. Elsa broke off a piece of the protein bar she had in her pocket, eating it thoughtfully as she strolled back down the path.

Chapter Thirty-three

"She knows."

"She doesn't know anything—you said yourself that she thinks you dropped the phone some other time."

"Do you really think that would hold up to any scrutiny? Get real, Kristen!"

"Well, what's your solution?"

"We're going to have to deal with her."

Immediately, Tiffany shook her head. "No," she said. "I'm not doing anything to Elsa Klossner."

"We have no choice."

The votive lights wavered dangerously as Tiffany jumped up from the pew. "Count me out!"

Elizabeth had summoned them to this emergency meeting in the chapel instead of the woods because all of them had exams in the morning and it was cold enough that being in the woods, even with a fire, was uncomfortable.

Elizabeth rose out of her seat. "You don't get that choice, Tiffany," she said in a low voice. "You sent Chelsea the original message, remember? And you were the one who found the scarf."

Kristen moaned once, but covered her mouth when Elizabeth looked at her.

"Listen, I know it's not pleasant, but do you want to be expelled?"

"Of course not!" Kristen said. "But this was supposed to stop with Chelsea."

"I know." Elizabeth leaned against the back of the pew behind her. "It's like a cancer, the doctor thinks it's just a small tumor only to open the patient and discover that it's spread to every organ."

"Elsa isn't Chelsea," Tiffany said.

"No, she's not a whore," Elizabeth said. "But she's a glutton. Just watching her eat makes me want to vomit."

"Okay, but that's not at the same level as Morgan and Chelsea. She's a nuisance, but she's not a problem for the school."

"It doesn't matter," Elizabeth said. "She knows and that's enough."

"But you have the phone. It would be her word against yours and no one's going to believe her."

"The police might. Do you want them snooping around? What's to say that Elsa won't suddenly put two and two together and tell the police? We can't take that chance."

Tiffany was mewling. "What are we going to do? I can't get expelled, my parents will kill me."

"Do you really think that's the worst thing that could happen?" Kristen snapped. "We need to think of something."

Elizabeth smiled. "Don't worry, I already have."

The invitation came via a text message that afternoon. It was cryptic: "Midnight at the tower." Nothing more, but that information was enough.

Elsa was so excited that she could barely concentrate on the rest of her classes and was reprimanded by a confused-looking Señora Velasquez for daydreaming during Spanish class.

By dinnertime, she was a nervous wreck. She changed outfits five times, unsure of what would look best for her first meeting.

"Do you have a date?" Stacy asked and Elsa bristled at the surprise in her voice.

"Is that so hard to believe?"

"No, not at all, but you're just not like this."

"Like what?"

Stacy waved her hands at the clothes piled up on Elsa's bed. "Since when do you care so much about clothes?"

"I care," Elsa said, feeling defensive. It was easy for someone like Stacy. She could just choose whatever she wanted to wear without having to think about how it looked. Sure, some clothes looked better on her than others, but all the clothes looked okay. She didn't have to worry about whether she'd fit or how a shiny shirt would make her stomach look fatter or whether a short-sleeve blouse would make her arms look huge.

It had always been painful to dress in the plus-size clothes, to see her reflection in the mirror. But now that she was losing weight, she'd even fit into a size 16 the other day for the first time in years, and she could see some difference in her body. Even the gym teacher noticed. She'd asked if she was losing weight and listened approvingly to Elsa's diet plans, giving her an enthusiastic "Good job!"

And now she was being invited to join the club she'd wanted to belong to for so long. She felt suddenly magnanimous toward her roommate, who, after all, had always been her friend even when Elsa was at her heaviest. "I've been dieting," she said. "I guess that's why I care more about clothes."

"That's great," Stacy said. "Congratulations!"

She agreed that she wouldn't say anything when Elsa was gone, though she did pester Elsa about where she was going. Stacy assumed it was to meet a guy and Elsa didn't correct her. She knew better than to say anything about the club, not if she wanted to be invited back.

Nicole waited until she heard Destiny breathing steadily before she got up. She was used to dressing in the dark now, used to feeling for the labels in her jeans and hooded sweatshirt in order to put them on the right way and to stepping carefully so that her sneakers didn't squeak and she didn't bump into the furniture.

When she was dressed, when she'd pocketed the small flashlight she kept hidden at the back of her desk drawer, she tiptoed to the door and opened it a crack.

The hallway was clear as far as she could see, the long stretch of red carpeting looking purplish under the dim flicker of the nighttime fluorescent lights mounted in sconces.

She walked quickly and quietly down the hall, conscious of every footfall and trying hard to keep them muffled by the carpet. There were faint sounds, someone snoring and a radiator hissing, but otherwise all she heard was the silence, which echoed in her ears as if it were a noise itself.

When she got close to Ms. Kavanaugh's door, Nicole held her breath. What if her teacher was awake? Nicole glanced at the door and then away, feeling the back of her neck get damp as she tried to think of an excuse to offer if Ms. Kavanaugh suddenly opened her apartment door.

No one came as she pushed through the outside door and she was careful to catch it and put a thin sliver of wood in the jamb before letting it close.

Wind whistled around the buildings, creating echoes, and she looked around constantly, feeling her heartbeats like someone running inside her, convinced every time she looked that someone was behind her.

The path toward the chapel was empty as far as she could see. She heard her footfalls soft on the concrete and had a sudden memory of walking in the Jardin Tulieries with her brother almost two years before. A winter's night in Paris, the noise from traffic only a few blocks away. The Louvre closed, the carousel shuttered for the night. The moon had been full just like tonight, a large pearl button in a sky studded with diamond pinpricks.

The wind had whistled through the trees just like now and she'd heard her footfalls loudly, scared enough to clutch Paul's hand as they passed through a gloomy section and she spotted a dark figure on a bench ahead.

"Let's go the other way," she'd begged, pulling on her brother's arm, but he'd resisted, laughing at her.

"There's nothing to be scared of," he said. "It's probably some old man."

And he'd been right, an old man resting on his cane who barely acknowledged them when they wished him good evening. Still, she'd walked past feeling his eyes on her back, and she could feel it now, the sense that every square inch of her body was alert to attack. She could remember, too, what she didn't have now—the comforting feel of her brother's larger hand encircling hers.

Thinking about Paul brought with it that intense longing for him that twisted her stomach like it was a dishcloth. She pressed a gloved hand against her abdomen, pushing against the pain, and then she saw another hooded figure standing on the path ahead and she ran toward her.

Tiffany smiled in greeting, but didn't speak until they were standing in the shadow of the chapel bell tower, on the far side where they wouldn't be visible if anyone should happen to look outside.

Elizabeth was already waiting there, leaning casually against the wall, her face hidden by the hood. Kristen was there, too, and she was talking with someone else.

Nicole paused for a moment, surprised, but then followed Tiffany until they were standing in a circle that included Elsa Klossner.

Elizabeth gestured with a hand and Kristen unearthed a

bottle of wine from a backpack and opened it, giggling as the corkscrew went in the wrong way. It took her a few tries, but at last the cork pulled from the bottle with a satisfying pop.

Nicole was surprised when Elizabeth only produced one glass. She poured a small amount of wine into the glass and passed it around the group, invoking the Oculus. Each girl took a sip in turn, but when Nicole extended it to Elsa, Elizabeth stopped her.

"Tonight we have someone new who wants to join our inner circle," she said. She refilled the glass and handed it to Elsa with a smile. "Drink up and celebrate your inclusion in this most exclusive of clubs."

Elsa dutifully took the glass, though Nicole noticed that her hands trembled. The girl took a small sip and tried to pass the cup back to Elizabeth, but she declined.

"No, it's all for you."

Elsa's white cheeks turned slightly pink. Nicole wondered if she were used to drinking wine. The heavyset girl took another sip, too big this time, and choked slightly.

"Careful, Elsa!" Kristen chided. "That's an expensive bottle, we don't want to waste it."

The pink staining her cheeks spread to her neck. Elsa took several more sips, her eyes darting nervously to the other members of the circle.

Nicole looked at Elizabeth, but she wore her usual enigmatic smile. Kristen, in contrast, wasn't smiling at all and even Tiffany's giggles seemed more nervous than amused.

"All the way down," Elizabeth said when Elsa seemed to flag with the glass still a quarter full. Elsa gulped it down and then Elizabeth simply filled it again, but this time passed it around to the whole group.

Somehow the glass ended at Elsa and Elizabeth again bade her drink up and not waste the wine. They did this same cycle two more times and then the bottle was empty.

This time it was Elsa who giggled as she handed back the

empty glass to Elizabeth. Kristen wrapped it in a towel and put it carefully in her backpack along with the empty bottle.

"Now what?" Elsa asked, her boldness brought on by alcohol, Nicole thought, noticing that she swayed slightly on her feet.

Nicole felt a bit light-headed, but she was far more used to wine and she'd had far less of it than Elsa.

"Now we go to the dining hall," Elizabeth said. "It's not good to drink on an empty stomach."

Tiffany giggled, but a sharp look from Elizabeth silenced her. Nicole had the feeling that something more was happening that she didn't understand, but she pulled her hood forward, dug her hands deep in the front pocket of her sweatshirt, and followed in Elizabeth's wake.

At night the dining hall seemed imposing, even scary. It was a newer building, but it had been built so its façade mimicked the older, stone buildings on campus, all the way down to the ivy that crept along the high walls.

Elizabeth fiddled with one of the wooden doors and then pulled it open. Nicole caught a glimpse of a key in her hand before she tucked it away. Elsa was in front of Nicole. She could hear her breathing, thick and heavy. Was it nervousness or exertion or both?

Tiffany exclaimed a muffled "Ow!" as she bumped into something.

"Quiet!" Elizabeth hissed. She lit the flashlight and led the way toward the kitchen.

Things that barely registered in the daytime became ominous in the dark. The most common objects seemed threatening: an enormous stainless-steel stand mixer, the magnetic strip lined with knives, their blades gleaming. Elizabeth ignored it all—the sinks wide and deep enough to hold a child, the long line of gas ranges and the copper-bottomed pots hanging from a rack over their heads.

They walked in single file along the tile floor and then

Elizabeth stopped. Nicole looked past her and saw they were standing in front of the freezer.

"Okay, Elsa, here's what we're going to do. You need to go in the freezer and get a carton of ice cream, but we don't want to eat just any old flavor. We only want to try it if it's good, so you have to try them all first. I want you to be the taste-tester."

"I can't eat ice cream," Elsa said, laughing a little, looking from Elizabeth to the other girls.

"Of course you can," Elizabeth said and she laughed, too. "You want to join the club, don't you?"

"But I'm on a diet," Elsa said in a low voice. "Ice cream's not allowed."

"You don't have to eat the whole thing," Elizabeth said. "C'mon, Elsa, don't you deserve a treat?" She smiled and her smile made Nicole smile, too. It was strange and goofy, but why not? She wanted to belong to the club, didn't she? It wasn't hazing, Nicole thought, because it wasn't cruel, not really.

Elizabeth held out a tablespoon and Elsa took it, her smile faltering. She looked as if she were going to say something, but Elizabeth prompted her. "Go on, then, get in the freezer."

Elsa struggled with the bulky metal latch for a moment before the heavy steel door swung open and a blast of icy air spilled out.

She stepped over the threshold and paused, looking back over her shoulder.

"Keep going," Elizabeth said, gesturing impatiently with her hand. "They're in the big containers in the back."

Elsa moved in her usual lumbering fashion, her clumsy gait more pronounced because of the alcohol. As she stepped toward the back of the freezer, the blue sweater she wore rode up to reveal an inch of white elastic and pink cotton underwear hovering above the waistline of her jeans.

Tiffany or Kristen giggled, Nicole didn't know whom, but she felt something akin to excitement herself, that anxious yet elated feeling of doing something forbidden. She was just about to call to Elsa to see which ice cream she'd found when Elizabeth touched her arm.

"We need someone to keep a lookout," she said. "Go wait outside."

Nicole didn't want to go back outside just when things were getting interesting and she certainly didn't want to go by herself. Elizabeth had already turned her attention back to the open freezer door, obviously assuming that Nicole would do as she asked. She was the leader, Nicole thought, and she moved reluctantly back the way they'd come.

She crossed the dark kitchen as quickly as she could, wishing she felt glad that Elizabeth had asked for her help. Instead she felt resentful. She was halfway across the spooky dining area when there was a loud bang like a door slamming.

Nicole dropped to her knees, sure that someone had discovered them. Pressing close against a table, she tried to become part of the furniture, her knees aching, her hands trembling against the scuffed floor. She listened for the sound of footsteps hammering across the floor.

Nothing. She could hear nothing except her own anxious breathing. She stood up slowly, careful not to bump the table, blinking in the dark. Clouds outside had shifted and there was a bit of moonlight streaming through the windows. The door was still in shadow, but she couldn't see anything around it.

She crept forward, keeping low until she reached the exit where she rose to her full height, looking around again before carefully pushing the door open. It was so still outside that she heard quite clearly the solitary and spooky call of an owl far off in the woods.

She shivered and blew on her hands, watching as little

clouds hovered in the air before vanishing. Suddenly Elizabeth was there, the other girls right behind her.

"Let's go," she said, grabbing Nicole by the hand and pulling her away from the dining hall. As they ran across the lawn, Elizabeth's hood fell off and her long blond hair rippled behind her like a moonlit stream.

It wasn't until she was back on the far side of the bell tower that Nicole realized someone was missing.

"Where's Elsa?"

Chapter Thirty-four

When the freezer door banged shut, Elsa didn't understand. She jumped at the noise and whirled around, but she
didn't feel alarmed. Not yet. It was a mistake, of course.
They must have stepped away from the heavy door and it
swung closed.

She stumbled back toward it, spoon clutched in her hand.
"Hey," she called. "Open up!" She laughed a little, the wine
making her feel dopey. It was funny, they'd all laugh together
when the door opened.

Only it didn't. Elsa shivered. It was damn cold in here
and she wasn't wearing a coat. She reached for the knob on
the door, but it was missing, there was only the stub of a
metal rod sticking out. She tried turning that, but it didn't
budge. She dropped the spoon and slapped the steel door.
"Open up!"

When nothing happened, Elsa felt the first little tendril of
fear uncurl in her stomach. She slammed both fists against
the door and shouted, "Hey! I'm in here! Open up!"

Pressing her ear close to the door, she tried to detect any
noise, but the door was insulated and solid. She could hear

nothing but her own rapid breaths and the hum of the freezer itself.

She pounded again, shouting along with it, until her fists were red and her throat raw. Panting and blinking back tears, she stepped back. Had they really left her here? Why? Was this some kind of initiation rite? If this was a joke, she didn't find it funny.

They've left, Elsa. They're not out there.

Panicked, Elsa fiddled with the metal rod again, wrapping the edge of her sweater around it and trying with all her strength to make it turn. She cried out with frustration when it didn't budge.

She was so cold. Her teeth chattered and she looked around to find something, anything to use to get the damn door open. She picked up an empty metal milk crate from a corner and hurled it at the door. It dented the steel and clattered to the floor. She did it again and then stood at a slight distance and tried kicking the door open. All that accomplished was a few more dents and a sore leg.

Was it colder than it had been? She wrapped her arms around her chest and walked the length of the freezer. Crates of milk stood next to large, cardboard tubs of ice cream, which were across from shelving that held stacks of eggs and boxes of butter. There was nothing in here but food.

She remembered a fantasy she'd had as a kid of getting locked in an ice cream store. She'd imagined moving at a leisurely pace from carton to carton, tasting all the flavors and lingering over her favorites. She'd imagined making triple scoop cones and banana splits and hot fudge sundaes with extra fudge and whipped cream.

There was nothing to stop her from eating all the ice cream in the freezer, but just thinking about it made her sick to her stomach. She didn't want any ice cream. All she wanted was to leave.

When were they going to come back? How long were

they going to keep up the joke? *They're not coming back, Elsa. This isn't a joke. The only joke is you thinking that they'd want you in their club.*

The tears fell then and she sobbed as she marched around the freezer with her hands pulled up in the sleeves of her sweater and her arms wrapped around her body.

She'd been so stupid to think that they wanted her. Why would they? She was just a fat loser. Elizabeth had wanted her phone back from her, nothing more. Then why hadn't she just taken it and left her alone? Because Elsa begged? No, that wasn't the reason. They were afraid of what Elsa might do. She might go to Sister Rose and tell her that she'd found Elizabeth's phone in the tunnel near Chelsea's body.

The full reality hit Elsa on her fourth circuit of the freezer. *They killed Chelsea and they're trying to kill you. They've left you here to die.*

Elsa screamed. She threw her body at the door over and over again until she tripped and fell in a sobbing heap on the floor.

Choking on sobs, she lumbered to her feet. She had to keep moving. If she stopped moving she'd freeze. The tears were freezing on her face; she scrubbed at her cheeks with the rough wool of her sweater.

She began another circuit of the freezer. When would someone find her? The cafeteria ladies. They'd come eventually. All she had to do was keep walking.

Her hands burned. She was so tired. There were thirteen steps to the back wall. Thirteen wasn't a lucky number. Take a bigger step and make it only twelve. Twelve back and then six for each side. Mix it up, change directions.

Each step seemed to take extra effort. She was so tired. Twelve steps back, one foot in front of the other. Done. If she just sat down for a minute it wouldn't matter. No, keep moving. Four, five, six. The back wall looked wavy. Was it moving? Eight, nine, ten. No, it was just out of focus. Eleven, twelve. Done. Tap the back wall and turn.

Each step back was slower. She had to stop, she was just too tired to continue. She saw some plastic milk crates at the front of the freezer. When she reached those she would just sit for a moment.

She sank onto a crate. That was a relief. It felt good to sit down, even if it was just for a moment. She stared at the door until it swam. Blink, blink and there it was whole again. She was so tired. If she just closed her eyes for a minute. She'd just close them for a minute, not even a whole minute, just thirty seconds. Her eyelids dropped like a final curtain.

Chapter Thirty-five

Elizabeth picked up the backpack she'd left against the wall of the bell tower. "Don't worry about Elsa," she said. She glanced at her watch. "We just have one more thing and then we need to go."

"But where is she?" Nicole said. "Did she get the ice cream?"

Instead of answering, Elizabeth dug in the backpack and brought out something small. Looking like a Valkyrie in the moonlight, Elizabeth turned to Nicole and beckoned her forward. Nicole moved toward her as Elizabeth revealed a circular tin sitting on her left palm. As Nicole watched, Elizabeth dipped a thumb in the tin and drew the sign of the cross against Nicole's forehead.

"You are anointed with the chrism of purification," Elizabeth said in a dramatic voice and Nicole felt warm oil branding her forehead. Then the leader stepped back and all three girls smiled. "Congratulations," she said. "You're official."

Nicole lightly touched her hand to the oil on her forehead and then she smiled, too. Elizabeth laughed and looked up at the sky, brushing silky strands of hair back from her face. "Look at the moon!" she whispered. "Isn't it lovely?"

It seemed to Nicole that she'd never looked at the moon in the same way or noticed how many stars filled the sky. The excitement she'd felt all evening had mellowed into some deeper, distant yet familiar feeling. It took her a moment to realize it was happiness.

Only one thing marred the moment, the nagging feeling that someone was missing. "Where's Elsa?" she asked again.

Kristen didn't meet Nicole's eyes, but Tiffany looked as if she had something to say, eyes brimming with some secret knowledge, but she didn't at a warning look from Elizabeth.

"She must have found her own way back," Elizabeth said. "It's late—we'll be missed."

They separated halfway across the lawn, each to her own dormitory. Nicole found the door just as she'd left it, and as she moved the sliver of wood she'd wedged in it, the quiet click of the door closing reminded her of the slamming door in the cafeteria. It hadn't been the main door, so what had that noise been?

She crept down the hall to her room and undressed in the dark, stuffing her clothes under the bed with her small flashlight wrapped in her sweatshirt. Her roommate stirred as Nicole sat down on the bed and she held her breath, but the other girl only groaned and rolled toward the wall. Nicole found her pajamas under the pillow and put them on before slipping under the covers.

She shivered between the cold sheets but even now, tired and cold, she couldn't sleep without again tasting the wine, or hearing the sound of Elizabeth's laughter, or seeing Elsa, poor, slow Elsa, lumbering into the freezer.

When she finally fell asleep it was to a vision of that long, blond hair streaming in the moonlight.

Chapter Thirty-six

There was snow on the ground. Lauren could see it in the dim light out her bedroom window, a thin layer lying untouched and perfect like white frosting on a sheet cake.

She'd woken to the noise of a car struggling to make it up the hill and now she could see its headlights as it crested the top. It was only 6:00 A.M.

Lying back down, she kept the curtain open, staring out at the lazy swirls of snowflakes that were still floating down from a pale gray sky.

It had snowed in Europe, but not like this. The most she'd seen was less than a half-inch in London, enough to dust statues and monuments and to melt in dirty puddles on the streets.

It had been cold, though, bitterly cold at times and the flat had a faulty heating system. She remembered the winter Sunday she'd spent huddled with Michael under an old comforter and layers of moth-eaten blankets talking about the snowfalls of her childhood.

She could see him as he'd looked then, the two of them lying face-to-face under the covers, bundled in jeans and sweaters because of the cold, their stocking feet entwined.

They'd warmed their hands on each other's bodies that cold winter, taking off the bare minimum, working their chilled fingers under each other's shirts and down each other's pants, eager to feel something other than that biting cold. In between bouts of sex, they'd emerge from the covers long enough to warm their hands on endless mugs of hot tea.

Michael liked his tea very sweet, stirring in heaping tea-spoons of sugar as he encouraged her to talk. She could still see his ink-stained fingers. His fingers had always been stained with ink and she'd assumed it was from writing his thesis. A doctoral candidate on the surface, but an oppor-tunist at heart.

He'd told her about his own childhood in the Midlands, stories about how he'd stolen candy from the local Tesco's and about how he and a mate once hotwired a neighbor's car and took it for a joyride.

She wondered, now, if those stories were true. Had it all just been a fishing expedition, give a little information in the hopes that she'd give more? *"Tell me about your childhood."*

On that cold Sunday she'd told him how the western Pennsylvania sky would turn a dirty white before a heavy snow, the clouds hanging lower with the weight of it, like a ceiling about to collapse. She described how the snow some-times fell in torrents, just like rain, and how it made a funny, crunching noise when she spread her arms and legs wide to make a snow angel. She thought of Amanda, then, and of sledding with the neighborhood kids down Buckeye Hill, their laughter echoing through the dark, barren trees in the park.

Michael listened, his fingers trailing over her body, com-ing to rest on the scar at her collarbone. He liked to touch her there, rubbing his fingers over it as if it were some sort of touchstone. *"Did it hurt?"*

She'd loved him so much that winter, believed so much in his love for her. It was painful to remember how naïve she'd been. She turned away from the snowfall, shaking off the memories. Once she'd longed for this weather and now here it was and all it meant was she'd have a hard time getting into town. Maybe somebody could give her a ride, or she'd have to cough up some money for a taxi.

While she was showering she thought she heard a high-pitched noise, but it had stopped by the time she got out. She was dressed before she heard it again. A siren. Lauren raced to the window and looked out just as an ambulance crested the hill and came racing along the long, circular drive.

Someone rapped on her door. Lauren expected to see some teacher with an explanation of what was happening, but instead it was Stacy Chin standing in pajamas and slippers.

"My roommate's gone."

Later, Lauren would reflect that this was the precise moment that she knew something was very, very wrong.

Betty Pachuk's old Dodge had trouble going the hill. She'd told Don that the guy at Sears told her the tires had to be replaced, but did he listen? He always thought he knew better, penny-pinching old fart, and she was the one who had to pay the price.

She gripped the wheel tightly and pressed her waffle-toed foot against the accelerator as gently as she could. "C'mon, sweetheart, you can do it," she said, coaxing her baby along just as she'd used to coax the horses on her father's farm all those years ago.

Christ, what had made her think of that? She was too old to go tripping down memory lane. The farm was a strip mall now, same as everywhere else in this country, not that she wanted to live in one of those Arab places. No thank you. Dressed in a veil didn't suit her and she'd had more than enough crap from men to last her a lifetime.

Truth was, the only reason she stayed with Don was because of the kids. Only little Bobby left at home now and he certainly wasn't little no more. Towering over her 5'5" height and easily lifting her to swing her around the kitchen when he was feeling happy, though she'd complain that he'd put his back out doing that, hefting her weight.

"Yeah," Don would chime in with that stupid laugh of his, "your mama never lost that baby weight."

Like he was some kind of god himself. Sitting there all slumped over in his recliner with what was left of his hair sticking up like weeds in an empty lot. Shoveling snacks into his mouth like someone was going to grab the bag away from him, mesmerized by whatever dumb-ass sport was playing on TV She had friends whose husbands were golfers or did woodwork. Not Don. His only hobby was watching TV sports.

Still, she wasn't supposed to complain because he came home to her at night and brought his paycheck with him. Jesus, women of her generation had been sold a bill of goods. Bow and scrape and spread your legs for a man who puts a little food on the table and doesn't beat the shit out of you or spend his whole paycheck at the track. Don't ride him if he drinks. Don't nag him if he never picks up a damn thing around the house. Don't worry if he looks at other women and comments on them in your presence just as long as he brings his naked, scratching self to your bed.

She was going to be fifty-five next year and by then she'd have enough saved to quit this job and quit this marriage and quit this town. Bobby would be off at college and she'd be free to go.

The Dodge crested the hill and she let up on the accelerator a little, steering with care as it drifted around the circle. She had to pump the brakes to make the turn into the back parking lot, but it was clear from the open slots that she'd beaten even Janet to work.

She had to fumble for the key to the dining hall door,

pulling off one thick glove to dig it out from amid the gum wrappers and lint in her parka pocket, but then it slid in right away. Almost as if the door was already open.

She stripped off her coat and hung it up on the coatrack in the small office. Punch in her time card, pull on the big industrial white apron she wore over her working whites, pull a cap snug over her graying curls, and she was good to go. She didn't put on the latex gloves until she was doing food prep; they just got in the way.

Janet came in while she was standing in the main kitchen reviewing the menu for the day. "Woo-ee, it's a bitch out there," she said. "Traffic's snarled all over the garden."

Betty noted that they were going to bake two batches of cookies that day in addition to the soup that needed to be ready for lunch. It was a good day for soup. She stepped toward the pantry and noticed something brown on the floor. Stooping over she picked up a brown oak leaf curled in on itself.

"Where did you come from?" she mused, carrying it over to deposit it in the trash can. But there was another one. She got that, too.

Janet came out of the office, tucking her short permed hair under her cap, and Betty waved the leaves at her. "Didn't we sweep this floor last night?"

" 'We' nothing. I did it."

"So where did these come from?"

Janet shrugged. "Better check we've got enough of the individual milks on hand because no way is that truck making it up the hill for delivery today."

"I'll do it," Betty said, brushing her hands free of crumbs. "Got to get the butter and eggs out anyway."

There was another leaf outside the freezer door and a tiny pile of dirt with it. Jesus, but Janet needed to get her eyes checked.

Shaking her head, Betty pulled the handle hard and the

door unlatched with a big sucking sound. She swung the door back and stepped inside.

What she saw propped on the milk crates made her forget about the leaves, about the cookies, about everything except keeping her breakfast down.

By the time Stephanie and Oz got the unmarked sedan up the hill to the scene, Harriet Wembley, thanks to her all-wheel-drive SUV, had already declared the probable cause of death "acute hypothermia" and the time somewhere between 11 and 2.

Crime scene tape circled the cafeteria and a crowd of students stood at its perimeters, along with several uniforms. Reporters weren't far behind. They were being kept at bay at the base of the hill by some ambitious patrolmen.

Stephanie and Oz ignored the students and stepped under the tape. Harriet was just packing up.

"About time you got here," she said and she looked unusually grim. She moved to the side and Stephanie saw the body of a heavyset girl sitting upright on a couple of plastic milk crates as if she were waiting for something. Or someone.

Harriet gave them the details and then she said, "You see that blue pallor? In a nutshell, she froze to death."

The girl was wearing a blue sweater and jeans—no coat—and she had her arms wrapped tightly around her body as if trying to ward off the cold.

"So she accidentally locked herself in here?" Oz said, looking around. "I thought freezers had latches or something on the inside to prevent that."

Stephanie examined the door. "The door's been tampered with—look, a knob is missing." There were also dents in it.

Oz bent down to look at it more closely. "So, she comes in here, but then she can't get out."

"*Why* did she come in here?" Stephanie looked around. On the floor near the plastic crates where the girl sat perched was a metal tablespoon. Stephanie picked it up. "Where did this come from?"

Oz looked away from his examination of the knob and Harriet Wembley shook her head. "No idea."

"A cafeteria worker found her, right?"

Harriet nodded. "Maybe she dropped it. She's in the main room with one of the officers who responded."

Stephanie wandered out there carrying the spoon. She saw two middle-aged women in white uniform shirts and slacks with clear plastic caps covering their hair talking to the formidable little headmistress.

Stephanie approached with caution, holding up the spoon. "Did either of you ladies drop this spoon in the freezer?"

The smaller woman with frizzy gray curls pointed to her bigger coworker. "That would be Betty."

"I never did," Betty said. "Sure, I found that poor girl, but I didn't carry nothing in with me. Certainly not no spoon." She looked affronted, as if Stephanie were accusing her of having killed the girl.

Stephanie led her through finding the body, the telling of which was done with great gusto and detail and Stephanie could sense that by the end of the day what had started as a tragic morning for this woman would become a pivotal tale in her life.

This seemed to be apparent to Sister Rose, too, if her demeanor was anything to go by. She listened intently as Betty described opening the freezer door and finding the girl and then she warned her not to talk to reporters.

"Clearly, this girl came to the dining hall for a snack and got trapped in the freezer," she said.

"Are students allowed access at night?"

"Of course not," Sister Rose said. "But as I'm sure you're aware by now, detective, a determined teenage girl can get anywhere she wants to. "

Stephanie nodded. "Who has access to this building?"

"Betty and Janet, obviously," Sister Rose said. "But there are others—our handyman, other workers, myself, and Mr. Pierce."

"And the students? Do any of them have access?"

"No, absolutely not."

"So this student"—Stephanie looked down at her note-book—"Elsa Klossner? How do you think she got in?"

The answer was harsh and immediate. "I have no idea."

"How long has the freezer's inside knob been missing?"

Janet looked surprised. "It was there yesterday—and it was working fine, too."

Betty nodded in agreement. "We use that door everyday, there's nothing wrong with it."

"Did you notice anything else this morning, anything that seemed odd or out of place?"

"Just leaves," Betty said. "There were some dried leaves on the ground. I thought Janet missed them when she swept yesterday."

"Oh, thanks very much." Janet grimaced.

"Never mind, it must have been that girl."

"Did either of you know Elsa Klossner?" Stephanie asked.

Betty shook her head. "Just by sight. We don't mix with the girls much—unless they get punishment duty."

"How often does that happen?" Stephanie asked Sister Rose, who shrugged.

"I don't know. Once a month or so? It's a standard pun-ishment for accruing too many demerits."

"Can you show me where you kept the keys?" Stephanie followed Betty and Janet into the small kitchen office, with Sister Rose trailing them.

The keys were kept on a small wall rack and there was more than one copy of the dining hall key. The honor system that the school operated under might be admirable, but it clearly wasn't working. It wouldn't be difficult to take a key if someone was motivated.

She didn't comment until she'd rejoined Oz, who stood just outside the freezer rubbing his arms. "About the only good thing to say about this crime scene is that I don't have to smell it," he muttered.

"Yeah, well you're going to love this—the keys to this place hang in plain sight in the office and students are assigned punishment work in the cafeteria. So basically everyone and their brother had access."

"Great." Oz grunted and stepped back in. "I suppose you don't think that this was just accidental—that she locked herself in here."

Stephanie shook her head. "According to the cafeteria ladies the door was in fine working order yesterday. So the door's been tampered with—c'mon, Oz."

"Okay, okay, I know." He sighed and looked at the door again. "So we've got someone doing this."

"Yes."

He sighed. "Christ, I'm getting tired of coming up here."

Daniel Stein got the jump on the latest death at St. Ursula's from a source he'd cultivated in Gashford. It was surprisingly easy to find people who'd do some watching and listening for him. People happy to think they were contributing to the news, who had the time to make phone calls and shrugged off the twenty-dollar bills he tried to offer.

Retirees typically, and this was one of them, one of the greatest generation who hung out at the diner in Gashford and knew the town's history's going back more than ten decades.

Edward Wilton was the kind of man who carried a pocket comb to smooth his silvered hair and wore a tie under his windbreaker. He probably wouldn't have hired a Stein or Goldberg or Cohen at the bank when he was manager, not that he ever said as much to Daniel. However, times had changed, as he was fond of saying, and Edward's days of a man of importance were so far in the past that the few moments of glory he experienced as an advisor to the *New York Times*—this was how Daniel couched it—meant something to him.

Edward's call came when Daniel was fresh from the shower and trying on the Brooks Brothers suit that had just come back from the tailor's. Having a good tailor was at least as important as having a good plumber and probably more so. Plumbers, after all, were a dime a dozen, but skilled tailors were a rare thing and his was an old woman who'd been trained in Eastern Europe and never blushed when she took his inseam.

When the phone rang, he dashed across the room, sure that it was from London. It was ironic that another death had occurred at the school just as he was circling closer to the truth about the mysterious Lauren Kavanaugh.

In the last week he'd finally gotten a tangible lead, locating the school where she'd last taught and adding a few more pieces to the puzzle.

Disappointment that it wasn't the call he was expecting gave way to excitement when he heard the news. He scribbled Edward's information down in one of his notebooks and changed out of his suit in a hurry, dressing in what he thought of as his country attire—khakis and a button-down—and stuffing a bag with a few essentials so he could stay longer to cover the story.

It wasn't good to get too excited, he thought as he drove his silver Prius out of Manhattan. By the time he got to Northern New Jersey, this could well turn out to be something completely unrelated to the other two deaths and the mysterious teacher. Edward had been sketchy with the details, but Daniel Stein's gut told him when something was worth pursuing and it was talking to him now.

Even if it did turn out to be a mistake, Daniel was determined to take the opportunity to talk to Lauren Kavanaugh again.

He'd called various police sources and used all of his considerable charm to have them check Lauren Kavanaugh and every one came up empty. No criminal record for Lauren Kavanaugh, not even so much as a parking ticket. For some reason that he couldn't explain, her very lack of a record just fueled Daniel's suspicions.

His visit to Denning High School in Hoboken, where she'd been a frequent substitute, confirmed what he already suspected—she had something to hide. A couple of teachers described her as "distant" and "secretive" and the principal, an effusive man who seemed happy to spend his lunch break talking with a *Times* reporter, mentioned that while she'd been a fine teacher they had no sense of the person behind the position.

"Teaching is a collaborative process," the principal said. "At Denning we pride ourselves on getting to know most of our teachers—even our substitutes—very well, but I'm afraid Ms. Kavanaugh remained as much of an enigma to me when she left as she did when she first arrived."

This only whetted Daniel's appetite for more information, but personnel records were private, so he employed an old trick.

"Did she talk much about her years at UVA?"

"UVA? You mean the University of Virginia? I don't know anything about that. I understood that her degree came from the University of London."

"Oh, maybe I was mistaken," Daniel murmured, jotting down "U London" in his notebook. The principal's somewhat-watery eyes narrowed.

"I thought this story was about teachers moving from the public to private sector?"

"Yes, well, it's in the information-gathering stage at the moment." Recognizing his cue, Daniel hopped off his seat and made his exit before any more questions.

He'd called the University of London yesterday, and after

numerous handoffs, ended up leaving voice mail for someone in the records office.

A day later he was heading toward the school again. If
Edward's info did turn out to be correct this could be huge.
Three teenage girls dead in less than two months? No matter
how the headmistress tried to spin it, these just couldn't be
accidents.

As he drove, Daniel wondered where Lauren Kavanaugh
factored in this. He couldn't think of the girls' deaths without thinking of the secretive teacher, but so far he could find
only two tangible links. First was the fact that the deaths occurred after she was hired. Second was the fact that she'd
found the first girl. And neither of these facts meant anything.

So why keep pursuing this? Maybe Lauren Kavanaugh
was just a nervous young woman. There were plenty of people who were anxious when they talked to reporters.

Except Daniel knew her face. He recognized her from
somewhere and she knew where—he'd seen it in her eyes, he
read it in her body language, he could feel it in his gut.

By the time Daniel made it to the entrance of St. Ursula's
the police had a roadblock set up to keep out the media and
any other interested bystanders, of which there were already
plenty. At least three news trucks and numerous small cars
lined the sides of the road.

That was obviously not going to do. He wasn't going to
waste his day hanging out with the dolts from the local TV
news. Or worse yet, the overly made-up, bubble-headed hosts
of the tabloid shows. Daniel shuddered and drove slowly
past the traffic, considering.

When he came back around he stopped next to the policeman guarding the entrance. "Sister Rose sent for me," he
said, flashing his ID with the confidence of a man fully expecting the barrier to move for him at once.

The young policeman, who looked like he was all of seventeen, didn't seem to know what to do with this information so he stubbornly repeated what he'd obviously been told to say: "No one in except police and school personnel."

He waved Daniel off as if he were a fly. Lesser men, men who looked down on reporters and thought of them as the vultures and hyenas of professional life, would have been angered by this casual dismissal. Not Daniel Stein. He'd faced rejection all of his professional life and he certainly wasn't about to let some low-level suburban cop dictate his presence at a story.

"Check," he said. "Sister Rose wants me here."

Not that this would necessarily work, but it gave him something to do while he explored other options. If this didn't get him in he could park farther down the road and hike in over the hills, but it looked easy to get lost and Daniel Stein was no great fan of the outdoors. He'd dropped out of Cub Scouts after the first camping trip, wondering why anybody would trade TV, indoor plumbing, and a restaurant meal for the dubious pleasures of tents, latrines, and smoky fires.

To his credit, police boy was doing as he'd been asked, calling in on the handheld radio while he kept one suspicious eye trained on Daniel and his car.

A lawn-care truck came clattering down the road, the two guys in the cab staring with interest at all the commotion near the school's entrance and the guy bouncing around in the back grinning out at the media like some sort of demented scarecrow. Daniel could almost hear the banjos.

Police boy was done on the phone. Daniel pushed the button on the window back down, prepared to thank the kid, but he was shaking his head. "No entry."

Chapter Thirty-seven

Classes were canceled at St. Ursula's, though as an official announcement it came somewhat late since many students were already packing their bags. The rest seemed to have gathered outside the dining hall, many with coats thrown over their pajamas, watching the police proceedings with all the excitement of celebrity seekers.

Lauren saw them as she crossed the campus to the main building to meet with the Klossner family. They'd flown in by private plane with their lawyer and she'd watched from a distance as they arrived at St. Ursula's in a chauffeured black Cadillac.

Sister Rose seemed to be in a state of denial. She'd called an emergency faculty meeting earlier in the morning, not long after the police arrived but long enough for the campus to be in an uproar. Anxious and harried faculty members crowded into the conference room in the main building, expecting to get clear answers about what, exactly, had happened overnight.

They were greeted by a headmistress who looked as calm as ever, the only evidence of stress being the presence of a somber-faced Ryland Pierce at her elbow.

"Classes are canceled and I'm asking all faculty members to help make calls to parents," she said in her usual calm manner. "If parents want their children to come home for the weekend, then we need to help them facilitate smooth departures."

"You're not canceling classes indefinitely?" an older teacher asked.

Sister Rose looked affronted. "Absolutely not. St. Ursula's will remain the calm port in the storm that it has always been. We may be buffeted by these unfortunate accidents, but we will not be defeated."

Far from being reassuring, Lauren found the older woman's stance disconcerting. She wasn't alone.

"These deaths can't be accidents," Alice LaRue said and others chimed in their agreement, but Sister Rose held up one small hand to silence them.

"We don't have time for this discussion," she said. "As you know, the police presence on campus is keeping the media at bay, but we must make sure that our girls aren't assaulted by reporters as they leave campus or when they return for classes on Monday morning."

When Alice and a few other teachers continued to argue, Ryland Pierce clapped his hands for order. "Elsa Klossner's parents are on there way here and an emergency session of the Board of Directors is being convened. We understand your concern, but these meetings have to take precedence. Please try and understand."

They'd filed out then, though not without muttering. Sister Rose plucked at Lauren's sleeve as she neared the door and pulled her aside.

"The Klossners will want to talk with you," she said. "We need to provide a united front on this, Miss Kavanaugh."

What could Lauren tell them? At some point in the night, Elsa had left her room and gone to the dining hall, but no one, not even her own roommate, had heard anything. At the same time that Elsa's body was found in the freezer, Stacy Chin had woken to discover Elsa's empty bed.

After Stacy showed up at her door, Lauren had conducted a search of Augustine House that ended only when she couldn't find Elsa or the clothes she'd worn the night before and she suddenly connected the sirens she'd heard with the girl's disappearance.

Lauren questioned all the other residents about when they'd last seen Elsa, but except for one student who dimly remembered hearing a door close sometime in the night, nobody could remember the last time they'd seen her.

Poor Elsa. A good-natured girl, but no genius. It seemed grossly unfair that she hadn't been given brains to compensate for her plain looks. All she had was pretty hair and a desperate need to be liked. Maybe it was the lack of something to compensate that had made her long for popularity all the more. She'd hung around the popular girls constantly, trying to be included.

And it had killed her. Lauren was sure of that. One of them, maybe all of them, had locked her in the freezer and left her to die. As soon as she'd heard the details, Lauren knew the truth, but there was no one to talk to, no one in whom to confide her suspicions, no one who would believe her.

Sister Rose certainly didn't, or wouldn't, believe this, and Lauren didn't dare tell the Klossners that their daughter probably met her fate at the hands of bullying students.

She smoothed the skirt of her gray suit and adjusted the cuffs of the lavender blouse she was wearing. Sister Rose met her in the hall, dropping her public face for just a moment so that Lauren saw that she was just as harried and shell-shocked as everybody else. "Don't sensationalize it," she whispered to Lauren before ushering her into the office. "Remember—it's just an unfortunate accident."

Sybil and Leo Klossner were like older versions of their

daughter, short and round with neat little features lost in faces ringed by fat. Sybil had obviously been sobbing; her face looked crumpled and red, her eyes swollen to little slits. She was also angry.

"This is outrageous," she said. "We sent our daughter to this school to protect her and look what happened."

Gashford had a Starbucks. Daniel Stein felt a rush of relief when he spotted the familiar logo at the edge of the main shopping district, though he probably shouldn't have been surprised. At that moment a Starbucks was probably opening in the Urals with a sign in the window advertising goat-milk lattes.

Daniel grinned as he pulled into the parking lot. Things were looking up. He hadn't been able to talk his way past the young cop, but he'd try again in another hour. In the meantime, he could enjoy a Venti Americano and check his e-mail.

The barista's eyes widened when he approached the counter, but Daniel ignored her. He stared out the window at Gashford's uninspiring streets while he waited and then carried the coffee over to a corner table and whisked his laptop out of his black messenger bag.

He dug out some headphones, clicked on iTunes and listened to the latest Gwen Stefani as he waited for his mail to load.

Sipping coffee in between, he ripped through thirty messages in ten minutes. A ping signaled the arrival of new mail. He didn't recognize the address but the message line caught him by surprise: Who is Lauren Kavanaugh?

Daniel choked on his coffee. Coughing and spluttering, he swiped at his watering eyes with one hand while clicking the message open with the other.

A single cryptic sentence that didn't seem to match the subject line at all: **Tom Donaldson has been sending letters to her for thirteen years.**

For one brief disappointing moment he thought it was spam, but just as his Google results for Donaldson came up on the screen, the name finishing rolling around the roulette wheel in his mind and landed in a slot. And just like that he knew why Lauren Kavanaugh looked familiar, why she'd been nervous, why his instincts had been correct.

"Yes!" Daniel Stein crowed, loudly enough that the baristas stopped moving and the line of customers stopped wondering why a "small" should be called "tall" and a "medium" was known as a "grande." They turned, en masse, to stare at the little man in the corner pumping his fists in the air like a miniature prizefighter.

The Klossners were the first parents to arrive, but others weren't far behind. The news spread fast that there had been yet another death at the school. When Lauren was crossing campus to meet with the Klossners she'd seen a Mercedes SUV pull into the main drive. On her way back, the single car had turned into a stream of vehicles.

The Klossners had left with their lawyer to claim their daughter's body, just as unhappy when they departed. There was nothing Lauren or Sister Rose or anybody could tell them that would make them feel better. Lauren knew this. She understood the need to blame someone and had sat quietly while they hurled invective at her. She'd been the target of anger before and she thought of Amanda and how she had responded differently, so full of bravado, when attacked. But that was years ago and Amanda was gone. Lauren couldn't find courage thinking of her, she couldn't bring the past back and undo what had happened.

She'd looked at the Klossners and seen the same anger and bewilderment she'd seen in other eyes. Was there anybody who made it through life without experiencing a tragedy that brought them smack up against the essential unfairness of the universe?

Parents who'd done the best for their children, who'd loved and cared for them with devotion, could still lose them in a blink. A car accident, a drowning, a fire. All the love in the world didn't make you immune to tragedy and it wasn't enough to help you recover from it.

Lauren had read about a study once that claimed clinically depressed people weren't guilty of distorted thinking, but of seeing the world quite clearly. They were depressed because they saw the world as it truly was, not like the eternal optimists who saw it as they'd like it to be.

She thought of this as she phoned for a taxi during the walk back to Augustine House. Girls passed her dragging suitcases. She ducked under police tape and surveyed the room that had been Elsa's. On one side of the room the bed was neatly made and the desk had a short, tidy pile of books piled on top, but it was otherwise barren. At that very moment Stacy Chin was sitting outside the main office with her suitcase by her side waiting for her neurosurgeon father to arrive from Manhattan. She had packed with remarkable efficiency; even the pictures were gone from the dresser as if she knew she wouldn't be coming back.

Elsa's side of the room, by contrast, looked as if she could come back at any moment. The bed not been slept in, but it was rumpled nonetheless and Lauren pictured the girl sprawled out on top of the covers reading a book.

A pair of blue school shoes rested on the floor at the foot of the bed as if they'd just been kicked off and a plaid skirt lay where it had been tossed on a desk chair.

It was what hung on the wall, though, that touched Lauren. Next to a ridiculous poster of Britney Spears was a piece of graph paper with Elsa's weight-loss program outlined and charted in little squares.

How many hours had Elsa spent thinking about her body? Stuck in a culture and time when normal-weight girls considered themselves fat and anorexia seemed to be a teenage rite of passage, Elsa must have suffered more than most of her peers.

Lauren knew she couldn't touch anything in the room, but she wanted so badly to take the chart down as if by doing so she could somehow protect Elsa from other people's harsh scrutiny of her less-than-perfect body.

She ducked back under the tape, needing to get away. Music drew her to another room and she stood in the doorway for a moment without being noticed, watching Nicole Morel packing a suitcase.

"So you're leaving," she said at last.

The girl spun around, a shirt clutched in her hands. She stared at Lauren for a moment then nodded. "Yes. My mother's arranged a train ticket for me."

She turned and folded the shirt once and then again, before finally, reluctantly, placing it in the suitcase. Lauren didn't move from the door. She waited and eventually the girl turned around to look at her.

"Why are you leaving, Nicole?" She spoke quietly as if it were a polite inquiry, nothing more, but they both knew it wasn't that. She could see the tension in the girl's hunched shoulders and the way one hand strayed to the handle of her suitcase as if she needed something to clutch.

"Are you afraid to stay here after what happened to Elsa?"

"Yes." The slight accent slipped through even on one word and the girl's eyes darted up and around Lauren, never quite meeting hers.

The girl moved back to her dresser and took a handful of socks from a top drawer.

"Where were you last night, Nicole?"

There was a split second's hesitation, but only that, and the girl turned toward the suitcase with the socks. "I was asleep."

"Really? So you don't know anything about what happened to Elsa?"

She dumped the socks in the bag. "No, why would I?"

"What happened, Nicole?"

The girl kept her back to her, arranging the clothes in the suitcase as if she were being graded for it, as if it were the only thing that mattered. "I don't know what you're talking about."

"I know that Elizabeth Lincoln was involved."

The name startled Nicole into looking at Lauren for a moment, eyes unguarded and vulnerable, but then she turned back to the clothes.

"Maybe Kristen, too."

"Why don't you talk to them, then?"

"They're your friends, right? You're all members of the club, isn't that right?"

"I don't have time for this." Nicole stalked to the closet, yanked clothes from hangers, marched back to the suitcase and thrust them in. No more careful folding.

"You mean you're not a member of Oculus?"

Surprise registered on the girl's face, followed by fear that she masked with a scowl. "I have no idea what you're talking about." She closed the lid on her bag, zipped it shut.

"Yes, you do. You definitely do. You and Elizabeth and Kristen and Tiffany. You're all part of the club."

The girl's hands shook a little as she dragged the bag off the bed and pulled up the expanding handle. Her face, however, was defiant. "So what if I am?"

"So who locked Elsa in the freezer?"

"She must have locked herself in."

"You know that's not true. You were there, weren't you? Did you lock her in?"

The girl backed up a step, a faint tremor passing through her body. "No, of course not. The club's not like that!"

"Then what's it like? Tell me."

The girl started to say something, but stopped, biting her lip. "I can't," she said after a minute. "It's part of the rules, you can't talk about the club. But it's not like that. Really."

"Yes it is, Nicole. Really. And you know it, don't you? You know what happened to Elsa."

The girl's face had two spots of color and she pushed past Lauren to get out the door, but Lauren caught her arm.

"Were you with Elsa last night?"

"No."

"That's a lie."

"Let go!" The girl struggled to pull free, but Lauren held fast.

"Listen to me," she said. "You are making a choice right now that is going to affect the rest of your life—don't make the wrong choice, Nicole."

"Let me go!"

"Not until you tell me the truth. Where were you last night?"

"Nowhere. Here. Asleep."

"I asked your roommate, Nicole. She's sitting at the office right now, waiting to go home. You see, I didn't believe you this morning when you told me you hadn't heard anything. You couldn't look me in the eye and I knew Destiny wanted to tell me something, but was afraid to in front of you."

"She's not scared of me!"

"Really? I thought the whole school was scared of the club."

The girl frowned, then shrugged in an unconvincing imitation of disinterest. "Believe what you want."

"I believe I know the truth when I hear it. And Destiny told me the truth. She said she woke up sometime after midnight and you weren't in bed. She thought you were in the bathroom, but we both know that's not the truth, don't we?"

"I don't have to listen to this!" Nicole wrestled to get free, but Lauren tightened her grip.

"You left the dorm with the other girls. You were with Elsa at the cafeteria. You shut her in the freezer."

"No! No, I didn't!"

"What did you tell her to get her in the freezer? What did you have to say?"

The girl stared at her and for a moment it looked as if she was going to say something, but a student looked out of the door next to Nicole's and Lauren loosened her grip. Nicole jerked her arm free.

"I don't know what you're talking about," she said.

"I understand that you're afraid, believe me I understand," Lauren said, talking fast. "And I know how hard it is to stand up to them, but you know it's the right thing to do."

There were sudden footsteps in the hall and another student appeared. She looked from Lauren to Nicole and back again. "Your taxi's here, Ms. Kavanaugh."

"Thank you." Lauren considered letting it go, but she had to get to the pharmacy. She had to find some proof and the pills were her best chance.

She stepped aside and Nicole pushed past her, suitcase in tow. Lauren caught her arm one last time. "Find the courage, Nicole."

The police report had been thorough and then thoroughly forgotten. "We checked it out," the officer who'd taken the complaint told Stephanie and Oz. "It was just a prank."

Bob Franklin had been a police officer for a long time, long enough to have gone from full-tonsured to comb-over, long enough to have known Stephanie's uncle when he was still on the job, long enough to think that women shouldn't be cops, much less detectives, even if they did have a family history with the job. He was a short, wide man with a gruff voice and he reminded Stephanie of a wounded animal. His was an anger directed at the whole world, but he'd willingly blame it all on the one hapless soul foolish enough to step in his path.

"You think I missed something?" he asked, leaning back in his chair, big arms crossed behind his head so the sweat stains were visible on his wash-and-wear uniform shirt. He was trying to look casual, but belligerence just oozed from him, like some repellant pheromone. The word repulsive came to Stephanie's mind whenever she had to deal with him.

"Don't you think this goes beyond a prank?" she said, tapping the section of the report that dealt, in detail, with just what a locker full of excrement looks like.

"Look, she named some girls she thought might have done it, but when we checked them out we found that they weren't the ones. This girl had bad blood with a lot of girls. Anyone could have done it."

"Do you have that list of girls she named?"

He bristled. "Why, you think I didn't do my job?"

"No, but we've got more going on now than a locker full of shit. We've got three dead girls."

Franklin dropped his arms and sat forward. "This has nothing to do with that. Believe me. This is some kid getting picked on and the mom making a big stink out of it, like her kid's never done wrong in her life."

"We need to see everything you got," Oz said.

Franklin sneered at Stephanie, but got up and slowly lumbered off to a far corner of the squad room where a long row of gray metal file cabinets held case files that hadn't been sent down to storage. He made a big production out of searching, and it took a few minutes, but eventually he came back with a slim folder and handed it over. "That's everything—my notes on the follow-up, everything. The girls' names are in there, but I'm telling you that I could find no proof that they had anything to do with it."

There were three names: Elizabeth Lincoln, Tiffany Bellam, and Kristen Townson. Stephanie made a copy of the report and the follow-up interviews with the girls and read them out loud while Oz drove back to the school.

"Notice that two of them say they were in class," Oz said. "I think that would be pretty easy to check."

"Well, what about the third one? This says she was in the infirmary. Couldn't she have slipped out?"

"I don't know, but c'mon, even if we do find out that they did this, that doesn't mean they had anything to do with all three deaths."

"Yeah, I know. Still, Franklin didn't exactly work the case hard."

"It was a nasty prank, but it was still a prank."

"Maybe they've escalated. I don't know. We've got nothing else at this point so we might as well spend a little time pursuing it. You okay with that?"

Oz shot her a look, but didn't say anything. She knew she was taking her frustration out on him, but her head hurt and she felt like she'd picked up Franklin's rage as if it were a virus.

She was angry there'd been another death, angry that they always seemed to be getting information late. She was angry that she was sleeping at her sister's and trying to figure out how to put the town house on the market when she and Alex couldn't even talk.

They hadn't spoken since she'd left. When she'd taken off the ring he'd had a shocked, sunken look on his face as if she'd punched him in the gut, but he hadn't called. Not that she was checking her cell phone for that reason. Sam's baby was due any day and she was expecting a call.

She hadn't been sleeping well since being at her sister's. The futon was kind of lumpy and she felt hyperconscious of being a third wheel. Not that Dan or Sam made her feel that way, not at all. If anything, they were making too much of an effort to include her in everything. But being included in another couple's joking banter made her painfully aware of being single again.

Struggling to relax enough to fall asleep in the room that was going to be her niece or nephew's nursery, she could hear the sounds of her sister and brother-in-law moving around their bedroom next door.

The room still smelled a little bit like paint. They'd chosen yellow because it was cheery. It depressed Stephanie even more. The thing she admitted to herself only at night was how much she missed Alex. During the day she could push him to the back of her mind, concentrate on her work, and tell herself that she was grateful not to be chained any longer to another person's demands.

At night, though, at night all that fell away and she was too tired to pretend that she didn't miss him like crazy. Sometimes she cataloged exactly what it was she missed. His hands, strong and so overtly masculine with their wide fingers and blunt nails and the way they'd felt cupped around her smaller hands. His blue eyes that reminded her of an ocean, the color going lighter or darker depending on his mood. She missed the taste of his mouth on hers, the look in his eyes when he slipped inside her and the feel of him moving in her, like he was the missing piece to the puzzle of her body.

She stared at the outline of the crib in the dark and thought about Alex demanding to know if she was ever going to care about him or their future children more than she did about the job. Thinking of that just made her angry all over again and effectively squashed any desire she had to call him.

"Hey, you okay?"

She looked up and realized they'd arrived at St. Ursula's. Oz had turned off the car, but was sitting there staring at her like she was crazy. Great, now she couldn't even focus on the job. Stephanie rubbed her eyes, which had the tight feeling of too little sleep, and opened her door. "I'm fine."

Things looked just the same at St. Ursula's, just like they always did, as if their motto was making sure that nothing, not even violent death, disrupted the routine. Maybe it was the religious component that made it possible, Stephanie didn't know. All she knew was that it was disconcerting to see students flowing into the dining hall for lunch just as if no body had been found in the freezer, and when they entered the main building they watched a group of girls giggling as they passed the roped-off door to the tunnel.

The secretary in the main office said the headmistress was in a meeting and they would have to wait, but just as they sat down the door to Sister Rose's office opened and the headmistress stepped out.

She looked truly shocked to see them and then she looked pleased, the reaction Stephanie was least expecting.

"This is serendipitous, detectives. I was just about to phone you."

"We've come to talk to you about the incident with the gym locker that happened last year," Oz said. "The one that caused Kathy Rice to leave the school."

Sister Rose frowned. "That's of little consequence now."

"You never found out who did it," Stephanie said. "Isn't that of consequence?"

"Not now. Aren't you interested in the deaths of our students anymore?" She didn't wait for an answer, ushering them ahead of her back into her office.

A tiny man was seated on one of the chairs in front of the desk. He was so small that for a second Stephanie thought he was a boy and when she realized the boy had a full five o'clock shadow, the next thought to cross her mind was that leprechauns really did exist.

He stood up from his seat and offered a manicured hand to both of them in turn to shake. "Daniel Stein," he said. *"New York Times."*

"We're not talking to the press," Oz said immediately.

"That's okay, I'm here to talk to you." Daniel Stein grinned like a pint-sized jackal. "I have some information that I think will interest you very, very much."

The closest pharmacy to St. Ursula's was at a chain store in a strip mall on the outskirts of Gashford. Lauren took a cab there and asked the driver to wait. Twenty minutes of waiting in a line of customers gave Lauren plenty of time to come up with a convincing story for the harried-looking, balding pharmacist in a white lab coat with "Bruce" stenciled in blue thread above the left breast.

"What can I do for you?" He gave Lauren a big, capped-tooth smile and brushed down his remaining brown hair.

She smiled just as brightly. "I'm helping my grandmother clear out some old medication and I found some pills that she'd apparently spilled and I need to know what they are so I can return them to the correct bottle." She handed over a plastic bag containing the pills.

Bruce extracted a pill and squinted at it through the reading glasses perched on his nose. "Hmm . . . let me just take these in back and see what I can find."

He disappeared behind a shelf crammed full of bottles of pills in various shapes, colors, and sizes. His assistant, an anorexic girl who'd obviously had breast enhancement, smiled at the customer waiting behind Lauren, so she stepped to the side to wait. Five long minutes passed while Lauren pondered the various merits of different brands of pantyhose and contemplated just how much shelf space was devoted to over-the-counter headache remedies.

At last Bruce returned and he was frowning. "These are Halcion," he said.

"What is it for?"

"It's used in short-term treatment of insomnia. Did you say your grandmother's on this?"

"Yes, well, I'm not really sure if she's still on it. I'm afraid she spilled some of these from a bottle."

"I think you need to talk to your grandmother's doctor. This is a very high dosage—0.5mg is the high end for this drug and it is addictive."

"Are there side effects?"

Bruce's head bobbed up and down rapidly. "Oh, yes. Absolutely. Halcion is from a family of drugs called benzodiazepines. Very, very potent."

"Could they cause delusions?"

"Why? Is your grandmother suffering from delusions?"

"Yes. Actually, she's exhibiting signs of dementia. Could it be the medication?"

"Yes, quite possibly, especially if she stopped taking this medication suddenly. Abrupt withdrawal from Halcion can lead to psychosis."

"Will it go away?"

"In most cases, yes, but there are some cases where the withdrawal symptoms persist for months, even years." He tossed the Baggie lightly in his hand and reluctantly passed them over. "You really need to talk to her doctor. This could be life threatening."

Lauren's hand trembled as she took the bag back from the pharmacist. After so long, to have the proof in her hands was almost too much. She slipped the Baggie in her pocket and kept her hand against it as she got back into the taxi.

The ride back to St. Ursula's seemed longer than it had coming. It was 3:30 when the cab crested the hill and she was back at the school.

The hallway in the main building was empty. Lauren walked briskly down the hall toward Sister Rose's office with the pills clutched in her hand.

She was brought up short when the door to the head-mistress's office opened and instead of just Sister Rose and her secretary she saw the two police detectives who'd questioned her in the past.

"I've discovered the truth," she said

Sister Rose came around her desk. "So have we, Miss Kavanaugh. Or should I say Amanda McBride?"

Chapter Thirty-eight

Lauren recoiled as if she'd been struck. "You are Amanda McBride, aren't you?" Sister Rose said.

They were in a semicircle: the headmistress, the counselor, the tiny reporter who'd recognized her, and both detectives. The detectives stood on either side, flanking the group as if she might attack them or maybe it was to prevent her from running. Neither was likely. She'd heard the expression "feeling rooted to the spot" but never understood it until now.

"No," she said. "Not anymore. I'm Lauren Kavanaugh. That's my legal name and has been for five years."

She wanted to say that Amanda had been dead for a lot longer than that, but they wouldn't understand. Her legs felt weak, but there was nowhere for her to sit. Something was rattling. Feeling as if everything had slowed, Lauren glanced dully down at the bag of pills twitching in her hand. She was shaking.

The female detective held out a piece of paper. It was a copy of a newspaper article, but Lauren didn't have to look too closely to know what it said.

Below a large headline that read, GIRLS GUILTY IN BURNING

DEATH OF CLASSMATE was a blurry newsprint photo of two girls passing through a phalanx of angry onlookers and reporters thrusting microphones and cameras.

Lauren's head hurt. She pressed her hand against her temple, pushing back the images, but they were too strong.

The room slipped away and she was back in that crowd, holding a jacket up to block her face, catching a glimpse of Whitney's scared face mirroring her own. It was the last time they would be together. Amanda McBride and Whitney Cernik. Murderers. Monsters. "Angel-faced killers" one article called them. Their yearbook photos would be reproduced over and over again. Articles would describe them as best friends since preschool, and use words like inseparable. Sleepovers and birthday parties, Brownies and ice skating. Everything together, just the two of them. Until Julia.

Be nice to her, Amanda's mother said, Julia's new. Julia trying to worm her way in, Julia always wanting to go where they were going, the tagalong whose mother knew their mothers, who lived in the house down the street from Amanda, who wanted to be included even though she so very clearly did not fit.

Lauren could hear their footsteps pounding the pavement, the two of them running down the street again, that same stretch of sidewalk she would run forever, returning there every time the sun slanted a certain way or she saw steps leading up to a similar-looking Victorian house.

"Amanda! Amanda, wait for me!"

That plaintive cry echoing over and over again. Their laughter following. Sometimes in the stillness of the night she'd hear that voice calling again, "Amanda! Amanda!" She would never be rid of that voice. It haunted her.

"Thirteen years ago you and a friend were responsible for the death of a classmate, Julia Donaldson," the female detective said. Lauren could hear her voice from a distance. The footsteps were louder.

Amanda and Whitney running hard side by side, breathless laughter escaping in little bursts as they turned to see Julia struggling to catch up. Up the steps to her house, giggling with Whitney, slamming the door on Julia, watching her fractured reflection through the etched-glass panel, giggling until her mother pulled her away, looking annoyed like she always did as if Amanda's very existence had been nothing more than an interruption in her life.

"Let your little friend in the house."

"She's not our friend."

"Don't be silly, Amanda, of course Julia's your friend."

The three of them sent to that formal dining room to eat bakery cookies arranged in a neat circle on a china plate, Whitney and Amanda giggling whenever they looked at each other. Julia smiled along in her usual dopey fashion as if she was actually part of something. All of them eavesdropping on their mothers' conversation over tea in the living room. "Your house is so lovely, Patricia!" There was never anything out of place in the McBride house, each piece of antique furniture hand chosen and authenticated, the crystal sparkling, the silver polished. And so cold, so very cold.

Which of them had come up with the idea to lock Julia in the shed? Amanda or Whitney, Whitney or Amanda? She couldn't remember anymore, but it had been both of them planning in the end. She was the one who'd first spotted the shed, walking past it once while taking a shortcut home. Tucked out of the way on the far corner of a playing field at the very back of the school grounds it was someplace no one would think to look.

They hadn't meant to kill Julia. On that she was clear. But what hadn't been clear as twelve-year-olds was that everything they'd done, everything they'd planned had led to Julia's death. They'd pushed her into that shed and padlocked it from the outside and stood there laughing as Julia screamed and pounded on the door. They'd laughed at her crying. They knew it was dark in the shed. They knew she'd be scared. Hadn't she confessed as much during one enforced play date? "I'm scared of the dark," she'd said.

"Julia still uses a nightlight," her mother confided to Amanda's mother.

"She's such a baby," Whitney commented when Amanda told her. They'd thought it was clever when they worked out a way to exploit that fear. Lock her in that dark and leave her there to scream where no one would hear her.

They'd gone home. Running down the sidewalk together, but this time without Julia behind them. Two glasses of milk instead of three. Fewer cookies on the plate. Just Whitney and Amanda, Amanda and Whitney the way it was supposed to be.

"Where's Julia?" her mother asked. They'd shrugged in response. "I don't know," she'd said when her mother persisted. "We didn't see her."

They ate the cookies while Julia's mother expressed her concern to the other two mothers; they drank their milk while Julia's mother hurried off down the block to her own house. Amanda's laughing eyes met Whitney's over the rim of her glass.

Later they strolled back to the school, saying they'd forgotten something, laughing as they talked about what, exactly, they'd left behind. The key to the lock sweating in Amanda's palm.

"She was trapped in a shed and couldn't escape the fire," the detective said.

They were going to let Julia out of the shed, they were going to tell her it had taken time to find the key. They'd unlock the door and let Julia out, claiming that it had been an accident and then she'd leave them alone. All according to plan. Except that they hadn't planned on the fire.

They were strolling, laughing and talking, coming over the hill when they saw a billowing cloud of gray smoke curling up into the sky. They ran then, Amanda running so hard that her chest hurt, but this time it was toward Julia, not away. As they got closer they could see the flames, the first little licks of orange peeking through the cracks in the old boards.

She could still hear the sound of wood cracking from pressure, the smell of burnt embers and the worse scent, sickly sweet, of burning flesh. She ran toward the shed with the key out and ready, grabbing for the lock but it burnt her hand, the heat singeing the pale hairs from her forearms and shins.

She heard screaming, but she'd never been sure if it was Julia's or theirs. The police and firefighters found them at the scene, burned, disheveled, and smoke-singed. At first they'd been treated with sympathy, people assuming that they were victims as much as Julia, until the lock was discovered.

Hours in the police station, hours of questions, both of them still in their uniforms, plaid skirts and white blouses singed with smoke. Shell-shocked and saying exactly what had happened, without the wisdom or experience to tailor their responses, to think about the impact they'd have re-peated as sound bites on TV and in the newspapers: "We hated her." "She was different." "We wanted to hurt her."

No one included the parts where they expressed remorse, except for the last little bit, the part where she'd said, "We didn't mean to kill her." And that was shown only at the trial to add support to the prosecution's case that here were two girls acting with reckless endangerment.

It didn't matter that they hadn't started the fire. It didn't matter that they hadn't know there was a can of gasoline in the shed and that in her panic to get out Julia had knocked it over. It didn't matter that she was the one who'd struck the match she found in a box sitting on a shelf.

The prosecution didn't buy that. They tried to suggest that the girls had put the box of matches in the shed, that they'd wanted Julia to find them.

Lauren stared at the photo in her hand. It had been taken the last day, but it could have been any day. There were crowds there all the time, angry townspeople screaming about what perverted girls they were and how they should be punished. *"We'll burn you in a shed!" "You should be fried!"*

Stories circulated about what had happened to Julia before they put her in the shed. They were accused of torturing Julia beforehand, of brutalizing her body before they locked her in the shed. It didn't seem to matter that none of this was true. No one seemed to pay attention when the stories were discredited by the police and their defense attorneys.

In the end, despite the controversy of the decision, they were tried as juveniles and sentenced to an indefinite term of imprisonment. At their sentencing, in a packed courtroom with television cameras rolling, the judge declared them to be "evidence that evil can exist even in the very young."

Her parents had been ashamed. More than ashamed. They had, in essence, disowned her. She still had the small collection of cards they'd sent during her years in the juvenile facility. Every holiday she received a card, the most generic of Christmas or birthday wishes, without any personal message, simply signed "Love, Mom and Dad."

The years had passed, a different world to the one she'd been used to. They were sent to two entirely different facilities and Amanda didn't know where Whitney was taken. She'd just never seen her again. Her own prison, though they called it a Juvenile Detention Facility, had been in a rural area of New York.

She'd replaced one ugly uniform with another and more structure than she'd cared for. In the grinding weeks and years that followed she found her way to some kind of peace. Except in her sleep. In her sleep that peace eluded her. She hadn't had one restful night's sleep since Julia's death and she had come to accept this as part of her punishment. She'd killed Julia. It was a small price to pay.

When word came that the killers of Julia Donaldson were going to be released, Amanda was eighteen. As a condition of their release, she and Whitney had to agree never to contact each other again. That was easily done; they hadn't seen each other in six years.

A letter arrived from her parents along with the lawyer on the day of her release. "Dear Amanda, We don't think it's wise for you to return home. Emotions still run high, here, surrounding the incident. We feel your return, and the ensuing commotion it is likely to cause, would disrupt the lives of your brothers and sister, who, after all, have done nothing to deserve this scrutiny. We've arranged for you to study in England."

So she'd spent her first night of freedom not, as she'd expected, back at the house where she'd grown up, but at her lawyer's home in Meadville. The next day she'd driven with her lawyer to buy clothes at a small shopping mall where she could be anonymous, and the day after that, she'd flown from Pennsylvania to England.

Only that became problematic almost immediately. It seemed that news of the release of Amanda McBride and her intention to cross the ocean had been leaked to the media. Her lawyer urged her to change her name. That was the day that Amanda disappeared forever.

She chose Lauren because it was her lawyer's first name and she liked it and Kavanaugh was her middle name and her mother's maiden name. Lauren Kavanaugh matriculated at the University of London and for that first year she moved hesitantly around a strange place with strange people, enjoying her first taste of freedom, but ashamed that she was enjoying it.

And then she'd met Michael. He'd approached her in a bar at the end of her first year, where she'd gone with other students to celebrate the end of exams. It was her first time in a bar; she hadn't known what to order to drink, much less how to handle the attention of strange men. She'd been ripe for the picking and he'd plucked her right up. She thought it was a mutual thing, this wonderful chance meeting with your one true love.

She'd been shockingly naïve and he'd exploited that, telling her how wonderful she was to him, telling her that they would always be together, that they were meant to share the rest of their lives together. Alone and lonely, she wanted to believe him.

She hadn't realized he took notes on all their conversations, cataloging everything she told him and turning it into fodder for a series of articles he sold to a British tabloid about how it felt to sleep with a child killer.

Ironically, the one thing he didn't know was that the first time she'd slept with him had been the day she received the first anniversary letter. It was a cold fall day and she'd finished classes and returned to her small apartment to find the letter waiting on the mat inside. A plain white envelope with her name, her new name, typed neatly in black ink.

She'd opened it eagerly, seeing the U.S. postage, assuming it to be a letter from the family that had all but disowned her. Instead, it was from the older brother of her victim. She'd gotten these letters in prison, too. They'd arrived like clockwork on the anniversaries of Julia's birth and death. But she thought that they'd come to an end. Surely, he wouldn't be able to find her if she was living under another name. Except that somehow he did.

"We will never forget how you killed her," the letter said. "You robbed our sister of the chance to lead a full life and we're going to rob you of the same. We want you to think of Julia each and every day and when you have something special happen we want you to remember that Julia can't experience that."

She'd saved all the letters. Somehow it seemed wrong to throw them away. Keeping them was part of her penance. Everything since Julia had been a penance.

"Yes, I'm Amanda," she said, looking slowly from Sister Rose to the Detectives. "How did you find me?"

"Just a little of my own detective work," Daniel Stein

said, speaking up. He sounded eager and he was bouncing on the soles of his gleaming black oxfords. "Remember, I told you that I recognized you."

"I believe you were tipped off by someone in turn, correct, Mr. Stein?" Sister Rose sounded less than enchanted with the *New York Times* reporter.

"Yeah, sure, someone sent me an e-mail saying it sounded like you, but I didn't know for sure until I did my own research."

Detective Land stepped toward Lauren. "You need to come down to the station and talk with us," she said.

"Why? I've told you everything I know."

"Ms. Kavanaugh, at the very least you've lied to us," the grizzled male detective said. "At the worst you've carried out several killings just like you did as a child."

"This is ridiculous," Lauren protested as she took a step back, "I haven't done anything." But the female detective slipped to her side and then the male cop flanked her on the other and suddenly she was being ushered from the office, her upper arms held tight in their grips.

"I have to teach this afternoon," Lauren said, struggling to break free.

"You won't be teaching at St. Ursula's ever again," Sister Rose said. "You're fired, Miss Kavanaugh."

The detectives marched Lauren out the door and past the curious eyes of students walking to morning classes. She was ushered into the back of a police car, her head protected by one of the male detective's large hands.

As they drove down the hill she turned and watched the school disappear from view out the back window. Everything she'd wanted to do had failed. There was nothing left.

As soon as Miss Kavanaugh left, Nicole dragged her suitcase back in her room and locked it behind her, before going in search of the other girls. She found Elizabeth standing in a crowd outside the dining hall and watching the activities of the police and other crime scene people. Bright yellow tape blocked off the path and there were police officers huddled within the tape and radios squawking. The thin layer of snow had turned black and muddy with boot prints and the sidewalk visible was wet and gray.

"Ms. Kavanaugh knows," Nicole said in a low voice when she'd reached Elizabeth's side.

Elizabeth fixed her with a bored look. "Knows what?"

"What happened with Elsa. She knows we were involved."

Elizabeth took her arm and pulled her out of the crowd, darting quick looks right and left. "What are you talking about?"

"Miss Kavanaugh knows we had something to do with Elsa."

"And how does she know that? What did you tell her?"

"Nothing. She came to me."

"What makes her think we were with Elsa?"

"I don't know. She asked me if I was anxious about staying because of Elsa and then she asked what I'd done to Elsa."

"So she thinks you hurt Elsa?"

Nicole nodded. "And you, and Kristen and Tiffany. She knows about the club."

"Did you tell her?"

"No, of course not."

Elizabeth shrugged and looked back at the cafeteria. "Then what's the problem? She doesn't know anything."

"Did you kill Elsa?"

"What are you talking about?"

"Did you lock Elsa in the freezer?"

Elizabeth stared at her for a moment and then she smiled. "Of course not."

"Then how did she die?"

"She must have locked herself in. I'm sure it was an accident."

"I don't believe that. You wanted Elsa gone, Elizabeth. She knew something, didn't she? What did she know about you, about Oculus?"

Elizabeth frowned. "Be quiet. Someone will hear you. Did you say anything to Miss Kavanaugh about all this?"

"Of course not."

"Listen, stop letting your imagination run away with you. We didn't hurt Elsa—we left her at the freezer when she said she'd changed her mind. She didn't want to join the club, so we left her there. End of story. We didn't do anything and it's not our fault if she decided to help herself to some food after we left."

"She was on a diet."

Elizabeth sighed. "Sure. Look, I'm busy now. Why don't we meet later, somewhere more private, to discuss it."

"I'm going home. If it was an accident why haven't you told the police?"

"What would be the point? Elsa's dead. Nothing will bring her back and I'm sure she wouldn't want us getting in trouble for nothing."

And she smiled again, that same charming smile that Nicole had desired so much in the first weeks of school, which seemed like years rather than weeks in the past.

This time it fell flat.

Kristen was balancing her cell phone on her shoulder and packing a third pink suitcase when Elizabeth appeared at her door. She snapped her fingers at Kristen and drew a finger across her throat.

"Listen, I've got to go, Mom," Kristen said, shifting the open bag so Elizabeth could sit down on the bed. "I'll call you once I'm in the car, okay? Love you, too. 'Bye." She made a smooching noise and snapped the phone shut. "What's up?"

"We've got a problem."

"Oh, Jesus, what now?" Kristen tossed the phone on top of her dresser and pulled more clothes from its bottom drawer.

"Nicole."

"What about her?"

"She's going to talk. I think she's already told that bitch of a teacher."

Kristen dumped the clothes in the bag and stared at her, mouth agape. "What the fuck is she thinking?"

"I don't think she is thinking. We need to take care of it."

"Oh, no." Kristen shook her head. "No way. I'm going home—I don't want to be involved."

"You are involved," Elizabeth said calmly. "Like it or not."

"It was your idea, you take care of it."

"Excuse me?" Elizabeth's voice dipped down. She stood up from the bed and Kristen swallowed, shifting her feet.

"You were the one who said it would be all over after Chelsea."

"And you were the one who dropped the phone in the tunnel, Kristen, remember?"

Kristen twirled a section of hair over her fingers, looping it around until it pulled too tight and then letting it go before starting again. It hurt her scalp, but she kept doing it.

"We shouldn't have hurt Elsa," she said, but her voice was weak.

"I didn't hear you say that when we closed the freezer door," Elizabeth said. She walked slowly toward Kristen, who backed away from her. "*You* were there, Kristen, *you* participated."

Kristen kept backing up until Elizabeth had literally backed her into a corner. She tried to make eye contact, but Elizabeth's eyes were frightening. Clear, cold, and hard, they reminded Kristen of a raptor she'd seen once at the zoo.

"Forget being expelled," Elizabeth said. "That would be

the least of our problems." She leaned in so close that Kristen could see her own reflection in her irises. "They'd send us to prison. Is that what you want?"

Kristen managed to shake her head.

"No, I didn't think so. Orange really isn't your color."

The taxi was overdue. Nicole paced beside her bag, stepped off the sidewalk and onto the asphalt road to try and spot any cars climbing the hill.

She'd been told to wait outside the main building for the cab, but the only traffic she'd seen in the last six minutes had been police cruisers, two going, one coming.

She turned at the sound of footsteps and saw a young girl, a pink-cheeked, baby-faced first year, running toward her.

"Are you Nicole Morel?"

"Yes."

"Here." The girl thrust a folded paper in her hands and took off before Nicole could say anything. She unfolded the pale blue paper and saw Sister Rose Merton's name embossed in dark blue ink across the top. Underneath it in neat cursive was one sentence: "Due to police traffic, your taxi will pick you up in the far parking lot."

She couldn't see what difference it made, but fine. If they wanted her to wait in the parking lot, she'd wait in the parking lot. The taxi had just better show up—she had a train to catch. Sighing, Nicole wheeled her bag down the exit side of the circular drive, following the sidewalk as it curved right toward the parking lots.

The parking lot on the right side, closer to the dining hall, was crowded with police and emergency vehicles. There were still a few hours until dusk, but all the headlights were on and the lights on top were spinning, casting red and blue shadows across shallow puddles left by melting snow.

She stepped off the sidewalk and headed left past the pine-tree border into the far lot. No sign of a taxi so far. She

walked along, bag bouncing on the old asphalt, and burrowed her free hand deeper into her coat pocket. It was so
cold. If it was this cold in October what did that say about
the coming winter?

There were only half a dozen cars in the lot. Most of the
teachers who lived off campus had left hours before and the
few students with car privileges were long gone. There was a
stone bench near the entrance to the one of the trails in the
woods and she dragged her bag over to it. She sat down, bag
propped next to her, and stuck her cold hand in her other
pocket.

It was so quiet. She looked up at the dark canopy of bare
trees overhead and shivered. A crow cawed somewhere in
the distance, its high-pitched cry echoing. Her nose was running, but she didn't have a tissue. She sniffled, the noise loud
in the silence. She wanted to be out of here so badly. Where
was the taxi?

She didn't know what she was going to say to her parents,
whether or not to burden them with what had happened, but
she knew she couldn't come back here. She wouldn't. She'd
refuse if they tried to make her.

If Paul had lived he could have helped her—no. She
wouldn't think that. Paul wasn't here. Paul was dead and no
amount of wanting him back could make it so. What had Ms.
Kavanaugh said? That it wasn't Nicole's fault that Paul had
been killed.

It was her fault, though, that Elsa was dead. She might
not have closed the freezer door, but she'd known, deep
down, what had happened. She was a coward for not demanding to know what had happened to the girl, for letting
them so easily convince her that Elsa had gone back on her
own to the dorm.

The cold of the freezing stone seeped through Nicole's
coat. She stood up and paced. Where was the taxi? What
could be taking it so long? She should call them, but cell

coverage was spotty out here and her phone was buried in the top slot of her luggage.

Each of her steps echoed. Weird. She stopped walking but the echo continued behind her. Nicole whirled around.

A hooded figure emerged from the trail, walking slowly across the road toward her.

"Wow, you scared me," Nicole said. "I didn't realize you were still here."

"Didn't you?" Elizabeth sounded bemused. She held something white in her hand.

Two more hooded figures emerged from the woods behind her.

"What's going on? Are we having a meeting?"

"Something like that," Elizabeth said. "You're the guest of honor."

Tiffany and Kristen didn't speak, moving silently to the right and left of Nicole. Tiffany walked toward the stone bench where Nicole had been sitting.

"What are you doing?" Nicole said, letting her eyes stray from Elizabeth's face to watch Tiffany. She grabbed the handle of Nicole's bag, began pulling it back toward the trail. "Hey, leave that alone!" Nicole said.

"Ssh," Elizabeth said. She raised her hand. It held a white cloth. She moved it toward Nicole's face.

"Stop it!" Nicole backed up, but ran straight into Kristen who pinned her arms to her side. The white cloth slammed against her face, covering her nose and mouth. Nicole struggled to break free, to breathe. The cloth was soaked in something. The fumes made her eyes water.

"Ssh," Elizabeth whispered. "Just breathe."

Chapter Thirty-nine

The last time Lauren had been in a police station, she was twelve years old. Her parents called her Mandy, but the police, frighteningly, referred to her as Amanda. Scared, covered in soot, with a burn on one arm and a keen awareness that she'd killed Julia, she'd sobbed as she waited for her parents, rubbing charcoal smears around her eyes.

She didn't cry this time. The room they left her in was plain, devoid of decoration on its cream-colored walls. The table was rectangular and of a boring industrial design in dull metal. There were matching chairs. One for her, one across the table, and one against the wall. A large round industrial clock ticked slowly high on the wall. She had been sitting in this room for almost thirty minutes. High up in one corner was a small, black security camera. Lauren wondered if they were observing her and knotted her hands together to keep from drumming on the table.

The door opened and Lauren flinched. Detectives Land and Plane entered and Detective Land sat down across from Lauren. She had a folder in her hands and put it down on the table, folding her hands neatly in front of her. Lauren noticed that her nails were very short, as if she'd bitten them to the quick.

The male detective placed what looked like a tape recorder on the table before leaning against the wall to the right of Lauren, so he was half in and half out of her peripheral vision. He loomed there, a large, bulky man in an ill-fitting suit.

Detective Land fiddled with the tape recorder for a moment before pressing a button. It struck Lauren that it looked out of date, but she supposed that police departments didn't always have state-of-the-art equipment.

"I'm Detective Stephanie Land and I'm conducting an interview with Ms. Amanda McBride—"

"I'm not Ms. McBride," Lauren said.

Detective Land pushed the pause button. "Excuse me?"

"I'm not Amanda McBride. She's been dead for a long time. I am legally Lauren Kavanaugh."

The detective seemed to think about this for a moment, absently stroking the end of her long brunette ponytail. She nodded briskly and switched back on the machine.

"Ms. Kavanaugh, we'd like to talk to you about the deaths of Morgan Wycoff, Chelsea Connor, and Elsa Klossner."

Here she paused, looking to Lauren for objection and finding none, nodded again, and opened the folder. "Let's talk about Morgan Wycoff first."

What followed and went on for more than an hour were endless questions. How did Lauren know Morgan, Chelsea, and Elsa? How did they first meet? What had her relationships with the girls been like? Were they friendly?

Lauren answered the questions, every one of them, before waiting for a slight pause to raise one of her own.

"I have an alibi for last night," she said. "The same is not true for Nicole Morel. I believe she was with Elizabeth Lincoln, Kristen Townson, and Tiffany Bellam. I believe they locked Elsa Klossner in the freezer. Why haven't you questioned these girls?"

She saw the detectives exchange a look, but then the burly male detective stood away from the wall and said, "This interview is about you, Ms. Kavanaugh, not about them."

Then both detectives asked more questions. Where was she the night before? Could someone vouch for that? Why had she hidden her past from the school?

"They wouldn't have hired me," she said. "I needed the job. I still need the job."

"Why teaching, Ms. Kavanaugh?" Detective Land spoke casually, but her eyes never left Lauren's face. It was an intense gaze and Lauren found it unnerving. She looked away.

"There was a teacher in the prison," she said in a low voice. "She was nice to me and I wanted to be like her."

They wouldn't believe her, but it didn't matter. None of it mattered anymore. Another girl had died, even though Lauren knew about the group. All she'd wanted was to give something back, make restitution by teaching, but it wasn't enough. She couldn't escape the past.

Frustrated and nervous, she ran her sweating palms against her jeans and felt something in her right pocket. The bag of pills. The shock of her past being uncovered had made her forget them.

"Look, I found these in Elizabeth Lincoln's room." She pulled the Baggie from her pocket and tossed it on the table. "The teacher who left the school before me was poisoned. These are Halcion. Elizabeth Lincoln probably gave these pills to Sister Agnes to make her sleep while they snuck out of the dorms at night, but the pills had another effect. They caused anxiety and paranoia and eventually, probably because she went off them so fast, dementia."

The detectives took turns looking at the pills, the burly detective tapping it with a pencil to avoid touching the bag.

"How did you get these?" Detective Land asked.

So Lauren explained about going into Elizabeth's room

and then she had to back up and explain about the journal entries and how she'd hunted for Sister Agnes.

She'd been carrying the journal entries with her and she pulled the folded pages from her jacket pocket. "I didn't know at the time that she'd used the initials of their last names," she said pointing to specific entries on the paper. "I didn't know who they stood for until I managed to find Sister Agnes."

It was dusk before they were done with her. Lauren left the police station stunned that they'd let her go, convinced even as she walked away that someone would stop her, come back and say that it had all been a mistake and she was under arrest.

They still could. Especially since they had her DNA. She'd given that willingly, allowing them to swab the inside of her cheek, only wondering as she watched the female detective walk out with the sample if they were going to somehow use it to charge her. Of course nothing could happen that fast. DNA analysis took time. They'd told her that while warning her about leaving town, the male detective especially talking to her like she was some kind of common criminal. She hadn't done anything, but there was no reason for them to believe her. She knew how it worked—once convicted, always convicted.

Her cell phone rang as she walked down the steps in front of the station. It took her a moment to recognize the number and she considered not returning it, but in the end hit the call back button out of curiosity.

Nicole Morel's mother answered with a breathless "hello," as if she'd run for the phone.

"This is Lauren Kavanaugh, returning your call."

"Ms. Kavanaugh," she said it with a sigh, "where is Nicole?"

"I don't know, I mean, she was packing to go home the

last time I saw her." Startled, Lauren tried to remember when she'd spoken to Nicole. Hours before.

"I think that was around one. I think she told me that she would take the two o'clock—"

"Train, yes, I know, this was the train she was supposed to take, but I was at Grand Central and she was not on it."

"Well, I guess she took a later one."

"No, I waited. I waited for three more trains. I'm still here and she isn't on any of the trains. What's happened, Ms. Kavanaugh? Where's my daughter?"

And just like that she knew. Call it a sudden flash of insight or intuition, whatever it was, she knew in her gut why Nicole wasn't on that train.

"I'll find her," she managed to reassure Mrs. Morel before hanging up on her. She was halfway up the steps back into the police station when better judgment halted her. There was no time for that. No time to explain, to try to convince. She had to get back to the school now.

She raced back down the steps to the street only to pause again when she realized that she had no way of getting there. Panicked, Lauren looked up and down the street, hoping to find a taxi, but there wasn't one in sight.

Taking a right, she ran along the street in the general direction of the school, hoping that she would find someone to drive her. Ahead of her was Sacred Heart Church. Someone there would drive her. Lauren ran toward the stone building just as a large boatlike sedan pulled into the driveway that led to the side entrance of the church and a gray-haired man in a faded suit got out, walked around to the passenger side, and opened the door for a stoop-shouldered, white-haired woman.

Lauren ran up the steps to the rectory and rang the bell. As she waited, she watched the man gently take the old woman's arm and walk her slowly up the long ramp that led into the side entrance of the church. The driver's-side door had been left open and Lauren could hear doo-wop floating through the air.

The radio was on. The keys had to be in the car. Lauren looked from the man to the car and back again. His back was to the car, he was concentrating fully on the elderly woman, whose forearm he held as they approached the arched oak doors of the church. Lauren hesitated only a moment before running across the lawn toward the sedan.

The keys were in the ignition. She looked once more at the man before opening the driver's-side door and sliding across the wide vinyl seat.

She hadn't driven a car in some time. She moved it into drive and pressed against the accelerator. The car lurched forward and she slammed on the brake. Through the windshield she saw the man turn at the noise and watched his mouth form an "O" of surprise. She didn't wait around to see his other reactions.

She floored it out of the driveway and turned, tires screeching, onto the road, just missing another car. Its horn blared as she sped past.

Chapter Forty

"Jesus, grand theft auto," she said out loud just as the singer declared "Stay with me, baby, stay with me."

She took a few wrong turns before finding the road that led to St. Ursula's. She floored it as much as possible, pausing for a microsecond at stop signs and running red lights as soon as she saw the way was clear. Amazingly, the police siren she expected to hear never came.

As soon as she crested the hill, she pulled the car over and ran toward Augustine House. It was dark by then, and the ivy that crawled along the brick walls looked like black lace by the light of the porch lamp.

She fumbled with her key for a second, but the door opened without it and she stepped inside. There was a distant thump of reverb from music playing on the second floor, but otherwise it was quiet in the hallway. Most of the students were gone.

She ran down the hall to Nicole's room, but wasn't surprised to find it empty. It was as if the girl had never been there. There was no Kristen in her room, either. Lauren paused and tried to think. Where were they?

Back out the door, she headed toward the main building, thinking maybe, just maybe, she'd find Sister Rose there or at least another teacher who'd be able to tell her whether anyone had seen Elizabeth Lincoln around campus.

The main building was dark, the corridors deserted, but a light shone from the main office. She ran toward it, hoping to find someone or something to help her search, but the door was locked. Frustrated, she turned to head back out the main door, only to stop short, startled, as Ryland Pierce appeared in front of her.

"Miss Kavanaugh, what are you doing here?" The guidance counselor's usually smarmy voice was cold. The debonair manner was gone. This was a man whose world was collapsing around him. Ryland's dress shirt was wrinkled and his hair looked as if he'd run his hands through it in frustration.

"Mrs. Morel called," Lauren said. "Nicole didn't make it to New York. Have you seen her?"

"No, I haven't. I'm surprised to see you, frankly. I thought Sister Rose made it very clear this afternoon—you no longer have a place on this campus."

"A parent called me. Nicole Morel was supposed to come home on the two o'clock train. She didn't arrive."

"That's not your concern anymore, Miss Kavanaugh."

"You don't understand."

"No, you don't understand—you are not to be on this campus. I'll just escort you out." He took her by the upper arm, but Lauren pulled free.

"Listen, I'll leave, but you have to find the girls—"

"Miss Kavanaugh, if you don't get off this campus this minute I'm going to have you arrested and charged with criminal trespass."

"No!" Lauren drew back, but Pierce lunged and grabbed her arm in his fist. He forcibly marched her toward the exit.

"You don't understand—they're going to kill her!"

"What I don't understand is why the police let you go.

But that will soon be remedied." He extracted a cell phone from a pants pocket with his free hand and Lauren watched him dial 911.

Desperate, she sunk her teeth into the arm holding hers, biting so hard that she felt the fine cotton of Ryland's dress shirt rip through and then she tasted his blood.

He screamed and released her, pain startling him just long enough for her to snatch the cell phone from his other hand.

"Give that back!" He clawed at her, but missed. "I'm going to have you arrested for assault!"

"Oh, God." Lauren swung the phone as hard as she could and hit Ryland Pierce square in the head.

Stephanie hit the rewind button and replayed the section of interview tape where Lauren Kavanaugh discussed her suspicions about the club at the school.

"I believe her," she said to Oz, who sat across from her at his own desk, feet propped up on one open drawer. He sighed as he pulled out an apple for a snack.

"She could have made all of that up to cover her tracks."

"What about the incident with Kathy Rice? That happened before her time."

"You heard what Franklin said." Oz took a chomp out of the apple and made a face as he chewed and swallowed. "Nothing checked out. These are top girls at the school, they couldn't prove anything."

"Still, it's worth checking."

"Yeah, but I want to do some more digging into Kavanaugh, too. Let's find someone who saw her on the nights in question."

The intercom on Stephanie's phone buzzed and Mabel Gery's voice came on the line.

"You there, Land?"

"Yeah, Sarge."

"You're not going to believe this, but we've got a report of auto theft in front of Sacred Heart and the perp matches the description of that suspect you just released."

"The teacher from St. Ursula's?"

"If that's the name of the skinny white girl with blond frizz you had in here not more than an hour ago."

Oz's feet hit the ground with a thud. "What the hell is she doing?"

"I don't know." Stephanie stood up and grabbed her jacket. "But we'd better find out."

The limestone crunched under her feet as she ran up the hill between the plane trees. Ryland Pierce was out, but maybe not for long. Would he follow her? She had to find the clearing first. Where had she gone off the path? Where was that place? She wasn't sure she would find it.

The marble statues of Stations of the Cross were like ghosts in the darkness. She remembered turning next to Veronica wipes the face of Jesus. She veered off the path, plunging into the woods, stumbling over twigs and roots of trees in her haste, low-hanging branches whipping at her face.

She should have brought a flashlight, she should have thought to bring something, but she had thought of nothing but getting here, not what she'd do once she'd arrived.

The trees were denser. What had seemed clear in the daylight was a confusing maze in the darkness. She held her hands out in front of her like a blind woman searching. Every few feet she would pause, listening, but the only sounds she could hear were the scrabbling noises of small nocturnal creatures and the hoarse, wheezy sound of her own frantic breaths.

"Nicole?" she called, desperate now, wondering if it was all a mistake, wondering if even now Nicole was on her way home with her mother. "Nicole, are you out here?"

Her voice seemed to echo in the blackness. She remembered feeling claustrophobic in all that unremitting green-
ness, the heat beating down on her as she ran through the
woods. Now it was unremitting darkness. Everything was
black or some similar shade. The tree trunks were black as
was the forest floor at her feet. The spaces between the trees
were charcoal.

Her ankle had started to ache and she could taste blood
from biting her lip. This was hopeless. There was no possible way to find that place and if she could find it then why on
earth had she imagined that they would be there? She was
just about to turn back when something changed. A shift in
the darkness between two trees. She moved toward it and it
was gone and she thought it had been her mind playing
tricks on her, but she moved forward again and there it was.
Not color per se, but light. She could see a light shining
through the trees. She moved toward it, running again and
then, just like the first time, she was suddenly in that clearing
and ahead of her was the source of the light, a lantern glowing next to the fire pit. She saw a figure moving near the pit.

"Nicole?" she called again.

"She can't hear you," a voice said behind her. She swung
around in just enough time to register a hooded figure and
someone swinging an arm, and then pain exploded in her
head and she slipped down, down, down into that darkness.

Chapter Forty-one

Darkness and light. The light came near her eyes and she knew she had to open them. Open. Open. And when she did it was too bright, so she closed them again. There were shadows, wings flying past her face. Lauren blinked and tried to focus, to make the shadows one. Someone was standing over her, she could feel the presence of another person, lightness again. She opened her eyes. Elizabeth Lincoln's grinning face looked down at her.

"I'm glad you decided not to sleep through the party," she said. "I wouldn't want you to miss the fun."

Something sticky on her forehead, a slow trickle into her eye. It stung. Lauren reached up, her hand moving slowly, and touched it. The light came back again just as she moved her hand away so that the red on her hand was startling. Blood.

She struggled to her feet and Elizabeth clicked her tongue. "Now, now, we didn't drag you to this spot just for you to leave."

The ground dipped and swayed and Lauren pressed a hand against her head, blinking against the pain. She could see the fire pit now, the glow from the lantern brighter, the circle illuminated. Something was lying in the center.

Another hooded figure came into view carrying an armful of branches. "This should do it," she said to Elizabeth. Lauren recognized it as Kristen Townson's voice.

The girl dumped the armful of wood in the fire pit and climbed in to arrange it. She was lifting the sack in the center and then something flopped forward. It was a hand.

"Who's that?" Lauren asked. Elizabeth ignored her. She beckoned to the figure holding the lantern.

"Put that down and come here."

The figure obeyed, setting the lantern down on a stump next to the pit and walking over to Elizabeth. "Here," she said, handing the girl something. Lauren caught a metallic glint. Then the figure swung it through the air and Lauren drew back. It was a large, serrated hunting knife.

"Keep it pointed at her," Elizabeth said. "If she moves at all—and I mean any little move—stab her."

The girl took the knife readily and pointed it at Lauren. Her hood was far enough forward that Lauren couldn't tell who she was, but she could see the smile.

"You should have minded your own business, teach." The voice was Tiffany Bellam's and she suddenly pushed back her hood as if to confirm this.

"Who's in the fire pit?"

"Who do you think it is?" Tiffany giggled, enjoying the game.

"Nicole Morel?"

"Got it in one!" Tiffany laughed. "I'm impressed—how did you guess?"

"They're looking for her," Lauren said. "They know she's missing."

Tiffany's smile faded a little. "But everyone thinks she went home."

"Her mother knows she didn't make it there. She contacted the school and the police."

The girl looked stunned by this news, but then she shrugged. "So, it doesn't matter."

"Why are you doing this, Tiffany?" Lauren kept her voice low and she forced a smile. "C'mon, this isn't you. You're not a killer. This was Elizabeth's idea, right?"

Tiffany looked from Lauren to Elizabeth, who was spraying something from a bottle onto the wood in the pit.

A strong oily smell made Lauren's nose twitch and her legs feel weak. It was an accelerant.

"Nobody misses these girls," Tiffany said.

"You're wrong, Tiffany. They do miss them. Elsa's parents are very upset. Nicole's parents will be, too."

The girl shrugged. "It was all just a joke, anyway. Elsa was just so stupid. It's not our fault the handle on the inside of the freezer door was broken."

"The handle was perfectly fine the day before—someone broke it."

Tiffany blinked. "I don't believe you."

Lauren shrugged. "It's the truth, but I bet it's not what Elizabeth told you."

The girl looked from Lauren to Elizabeth, who was laughing as she propelled the bottle of accelerant back and forth. Liquid flew in an arc and landed with a slap in the dry leaves piled near Nicole. Elizabeth swung again and a dark smear appeared across the trapped girl's pale hand. A dark stain appeared on her palm and dripped down to the ground.

"How do you know, anyway?" Tiffany demanded. "It's not like you were there."

"I heard the police talking about it. They know it was tampered with and they're going to find out who did it. Is that what you want, Tiffany? Do you want to go to prison?"

Suddenly Elizabeth was there. "Don't be ridiculous, Ms. Kavanaugh. We're not going anywhere."

"Did you break the handle on the freezer door?" Tiffany said.

Elizabeth laughed. "I can't believe you're listening to this nonsense."

"Did you?"

"Look, Tiffany, you're in this just like we are. She knew we were with Chelsea—okay? She was going to tell and then where would we be? At the very least you'd be expelled if not arrested. Is that what you want?"

"You killed Elsa." Tiffany sounded stunned.

Elizabeth laughed again, but this time it was bitter. "No, no, no. *We* killed Elsa. There is no I, here, Tiffany. We're all in this together."

"I didn't kill her!"

"Oh, yes, you did," Elizabeth was adamant. "Just like you killed Morgan and Chelsea. All of us, Tiffany—you, me, and Kristen."

She grabbed the knife from Tiffany's hand and used it to usher Lauren forward. "Get moving! Get in the pit!"

Lauren inched along, baby steps. "You don't have to go along with this," she said to Tiffany. "You didn't realize you were killing—the police will believe you."

Elizabeth snorted in disbelief. "Shut up!" She pushed Lauren with her hand to get her moving faster. "You don't know what you're talking about."

"They'll listen to you, Tiffany. I've shown them the pills she gave Sister Agnes."

"What pills?" Suddenly Kristen was there. She looked at Elizabeth. "What is she talking about?"

"Tell them, Elizabeth," Lauren said. "Tell them how you poisoned Sister Agnes."

"She was a snooping bitch just like you," Elizabeth said. Tiffany whimpered and Elizabeth swung on her. "Shut up!"

She turned back to Lauren and smiled. "Yes, I gave Sister Agnes Halcion. Mixed it right in with her nightly cup of tea.

She couldn't seem to sleep through the night so I helped her along. The dementia was just a little side benefit."

"Oh my God," Kristen said under her breath.

"No, not God. Me." Elizabeth laughed, but it had an angry sound. "No one else would do what needed to be done. No one else."

She'd stopped moving and Lauren stopped, too. *If I just keep her talking the police will come.* "Why did you kill Morgan?"

"Are you kidding me?" Elizabeth laughed again. "The question should be why did I wait so long?" She looked at Kristen to share the laugh, but the other girl stood as if she'd been frozen. "No one wanted to listen to her pagan ranting. No one. She was a fucking fruitcake. We just did what everyone else wanted to do to her—shut her up!"

Time was passing. Lauren had to keep her talking. "And Chelsea? Why did she deserve to die?"

"The Whore of Babylon?" Elizabeth sounded almost bored. "The world needed to be saved from that cunt."

"You said she saw us," Tiffany said. Tears were falling down her face. "You said we had to do it. Did you lie?"

"Oh stop that sniveling!" Elizabeth pretended to cry. "Boo-hoo, I killed the girl who'd spread her legs for anyone. You should be proud of the work you did. Think how many STDs you stopped."

"It's true, she slept around," Kristen said, turning to look at Lauren. It sounded like a plea.

"What did Elsa do to deserve that death?"

Tiffany's tears increased and Elizabeth gave her a withering look. "Jesus, what a cry baby you are." She looked back at Lauren. "What did Elsa do? You mean besides existing? She was a glutton, but that's not why we killed her."

"She found out the truth?"

"Oh, not yet. But she would have. Even Elsa would have gotten there eventually." Elizabeth shrugged. "Look, we gave her the happiest night of her life." She laughed again. "Except for the dying, of course."

"You won't get away with this, Elizabeth," Lauren said. "This is where it ends. They already know."

"Of course they know. They know about you."

"You're the one who told the reporter."

"I helped him along. Yes, Amanda McBride, we know all about you. The collection of love letters from your victim's brother helped. Nice of you to save them for us." She nudged Lauren again. "I didn't say to stop! Move it!"

Lauren inched forward. "They'll know it's you."

"No, they won't. They'll know it's you—you killed again just like you did when you were a child. You'd always been fascinated by fire, but this time you got trapped in it along with your last victim." She smiled. "My only regret is that you'll get the credit for all my work. But isn't that the way—most artists aren't appreciated in their own lifetime."

Her smiled disappeared. "Get in the pit! Now!"

Lauren lunged for the knife. Surprised, Elizabeth jerked back and lighter fluid splashed from the bottle and back onto her. Scowling, she darted forward and stabbed the back of Lauren's hand with the thin blade.

"No!" Lauren screamed, pulling away with another scream as the blade slipped painfully back out. She fell to her knees, clutching her hand, and watched as Elizabeth circled the pit, swinging the accelerant with more abandon. Some of the liquid arced back and spilled over her instead, running down her sweatshirt and dripping onto the grass at her feet.

A muffled cry startled Lauren. She saw Nicole gesturing from the pit, her mouth covered in a wide strip of duct tape. Her eyes were wild, the whites showing all the way round, and she was straining at the ropes binding her.

The panic in her face compelled Lauren to move. She pushed herself up ignoring the searing pain in her hand and throbbing in her head and moved resolutely toward the pit.

"You can't do this, Elizabeth," she said.

"I already am," Elizabeth said in a frighteningly indifferent voice. She dropped the bottle of accelerant and it fell over, dark liquid pooling around her as she stepped in front of Lauren with the knife raised.

Chapter Forty-two

Fear-induced adrenaline rushed through Lauren. She grabbed Elizabeth's wrist, stopping the knife's fall. The girl cried out in surprise and Lauren struggled to grab the knife with her other hand while she maintained her grip on Elizabeth's wrist. Elizabeth kept her grip on the handle and Lauren was forced to grab the knife by the blade. It cut through the flesh of her palm as Elizabeth twisted and pulled back, but Lauren wouldn't let go.

"I'll kill you, you bitch," Elizabeth snarled, grabbing her by the hair with her free hand. Lauren screamed at the eye-watering pain, but wouldn't release the knife blade. Blood poured from her palm and the blade was getting harder to grasp, but she couldn't let go. She knew with certainty that Elizabeth would stab her to death if she couldn't get the knife away from her, but the blade was sliding in her hand; she was going to lose her grip.

Her other hand ached with the effort of keeping Elizabeth's wrist suspended while Kristen slowly scalped the left side of her head, grunting with the effort. Lauren had nothing left to fight with other than her legs and she managed one solid kick and heard the girl groan with the impact, but that was the last connection. Kristen punched Lauren in the side. Howling with pain, she felt her grip on the knife give way.

Lauren's legs were trembling and she knew this was it. She would sink to the ground and Elizabeth would finish her here. It would all be over soon, all the misery. She would finally pay the price for what she'd done. She'd be with Julia. Her legs were buckling, she was moving down . . .

For a moment all noise seemed to cease as she watched the blood-slicked metal slip from her fingers. She felt strangely detached from her body and stared at the ground where strands of gold-colored hair blew about the leaves and then up at Elizabeth's face, a contorted mask that she didn't recognize. She looked back at her hands that were just barely holding on and she willed herself to let go, just let go.

"This is your penance, this is your penance for what you did to me." Julia's voice came from a great distance and she searched the trees for her. "I'm sorry," she sobbed. "I'm so sorry." She searched for Julia and saw the fire pit instead and Nicole lying in its center. Her vision blurred and it was a shed on fire and she was watching it, her hands burning from the hot metal of the lock.

She cried out, a sharp, high sound that pierced the silence and brought the present rushing back. Everything was startlingly clear. It wasn't just about Julia, it was about this girl, too.

The old man whose ancient Buick had been stolen interrupted all pertinent details to editorialize about the state of the world. Specifically, the state of the world since the "libbers" took over. He looked Stephanie up and down when they arrived and proceeded to direct all of his conversation to Oz.

"In my day, this never would have happened. We never had theft like this in Gashford. Never. And we certainly didn't have *girls* doing things like this."

"Which way did the *girl* head?" Stephanie interrupted.

The man glanced at her as if she were a pesky fly and continued talking to Oz as if she hadn't spoken. "Here I am walking Mother into church and this, this libber comes along as bold as brass and takes my car."

Oz made a sympathetic noise. "Which way did she head?"

"I turned around and she was in my car. My car! I'll tell you, I almost had a heart attack right there and then. I'm sure I felt it skip a beat."

Stephanie ran out of patience. She stepped in front of Oz. "Look, old man, do you want your car back or not?"

"What? What did you say to me?"

"Do you want your car back?"

"Of course I do, young lady."

"Detective Land." She grabbed one veiny hand and shook it. Spots of feverish color appeared on his cheekbones and the tip of his nose. He struggled to speak, looking from her to Oz and back, his wide jaw opening and closing.

"We need to know which way she headed." Stephanie gestured at the street. "Just point, sir. Right or left?"

Lauren tightened her grip on the blade of the knife as she lunged, sinking her teeth into the back of the hand that held the handle. It was her second bite of the night. Elizabeth roared and her fingers jerked up just long enough for Lauren to yank the handle out of her hand. The sudden release made them both stumble but Lauren kept hold of the knife. She slashed back with it and Kristen let go of her hair.

Lauren staggered backward, keeping a firm grip on the knife, fully expecting Elizabeth and Kristen to pursue her.

Instead Elizabeth stood where she was, fumbling with her sweatshirt. Lauren couldn't tell what she was doing until she saw the small pack of matches in her hand.

"Jesus! No!" she screamed as Elizabeth calmly tore a

match from the pack. "No, Elizabeth. Don't! You'll kill us all!"

"Shut up!" Elizabeth shrieked. "You stupid bitch! You just couldn't leave us alone!"

"Elizabeth, wait!" Kristen cried, but she was ignored. With a small moan, Tiffany took off, running toward the trees. Kristen's head swiveled back and forth, looking from Elizabeth to Tiffany and back again. "Don't do it!" she begged, inching back before she, too, broke into a run.

Lauren realized she could go, too. Without the other girls to help her, Elizabeth only had a knife. Lauren could outrun her. A strangled moan stopped her.

Nicole. She'd forgotten about Nicole. Elizabeth backed away from the pit, the match and its book held aloft in her hands. With a sudden flourish she lit the match and tossed it in the general direction of the fire pit. It arced like a shooting star and fell to the ground almost as fast, igniting the accelerant before it touched earth.

Chapter Forty-three

A map of fire rose instantly, racing along the lines and puddles of accelerant and tracing strange orange patterns on Elizabeth's and Nicole's clothes. Their cries mingled with the spitting and popping of flames licking branches and dry leaves and the roots of trees, curling moss into ash at the base of hundred-year-old oaks and maples and climbing their trunks with a speed no animal could match.

Lauren snatched the sweatshirt from the ground where it had fallen and leapt into the pit, beating down the knee-high flames to get to the struggling girl. She threw the sweatshirt on top of Nicole to smother the small blaze before snatching her from the smoldering debris. The charred rope fell apart as she tugged it. Turning with Nicole she froze at the sight of the inferno separating them from Elizabeth. The knee-high flames were now huge walls of fire and Lauren could barely see the girl through the orange-red curtain engulfing her.

"Elizabeth!" She couldn't get to the girl, or what was left of her in that writhing dark form. The wall of fire moved closer, undulating across the dry grass of the clearing like a wave. Intense heat knocked Lauren back, singeing her face and arms while smoke burned her throat and eyes. Coughing and gagging on the smells of smoke and accelerant, she stumbled backward with Nicole's hand gripped in hers, trying to find a way out, but an orange wall met them wherever they turned.

Oz drove as fast as he could toward St. Ursula's, siren wailing, blue light flashing. Cars parted on either side of the road and Stephanie saw people staring as they screamed past.

"She could have been leaving town," Oz said. "It's the same general direction and we've got no sighting of the car beyond this stretch of road."

"I don't think so." Stephanie pressed her right foot hard against the floor of the passenger side as if that could make the car go faster. "C'mon, c'mon."

"I'm doing ninety."

"Yeah, I know. I've just got a bad feeling. Why would she go back up to the school?"

"I don't know, but I hope you're wrong."

The road curved and the hill came into view. The leaves were in full color now, the green hillside awash with orange, yellow and red. And something else.

"Look." She pointed at the line where the trees met the sky. "Is that smoke?"

"Jesus," Oz said. "Call it in." Stephanie was already on the radio.

A new smell, charred but sweet, assaulted her and Lauren recognized it as burning flesh. This was it, she thought, she would die here just like she should have died in that shed all those years ago and she wondered if Julia felt this panic and despair just before her death. Maybe it would be quicker if she just stepped into the fire, but she couldn't bring herself to dive into the waves of flame. It wouldn't matter anyway because very soon she'd be swallowed up by this burning ocean.

She coughed and gagged on smoke, stumbling about, still clutching Nicole. It was getting harder and harder to breathe and then, suddenly, she saw a gap. A slight break in the wall of flames where an enormous tree had just fallen. She tugged Nicole's hand and pointed and the girl nodded, eyes streaming, both of them coughing and choking.

Head bent, Lauren ran for the log with Nicole beside her. She hoisted the girl onto it, clambered up herself, and then ran down its length, sliding off into woods only starting to smolder.

Lauren looked back once but all she saw was fire and then she ran and ran, sobbing and sucking in huge breaths of smoke-free air, tripping but managing not to fall, not to drop the hand of the girl she'd managed to save.

Stephanie tried to get off the back of the ambulance and a big hand pushed her gently but firmly back down. "You're not going anywhere," the enormous paramedic said in a kind but firm voice.

"But I need to know if they've found anyone—" Stephanie said.

"And I need to see if you've got any lung damage and treat you for smoke inhalation," the man cut her off, whipping out a stethoscope and blinding her with a penlight.

The first cop car had been joined by another, then by two fire trucks and an ambulance. Siren wails mixed with radio static and the chatter of newspeople reporting live, their SUVs and vans parked in every space not taken up by rescue vehicles. The bright revolving lights and the smoke, which was now billowing down the hillside, increased the pain in Stephanie's head.

She and Oz had been the first on the scene and she thought

she'd never forget the sight of those flames rising above the trees on that hillside. They'd barely crested the hill when she leapt from the car and took off running into the woods.

Instinct, she called it. Oz called it bad judgment. He'd grabbed her as she was running up the hillside, dragging her back down coughing and gagging.

"Are you out of your mind?" he'd asked. "Are you trying to get us killed?" He'd forced her to get looked at by the paramedics.

She heard a familiar voice that she thought she was imagining, but then an anxious-looking Sister Rose was escorted past the ambulance by several uniforms. Firefighters dragging huge hoses tramped past, effectively blocking her view, and she focused her attention on the enormous caramel-colored hands probing her face and listening to her chest.

"Need some oxygen here," the paramedic called over his shoulder and his partner responded with information of his own that Stephanie couldn't catch except for the last few words.

". . . female. Bleeding from something plus bad burns."

She moved before the paramedic turned around, hopping off the back of the ambulance and losing herself in the crowd of rescue personnel. She heard the man shouting behind her, but continued to move, up the steps onto the front lawn, pushing past people until she suddenly halted, staring at something dark emerging from the trees.

Two figures stumbled out of the woods coughing, their bodies covered in black soot, the hair on the side of the shorter figure completely burned away. Firefighters with hoses raced past and the blackened figures continued down the hill, unnoticed, Stephanie thought, except by her.

"Stop!" A male voice over a megaphone echoed over the hillside, commanding the attention of everyone, including the figures, who rocked to a standstill looking about with huge, stunned eyes that Stephanie recognized. "Let go of the girl," the voice over the megaphone commanded, "and put your hands on your head." Suddenly there were police everywhere, with guns drawn.

Stephanie struggled to push past several officers to get to Oz, who was wielding the megaphone. Lauren Kavanaugh let go of the girl's hand and she stumbled forward, moving numbly down the hill and into the arms of paramedics, who rushed forward to treat her.

Stephanie's eyes were riveted to the trembling, soot-covered figure standing alone on the hill. Lauren Kavanaugh faced a phalanx of police officers cautiously advancing, guns pointing at her, and Stephanie felt her heart contract as she noticed the woman's trembling.

She moved toward her instinctively and a young cop swiveled her way with a gun, his eyes filled with fear and adrenaline. Stephanie quickly held her hands up.

"I'm a detective," she said. "She needs medical help." She pointed at Lauren, who was following barked orders, slowly raising her hands before placing them on her head. Stephanie took another step toward her and the baby-faced policeman frantically waved his gun.

"Don't move, ma'am!" The young cop was obviously nervous. Stephanie just hoped he wasn't trigger-happy as well. She looked toward Lauren and saw her being handcuffed.

"Lauren Kavanaugh!" She screamed her name as loudly as she could and somehow, incredibly, over the crackling of the fire and the roar of voices and sirens, the other woman heard her, and haunting eyes rose to find a friendly face in the crowd.

Epilogue

The hospital existed in shades of white. White sheets, off-white walls, white intercoms and plastic jugs for water. White radiators that hummed when they switched on. A white landscape out the window, where the snow blanketed every inch of available space.

White was the color of pain when it got too bad, a pure, bright shrieking in her head, and of the soothing towels placed on her skin by physical therapists wearing white uniforms.

Lauren pushed the white button on the adjustable bed and it whirred her up into a sitting position. She looked down at her legs and arms. White was also the color of gauze bandages, wrapped loosely around one leg. Her skin was healing, they said when they checked her, but so far she didn't want to look.

The only spot to interrupt this whiteness was the plant on the windowsill. A beautiful green thing with great spiky leaves. A cactus, Candace said. *"Tough like you,"* the note attached to it read. She'd brought it by herself, hesitating in the doorway, but not, as Lauren supposed, because she was appalled at the sight of her charbroiled friend, but because of what she'd read in the newspapers along with the rest of the world.

"I don't know what to call you," she'd said after a few minutes of awkward silence.

"I'm Lauren."

"Not Amanda?"

"Amanda died a long time ago. I'm Lauren."

They'd talked about other things then, discussing Candace's new job at a high-tech lab and how other teachers from St. Ursula's had fared. Alice LaRue had moved to New Mexico to be near her daughter and throw pots. Leonard Whitecliff was teaching at a better prep school in New Hampshire.

Eventually the conversation slowed down, turned to the delicate subject of what Lauren would do when she came out of the burn unit.

"I don't know if I want to teach again," she said. "I might go back to school."

"How long will your leg take to heal?"

Lauren shrugged. She'd grown accustomed to indecisive answers from doctors. "I don't know. A month? I've got at least one more graft to go."

Candace hugged her when she left, extracted a promise to visit, and squeezed her gently as if she were a fragile thing. Perhaps she was. The nurses clucked over her weight and tried to tempt her with food. She stared out the hospital window and imagined running in the snow.

She was asleep when Nicole Morel arrived. She woke to find her standing at the foot of her bed. The girl's hair was growing back where it had burned off and the rest had been cropped short so it matched. The cut and the jaunty hat she wore made her look a little like a cancer patient, but her smile was bright.

"We're moving," she said. "I just wanted to say good-bye and thank you."

"Where are you going?"

"Back to Paris."

Lauren nodded. "You'll be going back to school?"

"Yes. In a new school, a day school."

"That sounds good."

The girl's smile faltered a little. "I don't want to be away from home just now."

"Of course."

She pulled a gaily wrapped package out from behind her back. "It's just a little present," she said.

It was a history of Paris. Lauren didn't think about Michael once when she read it.

"I know I'm a little biased, but isn't she beautiful?" Sam adjusted the blankets around baby Sidney, who slept on, undisturbed at having two generations of Land women looming over her bassinet.

"All babies are beautiful," Debbie Land declared.

Samantha rolled her eyes. "To their mothers, maybe, but I was talking as an objective person—"

"—not as a biased new mother," Stephanie added, trying and failing to hide a smile.

Sam threw up her arms. "Fine. You two are impossible." She led the way out of the baby's ridiculously pink nursery and back to the living room, where Dan and other members of his family were helping themselves to pieces of a bakery cake celebrating the baby's christening.

Piles of wrapped presents were stacked on a side table waiting to be opened.

"What a racket," Stephanie said to her sister, poking through the pile. "This is almost as much loot as you got for your wedding."

"Yeah, the free stuff is great," Sam said lightly. "You should try it." It took her a second to register what she'd said and then her cheeks flooded with color. "I'm sorry."

"Don't be," Steph said, but she pretended to be absorbed by a card so her sister wouldn't say anything more.

Things changed, life went on. Look at St. Ursula's. A school could stand on a hill for more than a hundred years and then, just like that, be gone. Why should relationships be any different?

She moved into the kitchen to refill her drink and heard the doorbell ring. Someone was late for the party. Sam's fridge was already covered with pictures of Sidney. Barely a month old and the little girl already dominated their lives.

"Don't kill me," Sam said from the doorway.

"What kind of intro is that?" Stephanie said, turning, and then she stopped talking. Alex stood next to her sister in the doorway.

"What are you doing here?" she said.

"Your sister invited me."

"I would have told you, but he didn't RSVP, so I didn't know if he was going to show," Sam said, giving Stephanie a too-bright, please-don't-be-pissed smile. "I'll leave you two alone." And she was gone before Stephanie could stop her.

"*I* wasn't sure I was going to show," Alex said.

Stephanie stared at him. He looked just the same, just as great as he always had. She wished that didn't make her long to touch him, to feel his arms wrap around her. She kept her voice deliberately cool, as if she didn't really care about his answer. "What made you change your mind?"

His answer when it came, was refreshingly brief. "You."

She kissed him then, breaking all the promises she'd made to herself about snubbing him if he tried to contact her.

"I'm not quitting my job," she managed to say when they came up for air.

"I don't want you to."

"That's a change."

They kissed some more and he pressed her up against the pantry door, his arms resting on either side of her. "I've missed you so much."

"I'm going to be a detective for just as long as I can be," she said. "You prepared for that?"

"I don't like the hours—"

She bristled, tried to slip under his arm. "They're part of the job."

"Wait." He held her in place. "Listen. Please. I don't like the hours, but I accept them."

"How magnanimous of you." She could feel the righteous anger now, it was just a few minutes too late.

"Listen," he repeated. "I'm sorry for all the shit I gave you. I'm so sorry. I didn't realize until you were gone just how much of an idiot I was and how much I love you. I love *you*. Not the hours. *You.* I'll take the job, I'll take the hours, because I want you."

"Even if we get woken up early in the morning?"

"Even if that damn cell phone rings at four every damn morning. Just as long as you're in my arms when it's ringing."

He leaned in to kiss her, but she pulled back and gave him a serious look. "There's just one more thing we need to address."

He looked worried. "What?"

"Your language. I'm not sure I can live with a man who sounds like a trucker." She began laughing before she finished the sentence.

He grinned at her. "Shut up, Stephanie."

She grinned back. "Make me."

Exactly one month after her last skin graft Lauren boarded a plane for southwestern Pennsylvania. It was a round-trip ticket and she took a cab straight from the airport to the cemetery.

"Please wait," she told the cabbie.

The cemetery was on a hillside covered in snow. She'd never been there before and had to consult the little map twice, wandering among the graves with her boots sinking into the soft, white carpet until at last she found it.

The marker was plain stone, piled high with snow that she brushed off carefully with one gloved hand. A single word was chiseled in the marble: JULIA.

Lauren unwrapped the roses from the cellophane and tucked them one by one against the stone. She stood for awhile, listening to the wind rushing through the trees, and the far-off sound of traffic. She thought she might hear Julia's voice, but she didn't. She didn't hear Amanda's either, or any of the voices from her past. They were gone, along with everything from her past, just as everything passed away. She would be gone one day, too, and whatever she'd done, both bad and good, would be forgotten.

She looked up at the sky, watching patches of blue struggling to break through the gray, and then she knelt in the snow in front of the grave and said an Act of Contrition.